NO TRESPASSING

"This is private property," I said with authority, "and you're interfering with my research. I'm asking you to leave. Now."

The stranger giggled, as if I was doing something naughty. "Don't ever take that tone with me, sweetie," he admonished, enunciating carefully. His voice was like a dry cornfield crawling with locusts. "You have no idea what kind of trouble smart talk will get you."

It was a good thing I was so mad; it let me ignore how much I was shaking. "Like I said before. This is private property. You're not welcome. Leave!"

He lifted his head and removed his sunglasses. He fixed me with a pair of icy gray eyes so pale that they looked almost white. "Sweetheart," he said, "there are people in this world that you do not mess with. I am one of them." He smiled foully, showing sharp canine teeth, savoring the confrontation. "I should just break your kneecaps."

He's out of his mind, I thought in a panic. *I mustn't let him know he's scaring me.*

I locked eyes with him, willing myself not to look away.

He sighed. "Baby, this is probably the biggest mistake of your life." He reached under his windbreaker and drew out a large pistol.

Which he aimed carefully at my head.

DANA CAMERON

SITE UNSEEN

AN EMMA FIELDING MYSTERY

AVON BOOKS
An Imprint of HarperCollinsPublishers

This is a work of fiction. Names, characters, places, and incidents are products of the author's imagination or are used fictitiously and are not to be construed as real. Any resemblance to actual events, locales, organizations, or persons, living or dead, is entirely coincidental.

AVON BOOKS
An Imprint of HarperCollins*Publishers*
10 East 53rd Street
New York, New York 10022-5299

Copyright © 2002 by Dana Cameron
ISBN: 0-380-81954-6
www.avonmystery.com

First Avon Books paperback printing: February 2002

Avon Trademark Reg. U.S. Pat. Off. and in Other Countries, Marca Registrada, Hecho en U.S.A.
HarperCollins ® is a registered trademark of HarperCollins Publishers Inc.

Printed in the U.S.A.

10 9 8 7 6 5 4 3 2 1

To the incomparable Diego:
This and all my love.

Acknowledgments

I would like to express my deepest thanks to the following, all of whom challenged me to be a better writer: Ann Barbier, Jessika Bella Mura, Cathy Bennett, Linda Blackbourn, Pam Crane, Janet Halpin, Mildred Jeffrey, Beth Krueger, Michael Levin, Roberta MacPhee, Peter Morrison, and Joan Sawyer. Thanks to everyone at Bread Loaf 1998, including Susanna Jones, Ronnie Klaskin, and Elizabeth Rouse, and especially David Bradley and Eric Darton. Thanks to my agent, Kit Ward, and Sarah Durand, my editor at Avon. Thanks most of all to my husband, who was right about everything.

SITE UNSEEN

Chapter 1

MY TROUSERS FELL TO THE FLOOR WITH A HEAVY, metallic thunk. My husband, Brian, complains that while other women undress with a whisper of silk, I tend to clank and require the services of a squire to disrobe. He doesn't mind, though, really; there's a certain cachet to being married to an archaeologist that he likes to think rubs off on him. I pulled my shirt off over my head without unbuttoning it, balled it up, and threw it in the general direction of the corner where the rest of my clothing from the week had been piling up, forming my own laundry midden. One thick, overworked sock followed the shirt, and then was followed by its mate, but the second sock went awry and landed on my desk amid piles of notes and books, scattering about a dozen empty film canisters onto the floor. I stared at the new disruption tiredly, took another sip of my well-deserved beer, and decided to take my shower instead of picking up. No one would have been able to tell where the new mess began and the old one ended anyway.

In the bathroom I reached over and set my beer bottle on the cracked tile ledge of the shower and turned on the water, hot and full blast. The shelf was a precarious perch for the beer, already crowded with my soap and shampoo, but it was worth the risk. The utter luxury of a cold beer going down my throat at the same time that steaming hot water poured over my body was not one to dismiss lightly. I could never decide which was more desirable, the beer or the shower, but the combination of the two was positively restorative. Life-giving.

Outside the shower, I got a start as I caught my reflection in the mirror and grinned: I was still wearing my baseball cap. I looked more closely at the lines that were developing around my eyes and mouth and decided that once again, the Red Sox had let me down. The crow's-feet made me look a little older, which I suppose, horrid to say, lends a little more credibility to me as a scholar. I could be as much a feminist as I liked, but I still had to admit that my age and sex were working against me. Academia is still very much a man's world.

Cynic, I chided myself. Stop feeling sorry for yourself. You're just tired, same as every other day—but there I stopped. Today was most certainly not like every other day.

The steam from the shower rolled across the room, fogging up the mirror, obscuring my reflected image. I was forced away from my morbid thoughts as I watched the steam creep down the mirror, blurring and then hiding the freckles on my nose. I batted my eyes in my best imitation of a Southern belle, convincing myself that I came off more like Scarlett O'Hara than Blanche DuBois. Hazel eyes, instead of green, notwithstanding, and red hair, closer to chestnut than black, though. Okay, so what if I was born in Connecticut, was presently working on the coast of Maine, and had never been within spitting distance of Georgia—it doesn't matter. Every girl needs to believe she's belle-quality indomitable. As the steam reached the bottom of the mirror, I made a kissing noise and bade my image farewell—y'all come back now, girl, y'hear? With that I slung the hat out of the bathroom door, shucked off my underwear, and prayed that the shower would work its magic.

The moment when that hot water hit my back was like my own private revival meeting. A moan escaped my lips, and I thought, if my muscles loosening could feel any better I'd be speaking in tongues. In fact, I realized I was already. I was chanting "Oh god, oh man, oh man, oh thank *you*—" as the water hit my head and worked its way through the sweat to my scalp. With another sip of the cold beer I thought my knees would buckle with pleasure, and as I got down to the serious business of trying to scrape the remains of the day's labor from my body and troubling thoughts from my mind, I began to believe that I might just make it.

When I'd finished, I stood under the water for an extra five minutes; not only was it one of the few moments of privacy that I would enjoy all day, but it was getting physically harder and harder to tackle this kind of work. I couldn't move around as carelessly as I did when I was eight when I started this work by trailing after Oscar, my grandfather and first mentor in archaeology, and I couldn't bound in and out of meter-deep pits the way I could when I was eighteen and starting my own small-scale digs. It was all Oscar's fault, I decided. If he hadn't introduced me to fieldwork, got me addicted, I'd be working in a nice air-conditioned office somewhere. A nice *boring* air-conditioned office.

At thirty I was in great shape for your typical American adult, but it was clear from the way that I was hitting the Advil this field season that I had to be better about delegating work if I was going to oversee things the way they deserved. I was just having a hard time convincing myself that the students could dig as well as I could, and for no good reason. After all, I'd trained most of them, except for Meg; it was just that I wanted to do it all myself. My role as project director was to organize and synthesize. Archaeology is no place for the incurious or the perfectionist: I couldn't dig the whole site by myself *and* expect to get the big picture. But who can resist trying?

Tomorrow, I thought as I groped for the taps. Tomorrow I'd definitely practice delegating.

The shower, as good as it was, had taken all the starch out of me. It was almost as if the dirt that seemed to fill every single one of my pores had been holding me up and, now that it was washed away, I was no longer capable of standing on my own. To hell with it, I thought, I'm going to make something real for dinner tonight and go to bed early. My notes are nearly done, and the rest of the paperwork I can do tomorrow. I'm doing laundry and calling a half holiday for myself. After what I'd seen today . . . I quashed the thought again. Never mind, Em, it's over now. Get on with life, because that rocky little patch of land called Penitence Point, Maine, is going to make your career, and you can't afford any distractions now, of all times.

I finished my beer and started to dry off. The towel felt harsh against my skin thanks to my growing collection of aches, bruises, scratches, and mosquito bites on top of the sunburn and windburn. Lucky for me the site had no poison ivy, else I would have been a real mess. Pulling on my clothes was a chore—I was really stiffening up now—but there's no way to describe the luxury of having that last pair of clean panties if you haven't spent all day sweating and soaking up bug spray. Fieldwork makes you appreciate the little things in life like you wouldn't believe.

Feeling much more human for the shower and my decision to take the night off, I started gathering up my laundry from around the room. I picked up my dirty work trousers and started to empty out the pockets. I found the usual miscellany: a piece of chalk, a tangle of string and bright orange flagging tape, three ballpoints and four markers, an eraser, two pennies, a small plastic bag, a dirty tissue, a pair of root clippers. And how did I end up with three tape measures? I must have absentmindedly picked up the two that weren't mine, trying to keep the site tidy. My husband has tried unsuccessfully to break me of the habit of stuffing my pockets like a chipmunk's cheeks, but then he has to admit that I always have an item when I need it. I picked up my Marshalltown trowel and affectionately placed it on top of my boots, where I'd find it tomorrow when I got dressed.

Laundry sorted into piles, I turned my thoughts kitchen-ward and to another cold beer. The students, with whom I was sharing this dorm as well as the work on the site, were unusually quiet. They'd already finished their dinners, I thought grumpily, but this subdued behavior was extraordinary and no one was in the common kitchen area. What generally went on was the sharing of six-packs and trading of improbable stories about fieldwork: who worked on the most unusual, most difficult, most boring, most exotic sites, with the most irascible, most inept, drunkest, or luckiest director. I knew that it wouldn't be long before this summer's stories became a part of that circulating canon of anecdotes. I mean, excavating the earliest English settlement on the American mainland should be enough for anyone, but I'd be interested to see what they made of this day's events in particular.

A piece of paper taped to the door caught my attention as soon as I tried to leave my room. I pulled down the scrawled note and read that Tony Markham would be visiting the site tomorrow. While this was an excellent opportunity, my heart also sank a little, realizing that my hopes of an early night were now dashed: I had to prepare for a state visit. Resigned, I headed for the fridge.

As I passed it, the phone on the wall rang right next to my head, startling me badly and providing yet another distraction from dinner.

"Yes?" I answered it impatiently.

"Em?" The welcome sound of a familiar man's voice came across the line.

"Brian? It's so good to hear you!" And it was; Brian Chang and I have been married for nearly five years, and even though we've been forced to spend a lot of it apart because of our respective jobs, just hearing his voice was enough to raise my downcast spirits.

"You too, Em. How're you doing?"

"Pretty well, I guess. I just got the message that I've got company coming tomorrow, in the form of Tony Markham."

"Who's that?"

"You haven't met him yet; he was away on sabbatical last year when I started. Tony's the other archaeologist in the department, a Mayanist. He's a big honcho and knows everyone, so it's nice he's taking an interest. Just means more work for me tonight."

"Poor Emma."

"Yeah, poor me. But he'll probably be the chair when Kellerman retires next year and it never hurts for me to start impressing folks with my tenure dance."

"Just so long as you keep all your veils on, hon. So what's this Markham want? Why's he bugging you? You want I should have a little talk with him?"

Since Brian is from southern California, his attempt to sound like a tough guy from the Bronx was laughable. Fortunately a laugh was what he was going for. "Yeah, sweetie, I think you should beat him senseless for me. Oh, wait," I pretended to remember something. "But that will mean you'll have to get your lazy butt off the sofa and indulge in some physical activity. It's too much for me to ask of you."

"Actually I know a physical activity that we can both do on the sofa—"

"And that's the only exercise you ever get! Not that I mind, of course."

"God." My husband pretended to yawn. "You East Coast types and your exercise. Life is too short."

"It is this summer." I laughed. "And now with an official state visit tomorrow, that means no rest tonight, if I want to show things off properly."

"Tell this Markham guy to take a flying leap. Tell him, 'I got better things to do than to cater to the whims of overindulged academics who privilege the white, androcentric hegemony!' "

I snickered. "Now I *know* chemists don't use that kind of language; you've been reading my books again."

Brian ignored me, however, wrapped up in his monologue. "You tell him, 'I got to get my work done so I can go home and play Warlord and the Slave Girl with my big, angry stud of a husband.' "

"Yeah, right!" The snicker was turning into a full-blown laugh now, and I tried to stifle it, hoping none of the students would pick just this moment to walk by. "I'll be sure to pass that one on."

Brian reverted to normal voice, warm, with just a hint of the Valley. "And just so we're clear, I want to be the warlord next time," he said, mock petulantly.

"We'll see," I said. "He did actually call up and let me know, which is nice. He could have just dropped in and surprised me, you know."

"I'm sure he's a prince," Brian observed. "So how're things going? You got the fort yet?"

"Not yet." I hated saying that, hated thinking what was riding on this project, but I knew that Brian had to ask and that I would have been hurt if he hadn't. "It's still early yet, but I think most everyone is down at least to the eighteenth century—"

"By most everyone, do you mean whatshisname is still lagging behind?"

"Alan's not the best excavator in the world," I admitted, my hand over the receiver, making sure I couldn't be overheard.

"Is he still drinking?" Brian asked.

"Rather more than usual," I said tonelessly. Down the hall, a door opened and someone went into the common bathroom. "I'm going to have to speak with him about this, and I shouldn't have to. Frankly, he's not cut out to be an archaeologist. I don't know why he keeps insisting he loves it when he's so defensive most of the time and plainly miserable the rest."

"I'd drink too, if my father taught in my department."
Brian was fascinated by the soap opera–like events that inevitably characterized the life on a dig. "That can't be easy."

"Nope. It's not a choice I would have made," I said tersely.
Oscar had never, *ever* pushed me like Rick pushed Alan. I
was sick of the whole mess and my role in the middle of it.
Rick Crabtree, Alan's father—whom Brian had once accu-
rately described as "the pudgy little weasel with glasses and a
combover"—was impossible to get along with and had been
loudly unhappy about Alan working with me. "Everyone else
is doing okay, but unfortunately, there's a little romance
blossoming in our midst."

"Em," Brian warned, "What those kids do is none of your
business. They're all over twenty-one."

"I know, I know," I said. "But it just seems like a recipe for
disaster—what if it doesn't work out? I'm not so worried
about Dian, she's sensible enough, but Rob tends to get
these . . . these *enthusiasms* and not consider the consequences. He just dives right in, and devil take the hindmost."

"I don't think that particular phrase has been used since
about 1790, hon," Brian pointed out. "You might want to
consider that when conversing with the rest of us ordinary
mortals. I like Rob, though, he'll be fine."

"You just like him because he's got the same warped sense
of humor as you," I groused. "But you should see him moon-
ing over Dian; you've never seen such big puppy eyes. Dian's
enjoying the attention, but I think she's still deciding about
him."

"Your new kid working out? The one who arrived last
week?"

"Meg's in good shape, I think. A bit prickly, yet, and I
don't just mean that spiky hair of hers, but I think she's just
sizing us up too. I wouldn't have had her in the program if I
didn't think she could do it. Any mail or anything?"

"Oh yeah, the department administrator called. The
goofy one."

"Chuck? Oh, be nice to Chuck. I like him and he puts my check in my mailbox. What did he want?"

"He left a message on the machine. 'Ah, Professor Fielding?' " Brian began to imitate Chuck's slow, hippy-surfer cadence. " 'Like, I know you're not there, but I thought you should know, it's time to order books for next semester, and I know you're rilly, rilly busy and all, doing the fieldwork thing—rave on!—so if you want to call me with the titles and all, I'll take care of it for you, 'kay?' "

I laughed. "Okay, I'll get back to Chuck." Then I was distracted by my rumbling stomach. "I gotta go, Bri, I'm starving."

"You haven't eaten yet?" Brian's voice was filled with alarm. Being hungry was about the worst thing he could imagine.

"Not yet, I've been trying to get something for the past half hour now." My stomach rumbled louder, as if in chorus to our discussion.

Brian sighed. "I'll be glad when this is over, hon."

"The dig's only a couple more weeks."

"No, when all *this* is over. When we can have a normal life together, and not spend all our time on the phone."

It was my turn to sigh. "I know, I know. It's not forever, but for now, we have to be where the work is. Somerville's not so far from Caldwell, maybe we can start looking for a new home someplace between Massachusetts and Maine when I'm finished here." I was employed at Caldwell, a small private college in Maine.

"Maybe look for a house?" He sounded hopeful.

"Not this year, sweetie." I hated to be a wet blanket, but we'd been over the finances every way till Sunday. It just wasn't in the cards with the dirt-pay of an as-yet-untenured assistant professor and a chemist who'd only recently made the change from prestigious but impoverishing postdoctoral research grants to a small company. "Besides, we don't need a house to be together."

Brian snorted. "We need a house if we're going to be to-gether in the same building as your books."

"Not if we clean out your record collection. No one listens to vinyl anymore anyway."

"You philistine." Then Brian began our traditional spiral of good-byes. "I miss you."

"I miss you too. I gotta go."

"I know, I know. Go get a sandwich. Come home this weekend?"

"I'll try."

"I love you."

"I love you too."

"And?"

It took me a minute to figure out what he was waiting for. "And next time you can be the warlord."

In the face of everything else, my husband's phone call had buoyed me, distracted me so that I hadn't even thought to tell him about this morning. Never mind; I'd tell him next time we spoke. I slapped together a peanut butter sandwich, stuck it in my mouth, and headed down to the dorm's laun-dry room with my basket. As much as I was grateful for the opportunity to rent the dorm space for the crew for the du-ration of the dig, hot showers and cold beer aside, I was a hundred times more grateful to be able to wash my field clothes on a regular basis. I may be a slob, but mine is a hy-gienic sort of clutter.

Not wanting to put the sandwich down on any of the gritty surfaces of the other washers, I held it in one hand while I loaded the washer with the other. I had just slapped the coin tray with my six quarters into the machine when my crew chief, Neal Fenn, came in with a duffel bag full of his own laundry.

One eye on the rising water in my tub, I nodded to him. "Hey."

"Hey." Neal ducked, his short sandy hair, streaked with

premature gray, just brushing one of the water pipes that were suspended from the ceiling. They weren't all that low, and I'm not a short woman; generally speaking, I had to stand well back to see all of Neal at once. He's not beefy-huge, but the fact that one is always left with an impression of legs, knees, and elbows seems to accentuate his height even more.

The water now covered my clothes, and I could see a bit of dried grass that had been stuck on my trousers floating on the top. I stuck my sandwich in my mouth again and measured out the soap. Watching the debris swirling on the surface of the water and now fully able to appreciate just how unfragrant I had been, I threw in an extra quarter cup of detergent.

"Things are quiet tonight," he began, shoving his glasses up his nose in a characteristic gesture. "I guess it's because of—"

"When's a good time to strategize for tomorrow?" I interrupted, licking some peanut butter off the back of my hand.

"How about now?" Neal answered.

"Okay." As I hopped up on the washer next to mine, I noticed Neal wasn't sorting his clothes, and I bit my tongue to keep from pointing out this fact. Neal was a grown adult; if he wanted to put the darks in with the whites, all on the hot water setting, that was up to him. "You first."

"Alan's down a little further than he was this morning." Neal tore the tops off a small package of detergent and one of powdered bleach; I shuddered as he threw both of them in at the same time, right on top of the dry clothes. "He'd have gotten more work done, but I had to get him to clean up his balks—they were bowing way in. Again."

He didn't have to say anything more; after two years of graduate school and this his second field season with me, Alan should have been able to keep the walls of his unit straight as he worked. Doing this would allow him to see the relationship between the layers of soil in the ground, the most important evidence that we use to reconstruct the history of a site. Alan's lack of progress and ability was a genuine concern.

I chewed my lip, thinking this over. "And then there was that little spat between him and Rob—"

Neal broke in. "Rob was teasing him about going so slowly. He didn't mean anything by it, he never does, but Alan took it too seriously and blew up at him. I just told Alan to cool down and then I took Rob aside and told him not to bug Alan anymore. He doesn't understand that Alan's *really* not getting it."

I sighed. "Okay, well, we're stuck with this situation for a couple more weeks. Nothing we can do about it. For this year," I finished significantly. "As for Alan's work, well, if his notes are okay, and he's not blowing through any significant features, we'll just keep him where he is and keep an eye on him. Otherwise, if it looks like he's going to miss the very early stuff, we'll . . . make other arrangements."

Translation: If Alan didn't show more care as he came down on the fragile seventeenth-century material, we'd move him to a less sensitive area. Which, to an archaeology student, was about the most humiliating thing that could happen. But better he learn on something that wasn't as delicate than destroy valuable data. Especially *my* valuable data, I thought protectively. And this on top of his moods and drinking.

I decided I needed to change the subject. "How's Rob doing over by the pine trees?"

Neal was silent for a moment, which was nothing unusual. He was a thoughtful guy, not a real chatterbox by nature. I'd learned to interpret his silences pretty well, I thought.

"Good," he finally said. He closed the lid of his washing machine and threw out his soap boxes. "Rob wasn't thrilled about moving from his old unit to the new one—I think he's, er, been enjoying working next to Dian—but he settled down to it and made good progress after lunch."

I nodded. "Did you tell him that I wanted to put Meg by Dian so that she could watch Dian's stratigraphy?"

"Yeah, he stopped slamming his tools around after that." Neal lowered his voice confidentially. "I think he thought you were trying to break them up or something."

"Well," I said with a sniff, "I do actually have better things to do than worry about his *affairs de coeur.*"

"He made a production out of setting up the unit very precisely," Neal said, "and then began digging like a champ after lunch." He paused, frowning. "He took his sweatshirt off. I warned him that he'd be covered with mosquito bites but—"

"But it's such a small price to pay for showing off one's brawny shoulders to two potentially adoring females," I observed dryly. "Besides, he's such a little gorilla that nothing could bite through all that hair. Did you explain that I think, judging by the lay of the land, that in addition to being an extension of the test pit near where Pauline found those first potsherds, he has a good chance of finding a defensive wall or ditch over there? If there's anything still left, that is." The ditch might not have looked like much of anything, just a shallow trench that eventually filled up with dirt over time. Nothing might remain of a masonry wall, if the stones were taken and reused by later generations. It was incredibly important to the project to determine what kind of defenses the English built and was a vote of confidence on my part to stick Rob there, despite his raging hormones.

"Yep, he very carefully explained that to Meg," Neal said. "You know, to bring her up to speed." He leaned against his washer and grinned knowingly. "Dian is in good shape—she thinks she might be hitting a seventeenth-century living surface; the soil's got that dark, greasy feel to it. She and Meg are getting on okay, and she thinks Meg is catching on just fine." Another small frown suddenly replaced his grin.

I hazarded a guess. "What about Meg?"

He shook his head, puzzled. "I don't know. She's going

awfully fast, for someone who's just started with us. She seems to talk a lot. She's not the easiest person to get along with." He fell silent suddenly.

I don't need this, I thought, not more friction. Alan's outbursts were enough, a blight on an otherwise great crew. "What's the problem?"

No answer. Then, "She's just got an attitude. She's not interested in accepting help where it's needed." Neal started rummaging through his pockets, picking out change.

Aha. I thought I might know. "Where was it needed?" I asked gently.

Neal colored. "Well, it was nothing in particular. I just offered to give her a hand, to get her started, and she blew me off."

"Is her work okay? Is that going to be a problem?"

"No, her work's good." Neal clammed up again for a few moments. He went over to the Coke machine and started putting his coins into the slot in a deliberate fashion. "She's just kinda brusque. Her work's fine, I guess." He got his soda and then began to clean the lint trap in the dryer he wasn't going to need for another twenty minutes.

And it was that anticipation, Neal's attention to detail, that was the key to the problem, I realized. Neal is very disciplined, very organized—that's what made me glad to hire him as the crew chief—but sometimes he was a little stiff when others, in his estimation, didn't measure up. Precision is a good quality in an archaeologist, but a good supervisor knows when to emphasize it and when to lay off.

I sighed and leaned over to check the progress of my wash. When Neal started in with the terse monosyllables, I knew he wasn't going to be any more generous with his thoughts.

"Who else?" I changed the subject. I'd talk to Meg myself tomorrow and see if I could figure out what was up from her side of things.

We ran down the list of other students, Neal offering his suggestions, me agreeing or reorganizing things so that we got the most work done with the most care possible. Finally, I gave him my plans.

"We're getting down to Fort Providence," I said. "Obviously, everyone has to be super cautious not to miss anything, from here on in. The English were only at this site for a little less than a year and they wouldn't have left much behind. If we're going to find anything of that period, we've got to keep an eye on every soil change, every little thing. We can't afford to blow it," I finished, almost to myself.

"Don't worry, Em, we'll get it. Your hunches have been right so far." Neal's words were comforting, but the sudden thought of all I had riding on this project made them fall flat.

"We need more than hunches and good luck." A thought struck me. "Oh, before I forget, I got your note about Professor Markham coming out to visit the site tomorrow. Did he say what time he'll be round?" The washer finished and I began loading the wet clothes into the dryer.

Neal shrugged. "He said he was having lunch with friends in the area and would drop by near closing time."

"You gave him directions?"

"He said he knew the way."

"Well, it's nice he's making the effort, even if we don't have any monumental architecture or gold treasures." I shut the door to the dryer and started it. "Just let everyone know that there will be a Divine Visitation; they already know they need to be on best behavior for me," I joked, "but extra-best behavior for Tony would be appreciated, of course."

"No problem, Em."

"Night, Neal."

I started up the stairs when Neal called out hesitantly. "Are you okay, Emma?"

I paused in the half shadows of the staircase, the smell of clean warm lint and detergent in the air, neither of us able to see the other's face. The sound of the washing machine and dryer filled the silence that hung between us. "Sure, Neal. Thanks."

"I mean," his words came out hurriedly, "I just mean, what with this morning and all."

"I'm fine. Really. Good night."

I turned on the steps and headed back to my room to wait for the clothes to dry, realizing just how long and odd a day it had been. It was funny how one bizarre occurrence could be so effectively blotted out by the minutiae of everyday life, as though your mind was struggling to divert itself elsewhere. The memory seemed to wink at me through the protective layers of daily duty and organization, letting me know it was still there, waiting for closer examination.

I closed the door to my room tightly and, robbed of my night off, began sorting paperwork in anticipation of the coming workday. But it was no good. Pushing my chair back, I went into the tiny bathroom, came back with my glass, poured a generous measure of bourbon into it, and then put the bottle away. I sat down, finally, to address the fact that I had stumbled across a corpse on the beach this morning.

Chapter 2

WHOEVER DECIDED THAT ARCHAEOLOGY WAS AN EARLY morning event was in a class with de Sade, I thought for the nth time as I rolled out of bed, cursed the sunlight, and scrubbed my sand-locked eyes open. Splashing a couple of handfuls of cold water on my face didn't do much except irritate me; what I really needed was coffee. Stumbling past piles of books and papers, I found that the only tidy spot in the room was the laundry basket, and I dressed, silently thanking whatever gods were attending the faithful at this hour of the morning for having let me impose that much order on my life. Nakedness covered, resentment temporarily subdued, but still bleary, I went to find salvation in the Mr. Coffee.

The doorknob slipped from my hand and the door slammed open with more force than I had intended. I vaguely understood that people—students—were gathered in the kitchen, talking and eating. I was grateful that they knew me well enough to give me the distance I needed in the morning, while I was still in the condition I had once described, in a moment of lucidity, as B.C.: Before Coffee. A pre-Columbian state, as it were. Voices were muted and no one yet tried to assail me with the problems that I was sure had already sprung, full-blown, from the newborn day. Rob hopped up and found me a mug, filled it with coffee, and just as I raised the cup to my lips, beginning to believe that I might attain humanity within the next half hour, a lone voice broke through the respectfully muted conversation.

"Morning, Emma!"

I jerked suddenly, splashing coffee down the front of my clean shirt. I brushed at the stain but to no avail. Not trusting myself to speak yet, I waved a hand in the direction of the speaker. The gesture might have been "stop!," it might have been "bye-bye," it might have been the barest of morning greetings, but it had the desired effect of stanching further attempts at conversation. I found my way back to my room and, with some finality, shut my door.

I swallowed greedily. As the coffee penetrated the somnolent recesses of my mind, I began my morning prayer of thanksgiving, a paraphrase of Vonnegut. "Aahhh, thank you God, for this magical bean. Thank you God, for letting me need coffee: It makes me more than talking mud." I felt my vision focusing and my thoughts sharpening, the universe suddenly revealing its inherent logic and my place in it.

And, now that I was a little more alert, I could also hear every single word that was being spoken in the kitchen. It was largely the fault of the dorm's thin walls and badly designed architecture, but I'm also very nosy. It works out nicely that nosy happens to be part of my job description.

One voice, the same one that so misguidedly greeted me minutes earlier, rose again in irate tones above the quieter murmur. "What the hell was that all about?"

So the new kid hadn't tried to wake me up on purpose, I thought. Ah, Meg. If you've been a good girl, the others will tell you how thin the walls are, how your words carry. If you haven't, well, we'll just see how far they let you go. Maybe they're counting on me being semiconscious.

Apparently no one was interested in saving Meg from

herself just yet, or maybe she already knew and didn't care. She did have an attitude, I'd noticed. "I've seen better manners at a drive-by shooting!" she announced.

Not bad, I thought, but inaccurate. I took a big sip of coffee. My manners are impeccable; they just happen to be dormant until about ten A.M. Everyone else knows this and loves me in spite of it. I put my mug down to examine the damage to my shirt.

"She's just not a morning person, that's all," a reedy voice I recognized as Alan's said quickly. "Just let her have the one cup, and then you can try conversation."

Rob, then, I guessed, chimed in. "Yeah, but no complex sentences until the second cup, and no problems till the pot's rinsed out."

Huh, the smartass! I never thought of it that way, but then I wasn't objective enough an observer at the critical times. I could have gotten away with the coffee-stained shirt—it was only going to get dirtier, after all—but seeing my trowel on my boots reminded me: I had senior faculty visiting today and needed to be as presentable as work would allow. My shoulders slumped as I realized I also needed to get going a little earlier so I could get the things organized for Tony's visit that I hadn't managed last night. I quickly unbuttoned my shirt and donned a clean one.

I laced up my boots and gathered up my notebooks and maps, then threw a couple more books on the pile. I'd need pictures to show Tony Markham the sort of things we were looking for, as we hadn't uncovered anything from the seventeenth century yet. With any luck, since we were so close to hitting the early surfaces, we might actually uncover some finds in time to really impress him. No sparing the lash today.

But I decided that I'd better make time to have another cup of coffee. Just in case. Gear and notes ready in a pile to leave with me, I put my trowel on top of them and went back to the kitchen. As I sucked down that cup of coffee even quicker than the first, I wondered for the eleventy-seventh time who it was I should be nominating for beatification, the CEO of Starbucks or Juan Valdez himself.

The students were making their lunches, and I slapped a sandwich together, thinking wistfully of Brian's cooking. I'd been eating too many sandwiches lately. Then I watched as Alan scraped a microscopically thin layer of peanut butter across a slice of bread and put that into a Baggie. I'd suggested before that he needed more lunch, but he always said it was too hot to eat. I worried about the pinched look of his face. I said nothing, but shook my head and emptied the rest of the pot into my travel mug.

"Let's go, let's go, guys," I called out. "Lots of work today."

"You say that every day," Dian said, reaching across the table for the pastrami.

"And it's true every day," I agreed. I put my sandwich in the cooler, and noticed that there was more than lunch construction going on. I stifled a groan: It was way too early for sexual displays.

Having leaned right across Rob to get the ingredients for her sandwich, Dian stretched to grab a new loaf of bread from on top of the fridge and then dropped the box of sandwich bags and bent over to retrieve them. Since Dian is built like a Hindu temple goddess, mostly luscious curves and brown curls, and since her cropped sweatshirt alternately rode up over her navel or gaped to reveal copious cleavage, she was guaranteed an audience. She looked up from her task, as if all innocence, and caught Rob staring. Looking straight at him, she licked the mustard off her knife. He dropped the apple he'd been holding, and it rolled away on the floor almost unnoticed.

I shook my head in disbelief, but then resigned myself to the fact that most field crews are just simmering cauldrons of lust. Brian was right, though. I had no business interfering.

"Fifteen minutes!" Neal yelled. "And keys! Who's got the keys to the big truck?"

"I do," Alan said, tossing them to him. Neal threw them to

me, and to my surprise, I snagged them one-handed. I just as quickly pitched them back to him.

"I have to bring my car today," I explained. "In case Professor Markham comes late, I don't want to keep you guys. And I'm heading up early, to get a few things set up for him."

I also had an ulterior motive. Generally speaking, if I get a few more minutes of semiconscious decompression, I'm not so likely to get the cognitive bends. Today I could get a little more thinking done if I was driving on my own.

"I'll come with you, Emma," Meg said unexpectedly. She already had her gear and lunch put together.

I didn't have time to argue. Shrugging, I said, "As long as you don't mind classical music and a contemplative driver, because it *is* a nice day for a drive-by—"

Meg flushed violently, and I continued as innocently as I could "—a nice drive by the river with Herr Beethoven. If you're ready, then let's get going."

I gave myself until we'd pulled off College Drive before I decided to examine last night's reflections in the cold light of morning. Literally cold, I shivered and turned on the battered old Civic's heat. Mornings are often chilly in Maine, no matter how warm the day shapes up to be, even in July.

I turned up my sonatas, let muscle memory guide me toward the site, and settled back to think. Last night I'd realized that there were two things that still particularly bothered me about my unfortunate discovery of Augie Brooks. The first was the awful sensation of actually, literally stumbling over his body. I'd been walking along the beach below the site, looking up at the eroding bank for any sign of the seventeenth-century English habitation, when my foot struck something soft but solid. I instantly thought of a life preserver lost on the beach, but it was far too heavy for that. I looked down slowly, hoping that it wasn't a dead seal—they usually were farther down the river, closer to its mouth and the ocean—and was grateful to see a dark red sweatshirt, half buried in the sand and tangled with seaweed. I thought it was something lost from one of the hundreds of sailboats and motorboats that travel the river until I saw how the flies swarmed around the bundle when I'd disturbed it. When I pulled my foot back, the body shifted and the sickly sweet smell of deteriorating flesh assailed me all at once. I gagged and stepped back. Please be a dead seal, please be a dead seal, I repeated to myself in the eternity it took for me to look closer. But I had already known the truth in an instant. I was just not willing to believe that I had found a human body.

The odd thing was that, after I convinced my breakfast to stay put, I'd mostly been curious, rather than horrified or nauseated. The fact is that, in our sanitized twenty-first-century lives, most of us seldom encounter a corpse outside of a hospital or a funeral parlor. The man, for male the body was, looked strangely out of place, and I couldn't for the life of me figure out why he didn't wake up, prodded by my heavy boot, or at least complain about me disturbing him. I stood staring at him for I don't know how many moments, not touching, but rather cataloguing what I saw, as if by analyzing what I observed I could make some sense of it.

The figure was facedown, left at the high-tide line. He was a short, stoutish, older man, say about sixty, based on the age spots, wearing a red sweatshirt and dark blue work trousers, the sort my mother calls "janitor pants." His dingy sweat socks and tennis shoes had seen better days. An overgrown fringe of thinning gray was all that was left of his hair, and I was grateful that his poor face was turned and half buried in the sand, for apart from some scary-looking bruises, when I noticed his shriveled white hand, I saw that the seagulls had been trying to make a meal of them. The mere thought of what the birds might have done to the soft tissue of his eyes and lips caused me to stumble back, and I decided suddenly that I should be initiating the modern rituals of death. I had hastened back up to the site, as calmly as I could, past the students, and went into the big gray house to call the authorities. Later I'd been told his name: Augie Brooks.

"Uh, Emma—"

Meg's warning woke me up to the present; I had been idling at a green light. I hurried through the intersection and picked up the thread of my thoughts a little more cautiously as I hit the highway.

I suppose that in a way I am constantly prepared to find bodies, although I expect that they will have been dead for a much longer time and be nicely, cleanly fleshless. I've worked on human remains in the field on many occasions, and I believe that I've become pretty good at remembering that the bones were once people, with all their attendant worries and hopes, good qualities and bad. I try to remember that their probate inventories, letters, diaries, and bills were not created just to be fodder for my research, but were real parts of many lives. Folks consider me pretty sensitive when it comes to dealing with the dead, but I have to admit, it is the immediacy of flesh on bone that brings that humanity much more forcefully to mind. Knowing a name doesn't hurt either.

Signaling to turn off to a secondary road, I mentally shook my head. After all, I'd just been walking, trying to sort out some site questions, and happened upon this quiet, almost private scene, purely by chance. A decision to walk down the dirt road instead of the pebbly beach and I would have never seen it. There was the second thing that bothered me: Why did Augie prey on my mind so? I didn't know him and, really, hadn't been terribly upset by the mere fact of my discovery.

Finally I decided that I resented his proximity to Greycliff, a place that meant so much to me all through my life and was now the focus of my professional scrutiny as well. You get protective about any site you've worked on, no matter how scrubby-looking it is or uninformative it turns out to be. Never mind that this had occurred practically at the front doorstep of my friend Pauline Westlake, who happened to own the site.

That rational explanation didn't sit quite right, however. There was a pricking in my thumbs that persisted in the face of all that good sense. Forget it, Emma, I scolded myself, there's work to do. As I pulled down the last, pine tree–lined road that led to the site, I reached the conclusion, not for the first time, that I think too much for my own good.

"So, what's up?" I said, finally addressing Meg. "Any particular reason you wanted to join me?"

"Nothing much," she answered. "Just wanted to get out a little early. I think I'm changing levels, and I wanted to get a look at the dirt in the direct sunlight, before we get the shadows."

"Good enough. You're close to Dian's depth, so keep a sharp eye out."

"I always keep a sharp eye out," came the prompt reply. Not shirty, but a little too self-assured, perhaps.

I raised an eyebrow but kept my response mild. "It's just an expression, but we *are* getting close to the seventeenth-century levels, and one careless swipe of the trowel could do a lot of damage."

"Right."

"You can get right to it. I'll check in with Pauline and then get my stuff sorted out for Tony, er, Professor Markham."

We pulled into the drive and got out. As trite as it sounds, the smell of salt air and fresh dirt really has a powerful effect on me, like a call to battle. If a shower strips you down emotionally at the end of the day, when you can only see the huge amount of work that still remains to be done and the problems you still haven't solved, then the arrival on a site equally brings the sense of new beginnings, the opportunity to figure it all out, another chance to solve all the mysteries.

I'd just grabbed my notebook when I noticed a black car, some sort of Camaro or Corvette or something, drive slowly up to the house. It almost came to a stop, but then suddenly speeded up and tore off up the road. I frowned: This end of the road was well away from the beach that attracted so many tourists, and the locals were usually much more cautious about speeding around the twists and turns. Guy must be lost, I thought.

As I walked down the driveway I could see that Pauline was already on the porch of the large gray house that was built before the turn of the century, and named Greycliff for the gray granite outcropping behind it. Pauline professed to hate the name, bestowed by the sentimental, Scot-loving Victorians who'd built the place, but unless she wanted to take a hacksaw to the fancy wrought-iron fence plate that spelled out the name, she was stuck with it. No one could have had the heart to undo that beautiful ironwork, though, no matter how good the cause.

Even from a distance one could see that Pauline Westlake was tall and slender and indomitable. Her erect posture had, in the past, occasionally been echoed by a silent armada of lanky Siamese cats, who periodically aligned themselves around their mistress, as if subjecting her guests to the same sharp scrutiny that she was too polite to make obvious. They were gone now. When the last one, the patriarch, had been carried off by one of the eagles that soared over the river, she hadn't had the heart to replace him.

I had first met Pauline when I was eight, the age at which my grandfather believed that children ought to start being introduced into the adult world. She was already nearly sixty then and she'd scared the hell out of me. My mistake had been in assuming that she was not kind simply because she'd not spoken down to me, a child. I eventually learned over the years that although Pauline did not tolerate silliness, she had a great capacity for good humor and, on occasion, an impulsive sense of daring that took my breath away.

The passage of time had little altered my friend (surely too pallid a term for our relationship, but we had negotiated our relationship carefully over the years and earned the finer connotations of the word). The years only appeared to have distilled her to an even more essential form of herself.

Pauline's hair was whiter, and still carefully bobbed to just above her chin, her posture not a whit relaxed from its military bearing. She still dressed with crisp orderliness in the jeans and men's shirts she'd worn since time immemorial. Pauline had always been a remarkable woman, and even now seemed to possess the secret, if not to eternal youth, then to eternal vitality. She'd done nearly as much as Grandpa had in making me the adult I am today, by sharing her tales of travel in far-off lands and her love of the objects she brought back from those solitary journeys.

"Morning," Pauline greeted me. She held up the mug that I'd come to think of as my own. "Coffee?"

"No, thanks," I said as I took the mug. "I hear caffeine is bad for you." I sat down on the swing next to her and drank deeply. "Oooh, plasma."

"Close. Jamaican Blue Mountain," Pauline said. Her words were Beacon Hill Yankee, with the patina of antique family money. I loved listening to her speak.

We rocked back and forth for a moment, enjoying the morning sounds of birds and wind on the river, which we could see in an unparalleled view from the porch. We could see Meg beginning to work below us, but were too far away to hear the sound of her trowel on the soil. On the far bank, a few scattered houses peeped through a dense, dark green wall of trees. On the river, moored sailboats bobbed lazily on the wake of two lobster boats chugging past. The sun was rising quickly now, burning the mist off the river.

"What's the plan for today?" Her words were the same every morning, and if they had not been, I would have worried.

"We're getting down through the eighteenth century, I think. If we get through that burn layer I've been seeing—you remember?—we may be close to Fort Providence. Today could be the day," I said carefully, with no other emphasis.

"That's something, isn't it?" Pauline said, staring out at the water. "An English site that was settled before Jamestown?

That predates the Pilgrims at Plymouth by almost two decades? And I have a front-row seat to it all."

That thought jarred my memory and my worries of the morning. "Paul? Weren't you bothered by . . . what happened yesterday?"

"What happened yesterday?"

At first I thought she was teasing me, but then I realized Pauline would never joke like that. "The body? Down by the shore?"

"Oh no." Pauline shook her head. "No. Dear me, Emma, from what you told me of it, I've seen much worse, and they had him all neatly covered up by the time the ambulance came, so I didn't even see that. And Augie Brooks? It's a sad thing, certainly, but anyone who knew him would have bet that he would have come to just this sort of end. Really, we were prepared for it after they found his motorboat without him in it. The man wasted every chance everyone, including God, ever gave him." She looked at me. "*You* are bothered, though, aren't you?"

I shrugged. "I guess I was wondering: Why here?"

Pauline laughed. "Well, why not here? They say if you stay in one place long enough, the entire world comes to your door, and if I'm lucky enough to have Fort Providence, then surely one drunken old fool should come as no surprise. Augie Brooks was never handy on the water; too nervous." She sighed. "He must have been on quite a bender."

"I couldn't see everything," I said hesitantly. The deputies had said it was an accident, but it looked worse than that to me. I couldn't shake off the memory of those bruises. "But from what I could see, his face was . . ." I decided there was no point in finishing.

Pauline patted my arm. "I'm sorry you had to be the one, but the way I see it, better Augie should land here than downriver, on the public beach, for some poor tourist to find. This way we can take care of our own."

"That's what the officer said." I watched the fair-weather

clouds glide over the Point and realized that I needed to get to work.

Pauline nodded her approval. "That Dave Stannard's the best kind of man. Not too pleased with his badge and his title, like some sheriffs we've had. Sensible, fair. And his wife's a dear, one of the best cooks I've ever met."

It was my turn to laugh as I got off the swing. "And that's got exactly what to do with his qualities as a cop?"

"Sheriff. Nothing, only it's nice to see good people with good people every once in a while. Speaking of which, when will Brian be by for a visit?"

"I hope in a week or two. He's pretty busy right now, something big's happening at the lab, I guess." That reminded me. "Oh, I wanted to give you the heads-up. I've got a visitor stopping by today, a sahib from the department, Dr. Tony Markham. So if you see anyone wandering around . . ."

Pauline nodded. "I'll send him your way. As if anyone would mistake what's happening down there for a polo match. I'll be down later." She reached out her hand for my mug, and I reluctantly gave it to her.

I stood watching Meg and chewing my lip. Pauline gave me a gentle push in the small of the back.

"Go on. No more brooding over Augie. Go find my fort."

On the scrubby lawn below the house and toward the river was The Site. My site. Even though I had visited a thousand times as a kid, it was now mine eternally, because I had put spade to earth there. All my history in the house, and all that history waiting for me under the lawn—it made me dizzy to think about it.

I marveled over the events that seemed, like fate, to lead me to this amazing site, but it was really the indirect cause of my acquaintance with Pauline to begin with. Grandpa Oscar had met Pauline during one of his searches for Native American sites in the area more than thirty years ago. The area was a strategic location for hunting and a center for politics and religion. When he approached Pauline about permission to survey her property, a situation that could easily have turned into a hostile encounter, their mutual interest in antiquity had sprung into lasting friendship.

Last fall, a few years after Oscar's death, I had been visiting Pauline at Greycliff, pacing restlessly in the living room, confiding to her my fears about the whole academic roller coaster over tea and sympathy.

"There's just so much at stake," I remembered saying to her. "There's so much other work to juggle before you can even think about doing your own research. I can't afford to screw up, not in the least little way, not if I want to keep this job. And the landowner at the MacGuire farm has suddenly decided that he doesn't like the idea of me working on his property this summer. So now I'm out of luck for this season."

Pauline just sat listening, watching me, waiting until I ran out of steam before she offered any advice.

I went over to look at a picture of Oscar that resided among the collection of photos on the mantelpiece. He was with a group of Native American men, the only one in the photograph who had a beard. Pauline had an array of things on the mantel with the picture, and at first I'd taken it for granted that they were more costly souvenirs from her travels, small pieces of the art she loved so much. But it was a dirty piece of dull green-glazed pottery that caught my attention and forced me to examine them all more carefully. I picked one up and turned it over and over, not willing to believe what I was seeing. It couldn't be . . .

I looked at my friend in shock. "Paul, where did you get these?" They weren't beautiful or expensive things at all; they were broken, dirty, and, to many eyes, nondescript.

She rose and joined me at the mantel. "Oh, I'm glad you saw them. I've been meaning to ask you about them. I found them when that old pine down front finally uprooted last winter. These things came up in the roots. What are they?"

"You found them *here*?" I asked excitedly. "Pauline,

they're about four hundred years old! They're European, I think they're English! What the hell are they doing here? Could they be—?"

Pauline was silent a moment. "Everyone's heard of Fort Providence, of course. There's even been a number of attempts to locate the site of it—Oscar was mildly interested, but his first love was the Indian history around here. He believed that it was upriver, where Fort Archer is now. And I never thought that there was anything but the remains of the eighteenth-century farm around here, myself." She laughed. "There were all sorts of stories about buried treasure—gold—in Fort Providence, and of course that's what people always thought of, not that it was the first English settlement in New England."

"And no one's ever found it," I said, amazed. "No traces of it ever turned up?"

"There were just a couple attempts in the sixties, but Oscar told me that because there were so few documents associated with it, it was practically impossible to locate the site. People knew it was on the Saugatuck River, but it's a very long river with a very long history."

We exchanged a glance. "Do you really think they could be from Fort Providence?" she asked. "All the way from 1605?"

I hardly dared to believe it was possible. "It could be. Why don't you show me where you found them, and then, well, it's worth a few test pits, that's for sure."

And it was at that point that I began to believe that I could initiate a fresh search for the earliest English site on the American mainland.

A seagull screeched overhead and I paused in my reflections to scan the site. To the south was the dirt road and a slight rise in back of Pauline's house, which faced the river. To the east, a cluster of scrubby pines and oaks marked the edge of the property, as well as another edge of the land itself, and threatened to overwhelm an ancient barn that was standing more out of habit than structural integrity, but still

saw use as our storage depot. The western boundary was
proclaimed by a sparse line of silver birches, planted when
the property was sold and the house constructed. A compar-
atively flat stretch of land lay below the slope on which the
house sat. It had once been a field and probably an unpro-
ductive one for all of that, now roughly mown so that we
could work. To the north of this field there was another
slight slope, then the bluff dropped off to the river, literally
and figuratively: It was eroding quickly. At the northeast corner was a staircase of disintegrating concrete steps with the
rusting remains of a railing that led down to the water. An
equally rusted iron ring remained at the base, once used for
tying up dinghies. I just told the students to stay away from
the whole crumbling mess. The excavation areas were in the
field, to the west of the barn and pine trees.

Now I had to get to work and prove to everyone else what
I already suspected, that I was on the track of an extremely
hot site. I tried not to think about how much I had riding on
this work, emotionally and professionally. My whole future
and my whole past.

I sauntered down the hill and, nodding to Meg, who was
finishing scraping the last bit of soil from a corner into a
dustpan, squatted well away from the edge of the unit to pre-
vent knocking anything into the unit she was working so
hard to clean. Meg dumped the soil into a galvanized bucket
and went to the sifter screen. Like everyone else, I noticed,
she had uncovered the scorched layer yesterday, but was
moving quickly this morning, just as Neal had indicated to
me last night, and was nearly through that already. I looked
at the unit, a one-by-two-meter oblong trench cut into the
ground, nearly a half meter—or about a foot and a half—
deep. If her walls were any indication, she had everything
well under control: They were surgically clean, the corners
were square, and the soil carefully sifted through a screen
into a pile off to the right. In her artifact bucket, she had
plastic bags marked with the state site designation number,
ME343–1, the unit number, and the number of the level in

which she was presently working, with the date and her initials at the bottom. Good; everything we'd need to keep track of where the artifacts had come from. This information would also be marked on the artifacts after we washed them.

The sound of the dirt rasping on the screen stopped momentarily, and I watched as Meg examined what had not passed through the mesh. She was maybe four inches shorter than I, maybe five-four or so, and well muscled; I could tell that she had spent a lot of time in the gym. Her hair was cut short and spiked and was bleached almost to a platinum. A row of earrings lined each ear, giving her a tribal appearance. Her every move seemed to bespeak aggression, or maybe *confidence* was the better word.

Systematically Meg began at the top of the screen and scanned back and forth, occasionally stopping to look more closely at something that caught her attention. The student used her trowel to flick at some clusters of pebbles, checking for artifacts that might be mixed in with them. After she'd collected everything she could see, she gave the screen one more shake, took another quick look at the contents, and then, satisfied that she had missed nothing, turned the screen over, dumping out the pebbles and other non-artifactual detritus. I watched as she knocked the overturned screen to loosen anything that might have stuck between the mesh and the wood frame and then cast a glance at what had knocked out onto the top of the spoils heap. Perfect technique.

"Nice stuff," I said, returning the artifacts I'd been looking at to her bucket. "A little local redware, a piece of English creamware, nails and such. Just not a lot of it."

"I think I'm coming to the end of the eighteenth-century level," Meg said. She started sorting her finds from the screen. "What was going on back then?"

"Not much, down here, at any rate. The farmstead had been abandoned, burned in the 1770s or so—that was off a ways to the west. This area's always been a strategic location. There's probably a few shipwrecks to be found out there too, what with all the river traffic."

Meg hesitated, then, a little embarrassed, came out with her next question. "When I told folks at Caldwell that I was going to work out here, everyone kept saying that there was supposed to be treasure out this way."

I nodded; it was a common rumor, one that seemed to dog every site. "Yeah, those legends seem to be particularly thick around here, don't they? I haven't tried to trace the source of the legend yet, but I'm willing to bet that it's probably just something that the local nineteenth-century hotel operators came up with, to attract interest."

I cast a glance in her artifact bucket. "I noticed you've already divided the artifacts into smaller bags by type," I remarked. "That's nice, but I usually wait until we're in the lab for that. Saves the bags for use in the field, so we don't need to go running around looking for sandwich baggies to substitute when we run out in the middle of the dig."

Meg looked put out and arched an unbleached eyebrow at me. "Sorry. That's how we used to do it for Schoss back in Colorado." She didn't sound sorry and just continued sorting her artifacts.

"Ah, but Professor Schoss had the finances of the National Geographic Society filling his pockets, and we, alas, do not," I said. "Looks like you've got a change of soil coming up there." I pointed to the corner. "You uncovering a little feature there, or is it just the light? Looks like the soil is a little lighter, a little more mottled in color."

Again Meg looked at me impatiently.

Oh kiddo, I thought, if you can't take a little cooperative observation, what's going to happen when I really have to criticize you? A little knife between the shoulder blades? I'm on your side, really.

Finally she dropped the last of her artifacts into the bags and turned to look where I was pointing. "I think you're right," she said, after a minute. "I wasn't sure. I'll start a feature sheet along with the new level."

And that was that, or would have been, but I wasn't about to be psyched out of checking her record sheets just because she had a chip on her shoulder. "Mind if I go over your notes? Just to make sure I can read them." I am the big dog here, I thought, and I have just as much attitude as you do. And if you aren't up to snuff, I'm going to let you know. In the nicest way possible, of course.

"Here you go." She handed me the clipboard.

I flipped through the sheets, checking her descriptions and observations. "Good, good. Lots of nice, precise adjectives. Your mapping looks right on, just add the scale, okay? Excellent work." I smiled at Meg, who seemed surprised.

"Thanks." A pause. "I'll draw a plan showing that feature when it's a bit better defined." She hazarded a smile as I returned her notes.

I hunkered down in a squat and took out my creased little notebook so I could write down my own impressions while they were still fresh in my mind. "You know," I said as I scribbled, "one of the things I love about fieldwork is that everyone gets to own it. I mean, everyone contributes and everyone gets to take some pride in it. The community of a project gives it its identity and we've got a good one going here. Give and take, everyone working toward the same goals. A *group* effort, know what I mean?"

Meg's brow was furrowed in concentration. She stopped trying to define the edge of the stain with her trowel to look at me. "Yeah, I suppose so."

"I've got to get some stuff together for Tony. Let me know if that stain turns into anything."

"Sure. Hey, Emma? Who's that?"

The student pointed down the slope. I saw someone coming up the stairs at the edge of the site. That in itself was unusual enough to alarm me, but my heart nigh on stopped when I saw the stranger fiddling with a metal detector. I realized that he was a pothunter, a looter. Whatever you wanted to call him, I wasn't about to let him steal anything from my site.

"Emma, should you—" Meg began, but I was already tearing off down the slope.

I gasped and began to run when I saw the stranger lean over and pull out one of the nails that held the strings that delineated the nearest of our units to the stairs. The nail out of his way, he made another pass with the metal detector and then tried a few more adjustments.

"Hey, leave that alone!" I shouted as I approached. It didn't matter that we'd already abandoned that unit. "This is private property—"

The stranger, a man, looked my way expressionlessly and then turned away again to play with the knobs on the metal detector. Call it intuition, call it pheromones, but I instantly knew this guy wasn't just some tourist with no clue. *He* was nothing but trouble. Tall and thin, he wore a greasy pair of jeans, a light blue windbreaker, and a pair of badly worn black leather cowboy boots. His eyes were concealed behind a pair of wire-rimmed aviator-style sunglasses. His face was lean and tan and weather-beaten, and his mouth was busily working a piece of gum. I was pretty sure that he was no younger than forty, and nearly positive he wasn't any older than sixty, but beyond that, I couldn't be certain of his age. His hair was yellowing white and shoulder length; it blew about in the wind, and he made no move to remove the strands that caught across his sunglasses as he turned his attention back to me.

I said with more authority, "You're trespassing. This is private property and you're interfering with my research. I'm asking you to leave. Now."

The stranger giggled, as if I were doing something naughty, and then shook his head regretfully. "Don't ever take that tone with me, sweetie," he admonished, enunciating carefully. His voice was like a dry cornfield crawling with locusts. "You have no idea what kind of trouble smart talk will get you. You want to end up like Augie Brooks?" He bowed his head back over the controls he was studying.

I couldn't believe he'd just said what he'd said. Surely I must have heard wrong . . . I couldn't believe any of this was happening. End up like Augie? Hostility was coming off this

guy in waves. It was a good thing I was so mad; it let me ignore how much I was shaking. My only concern now was to
get him away from the site, away from Pauline's house, as
soon as I could. "Like I said before, this is private property.
You're not welcome. Leave!"

The stranger didn't even bother to look up at me. "Why
don't you just fuck off and mind your own business?" He
stepped forward, clearly intending to use the detector.

I stepped directly into his path. Look at me, you maggot, I
thought.

Realizing that I was not going to move out of his way, the
stranger sighed, and placed one hand on his hip, as though
trying to summon up patience. His eyes did not move from
the ground near my feet. He removed the headphones, letting them rest around his neck. The wind fanned his white
hair into a demonic halo.

"Sweetheart," he said, "there are people in this world that
you do not fuck with. I am one of them. And you are starting
to bug me."

He finally lifted his head and removed his sunglasses impatiently, then fixed me with a pair of icy gray eyes so pale
that they almost looked white. With the shades off, there was
no way of hiding their intense malignancy, as systematic and
uncaring as a virus.

"Why don't you just save yourself a lot of trouble and take
a hike?" I said. "You're not going to use that thing around
here."

He smiled foully, showing sharp canine teeth. He was savoring the confrontation. I was shaking from indignation
mixed with fear.

The stranger cocked his head, considering the situation.
"I should just break your kneecaps, bitch," he said regretfully.

He's out of his mind, I thought in a panic. I mustn't let
him know he's scaring me. I locked eyes with him, willing
myself not to look away. Not to run away.

The stranger held my gaze for another moment. "Baby,

this is probably the biggest mistake of your life." With another sigh, he reached under his windbreaker and drew out a
large pistol, which he aimed carefully at my head.

I felt my face freeze into a blank mask that concealed my
fear. It was a curious sensation, maintaining that kind of
control while you are feeling just the opposite. With the
weapon no more than a meter from my face, my mind
churned over a thousand thoughts at once. I prayed that
Meg would stay still and not do anything to make this nut
pull the trigger. I hoped that my knees would not buckle.
Anger at the absolute wrongness of the situation and the
stranger bewildered me. At the same time, I foolishly wanted
to shush the seagulls, squabbling overhead with no concern
for my predicament, so that I could think without distraction.

The wind whipped his hair around crazily and billowed
my shirttails, lending frenzied motion to an otherwise static
tableau. All the while the arctic wastes behind those pale eyes
froze me to the marrow.

"It would be so easy for me just to blow your whole fucking head off right this minute. Her too." His words were filled
with awe at the simplicity, the efficiency of his solution. The
stranger gestured with the pistol at where Meg was standing,
stock still, by her unit; I couldn't help but follow his gesture.
"Wouldn't take but another second."

I remained rooted to the ground, never letting my eyes
move away from his. Another moment passed.

"I'm getting bored," the stranger said irritably. "You act
snotty, you get in the way of my livelihood, my living. Now
you're fucking with me, and I told you, I am one of those
people you do not f—"

Pretty limited vocabulary, I thought hysterically, blocking
out the last of his words. Pretty repetitive. The gun looked
heavy and very deadly. A giggle almost broke the surface, and
yet I knew my face was still impassive. But I was very close to
the edge and could feel my reserve giving way.

There's nothing I can say, I thought, as the stranger returned my stare. That gun's too close, he can't miss. There's nowhere to run.

But I can't just stand here and let him shoot me . . .

I had absolutely no idea what to do. So the stranger made my decision for me.

Chapter 3

THE SOUND OF SLAMMING TRUCK DOORS CAUSED US both to look up the slope. The rest of the students had arrived. I saw that Alan and Pauline were staring in shock down at me and the stranger. Panic welled up in me as he spoke again.

"All right, sweetie, I haven't got time for this shit." Straightening his arm, improving the already point-blank range, he then suddenly lowered the pistol, turned on his heel, and headed for the crumbly cement stairs leading to the narrow shingle. He pivoted, still brandishing the gun, still carrying the damned metal detector. "I haven't got time for this now. I've got important business. But if I ever see you again, it's all over." Then he simply stalked down the stairs and out of sight.

I was frozen in place, expecting him to rush back if I moved. Eventually anger and prudence took control again, and I forced myself to walk over to the crumbly staircase that led from the bluff to the beach. The stranger was nowhere in sight. He moves fast, there's no trace . . . wait a minute, just below the cobbles at the high-water line. I saw footprints heading east round the bend, toward the public beach and the parking lot a mile away. I needed to call the sheriff's department before he got too far. As I picked my way back up to the trenches, I found myself starting to tremble even more violently, sweat coursing down the inside of my shirt, and the hair on the back of my neck stood on end. That didn't just happen, I kept telling myself. People don't act like that—

I turned and saw Meg flying down the hill toward me, and the adrenaline rush that had been supporting me suddenly fled my system. My hands were like ice, and the prickling down my scalp and spine competed with the roiling in my stomach. I tried to call out to her and had to swallow several times before I could actually speak. The dry taste of dirty pennies wouldn't go away. I started to shake violently again and couldn't stop. Typical fight-or-flight reaction, I thought, cataloguing my symptoms as though they belonged to someone else. Quite an impressive thing to experience firsthand, I pointed out to the part of me that was screaming inside.

"Emma, oh my God, are you all right?" Meg was having no problems with her voice; she had grabbed my arm and was practically screaming in my ear. "I can't believe it! He pulled an automatic on you!"

"Yeah, I know." I began to giggle, I couldn't help it. Automatic? That what that thing was? "Yeah, I *saw* the gun, Meg."

I clamped down hard on the nervous laughter that threatened to well out of me; it scared me almost as badly as the stranger did. "I'm sorry, I'm a little shaky. Are you okay?"

Meg looked at me, amazed. "I'm fine. I just can't believe it. I mean, that doesn't happen out here, does it? I mean, you can hear about people pulling that sort of crap back home in Colorado, but out East . . . that just doesn't happen here, does it? You were so calm about it all—"

She must be in a state of shock; I didn't think she was a fool. "We need to call the sheriff's department right away. Were you able to hear any of what happened?" I wondered if my legs would carry me up to the house.

"No, no, the wind carried off most of it," Meg said apologetically. She continued on in something that sounded to me dangerously like awe. "It was amazing, the way you stared him down. You just faced him out."

I didn't do anything so useful, I thought, disgusted with myself. Out loud I said, "The only thing going through my mind was how to keep from getting killed. Getting us killed. I certainly wasn't going to do anything to make him want to pull the trigger." My teeth began to chatter now, but Meg didn't seem to notice.

"I know, but I felt so helpless," she repeated. "It was horrible. I didn't have—"

I didn't want her to dwell on these thoughts and she didn't seem to be able to shut them off. I grabbed her hands, though I could barely feel them with my own numb ones. "I'm really glad that you stayed put," I said emphatically, locking her gaze in my own. "There was nothing you could have done, and with someone as crazy as he is . . . any kind of distraction would have been . . . been bad."

Meg started to protest, but I cut her off. "Look, I don't know about you, but I'm freezing. Let's get up to the house and phone the sheriff right now."

"You're sure you're all right?" I asked Meg again, as we climbed up the slope.

"Yeah, fine. A little pumped is all." Leave it to the young; Meg didn't look as rattled as I felt.

We didn't even have the few moments that it usually would have taken us to reach the house; everyone, including Pauline, had rushed down to meet us halfway. Alan looked a little sick, but even that didn't keep him from piping up with the others.

"Emma, who was that?"

"Was that a *gun* he had—?"

"What was he doing there?"

As glad as I was to see everyone—I had to believe that their appearance saved my life—I couldn't suppress a little feeling of annoyance at their questions and concern. I didn't want to recount what had just happened to me; it was still too close and I still didn't know what I made of it all myself.

I turned to Pauline. "Could you see him? Did you hear anything he said?"

"No, Emma, it was too far away. Are you okay?"

"I'm fine, I'm not hurt. I'll be right back. I'm going to call the sheriff."

I trotted up the steps of the porch and into the kitchen. The phone book was still opened to the municipal pages listing the number of the sheriff's department, left from when I called yesterday. I was put through right away and related my version of the incident to the sheriff, the quiet-spoken bloke named Stannard, who'd been kind enough to me yesterday after I found Augie Brooks's body. I felt stupid actually saying things like *pistol* and *threat,* but I had to accept that those were the words to describe what happened.

The sheriff recognized my description of the stranger. "Ah, me. It sounds like Grahame Tichnor." He sounded weary. "Not the first time we've had problems with him, but this is unusual, even for him. I'll come out and have a look around and then you should come down to the station and have a look at some photos, see if you can identify him."

I irrationally thought of all the work I'd planned for today. "But I'm sort of busy right now—"

"Me too," the sheriff said good-naturedly. "It will only take a minute."

I sighed. "You're right, I'm sorry. When can you get here?"

"About a half hour. I doubt our friend will be back any time soon, he's just not the type. But just to be sure, I'll have a car swing by the Point every so often, keep an eye out. And you tell Ms. Westlake to lock up good, come night. I'll see you shortly."

I hung up and watched as Pauline came in and began to clear up her breakfast things.

"What'd he say?" she asked.

"He's coming out. He said to tell you to lock up at night and that they'd send someone around every once in a while, just as a precaution. You put your alarm on every night, right?"

Pauline looked back over her shoulder and shrugged. "I forget mostly. Who'd want my old things anyway?"

"Pauline, don't be funny! Never mind your stuff, I'm worried about you! Promise me you'll set your alarm and be careful!"

"I wish you wouldn't make such an issue about the alarm," Pauline said. "I'm not the one he was pointing that horrible thing at. I'm more concerned about you." She took a towel down from the dish rack, and turned to face me as she dried her hands off, leaning against the island.

"Paul, an issue? You need to take care! All sorts of things are happening around here—yesterday a body on the beach, and now this guy—Tichnor, his name is—"

"Oh Lord. *That* poor excuse for a—"

"—he's dangerous! He had a *gun!*"

Pauline waved my concerns aside. "Don't fret so, I managed to totter round the globe several times before you were born without coming to too much grief. I think I can just about manage locking the door at night. Grahame Tichnor has been a nuisance for more years than anyone cares to count; I'm not afraid of him and he's not worth your worry. I'm not going to let some noisome little cretin boss me around my own place. And anyway, I've got people coming tonight, and I'll be in Boston all next week, and the beginning of the next—so don't worry about me. Honestly. I'm more worried about you. That must have been terrifying—"

"I'm fine," I insisted. "I'm just a little . . . pumped, is all." And I was fine, I told myself. Absolutely.

"If you're sure." Pauline folded the towel, gave me a peck on the cheek, and the matter was closed. The phone rang. "I'll just take it in the other room, dear. And yes, for you, I'll set the damned alarm."

I went back toward the door, but something made me stop. Through the window I could hear Meg talking to the other students about the incident.

"—I just couldn't believe it!"

"What did *you* do?" Alan asked. He'd been following Meg around the site ever since she'd arrived.

"Me? Nothing. There was nothing I could have done, without getting—"

"What did Emma do?" I heard Dian ask.

"She was the amazing one," Meg said. "She just stared him out, didn't back off or anything. The wilder he got, the calmer she got, just like a standoff. It was un-*real*."

"No way!"

"I'm telling you, she's got icewater for blood!"

Utter nonsense. It was at that point that I decided to go out there and explain exactly what happened and how there was nothing heroic in what I had done, or more precisely, not done, but when I reached for the door I realized that I was trembling violently again. I couldn't feel my fingers, and the acid weight congealed in my stomach. Instead of going outside, I went into the little bathroom off the kitchen and ran hot water over my wrists until I was sure the trembling had stopped.

By the time I'd recovered my composure, answered the rest of the questions the students had, and got them settled into work, a new Jeep Cherokee with a "Fordham County Sheriff's Department" logo arrived. I recognized the sheriff right away, average height, medium brown hair a little sun-bleached, and dark eyes. Nice-looking guy.

"Professor Fielding," he said, offering me his hand. "This is starting to be a habit with us."

"Hey, don't look at me," I protested, even though I knew it was probably a joke.

The sheriff's face sobered. "You're okay, though?"

"Yes. A little taken aback by it all."

"Why don't you show me where it happened and walk me through it?"

I led him past the working students to where Tichnor had kicked out the lines of that abandoned unit. The sheriff listened to my story, asking a question here and there for clarification, as he scanned the site, the working students, and the river. He walked over to the stairs and had a look at them and then the footprints that were still impressed into the sand. That was what reminded me.

"I don't think I said anything to you about it when I called," I began apprehensively, "but he, Tichnor I mean, said something about Augie Brooks. He said . . . said that I didn't want to end up like Augie Brooks. Does that mean . . . do you think he had something to do with . . . the body?"

The sheriff shook his head. "I doubt it, he probably just meant dead, is all. The autopsy is scheduled for this afternoon, but it seems pretty clear so far that Augie had an accident. This time, it wasn't one we could save him from. I think our friend Tichnor was adding a little color, is all."

"But what about his threats?" I protested. "He's crazy, certifiable! We can't rely on him to behave rationally enough to want to stay out of trouble! There's too much going on here, all of a sudden."

The sheriff nodded. "We've been looking for him already and now we'll book him for assault, just as soon as we find him. Like I said before, though, he's probably going to do a fade for a while, now that he thinks he's made his point. Just to be on the safe side, there's safety in numbers, don't forget."

"Isn't there anything else we can do?" Out of habit, I reached for my pen to chew on, a security blanket that was socially acceptable in academia, but caught myself and thought the better of it.

"Yes there is. If you and Ms., uh—" Stannard checked Meg's name in his notebook. "Ms. Garrity up there could stop by the sheriff's department later on and look at a few pictures, that would help. Also, if you would be so kind as to write up a couple of descriptions of what happened, it would be a big help."

"I'll do that," I said, determined. "We'll have them for you this evening."

Stannard waved my proposed haste aside. "No hurry. You drop 'em by if you get the chance, or you can mail them in later if that's more convenient."

"You don't seem really troubled by this," I said, annoyed. "I mean, look at what's been going on here—"

"I am troubled, I'm sorry it happened," he broke in. "I'm doing what I can legally do about it all, but the reality of it is, summer brings out the nuts from wherever they hide during the winter. It's what happens." The sheriff saw that I wasn't convinced and continued. "Look, I don't want anything to happen to you, any more than you do, okay? We'll do our best to find him and put everyone's mind at rest."

His eyes strayed back up toward the excavations, and he squinted, trying to concentrate. "So, tell me what's going on here."

"Well, we're trying to identify whether this is the site of Fort Providence, which was built in 1605 as a stronghold, especially against the French—"

"If that's the case, why isn't the Point called Providence today?" the sheriff asked.

Good question, I thought. "Well, the seventeenth-century settlers had had a stormy passage, complete with a couple of sea battles, and were pretty pleased to make it over here alive—hence the name Providence. I suspect the Penitence name came long after, when the area was resettled for good and people tried to farm around here."

We could both hear the ring of the students' trowels on the stony soil, a good reminder of why fishing was a much more lucrative endeavor than farming in this area.

"Anyway, the fort predates Jamestown by a couple of years and Plymouth in Massachusetts by fifteen. If it had lasted more than a year, more people might know about it from the history books."

Sheriff Stannard whistled, low and long. "So how do you know where to look?"

"That's a matter of a bit of luck, in this case. There's a lot of places along this river that it could have been, but the reason that I'm looking here is because artifacts of the right date were found here, and unless a collector dropped them or they were brought over as ship's ballast, it's real likely that this is where the settlement was."

He ran his hand through his hair in thought, leaving some standing on end. "So what did it look like? You really don't know what you're going to find?"

"In archaeology you never know what you'll find. Let's put it this way: I've got data from forts built by the English about the same time as this one, in Virginia, Ireland, and the Caribbean. You read what other people have excavated on those sites, and maybe we'll find the same thing here. And there was lots written at the time about how to set up a fort, picking out the right kind of land, looking for a defensible area, fresh water, and that sort of thing. So a lot of this work is based on educated guesses, but very well-informed educated guesses."

He nodded slowly, observing the working crew. "And you dig down and find . . . what?"

"So far, we've got mostly sherds of pottery, a few animal bones, parts of clay smoking pipes, that sort of thing, but these are all late eighteenth-century artifacts. There wasn't a whole lot going on down this end of the property before that, except for some farming."

"Interesting," he commented.

I nodded. "And what we do is dig down through the centuries, the most recent stuff, then older, and older as you go down. And we haven't hit the seventeenth-century strata yet, but when we do, I'm betting we'll find things, well, things that belonged to a fort, an outpost. You know, lead shot, trade items for the Native Americans, parts of weapons, in addition to the usual glass, pottery, and personal effects. Neat stuff."

I thought about how archaeology is like visiting another country, where you may be well versed in the mores of the place, but where surprises still lurked around every corner. Historical culture shock with the lure of discovery.

"Sounds good," the sheriff agreed, and we started to walk back up to where his Cherokee was parked. "My kids would love this. Could I bring them by, sometime? We wouldn't get in the way or anything. I like to show my girls what all sorts of people do for work, you know?"

"Sure, any time." We shook hands again, and as he left, I was surprised to find just how normal I felt again. Clever of the sheriff, I realized, to get me talking about my work. Settled me right down. Trying to capitalize on that feeling and trying to get some work done this morning, I went back down to check on the students.

I sensed a faint salt smell mingling with warm grass as I stopped by Alan's unit first. As much as I knew he was trying hard, he just wasn't cutting it. Unlike Meg's unit, his balks or walls were sloping in, and he had dug so far down in one corner that he might have changed soil levels and not known it, for all I could see. On top of that he was painfully thin; I'd worried about this watching him eat, or rather not eat: He never did anything more than push the food around his plate. I suspected it was trouble with his family; more than heroin-thin chic, he was starved for something that no one could give him. Aside from his last name, he didn't seem to share any of his father's characteristics. Alan was thin where his father, Rick, was closer to egg-shaped; had light brown hair that he let grow past his ears in a sort of dramatic, romantic MTV style that didn't work, whereas his father was nearly bald. Alan claimed to be interested in historical archaeology; his father, a cultural anthropologist, didn't see the reason for digging when "there were documents to tell you what happened," as he so often told me. More than anything, Alan generally looked uneasy and hyperaware, where his father had a much thicker skin.

I remembered the famous criticism of a fictitious archaeologist and silently applied it to Alan Crabtree: The poor kid couldn't dig his way out of a box of kitty litter. I sighed. I had done my patient best to remind him what was supposed to happen when he was working. Taking a deep breath, I tried again.

"Hey, Alan? Looks like you're getting a little low over on that side, by a couple of centimeters. You'd better bring everything else down level with that before you go any further. Then you can take the elevations and start a new level, if you have to, but it's getting away from you now."

Alan sighed and looked down into the messy little ditch he was digging for himself. He'd heard it all before and it still wasn't taking. He didn't look at me, and I wondered whether he'd heard me.

"Okay," he said finally.

"Just try to remember what we talked about last week— you dig a few centimeters down, evenly across the whole unit, you sift that, write about what you see. If you get that rhythm going, that will help keep track of what you're finding."

"I *know*, I'll try again." He stood back and tried to see where to continue.

"Great," I said, ignoring his testy tone. "Why don't you work on cleaning up that level, and then trim those balks back—don't bother saving any of the artifacts out of the cleanup; they're no good to us if we don't know what level they came from"—I shouldn't have to be telling him this; it was something a freshman would have mastered—"then I'll come back and go over your notes with you."

"Okay, whatever."

Maybe because he was just sick of my pestering, he still refused to make eye contact. Tough, I thought.

Alan took a deep breath and, holding it, began to follow my directions doggedly. He was still holding his breath as I walked away toward the other cluster of units that were positioned to identify what might have been in the fort's interior.

Not for the first time, I cursed the ego of a father who would keep his kid in a place where he had no talent. I wondered again what department Alan might have chosen if his father hadn't been an anthropologist and determined to have a son follow in his footsteps. Rick made it plain that he thought I was trying to play Alan off him, but nothing could have been further from the truth: I would have given anything to keep myself out of the middle of their dysfunctional family mess.

I continued down the slope, off to the east where Dian had abandoned her own unit to help Rob do some mapping. I could see their two heads close together and I hoped they were talking about the coordinates they were ostensibly taking.

"Hey, Em, we've got some bad news for you," Rob called out. "We've got a—"

"If you found a skeleton," I cut him off, "bury it and don't tell me about it." I was joking of course, but human remains required us to stop digging and notify local and state bureaucracies. They were a real nuisance, legally speaking, in spite of the wealth of data they represented.

"No, nothing that bad," he replied. "That feature we've been mapping so carefully?" He held up a small bluish bottle. "Nineteenth century."

"Well, it happens." I looked at the bottle and its side seams. "Yep, that medicine bottle didn't come over on *The Endeavour* in 1605." I looked at the unit and said, "Well, it looks like you've still got a ways to go before you get down to where Meg is. You can still get some undisturbed seventeenth-century remains if that's as deep as that little pit goes—what is it, a planting hole? I wasn't real hopeful about that, though. It's still a little high. Keep at it."

"Yes'm."

I eyed Dian. "I bet Rob can dig the rest of this by himself, if you're done with the plan."

She smiled, pouting a little, knowing exactly what I was saying. "I'm done. I was just initialing the map, Em. I'm almost through the burn layer in my unit and I'm not getting much." She retied her hair, preparing to get back into the dirt. "A little eighteenth-century stuff."

"That's what Meg's got. You guys go up and see what she's up to, see if you're getting the same sorts of soil changes down here as she is up there."

"You got it."

I looked around. "Where's Neal?"

"Over with Meg," Dian said. Then, deadpanning, "Maybe he's helping her map her unit."

I gave her a sour look. "I'll be writing notes if anyone wants me. Back to work, you."

She smiled again, showing all her teeth. I liked Dian but didn't fancy Rob's chances if she decided to respond to his advances.

On my way upslope, however, I paused, noticing that the black car I'd seen earlier had returned and was now idling in the road above the driveway. I could see the driver this time—or more of him, at any rate—a tangle of light hair, baseball cap, a mustache. He seemed familiar to me, but just before I could dig up the identifying memory, he roared off again. Car needs a tune-up, I thought, frowning. Still unable to place the driver's face, I decided that if he was really interested in the dig, he'd get out and ask a few questions.

At last I was finally able to settle down to take my opening notes. Near the top of the slope, I had set up a card table between the barn and the bulk of the excavation units to keep my maps and notes on. We'd collected beach cobbles the first day, just to weigh down the papers that were constantly threatened by the wind off the river. It was a little up to the north of all of the work areas, where I could have a decent view of everyone and keep an ear and eye open while I sorted out my thoughts. The notes were inevitably, at this stage, a jumble of observations, reflections, memos to myself, even personal impressions of morale and activity. Already I was able to start making connections between finds and stratigraphy across the site, even a few tentative correlations between the court documents that were generated by the legal proceedings at the expedition's demise. By the end of the month I had in the field, I might be able to determine whether we actually had sufficient evidence of the location of the site. And much later, during the long, cold winter that would be spent in my lab at Caldwell College, all those notes would trigger my memories of the site and aid in the interpretation of it all, continuing to compare with what others at other sites had been able to piece together before me.

I finished, then watched Neal looking over Meg's shoulder, thinking I might be able to figure out what the problem was between those two. I kept my head down over my notes and kept my ears wide open. I make no apologies for eavesdropping. For one thing, it was my site, and that meant I was god of my small universe and therefore got to be omniscient when I chose. The other thing was that a good half of directing came down to personnel management.

My worktable was a little too conveniently placed at the moment; I could see and hear everything that was going on in Meg's unit. That was not a coincidence—I had no idea how much of an eye I'd have to keep on this newest student, but as it turned out, her excavating ability wasn't a problem at all. Quite the opposite. But considering Neal's vehemence last night, I thought I'd better pay heed.

"What you got there?" I heard Neal ask. "It looks like it's shaping up into a posthole."

"It is and I *just* got a piece of shot," Meg said excitedly. "I think it's early enough to be from Fort Providence! I'm just getting ready to take it out now."

I almost started out of my seat when I heard that. If the lead ball was the size used in muskets of the early seventeenth century, then this would be the first artifact we found *in situ* that was associated with the site! The first one that might confirm the early, sustained presence of the English in New England before the Pilgrims! I managed to get control of myself, however, because Meg should have the pleasure of getting to call me over to see her find. I wondered if she'd be the type to yell it out, once she was sure, or come over quietly and get me. In either case, it was her right. I also wanted her to be certain, just in case it was another later feature and not part of the fort. That was also her right, so I sat as tight as I could, under the circumstances.

"Check it out!" she said a moment later. "It sure looks okay!"

"Wow." Neal was appropriately awed. I saw her beaming at him and his faraway look at the realization of what she might have found. And then the pleasant tableau was shattered when Neal shook himself and then reached over into her unit.

"Look, I'll just clean this up for you and you go tell Emma."

His words hit me just a nanosecond before they sunk in for Meg. Oh Neal, don't! I thought. Don't rob her of this moment, her moment, with your obsessiveness.

As Meg realized what Neal was going to do, the smile faded from her face and she put her hand on his arm before he could touch anything. "You don't need to clean anything up." She spoke quickly, deliberately casual. "It's fine the way it is."

I watched as Neal furrowed his brow in the face of this unexpected resistance, and I prayed he'd just let Meg alone. "There's a lot of loose dirt," he insisted, trying to be helpful. "I'll *help* you take care of it." He reached forward again and Meg stepped in front of him.

"Don't." Meg ran a hand over her forehead and through her hair, leaving a dirty stain in the sweat that looked like war paint. "Look. The floor is pristine, nice and level. If it wasn't *I'd* fix it." She shrugged.

I thought about going over, but realized they needed to have this out. Neal was not used to being challenged, and was getting flustered. "What *is* your *problem*? I've told you before, I'm trying to help you!"

"Like I said yesterday, I don't need help, and I don't want you to mess with my work without asking." She paused, obviously struggling with her temper. "It's rude. It's unnecessary."

"I'm rude? *I'm* rude? You're whacked!" Neal was almost

shouting. As interesting as I found his unusual display of temper, I knew that name calling was my cue to get in there and referee. They weren't going to sort this out on their own.

"Hey, guys—" I began in an authoritative way, but I was interrupted by a loud clanging from down south of us. It was Dian signaling noontime by bashing her trowel against her metal dustpan. Meg and Neal looked at me expectantly and guiltily, aware that they'd been caught fighting.

"Lunchtime," I called out brightly.

Chapter 4

Neal shot Meg a last dirty look. "We can discuss this later."

"I'll be here." We both watched as he stalked off for the cooler.

There's the bell, head back to your corners, I thought. I ambled over to where Meg was. "Something up?"

I watched, amused, as she struggled to remember what had occasioned the disagreement and her face suddenly lit up again. She held her prize out to me. "Yeah, piece of ordnance. I think it's the right size for Fort Providence. And"—she stepped out of the way so I could see better—"it came out of this area. It looks like a posthole." This was all done with the immense, jaded cool of the self-satisfied. But then she raised her eyebrows and smiled at me in triumph. "Right where you saw that soil change."

I was taken aback and pleased; I didn't expect her to be so gracious. "Well, you found it and defined it quickly enough. Good job, first rate." I looked at the piece of lead, holding my breath. "Yep, it's looking like Fort Providence all right. Way to go." I smiled back at her and then cupped my hands into a megaphone. "Hey guys!" I called to the rest of the crew. "C'mere a second!"

I handed the piece of lead back to Meg while the others gathered around.

"The clock's ticking, Em, it's lunchtime!" Rob protested.

"I think you'll want to see this. Meg?"

She held up the piece of shot for everyone to see. In his eagerness, Alan stepped a little too closely to the side of the unit and caved some loose dirt onto the immaculate surface. "Hey, c'mon, man!" she protested. "You're killing me here." She let out a sigh of impatience; Alan had been following her around like a lost stray for the past week.

Rob grabbed Alan by the scruff of the T-shirt and yanked him out of the way. "Dork." He said it almost lovingly, as though this was all that could be expected of Alan. The two students wrestled for a moment, and Alan almost succeeded in pulling Rob's shirt off. He was breathing heavily, his reaction a little too aggressive for mere play.

"Hey, now!" I admonished.

"Enough foreplay, you guys," Neal said. "You're missing the point. Look."

The crew quieted until they realized the significance of what they were looking at.

"A posthole!"

"No way! The ball came from there?!"

"Is that right, Emma?"

"Sure is," I said. "Meg's got it, it looks like."

"All right Meg!" Dian cheered. "Woman!"

The others followed with congratulations, slapping Meg on the back and rubbing her head until her blond spikes looked even more barbaric than usual. "Hey, all right, all right," she said. But she looked really pleased with herself.

"So keep your eyes open—that's what other postholes will look like here, and there's a good chance we could hit another one any minute," I cautioned them. "So move it, faster, deeper! We want to confirm that these are really seventeenth century. But for now, get eating."

The others went back to the tree line where the cooler was, chattering excitedly about the find. I turned to Meg, who was still beaming, and handed her an empty film canister from my pocket. I watched as she marked the canister with the provenience and decided to bring up her argument with Neal. She'd had her moment, the others were gone, now was as good a time as any.

"You seemed to be disagreeing with Neal back there," I said calmly, as she handed me the find. "Things a little tense, huh?"

Her smile faded and something of the icy shell returned. After a moment she said, "I thought he was getting pushy."

"Well, it is his job to keep an eye on things." I waited a moment, looking thoughtfully at the piece of lead shot. "He sometimes gets a little overeager, but he's got high standards."

"Well, my standards are pretty high too," Meg said in a huff, then she caught my eye.

I looked at her hard for a moment, letting her know that she could make this better right now. She took the hint and swallowed.

"Maybe I won't take it so personally, seeing as he's got control issues."

I shrugged. "That could work. I'll suggest that he can afford to refocus his energies as well." The lesson was over. "Come on," I said. "I'm starving. And I want to recheck the maps."

But I couldn't stay away. As much as I love the scant moments I allotted for lunch, a moment to let my subconscious sort things out, I couldn't leave that posthole alone. So I scarfed down my lunch, heartily sick of sandwiches but unwilling to go hungry. It was a relief to get away from the antics at lunch today. For whatever reason, Alan moved away almost immediately after I sat down near him. He barely touched his stingy half sandwich, making me wonder if he wasn't anorexic. In any case, it was kind of heartbreaking to watch Alan traipse after Meg, laughing too loudly at her jokes. I didn't worry about Rob or Dian; they would be fine if things didn't work out between them. But Alan was hollow all the way through, with no core and no reserves.

I went back to my table with the maps, not that it did any good. Without the faintest idea of the construction of the fort or the buildings inside, the location of one posthole—if it was indeed early seventeenth century—didn't really clarify things. One point does not extrapolate to a wall, until you find its fellows. If they had also survived. Too many unknowns, I thought, putting the maps away, there's nothing to see here, yet. So I went and stared at the dirt for a while.

Tapping my pen against my teeth, I looked at the floor of the unit. It was just a circle of differently colored soil, mottled yellow and red sand, framed within the uniform brown of the surrounding level. It was *definitely* a feature, *most likely* a posthole, *maybe* dating to the seventeenth century, *possibly* as early as the Jacobean fort. Way too many unknowns, and there was nothing else to do but wait and see if others like it showed up.

Wait and see. The idea was not as easy as it sounded. Never mind that it might be the beginning of the fort, never mind that it might be the best evidence yet for this history-shattering discovery, never mind that it could make my career, I thought. I had to wait and I was pretty sure the suspense was going to kill me.

I realized that now I was chewing the pen cap, gnawing hard on the plastic. I carefully replaced the pen in my back pocket before I could break it or a tooth. As I turned, I noticed that Neal had joined me.

"Pretty neat," he said, nodding at the feature.

"Yep. It could be it." The thought alone made me long for my pen cap.

"What's the plan, then?" he asked.

"Well, I'm going up to tell Pauline about this. Give the others ten more minutes to finish up—we started late—and then get an elevation on this. The others need to know when things might start happening in their units. After that, we keep digging."

Neal was silent for a moment then said, "It seems like we should be able to do more, once we've got this."

"We're doing what needs to be done," I said. "You're right though, just carrying on seems like so little. Oh," I continued, as if with an afterthought. "There seems to be a little tension between you and Meg. That what you were telling me about last night?"

The crew chief immediately flushed red.

"I had a word with Meg. I think she'll be a little more open to suggestion in the future." We walked up the slope a bit together. "Her work looks pretty good, don't you think?"

He nodded, still red.

"Not everyone would have seen that transition right at the top like that. Most folks would have gone down a bit before they picked up on it."

Neal shrugged.

"I mean, I think we can be more confident about her." I stopped and caught Neal's eye. "Which is good, you know, because that frees you up for your work and for watching out for Alan, right? Everybody wins."

He nodded. "Gotcha, Em."

"Good. Back in a bit."

Congratulating myself on handling things so effectively, I went up to the house. I found Pauline working steadily in the front flower beds, pulling weeds and deadheading faded blooms.

"Hey Paul," I hailed her. "Got a minute?"

She smiled. "Of course." After she carefully wiped off her shears, we sat on the steps leading to the big wraparound porch. I told her about Meg's find of the lead ball and the posthole, but she was curiously unmoved by these discoveries. She sat leaning against one of the porch posts, watching the terns wheel against the backdrop of the opposite shore, her eyes half closed.

I began to get worried; surely she wasn't ill? "You see? It's possible we've got the first hard, in-ground evidence for the fort."

Her eyes were closed completely now. "I do see. It's great news, isn't it?"

I put my hand on her arm. "Paul, forgive me for saying so, but you don't seem, well, *excited*," I said. "Are you okay? You should come over, have a look at Meg's feature."

"I'll stop by later, as usual," she said unhurriedly. Pauline picked up on my concern, however, and opened her eyes again. "I'm thrilled, of course," she explained. "But if I'm not capering, it's because I thoroughly expected you to find the fort, dear. It was only a matter of time."

I stared at her. "It wasn't just a matter of time, we had practically nothing—we still don't even know if that's what we've got!"

"You've got it, don't worry."

I chewed my lip. "I wish I could be as sure as you are."

Pauline laughed. "Relax, Emma. Oscar taught you well."

I frowned; the posthole's appearance had nothing to do with Grandpa. I decided to change the subject. "Oscar would have loved this, wouldn't he?"

"He would have indeed," she replied, nodding. Her gaze was still dreamy, though. "Oscar would have been right in his element watching you work and it would have meant more to him than all those professional accolades he accumulated." She turned to me now and cocked her head thoughtfully.

I had never asked about her precise relationship with Grandpa. Grandma Ida had died only two years before Oscar, and he and Pauline had been friends for more than thirty years. I found myself wondering again if they had been lovers, and immediately reprimanded myself. I hated falling into the prurient trap of automatically assuming such a thing. It didn't matter, anyway.

"I can see a little of him in you, Emma, about the eyes, the chin."

"Do you?" was all I asked. I didn't dare hope.

"Yes, particularly when I see you directing the crew, you move like him." She patted my arm. "Though Oscar was a bit more brusque about it—"

"Oscar was an ogre to his students and they worshipped him," I broke in, "though not always at the same time!" I sat back down, able to recall many occasions of bellowing and roaring with stuttering replies. "But Bucky's the one who looks like Oscar."

"Your sister certainly resembles him," she agreed, "but you got his soul, Emma."

I didn't quite know what to make of that. It was unlike Pauline to dwell on such abstractions—she was so full of life, so devoted to doing rather than wondering, that I was a little concerned. But she didn't seem gloomy at all, just contemplative and content. I pulled myself off the stairs reluctantly, brushed off the seat of my pants, and let out a piercing whistle, the kind you can only make with both pinkies. Down the slope, I could see students looking up from their lunches.

"Whaddya lying around for?" I belted out. "Meg's only been out here a week and already she's found the fort! The rest of you waiting for an invitation or something?"

That's one of the things I love about Pauline; when she laughs, she doesn't mess around with ladylike titters. With her, it's belly laughs or nothing.

Much later that afternoon Pauline did stop by to visit the progress in each of the units. Although no one else had yet found another posthole or uncovered the top of the seventeenth-century layer, excitement and morale were running high with the eagerness to find that next clue. I was just kneeling to show her Meg's posthole when a shadow fell over me. The sudden cool shade from the sun made me shiver, and for an instant I feared that Grahame Tichnor had returned. But then, with a sinking heart, I suddenly recalled what I should have been planning all day.

"Hey, Emma, Professor Markham's here!" Neal called be-latedly.

I looked up, squinting into the sunlight, and hastily rose, dusting myself off, but all in vain. As hard as I'd tried to keep myself presentable, I was sweaty and covered with a noticeable film of dirt. It didn't help that I had broken into a cold sweat immediately after my encounter with Grahame Tichnor; I was now caked with grime. This was definitely not the image I had in mind for my meeting with my august colleague.

Tony, on the other hand, was immaculately outfitted in the traditional khakis and blue oxford cloth shirt so beloved by the men of my academic tribe, and seemed to be immune to the heat of the day. His close-cropped beard and hair were meticulously groomed, a little remaining brown overtaken by white. I got the impression that he was the kind of archaeologist who could go into the field wearing white and come out spotless at the end of the day. He didn't come off as prissy or fastidious, though; it just added to his charisma. Me, I'd seen garbage men look less disheveled than I did after work.

"Hello, Tony. Sorry, I lost track of time, what with all the excitement around here. Pauline, this is Dr. Anthony Markham, a colleague from the Caldwell College Anthropology Department. Tony, this is my friend Pauline Westlake. This is Pauline's property."

Pauline smiled graciously. "How do you do, Dr. Markham?"

"Tony, please," he said, smiling back, Southern charm instantly activated by Pauline's regal bearing.

"I don't know whether you've met Meg Garrity, who'll be starting with us this fall?"

"Oh, I had a chance to talk with Miss Garrity before she joined you here," Tony said, his words full of irony. I wondered if Meg had impressed him as she'd impressed me.

"Hi, Tony," Meg said, looking up from her note taking.

"Emma, I need to get ready for this evening," Pauline excused herself. "A pleasure, Tony."

"Ms. Westlake." Tony watched Pauline return to her house. "Wonderful old place," he commented.

"There was a building boom in the nineteenth century," I said, "when seaside touring was the vogue. A lot of nice places were built then, which is kind of ironic when you think how impoverished it was around here before the price of real estate shot up."

"And this all looks very impressive," he said, gesturing to the units all around me.

I suppressed a triumphant smile. "Let me show you around a bit—"

Meg interrupted. "Sorry, Emma, but what time are we expected at the sheriff's department?"

I couldn't tell for sure, but I thought I detected a note of humor in her voice. It was not, I had to concede, a question one asked every day.

Cursing to myself, I checked my watch and realized not only that had I forgotten my promise to the sheriff, but also that it was time for the crew to start cleaning up for the day.

Tony was too polite to ask, but a raised eyebrow indicated his curiosity.

"I had a nasty run-in with an armed pothunter today," I hastened to explain, "and I did tell the sheriff I would stop by and look at some photos, you know, to identify the guy."

Tony looked startled. "Goodness."

I checked my watch. "Excuse me, Tony. Hey guys," I called to the crew through cupped hands. "Time to wrap it up." I turned back to Tony, trying to figure out how I could salvage as much of this botched opportunity as possible. "Well, I've got about twenty minutes to show you around, and then I've got to get to the sheriff's department. I'm so sorry about this—"

"Don't worry about that," Tony said. He thought a moment. "Will that take long?"

I shrugged. "I don't imagine so."

"Well, by all means, I'll follow you there," Tony drawled.

"And after I'll buy you a drink and we can chat."

I brightened. "Sure, if you don't mind the wait."

"Not a bit. I've never been to a mug shot party before."

"Then, if you'll just let me get the crew sorted out, I'll give you the Cook's tour. Hey Neal," I yelled.

He ambled over. "I can get everything closed up for the night, Em, don't worry."

Sure enough, students were already pulling blue plastic tarps over the units to protect them for the night.

"Excellent, thanks. Meg and I are going to the sheriff's department, then I'm going to get a drink with Professor Markham. The beer's on me tonight—" I rummaged in my pockets and handed him a couple of crumpled bills, but Neal was already thinking ahead.

"So how's Meg going to get back?"

I thought about it for a minute; there were two other vehicles, but not enough room in just one of them for all the rest of the crew. I surely didn't want Meg tagging along while I spoke with Tony . . .

But then a solution presented itself in the unlikely form of Alan, who had joined us. "Emma, I could wait and go back with Meg. That'll leave enough room in the other truck, and I've got a little bit more to finish here anyway," he offered eagerly.

I realized that whatever antipathy he'd developed toward me was secondary to anything that might allow him a little alone time with the object of his desire. It was a solution, however. "Great, Alan, thanks. If you don't mind a trip to the sheriff's, that'll work fine."

I saw Meg roll her eyes at the thought of the long ride home with Alan, but to her credit, she did it so he couldn't see.

"Then we're all set. Shall we?" I turned to Tony and led the way to the bottom of the site, so I could orient him. "Did you have any trouble finding the site?"

Dr. Markham waved off my inquiry. "Just a little, the fort on the map I had was the wrong one. I thought you meant the historic site."

"That's Fort Archer. Easy mistake, you just went past us, too far upriver. I took the students over there for a field trip. It's a neat site, dates to the mid-eighteenth century." I grinned. "But all that's nothing compared to this."

I took a deep breath. "Welcome to Fort Providence." I began walking and giving my patented spiel, hitting on the terrible weather, the dismal relations with the Indians, and the lack of funds that all ultimately contributed to the downfall of the installation.

"Imagine a particularly bad Maine winter without benefit of L. L. Bean, central heating—"

Tony scowled. "I'm from Georgia. Give me the Yucatán every time."

I nodded. "Most of the information that was sent back about Virginia—yes, even this far up was Virginia in those days, Northern Virginia—was real propaganda. The early tracts promised temperate weather and fruit, vegetables, and gold for the taking, along with benevolent natives. None of which turned out to be true; the settlers who stayed didn't have enough supplies to last the winter, there were no sources of gold or gems to be found, and relations with the native people soon disintegrated, most stories say because of the bad behavior of the English. In any case, virtually no descriptions of the fort or site remain, and I have to rely on comparanda from other sites to guess at what might be here."

Interest lit Tony's face. "What sort of buildings do you expect?"

I stopped to think. "If Fort Providence was anything like the forts drawn by the English military cartographers, probably a storehouse, a couple of barracks for the soldiers, maybe a chapel or kitchen house. Other than that, we're hoping to recover part of the ditch or other fortifications— we're expecting they'd follow the contour of the land. That's what I'm basing my testing design on."

"Have you found anything yet?" Tony seemed to be captivated by the site, staring out to the river. I couldn't blame him; I was working in one of the most beautiful spots on earth.

I stopped by Meg's unit. "How kind of you to ask. Just today, Meg Garrity found a posthole. It was beneath the known late eighteenth-century level, the earliest time for which we definitely know there was an Anglo site here. And since we know that the English built many of their buildings by setting huge posts in the ground instead of using foundations, we're hoping it's early enough to be from Fort Providence. And to top it off . . ." Here I paused to pull the tarp back. "We found a piece of lead shot that dates to the correct period. I'm keeping my fingers crossed, but it looks really good."

Tony stood a moment, taking it all in. "But if what you say is correct, this is a find of the utmost importance! A scientifically recovered site that is earlier than . . . ?"

I couldn't conceal a wide grin. "You got it!"

My colleague's brow furrowed. "How come no one ever thought to look for it before? Why wasn't it known before this? I beg your pardon, Emma, but I do try to keep up on other aspects of the discipline outside my own—why haven't I heard about this?"

"Just one of those things," I said. "An accident of history. The settlement failed after less than a year—we both know how little can be left behind on a site after such a short duration—and naturally, better-known sites took precedence once they were found. There was a little interest in the site in the nineteenth century, with the colonial revival movement, but since no one knew precisely where it was, everyone tended to focus on the Revolutionary War history in the area. You see, there are so many points and coves along this river, it could have been anywhere. There has always a bit of local interest, and even Oscar—" But here I clammed up.

Tony pounced on my slip, however. "I've been meaning to ask you about that. Your grandfather, pardon me for asking, but he was *the* Oscar Fielding, wasn't he?"

I paused a little too long, phrasing a polite answer.

"I'm sorry, I didn't mean to pry," Tony said, but it was clear he was still curious. "Let me give you a hand with these tarps. You've got to get to the sheriff's department."

"Thanks, you're right. We'd better get going."

Since Tony drove his own car and Alan and Meg were following mine, I was left alone with my thoughts as I led the winding way back to Fordham, the county seat, and the sheriff's department after we closed up the site. The exterior had not changed since the first time I'd seen the chunky gothic building, about thirteen years ago, but the soot of the ages had been cleaned from the red sandstone recently and the building looked pretty spruce, comfortable and stolid, like a longtime citizen with old-fashioned values. Inside, more substantial changes had taken place, and recently too. I remembered that the interior had been a dim cave of old linoleum and cobwebs when I'd seen it years ago. Now, however, the lighting was new and bright, the floors had been replaced with, well, cleaner, uncracked linoleum—it wouldn't have made sense to put carpet in, I supposed. There was a nice little waiting area, with a rubber tree, even, off to one side.

After I gave my name to a deputy at the desk, Tony and I sat on a chrome and faux leather couch waiting for my turn in the sheriff's department. Alan sat across from us, trying to avoid my glance while watching but not daring to follow Meg as she poked around the corridors. Just as I was casting about for some reason to call her back, a gangly deputy politely asked her to stay in the area. I was just wondering what sort of chitchat one made with eminent colleagues and students while in the sheriff's department, when a curious distraction presented itself.

We didn't even need to strain to hear what was transpiring. Two voices were coming down the hallway; a man's voice, low tones and moderately paced, frequently interrupted by an insistent woman's, or what I assumed was a woman's because of its higher pitch. That second one was an odd voice, not exactly whiny but sounding like machinery that's been left in the rain; grating, rusting, resentful. Before I even realized I was eavesdropping, I was fascinated by that voice, wheedling but at the same time shot through with the threat of too much interest, curiosity that boded no good for anyone under her scrutiny. It took me a moment to get the hang of her accent underneath the oddness of her voice. I noticed that Tony's brow was furrowed, Alan wasn't paying attention, and Meg just looked plain delighted.

"—but those bruises were classic defensive wounds," the woman's voice persisted, and I realized with growing horror that I was listening to an addict's pleading, though I didn't know what the source of that desperation could be.

The man's voice responded firmly: I recognized it as belonging to the sheriff. "Yes, defensive wounds from the fight earlier in the evening—"

"They might indicate that it was no accident he ended up in the water—"

"But there's no way of telling when the two incidents were less than twenty-four hours apart and there's clear tissue alteration due to the period of immersion, and—Terry, are you listening?—even if we were inclined to fly in all the face of this evidence and suggest foul play, our best suspect was also our guest in lockup number two last night. Can't really argue with that now, can we? Occam's razor, Terry."

The woman's response was indiscernible and unhappy, but I caught the last few words. "—watch out you don't cut yourself with it, smartypants."

"Do you know what I think?" said the sheriff.

There was no answer and the sheriff continued.

"I think that you're stretching some fairly dubious possibilities into something they're not because you're *bored*. Don't worry, I'm still looking into it all, but in the meantime, do a crossword puzzle, for Pete's sake. Don't go looking for trouble."

"Huh!"

"Can it, Terry," Stannard said patiently.

The footsteps grew louder and suddenly the speakers turned the corner toward us. Dave Stannard was walking with a woman, and her appearance took me aback. She was a wizened little stump in a stained white lab coat. God help me, she looked like an evil gnome, with a tight bun of coarse black and gray hair. She was worrying an unlit, unfiltered Camel cigarette in one clawlike hand, and she had another tucked behind her ear, both apparently ready and waiting to have the life sucked out of them at the earliest opportunity.

"Dr. Fielding." The sheriff stopped in front of us. "Nice to see you. Again."

I giggled a little at the "again," all composure shot in the face of legal authority. I introduced the rest of our group and explained the sheriff's words to Tony. "I stopped by a couple of weeks ago to let folks here know I was going to be digging at the Point—"

The short woman in the lab coat broke in insistently. "Digging? Digging for what?"

I ignored the interruption. "—and then yesterday, there was a body washed up near us and I was there for that too."

Tony shook his head in amazement. "You found a *body*? I thought this was about a pothunter!"

"You the one found Augie Brooks?" the woman wheezed, then snapped her gum, suddenly interested. "Lots going on down the Point." She looked at the sheriff. "All of a sudden."

The sheriff kindly stepped in to rescue me. "Things happen near rivers, Terry, for all sorts of reasons. This is Dr. Emma Fielding. She's an archaeologist, doing some research out at the Point."

"Archaeologist, huh? And all of a sudden Augie washes up on your shore, looking a little the worse for wear."

Stannard coughed a little and gave the woman a look. She viewed me with the utmost distaste. "So, you dig up bodies and stuff?"

"Excuse me? What?" I was thrown for a minute, because I had suddenly realized that the woman sounded just like the wicked witch from *The Wizard of Oz*. Margaret Hamilton with a Down East twist, rusty Victorian hinges and squeaky blackboards. "Well, we haven't found any human remains yet, but—"

"Except for Augie." She snapped her gum again pointedly, and the sickly sweet smell of cinnamon reached me.

"Well, he wasn't exactly an archaeological find"—I risked a quick smile at Tony—"but we have found pottery sherds, things like that. We hope to find more before we're done."

"Huh." She looked me up and down appraisingly. "You've got to be some kind of nut, looking for that kind of stuff, nosing around people's business like that."

Meg muttered crossly under her breath. "Well, perhaps," I said stiffly, "but we may have just found evidence of the earliest English settlement on the East Coast today."

Sheriff Stannard stepped in. "Dr. Fielding, this is Dr. Theresa Moretti." He let a beat pass. "Our consulting medical examiner."

Chapter 5

THE MEDICAL EXAMINER AND I STARED AT EACH OTHER with distaste. "Dr. Moretti's just concluded her exam of Augie Brooks. It looks like it was just a nasty accident," the sheriff said firmly. "He was drunk, fell over, hit his head on the way out of the boat, and drowned. Still don't know where he went in, though."

"Still lots of questions—" the ME growled.

"Terry—"

"But why was he out on the water at night at all?" I interrupted. The two officials turned and stared at me.

"I mean," I said hastily, "he wasn't too keen on the water, as I understand it."

Dr. Moretti gave me another sharp look, then snapped her gum expectantly, then looked at the sheriff, waiting for his answer.

"We're still looking into it," he said pleasantly.

"Yeah, well." Dr. Moretti shot Stannard a withering glance. "I've got crosswords to do."

We watched the woman scurry off back down the hall. Stannard looked like he was going to say something and then apparently thought better of it. "If you'll give me a second, I'll get the photos."

He stepped into an office, and through the door I could see that it had not been subject to the same renovations as the rest of the building. That room looked a little less renovated but also a little more relaxed, and I could see a couple of framed finger paintings proudly hanging behind the desk. The sheriff pulled a file and returned, holding out a piece of construction paper in front of me. It was covered with a half-dozen Polaroids. I pointed out the one of the stranger—Tichnor—immediately; you couldn't miss that malevolent look, even without the sunglasses. The hair was also a pretty good clue.

Meg also picked out the same picture. Alan looked over her shoulder and said, "Is that him?"

Stannard held it out so that he and Tony could see. "Got it in one," he said. "That's Grahame Tichnor, figured it was him. And he was vandalizing your work when you confronted him?"

"Yes." I felt a rush of heat in my face, and I realized that I hated admitting that the guy intimidated me, that I was a victim of any sort.

"You wouldn't believe the sort of damage treasure hunters have done to sites down where I work, in Mexico," Tony added. "It's a global crisis, really."

"Well, if I'm right, he's the one responsible for the damage to sites around here too," the sheriff said, surprising me. "There's been a complaint from Fort Archer. Someone's been digging little holes all over the historic site. Maybe looking for the legendary Fordham County gold. I know it kept my girls busy on the beach last year." His grin suddenly turned into a frown. "No chance it's another professional looking around there?"

"None," I said firmly. "Professionals get permission and dig with a goal, a research goal, in mind. And I don't know of anyone else working around here this year."

The sheriff nodded at Meg and Alan. "What about the rest of your students?"

"If I even suspected one of them of doing such a thing, I'd skin him alive!"

The sheriff was taken aback by my vehemence. Tony just laughed, and Meg and Alan hurriedly shook their heads.

"Well, then I'm willing to bet we've got our man," Stannard said. "We're looking for Tichnor now—we want to ask him about a few other things too—and bring him in if we find him, of course, but I'm betting he'll do a fade job for a couple of weeks. Don't worry about it."

"Just so long as Pauline's safe," I said. "She'll be away next week for a week or so, and I'm glad of that."

"He won't be back," the sheriff said confidently. "I'll let you know when we pick him up. You're willing to press charges?"

"Of course!"

The sheriff led us politely but quite unmistakably toward the front door. "So you think you hit Fort Providence today? That's pretty exciting. You'll do a talk around here, I hope, let folks know what you've got? Maybe at the elementary school? Like I said, the kids would love this."

"Oh sure. I always like to keep people informed of what I'm finding."

"Good, good. Thanks for your help."

I was surprised to see the sun still shining when we got out of the station; it seemed to me that we'd been in there a long time.

"Now, how about that drink?" Tony offered.

"That sounds great. You're sure?"

"Of course."

Meg perked up, obviously hoping to be asked along, but Alan insisted that he wanted to get going, so they excused themselves.

"I know a place nearby," I said to Tony. "They know me, and won't mind my grubby clothes."

It was just a couple of blocks to the bar, the Goat and Grapes. I suppose years ago it had been a fairly posh place—there was still a lot of good wainscoting in there—but now it had lost all its pretensions to plastic red-checked tablecloths and beer posters. I didn't mind, however; I never knew it any other way, and besides, I went there because the folks were nice and the beer was just cold enough. The television was usually off too.

I didn't see anyone I knew besides the bartender. "Hey, Nick," I called, as I slid into a booth.

A short, slight, balding fellow with glasses worried a toothpick in his mouth and squinted at me as he came to the table. "Hey, Emma! Been a while hasn't it?"

"Too long. How's things?"

Nick snorted. "Same as ever—we're not real big on change around here. What can I get you?"

"Amber, please. Tony?"

"The same."

"I think I can manage that." Nick left us to our conversation.

"I didn't mean to dodge your question back there at the site," I apologized in a rush. "About Oscar. It . . . I just tend to avoid talking about my grandfather in a professional sense. I mean, the relationship's no big secret, but I want to be known as Emma Fielding, not Oscar Fielding's granddaughter, if you know what I mean."

"Of course." Tony nodded. "I can see the difficulty, but I really don't think that it's something to worry about. Forget about comparisons, or anything like that. It's a different world today."

I gave him a look and a brief smile.

"Of course we Southerners tend to trot out the family tree on any and all occasions," Tony continued. "It's a sort of familial jousting tournament, who's got the most colonels or the most decaying moss-covered mansions."

I laughed. "I'm ferociously proud of him, don't get me

wrong. It's just odd sometimes, to hear the way that people talk about Oscar. He was a big deal to the archaeological community of course, but he was just Grandpa to me, when I was a kid. Just doing what grandfathers did, I thought."

"I've got this mental image of you, Emma," Tony said, "as a lisping urchin, clutching a projectile point in one grubby hand and a copper bead in the other."

"Not too far off, I guess." I took a sip of beer. "It's how I got my start, following Oscar around. I picked up a lot of the mindset before I even knew what was happening. It was a bit of a shock to start college and see his name in textbooks, with all those verbal laurel leaves. I was glad to be able to relate to him professionally, though, for that little while he was alive. He died a couple of years before I took the position at Caldwell. I'm the only one in the family who followed in his footsteps."

I swallowed another mouthful as I thought about the welter of emotions, the pride, the worry that I wouldn't measure up, the love I had for him, the fear that people would expect too much of me. That I would disappoint him. "Graduate school's when I started to be shy about it. Too many people would ask me what Oscar was *really* like. He was of the old school, demanding, scathing, at times. John Houseman in *The Paper Chase* crossed with a Marine staff sergeant. But what was I supposed to answer? He was Grandpa." I shrugged.

Tony seemed to be deep in thought himself. "I met Oscar on several occasions, but never knew him well. I suspect few people would have been privileged to see his family life. He had such a reputation for, er, demanding exactitude," he said, carefully polite.

When I was very little, I had thought that Oscar was a pirate. His bushy red beard and growls ensured that most people never grew out of that superficial impression. I never minded, though, because I wanted to be a pirate too, stomping through the woods, looking for treasure, and then telling stories about it. It was just a by-product of my affection for him that by the time I was in high school, I'd already had more field experience than most graduate students.

I changed the subject. "So what brings you to the area? We're a ways from the college."

Tony settled back into the booth. "I was having lunch with a friend nearby; he's got a summer place near here. And I thought as long as I was around, I'd drop by. What with my sabbatical and your workload, I figured we could stand to get better acquainted."

"It's been a busy year." I thought about the amount of work that gets heaped on new professors. "I'm hoping that things will settle down this semester."

Tony laughed humorlessly. "It will never settle down. Academia's a grind, so you just have to find your own approach to dealing with it. I'll tell you a secret." He leaned over across the table. "The more you seem to disdain the process—while completing all the obvious tasks you need to get tenure—the more that people will think you know something they don't. The more they will defer to you. The more you will succeed, through appearing to scorn the scene. By seeming to reject the process, you will triumph over it."

"That's sort of the cat theory of academic advancement, isn't it? The more you ignore your keepers, the more desirable you become?"

"That's it precisely." He took another deep draft of beer. "Enough about this. Tell me about the site."

"Not too much besides what I told you out on the site. We're still getting down to the right levels. The locals, for the most part, our maniacal friend today quite excepted, have been great, very supportive. We'll be out working for another couple of weeks, and then back to classes. I'm extremely hopeful about what we're going to find."

"It is exciting and you should make the most of it, because these opportunities don't come along that often." Tony continued, "particularly since Rick Crabtree wants to give the nonmajors' introductory class to you again this year. Says it will help your tenure review. Though how Lifestyles of the Dead and Famous could help anyone is beyond me." He smiled briefly, meaningfully.

"I always thought of it as Ancient Thrills for Jocks and Jills." I put my glass down carefully. This was great kindness in Tony, to let me know what Rick, who was probably my greatest obstacle in the department, was thinking. "I'll see if I can't offer Chairman Kellerman a more attractive option instead."

"Good idea. You've got a lot riding on this, of course."

"You don't need to tell me. I don't know what I'll do if this doesn't work out," I admitted. "Everyone knows the tenure statistics . . ." I laughed awkwardly. "There's not a huge market for slightly used assistant professors out there . . ."

"Look, let me tell you about my field season," Tony offered, as eager to change the subject as I was. "We've been finding just the most . . ."

We spent the next half hour trading war stories and gossip, a decent end to the day.

". . . and that was when I realized that in addition to telling the new students which plants to avoid touching, I really did have to warn them to use the official, cleared latrine sites. Imagine a snakebite . . ." Tony paused, then chuckled a little into his beer glass. "Well, the poor lad lost all interest in archaeology after that."

"Oh, I can imagine. Poison ivy's bad enough."

Suddenly Tony set his glass down rather decisively, almost impatiently. He reached over and brushed his thumb across my wrist and down my index finger. "Look, will you have dinner with me tonight?"

A thrill ran up that arm and down my spine. I sat transfixed, shocked, disbelieving for the second time today. "Wha-what?"

Tony reddened, but persisted. "Dinner. Would you have dinner with me? I'm asking you on a date."

Startled, I started to snatch my hand away from his, and then imagining what kind of rejection that must look like, I pulled away more gently. "Uh. Tony, thanks, but I'm . . . I'm married, you know?"

He stared at me, swallowed, and looked away, compressing his lips. "No, no I did not know that." Tony exhaled and smiled embarrassedly. "I did not know, I'm not in the habit of asking out married women. I didn't see a ring, else I wouldn't have asked."

Now I felt guilty, like an idiot. "No, you didn't. I don't wear jewelry in the field. It's not your fault. I'm sorry."

"No, I'm sorry, really." He looked away, pained.

We sat there, supremely uncomfortable, for an interminable thirty seconds.

"Look," I started hastily. "How about another beer?"

"No, no thanks. I've got to get going." Tony got up and waved aside my offer to pay for another round or even my half of this one. "I won't hear of it, I invited you out." He threw down some bills on the table, leaving a decent tip.

"I'm sorry, really," I repeated.

Tony reached over as if to touch my shoulder, but then pulled back, thinking better of it. "We are fine, here," he said. "Really. It was a simple misunderstanding." He peered at me, cocking his head. "Right? We're good?"

I nodded. "Sure."

"Okay. Now. Thanks for the tour, it was even more interesting than I expected." He shook his head. "Everyone seems to think that we Mesoamericanists are the inheritors of Indiana Jones's reputation, but you—you're right in the middle of it all! It's not every day I get to see medical examiners and mug shots."

"Well, I'm not used to it either," I said. "It's not a regular thing for me."

"Fair enough." He looked uncomfortable, then laughed again, offering his hand to me. I took it and probably shook it a little too long, trying to make up for the misunderstanding. "Thanks again. See you in a month or so."

"See you, Tony."

I leaned back against the booth a moment after he left and groaned to myself. In the few meetings we'd had during my interview at Caldwell, Tony seemed rather detached, but that made sense in light of his views on how one gets ahead. He reminded me a bit of Oscar, age difference apart. There was the same old-school flair for the dramatic, the same sort of encyclopedic mind, a similar sense of humor. But no matter how honest the mistake, I had blown him off. Great.

I went over and sat down at the bar and rubbed my head; the day was settling down on me. "Another one, Nick?"

"You bet." He pulled on the optic and glanced over at me, a toothpick working between his lips. "You okay?"

"Yeah. It's been a hell of a day. I've got a headache, is all." I sipped at the beer, trying to assimilate what I'd been through in the past twelve hours. Tichnor's appearance, the potential of the posthole, the decidedly odd scene at the sheriff's office . . . And then there was Tony's visit, replete with its own drama. Really, it was just too much.

"Ah, to hell with it," I muttered, setting the glass down. I'd handled everything just fine, everything was covered. I looked at Nick, who was drying glasses. "I got better things to worry about."

He switched his toothpick from one side of his mouth to the other. "You say so. Say, I heard you were the one who found Augie."

"Yeah. Bit of a shock." I thought about the disagreement I'd overheard at the sheriff's department. "Say, Nick, did Augie get into a lot of fights? You know, fistfights?"

"Oh, more'n most people, less than some." He shrugged. "Get to drinking, get wound up about something. He was more of a weepy drunk, but every so often he'd get scrappy. The other night, night before he died, that was the first time in a while. Why'd you ask?"

"Just wondering," I said. "He looked pretty beat up to me when I found him. All sorts of fun at the Point. Had some nutcase named Tichnor out there today. Sonofabitch threatened me, can you imagine?" I kept my tone light; it *was* sort of amusing, well after the fact. Two people facing off over holes in the ground.

Nick's toothpick stopped dead in its migration. "No shit? Tichnor, you know, he and Augie ran around together sometimes. They were in here the night before last."

I put my glass down, thinking hard. "Yeah? How'd they get along?"

"Like spoons in a drawer; now Tichnor's going to have to find someone else to listen to his big talk. The three of them were in here that other night, those two and Billy. Tichnor left early, before the serious drinking got started, but then later on, Augie and Billy started trouble and I had to call the cops." He pulled out a sawed-off baseball bat from under the bar to show me how the bar's tranquillity had been restored. "Takes someone as mean as Billy Griggs not to quiet down when I'm trying to get a point across."

I had just taken another sip and nearly dropped my beer glass at his words. The blood rushed out of my face. "You . . . you didn't just say Billy Griggs?"

"Yeah, sure. But you wouldn't know *him*, he's a real bast—"

"About my age, my height, bad skin, ratty hair?" I said. "*Serious* personality deficiencies?"

Nick nodded incredulously. "Emma, when did you ever run into him?"

I didn't answer right away. My mind raced. The instant that Nick had said the name, I realized why the driver of the black car that drove by Pauline's had looked so familiar. My stomach did a flip-flop. There was no way that Billy could remember me—it had been more than ten years ago—or even recognize me from that distance, I thought hurriedly. It had to be a coincidence, but all at once, there were far too many coincidences occurring down at the Point.

"You okay, Emma?" Nick looked worried. "You look a little rough, there."

Thinking furiously, I said, "Billy Griggs was the one who beat up on Augie?"

"Sure."

"Does the sheriff's department know this?"

"Yeah, they were the ones gave Billy a free night's lodging for drunk and disorderly and then gave Augie a lift home so he wouldn't get into any more trouble." Nick stretched and shrugged. "Shoulda baby-sat him too, for all the good that did."

Okay, I thought, that rules out Billy. He must have been the "best suspect" I heard Sheriff Stannard and Dr. Moretti arguing about. "What about Grahame Tichnor?"

The bartender waved a hand dismissively. "He was gone long before the other two got bored enough to start in on each other. What are you thinking?"

"Just trying to make sense of what's been going on around me," I replied.

"Well, the cops know all this." He looked uneasy. "Not to add to your worries, but I think we had one of your kids in here that night too."

"Oh?" But my heart sank; I already knew who it must have been.

"Yeah, tall drink of water, puss on him like one of those sad clown pictures. Already pretty sloppy. I refused him." The bartender swiped at a glass uneasily. "I thought you oughta know . . ."

Alan, of course. "It's okay, Nick. I appreciate the heads-up."

"And if Tichnor shows up here again, I'll let him know not to bother you." He nodded at the baseball bat meaningfully. "No call for that kind of crap."

"Thanks," I said gratefully. It was like family around here, everyone looking out for everyone else. I drained my glass. It was time to get going myself.

"I'll see you." I slid off the stool and left some bills on the counter. "Work to be done."

"Take it easy, Emma."

*   *   *

When I got back to the dorm I wandered down the hall to the kitchen to see if there was anything to gnaw. On the way to a little caloric therapy, however, I passed Neal's room, where I witnessed something that was guaranteed to keep my stomach rumbling and my head aching. I know for certain that if they had seen me coming down the hallway, I might never have seen this little slice of private life.

The door to Neal's room was open. Someone was standing in the doorway with his back to me.

I heard a vehement, what—denial? "You don't know what the hell you're talking about!" That voice was Neal's but he wasn't the shadow in the doorway.

"What do you mean by that?" the other voice demanded. I couldn't make that one out yet.

"Just what I'm saying." Neal's voice was low and emphatic. "You have no idea of what's going on and it's not fair to Emma to assume you do."

My ears pricked up.

"You saw what happened out there today! But I know what you think of me—"

"You don't—" Neal interrupted.

"Oh, I'm not so stupid that I can't see you making fun of me with the others—"

"God damn, you're paranoid!"

"—and I'm just saying, you should stay away from her—"

It was at that point that the form outlined in the doorway turned and saw me. I almost didn't recognize Alan, his face was red and he was breathing through clenched teeth. If it had been anyone else, he might have been able to cover the quality of emotion that possessed him, but Alan was ill-suited to subtlety. Add to that a chronic, misinformed sense of being outclassed and ridiculed and you had a walking time bomb.

"Something wrong, Alan?" I asked as nonchalantly as I could.

Like I said, he's no good at concealment. When it finally

dawned on Alan that he was staring at me, the barely checked emotion—what was it? anger? frustration? jealousy?—shifted immediately into fear.

I figured I would get some explanation at least, but he all but ran past me.

I looked into the room and saw Neal. He was standing and caught in the grips of some violent passion, fists clenched and feet apart. He looked up and caught my eye and swallowed. "Care to clue me in?" I asked. "What's going on here?" I took an authoritative tone, to startle him into telling me what had just transpired. Maybe it wasn't fair of me to try and get it out of Neal, but I knew I had a better chance of finding out from him.

"I can't." Simple as that. Behind Neal's eyes, doors slammed shut, shades were pulled down, and the phone was taken off the hook.

"I beg your pardon?" I said in my best arched-eyebrow, skeptical professor voice. "What do you mean you can't?"

"It wouldn't do any good," he said after a moment's consideration. "Trust me."

I shifted tack a little, added a little soupçon of guilt. "Neal, I do trust you. I'm sure if I needed to know about it, you'd tell me, right?"

He only nodded, and I knew right then and there that I could ask all night and I still wouldn't find out what was making him look so miserable and Alan look so scared. So I went back to my room and tried without luck not to stay up wondering about the reappearance of Billy Griggs at this unfortunate juncture in my life.

Chapter 6

I WAS FACE TO FACE WITH THE DIRT, LYING ON MY BELLY with my legs stretched out behind me, something you only do with the closest of close work, when something begs your attention and you wonder whether that something will suddenly transform itself from the merely curious into the important. It was the Thursday after my discovery of the body on the beach, my run-in with Grahame Tichnor, who was only a shadow hovering at the edge of my thoughts. I occasionally flinched at unexpected noises, but eventually I had to stop simply because I didn't have the time to pay attention to them all. My drink with Tony, Billy's appearance, and my interruption of Neal and Alan's argument, all of these events were banished from memory in the light of our most recent finds.

The smell of the sun-warmed earth and parched grass enveloped me, even down inside the cool of the unit. As I studied the posthole, Meg hovered anxiously behind me. Anxious despite herself, her protective shell of cool cracked and tossed away in the face of what she was working on. This was Meg's second posthole, bringing the total number to three on the site including her first one. The other two post-holes were even better preserved and the really big news was that all three appeared to be in a line, better yet. There's the old archaeological saw that if you have two postholes, no matter where they are on a site, you can make them line up into anything you want, but if you have three, and they are in a line, well, that is starting to look something like real evidence.

That line could mean a wall of a building, and that would mean that we had a seventeenth-century English building in New England almost fifteen years before the Pilgrims landed at Plymouth, a settlement that was abandoned a year before Jamestown was established in 1607. It hadn't lasted, so no one knew of it like they knew Plymouth and Jamestown, not the history books, not the scholars, not the specialists. And those who had done work in the area didn't believe the fort could be found, without a map or better proof, or if it did, it might have eroded into the river or been destroyed, robbed out, built over, or any of the myriad disastrous fates a fragile site can suffer. So what we were in the process of uncovering was going to change those history books, inform those scholars, and make the specialists reconsider their specialty in a whole new way. My heart had been beating so fast for so long since we'd found the first posthole that I was slightly giddy, over-oxygenated, atingle with the possibility of what we'd been revealing.

So I was glad Meg looked anxious. I might have shaken her otherwise.

I used my abdominal muscles to pull my head and torso out of the unit, trying not to touch the edges of it lest I collapse the drying soil of the walls that Meg had worked so hard to keep straight and clean. Looking back into the unit, the hole that had been dug nearly four hundred years ago to accommodate the post had been neatly reexcavated by Meg, who had carefully followed the soil distinctions to reveal the exact shape of the original hole. Imagine a perfectly square hole like a telephone booth cut into the soil—our unit—

with a rough circle of mottled earth—the original, filled-in posthole—appearing in the bottom of that. Meg had brought down half of the unit deeper than the other and bisected the posthole, so that for a while we could see a neat profile of the hole itself, with a stain where the post had been and small rocks that had been thrown in to prop up the post while its hole was being refilled. We had drawn that and photographed it to within an inch of its existence. It was perfectly defined and distinct, the sort of thing you never find.

But nothing that good ever comes without complications: The unit was not directly lit by the sun, it was overhung with branches and so was dappled with shadows, making photography difficult. We'd used a white sheet to block out most of the shadows, then tried long exposures and a flash to add an even light, and prayed like mad that some of it would be preserved clearly on film. You never know until you get it back whether your work—now destroyed, excavated, filled in, and gone forever—will show up, so you also do measured drawings and verbal descriptions in notes. Triple, extra, super-redundancy, whatever you can think of, to preserve this vital information.

After we had recorded the excavated half of the bisected posthole in relation to the other stratigraphy, Meg had removed the remaining part of the posthole as well, in the hopes of recovering an artifact—a hand-wrought nail perhaps, or even better, a button or piece of pottery that could be more closely dated—but had come up with nothing. Since we had even found a tiny, precious sliver of the original post, worn down and disintegrating from a huge structural member to a splinter the size of a cigar, another dateable artifact would have been too much to ask for, in light of the perfect preservation of this most recent trace of Fort Providence.

I dusted off my hands and then, out of habit, automatically brushed at my chest. A crew of women doing close, nose-to-the-soil archaeology can end up looking like a Wagnerian chorus, perfectly round, brown-colored breast shields imprinted on T-shirts, pressed into the soil by the flesh beneath the fabric.

"Yeah, that's it," I said at last, "but it's a real pain in the butt to see in this light. Good job, though; I think you got it all out of there."

"Thanks, Em." She was pleased with herself and the find and me too, I thought. She knew how big a deal this was.

Something suddenly caught my eye. "There is a little dark stain over there. I thought it was a stain from a disintegrating rock in the subsoil when I was down there." I gestured with my trowel to the far side of the posthole, now in shadow. "Can you see that dark patch in the very bottom, by the south wall over there?"

Meg squinted, a small frown quickly replacing her smile. "I can't see."

I lowered myself down again, balancing so that I could see and still not obscure her view. "The light down here stinks. Just now, I thought it looked different. Probably nothing . . ."

Letting my eyes adjust to the gloom of the small hole again, I scraped gingerly at the area I wondered about. The disintegrating rock theory seemed to be confirmed when the soft, dry sound of the trowel against loose soil suddenly changed to a metallic rasp. A dark shape fell out of the wall to the bottom of the hole.

I reached for it, and when my fingers closed around a thin flat object instead of a small, spherical one, my breath caught. Holy shit, I thought.

Twenty times a day on a site when you might be getting down to what you're looking for, you pause, and your heart stops. Then your breath catches because your brain has been tricked into seeing something that might be *something*, but turns out to be a rock, or a twig, or just another piece of modern brick. That's always what happens, and you feel silly and a little disappointed and you carry on.

Except this time, even without seeing it, I instinctively knew it was a coin I held in my hand.

I pulled myself out of the unit, heart pounding, trying to

keep my cool until I could be absolutely sure, but trying also to prolong the moment in case it was indeed what I thought it was. These moments come seldom in the course of a career, and sometimes they never come. Seating myself by the edge of the unit, I closed my eyes briefly, collecting myself before I turned my closed fist over and opened it. Forget buried treasure, if this was what I thought it was . . .

This could change everything, I thought. My God. It could be the cover of the book. It could be the front page of the *New York Times*.

"What is it?" Meg said. She walked around the unit to my side, the better to see.

Carefully I opened my fingers, and there in my palm was a small, gray, flat circle, a crust of dirt discolored with dark, almost purple flecks of corrosion still sticking to it. I brushed at it carefully, so carefully, holding my breath lest even that gentle action destroy some vital evidence. A date, I thought, what is the date? My eyes strained to focus, to read what was on the side of the disc, and I thought I'd burst with anticipation. I couldn't see a date, couldn't even remember whether there should be a date on the coin, the one thing that would provide incontrovertible proof of what I'd been working on. But then there in my hand, I thought I saw the faint outline of a minute flower to one side of a face—

"Emma, what *is* it?"

It was a rose. A Tudor rose.

"Holy shit," I whispered. I looked up at Meg and held my opened hand for her to see. "Holy—"

"Oh my God," Meg whispered back. Her voice rose in excitement. "Is that a . . . is that what I think it is . . . ?"

"Yeah." I stared at the thing. "My God, it is. I can't . . . I don't believe it!"

"Turn it over, quick!" I wouldn't have believed that Meg could squeal.

I shook myself, tried to concentrate, turned it over, and again brushed carefully. The other side of the silver coin was worn smooth, but the faint outline of a crown was still visible. The edges were worn as well, and though the lettering had long ago been worn by acts of everyday commerce, changing hand to hand, traveling in a pouch, being hoarded in a wooden casket, I knew from the rest of the imprint that the letters would have spelled out "ELIZABETH D. G. ANG FRA ET HIB REGINA": "Elizabeth, by the grace of God, Queen of England, France, and Ireland."

"It's Elizabeth," I said, starting to stand. "I can't remember the issue date of this coin, but it's—"

"It's definitely early enough," Meg finished for me. Her eyes were shining and her voice was getting higher and higher with excitement. "More than early enough, it's just too perfect. I mean, they draw stuff like this for a textbook, right? Guy comes along, digs a hole to set his post in, ooops! accidentally, conveniently for us, drops in a coin with a date to tell us the date after which the house was built, fills it in, builds the house around the post, leaves it, and voilà! We come along after a couple of centuries and—"

She was really starting to babble. "Yeah, Meg I know," I said. "I *know*." The last word was a little strangled and I realized that I wasn't breathing evenly. In fact, I found myself having to sit down again; the sky was starting to close in on me.

"Are you okay?" Meg asked.

I shook my head, trying to clear it, and then tried to nod at the same time, lest I further worry Meg. "Yeah, just a little . . . we need to get a box or something rigid we can pad. I don't want this to get any more damaged than it already is."

The student rummaged around frantically in her kit and handed me a small cardboard box.

"Poke a couple of small holes in it, so the condensation can escape," I added, and when she had done so and put a piece of paper towel in the bottom of the box—the best we could do for field conservation—I gingerly slid an envelope into the box for added protection. Coins from the early part of the seventeenth century or earlier are very rare, but it was valuable to me for far more than its numismatic worth. It

confirmed that what we'd been finding was the early fort beyond a shadow of a doubt.

"Shouldn't we . . . ?" Meg gestured with her head down
the slope to where the rest of the students were working.

"Yeah, we should. Just give me a sec, okay?" I stared at the
coin a moment longer, as if burning it into memory, and
then nodded. "You go ahead. It's your posthole."

She shook her head. "You found it. You at least get their
attention."

I gave one of my piercing pinkie whistles and as the heads
turned around, Meg cupped her hands to her mouth and
shouted the call that every dig member hopes they'll get to
make someday. "Hey, guys! Look what we've got!"

And then, suddenly, later that morning, there was the "click."
I was sitting down to review my notes with the whole site
spread out before me, as the river below continued its end-
less rush to the ocean, when it came. It's not like Tennessee
Williams or anything; I certainly hadn't been drinking,
though with the click, there always comes a mighty buzz.
The click was how I described it when, suddenly, I understood my site entirely.

Sure, every site, every season is full of discoveries, but for
everything to snap into place so completely? One all-encom-
passing, road-to-Damascus insight? It's the stuff dreams and
careers are made on. And every minute longer we spent on
this site proved conclusively that we were on the actual site of
Fort Providence, the site that was going to rewrite history
and make my career, not necessarily in that order.

Even with all the work that was left to be done, the sorting, the analysis, the writing and researching, I felt more and
more confident that I would no longer have to look over my
shoulder to see who was gaining on me, waiting for me to
slip and fail in my bid for tenure. I could unpack my bags,
metaphorically speaking. I watched the cormorants flapping
their wings on the water; I had absolutely no idea why they

did it, but it sounded remarkably like applause. After years of work, struggle, scrabbling, and trying to kiss as little ass as possible, I would have arrived.

But even that potential paled in comparison to what we were uncovering; it made me start to shake just to think about it. Archaeologists are romantics at heart; otherwise they'd be historians or crossword puzzle writers. Every one of us, no matter how stodgy a devotee to the scientific method one claims to be, wants desperately to *touch* the past. Not just acquire a deeper factual understanding, we want to feel what the people who lived hundreds of years ago felt, get inside their hearts and minds, and know what it was that made their world for them. And for archaeologists, the shortest path, the most satisfying of unsatisfying solutions short of a time machine, is to handle the artifacts, walk the ground, and breathe the air that filled the lungs of our predecessors on a site.

I could hardly wait until Pauline got back—what this would mean to her! I got excited just thinking of telling her about it. Oscar had given me a passion and the tools to recover the past, but Pauline had given me an understanding of culture and the site itself. And now I could finally return the favor and reconstruct Jacobean culture transplanted in her front yard. After all these years, I could finally start to pay the two of them back for their gifts to me.

My euphoria was conducive to interpretation. I imagined that the English garrison must have had days like this four hundred years ago, when the hideous winter was a bad memory, the food was abundant, and the "savages" didn't seem quite so alien. It must been on days like this that the months of voyage, the sickness, fear, and violent death seemed justified; the adventure was worth it all. An entire continent to explore—imagine what even this small, clean stretch of coastline would have looked like to some poor soldier raised in the smoky squalor of late sixteenth-century London. A line from *The Tempest* came to me: "The isle is full of noises, sounds, and sweet airs, that give delight and hurt not . . ."

Imagine . . .

A cluster of small buildings, made in the English half-timbered style but of New World materials. Smoke rose from the chimneys even on a hot summer day, for food must be cooked and tools mended and lead poured into molds to replace diminishing supplies of shot. A hard-baked and stony garden yielding a growing store of vegetables, just beyond the ditch and the rampart. The gates are open today, for there is no threat by the land, and seems to be none on the sea from France or Spain—the guard keeps only a distracted watch. Men drill in military exercises, others hunt, others begin to lay plans for exploring farther up the river, which may lead to the Great Southern Sea and China . . .

And what about the native people? It could have been on such a day that it might have seemed possible, for however short a time, that they could live in peace with these pale, curious, ungainly strangers lately come upon their shore. A chance to understand some of their bizarre behavior that seemed so contrary to a reasonable way of life . . .

Imagine . . .

A small group of men trying to trade good pelts for a cold iron ax head, beads, and other curiosities. Sometimes the exchanges succeed with these queer foreigners, sometimes not. A European pot falls into a cooking fire, leaving a little piece of North Devon behind in a New English trash heap of ashes, stone flakes, and bone . . .

I took out my notebook and started to write.

The siren call of the site completely seduced me, and the words came forth faster than my pen could work across the page. That capricious rascal, my muse, had come back from her extended vacation and was making up for lost time. I hardly noticed the dry, prickly grass poking into my backside, or the line of ants marching purposefully across my left boot. Even the cormorants' clapping no longer intruded into my thoughts. Yesterday it seemed impossible to make sense all of the stratigraphic sequences that shaped the site; today they obediently slipped into logical order and gave up their secrets. The ghosts of people long dead were inclined to share their knowledge with me, at last. Passages from the eighteenth-century deeds, inventories, maps that I'd studied all winter suddenly sprang to mind, to explain that scatter of stones, or this artifact distribution. I thought of other research from the South, from the Caribbean, from Ireland and England in relation to my own, and for the first time I felt as though I could begin to understand the personalities involved, the cultural dynamics of the place, the introduction of the Old World to the New in the early seventeenth century.

The calm with which I worked was mystic, and it wasn't until I felt someone, Rob, nudge my foot with his that I came back to the present, but I was so grounded, so in tune with everything, that his insistent tapping was merely one more sensation to appreciate. I finished my sentence, scanned the rest of my notes to make sure it was all still there, and smiled at him beatifically.

"Sorry, Em, but you didn't seem to hear when I called. Neal's got everyone packed up, and we're ready to roll." He offered me a hand up, and I dusted myself off, after a spine-crunching stretch.

"Why? We going out for lunch?" My stomach suddenly indicated its long neglect, but otherwise, I felt the way I did after a fabulous run; high and focused, perfectly calm and alert to everything. Odd; Rob usually took until the end of the day to get those ridiculous, baggy shorts of his that filthy. He must really be wallowing today, probably another phase of his chimp mating display for Dian.

"No, Emma. Lunch was over four hours ago. It's time to go home now." He spoke slowly, as though plain American English might be beyond my ken. "Neal didn't want to bother you, as you seemed a little tuned out and didn't come when we hollered for you." Like Brian, Rob wasn't the sort to appreciate what might cause one to miss a meal, outside of some catastrophe, and gave me a look that spoke of worry for my sanity.

I rolled my head around my shoulders and another volley of bone cracks followed. "I thought it had clouded up a bit," I said, realizing the sun had moved clear across the sky. "Preoccupied, yeah. Got a lot of work done though." I bestowed another hundred-watt blast of my patented St. Emma valedictory smile on him, and got another bewildered look for my trouble.

Perhaps I was showing a few too many teeth—ah, but he couldn't have known that I had been strolling on Mount Parnassus. Poor mortal, I thought charitably as I followed him up to the trucks, perhaps someday he'll know what it's like to be the first person to set foot on Mars, or hear the National Anthem played for his victory at the Olympics. Or see a seventeenth-century English soldier standing alone on the beach, filled with homesickness and hopefulness.

"You're kidding me, right?" Brian's voice was incredulous on the phone later that night. I had been telling him about the day's discoveries, saving the best for last. "My God, Emma, that's fabulous! Oh man, that's so excellent!"

"I think it will really be an excellent cover for the monograph," I said. "I'm thinking of a couple of overlays, a contemporary painting of a fort, a topographic map of the site, and then the coin, bang, right in the middle."

It was nice to be the bearer of good news, for a change. I'd already been through several emotional peaks since we'd found the coin and was tired enough to act a little jaded about it. National interest was assured, international was probable, and just having the beginnings of the project show such results—for the three postholes had become five, and not indicating one building but *two*—was grant bait of the first water. Grants begetting grants. Hello, National Geographic Society. Hello, National Endowment for the Humanities.

"But wait. Isn't a 1590 sixpence too early?" Brian's voice

filled with worry. "Don't you need it to be closer to 1605 and King James or something for it to work for you, date-wise?"

"No, it's fine as long as it's the same exact date or earlier," I reassured him. "The same way that you can use a quarter that was minted when Nixon was president, but you couldn't have a quarter from ten years from now, because they wouldn't exist yet. In fact, you're more likely to have an older coin, because the newer ones wouldn't have had as much time to get into circulation, right?"

"I get it. What does Pauline think? She must be excited, huh?"

"She doesn't know yet, she's still in Boston, till next Wednesday, I think. But I'll have a hell of a surprise for her then."

"Speaking of the weekend, I know this is exciting and everything, but are you going to be able to come home this weekend?" Brian sounded wistful. "I mean, I don't want to drag you away from your work, or anything . . ."

"I'll be there, hon. Since we've got that line of postholes now, I do want to try and get as much out of it as we can— we've only got about a week left, and everyone knows that any archaeological crew worth its salt always finds the best and least explicable stuff right before you're supposed to close down. The weather's supposed to be bad tomorrow, so if it rains I'll be home that much earlier." I twined the phone cord around my hand. "Don't make any plans for this weekend, 'kay?"

I heard Brian pause. "Naturally, had I known your plans for sure, I wouldn't have dreamed of it," he said slowly. "But I did sort of tell Kam to come over for dinner tomorrow night. That's okay, isn't it?"

It was my turn to be sheepish. "Well, yeah, especially since I just remembered I told Marty to come over for a visit then. It's her only free night in Boston this weekend."

"Tell her to stick around for food, then."

"You know," I mused. "I'd always wondered if they

mightn't get along rather nicely together. They seemed to get pretty chummy at dinner that time."

"Emma, don't!" Brian pleaded. "Kamil Shah's my oldest friend, and what's more, he's my boss—"

"Pish, something in title only," I said.

"Yeah, well, I don't want you messing around with two perfectly good friends and trying to make them into something else," he insisted. "It will just get complicated and screw everyone up if it doesn't work out. And these things never do."

I wasn't about to be put off; my idea was *great*. "But what if it works? Don't you want Kam to be happy like us?"

"Kam is happy with a gym with large mirrors and women in spandex. Kam is happy with his uncomplicated serial dating. I like Kam happy the way he is."

"Never mind, then." I just wouldn't say anything more about it to Brian. "It was just a thought."

"Good." Brian sounded relieved. "So I'll see you tomorrow night, maybe earlier?"

"You got it. And we should make a point of celebrating."

"Right. I'll get the wine with the real cork this time."

"And don't get the pizza from that place down the street—they have soggy crust."

"Anything for you, my queen. See you then, love."

"I'll see you, sweetie."

"I'm so proud of you."

"Me too. I love you. Bye."

True to the forecaster's predictions, rain was just heavy enough on Friday morning to drive us out of the field and back to our makeshift lab at the dorm. When one says the word *lab*, one thinks of white-coated technicians rigorously observing the results of experiments conducted in gleaming glassware and complex-looking, state-of-the-art computerized equipment. While the pharmaceutical lab where Brian

worked as a chemist might closely resemble that ideal—
gleaming pipettes, bottles of chemicals, and all—an archaeological field lab almost never did. We used dishpans and
sieves and toothbrushes bought from the supermarket to
wash the artifacts, and then we dried them on ordinary window screens, newspaper, or even beer flats. The highest technology we had in our field lab, if we were lucky, was
somebody's portable CD player. And what we were doing
was hardly demanding, even if it did require patience and
care; we were washing trash discarded several centuries ago.
Pretty funny, when you stopped to think about it.

Normally labwork is something to be delayed as long as
possible, because washing every one of those thousands of
little pieces of ceramic and glass is the most tedious task on
earth. There is never any good way to work; either the plastic
washtubs are too high on the table, and you have to stand, or
too low, and you have to hunch over. Fingertips inevitably
become cramped from holding the artifacts tightly, scrubbed
raw from brushing them, and wrinkled from being sub-
merged in water for hours on end. Labeling the artifacts with
their context coordinates is even worse, with the fumes from
the marking pens and the clear varnish used to protect the
labels making the students dizzy, even with the windows
open.

Even I helped out this time; usually I just excused myself
from the odious chore, pulling rank and using the excuse of
seniority. But now we had the opportunity to get a closer
look at the artifacts associated with the early settlement, and
so the drudgery was mitigated for everyone.

I squinted at the piece of pottery that I held between my
water-pruned thumb and index finger. Water dripped off the
ceramic potsherd that looked better for washing, but was really not much more than mud that had been hard-fired into
shape. No wonder we had so many of the ugly, rough, brown
potsherds; whoever had been in charge of outfitting the settlement at Fort Providence certainly hadn't put the money

into sturdy ceramic storage vessels. With walls this thin and unrefined, they must have broken if someone looked at them sideways.

I sighed and put the sherd with its fellows. After my revelatory experiences of the day before, I chafed at being locked up away from the site. So far in the artifact assemblage there wasn't anything that stuck out, gave a blinding new insight into life at Fort Providence. That would come with closer examination. Later.

"Mine's smaller than yours!"

That unlikely challenge caught my ear and I looked up. Rob was holding up a minute piece of eighteenth-century glass for Alan's inspection.

"You can't even read the provenience!" Alan shot back. "That doesn't count!"

"You can so," Rob insisted. He handed the sherd to Neal.

"ME 343–1–2F3" Neal read out loud. He looked at Rob. "That right?"

Rob looked smug. "That's it all right."

"Of course you'd take his side," Alan told Neal.

The crew, as one, sighed. Alan's passive-aggressive behavior around Neal had been increasingly less passive, more painful to listen to, and harder to ignore.

"It's just a stupid game," Meg said. "No one really cares who can write the smallest, just so it's legible."

"Calm down, Al," Dian said, not looking up from her own work.

"This sucks," Alan announced. He threw his marking pen down and stalked out of the room.

"For God's sake," Rob muttered. Everyone else looked at me.

I sighed but spoke decisively. "Finish the bag you're working on and then let's knock it off for now, before I get sued for exposing you all to carcinogens. We'll let the freshmen do the rest of the later stuff in September. When you're done cleaning up, we'll break for the weekend." It was clear to me that we'd hit the boiling point during the dig, the time at which tempers that had been kept in check at the beginning were fraying and people were starting to get on each other's nerves. "G'wan, get out of here."

With a collective stretch and a groan of relief, they straightened up and started carefully moving the artifact screens out of the way to dry. Neal looked at me and I nodded, sighing. "Back in a minute."

After everything was put away, I walked down the hall and knocked on Alan's door.

"Go away," came the muffled reply.

"It's Emma." So you don't get to say that to me, I thought.

There was no answer, but I could hear movement inside the room.

"Alan, you've been really on edge lately," I said through the door. More than usual, I said to myself. "You've barely said two words to me in the past week. What's going on?"

Still there was nothing.

I sighed again and summoned up the wherewithal to pursue this. "Alan, I'd rather not have this conversation out here in the hallway, through a closed door, but we are going to have it. It's up to you."

Suddenly the door opened. I composed myself and prepared to confront Alan once and for all, but that was not going to be possible. He had a full duffel bag with him and pulled the door shut after him.

"Everyone else is heading out too," I said neutrally.

Alan looked startled at this, and I realized that he had been planning to leave, bad weather, chemical fumes, or no. His face was red and tormented, looking anywhere but at me.

"Alan, what's going on?" I asked gently.

"I'm leaving . . . I can't stand . . . I don't . . ." He rested his head against the closed door and I could see a vein pulsing in his temple, his jaw working. The hand that still clenched the doorknob was white-knuckled.

"Something's really troubling you," I said. "Please tell me."

"You're the last person I can tell," he answered abruptly. He turned away from me completely. "I'm sorry about what happened, but I just can't keep . . . oh, forget it."

He headed away down the hallway and I asked quietly, "Alan, are you coming back?"

He stopped. "I want . . . I can't . . . I don't know." He then simply fled down the hallway and out into the stairwell, while I stared after him, no better informed and much more confused.

Chapter 7

ENOUGH, I TOLD MYSELF, I'M GETTING OUT OF HERE. I went upstairs to my room, grabbed a backpack and stuffed a couple of clean pairs of underwear and shirts into it, thought about leaving my notebook behind, and then thought the better of it and threw it in anyway. You never know when inspiration will strike. I shouted, "See you Sunday night!" in the general direction of the students' rooms and bolted down the stairwell to the parking lot and my beat-up Civic.

Quite apart from the emotional turmoil that seemed to be compounding in our little group, and even in the face of the week's staggering finds, it is always something of a relief to get away from the site. A little distance never hurts, and downtime becomes even more important when you're overwhelmed with a deluge of data, particularly of this caliber. Your judgment gets worn out, otherwise. So it was with only a very small pang of guilt that I began the three-hour drive toward Boston, grateful that it was my week to have the car and I could be self-propelled.

It wasn't such a bad arrangement. The drive helped take

the edge off, and since I was driving south, I had a clear sail to the New Hampshire border. The rain lessened to dull skies as I headed south, and I pitied the poor vacationers just starting to meld into a logjam on the northbound side of I-95.

Our apartment was in Somerville, a city with a high density of Boston and Cambridge academic types who can't afford to live in Boston or Cambridge or the more remote suburbs. It wasn't a bad apartment—it was in a place with nice a sense of neighborhood—but it was on the smallish side and getting smaller every year, it seemed, with the growing library collections Brian and I were both accumulating.

The worst thing about it was that I was almost never able to be there except on weekends, even during the school year. We got it when Brian was hired by his friend Kam to work in a Cambridge lab, and when the Caldwell job came up for me in southern Maine, we simply decided that it would be easier and cheaper for me to take advantage of the on-campus housing rather than trying to make an untenable commute between Massachusetts and Maine every day. We knew we'd need to move sooner rather than later, but it had always been our hope that a house would materialize in our future, and so put off moving with that hope in mind. Lately we'd given up and just thought about a bigger apartment someplace in between.

I parked in a huge puddle in front of our place and saw that Kam's Jaguar was already parked up the street, a marked contrast to the econoboxes that belonged to the folks who lived in the double-deckers around us. He's always been loaded, but there you are; the jerk is also gorgeous. At least he's got the good taste that so many rich folks seem to lack.

I tch-tched over the lack of our lawn, now mud. The little patch of dirt in front of the house was merely a collecting place for weeds and the occasional plastic bag. Our landlady was charmed when we put an ironical ceramic gnome out there. It was just to fill up space because the soil would support only a couple of spring bulbs, which took more fertilizer than it was actually worth to get them to grow.

Grabbing my backpack I bounded up the stairs, so light of

heart that I didn't even notice the other people crowding our second-floor hallway until I had practically landed on them. Two faces, one startled and one serene with only a raised eyebrow, turned to greet me.

"Marty! Kam!" I cried. "This is good timing, when we all three show up at exactly the same moment! Couldn't have timed it better!"

"*Jesu*, Emma, you scared the wits out of me," Marty complained. She fumbled her enormous Chanel handbag out of the way and reached out her arms to me. "It's good to see you, dearie." Mariam Asefi—Marty—was my oldest friend, an improbable roommate from college days. She was a petite, dark-headed, porcelain-skinned creature, urban and urbane, with a talent for hyperbole.

"Yes, excellent timing," Kam added, still doing his imitation of Mr. Spock. He was like a cat who had grown out of kittenish bounding, and although tolerant of bounding in others, was more disposed to dignified propriety for himself. He was elegantly thin, a clotheshorse of the first water, with dark eyes that made you want to drown yourself in them.

I gave my friends a hug and the door suddenly opened. "Brian!" I dropped away from them to assault my husband. He was the perfect fit; not too much taller than me, not so broad that I couldn't steal his shirts and sweaters when necessary. His Chinese ancestry gave him a slightly exotic look, but other than that, I'd really married the all-American boy.

"Sweetie!" I stuck my nose on his neck. God, you smell good!" Warm man and shampoo; there's nothing more intoxicating.

He nuzzled me back. "You too. I've missed you."

We were lost in private welcome for a moment too long.

"Ahem."

"Leave them be, Kam."

"Well, they've gone so far as to invite us to dinner, they might consider our presence," Kam complained.

"You're just jealous because I don't kiss you like that," Brian retorted, giving me a final kiss and setting me aside.

"Enough," I said. "I've got amazing news—"

"So do I," said Kam. Brian exchanged a look with him and he nodded.

"I have some news that will wait for later, but a thirst that burns now," Marty said. "I require immediate attention."

"Allow me." Kam pulled out two bottles of what even I could recognize was hideously expensive champagne. Sure enough French.

I looked incredulous as Brian suddenly materialized with our champagne flutes, wedding presents that had seen very little use over the past five years. I could have sworn that they had been lost, languishing in the back of some cupboard. "What the hell is going on here?" I asked.

Marty looked as startled as I felt. "Don't look at me. I have no idea. About *this*, I mean."

Brian set the glasses on the table with a flourish while Kam wrestled with the first bottle. Then Brian took my backpack away from me, waltzed me away from the door and into the middle of the room, then swung back to escort Marty next to me. He shut the door just in time to take the first glass that his friend had filled and hand it to me.

"Brian? What is it?" I said.

He smiled devilishly and put his finger up to his lips. "Don't worry, hon. It's cool. Extremely cool."

Marty looked impatiently at Kam; the small bubbles were obviously calling to her, but it was clear that Kam was going to make a toast. "So?"

"So." He paused a moment further, then raised his glass dramatically. "To United Pharmaceuticals."

"United Pharmaceuticals," Brian echoed. They drained their glasses, while Marty and I simply stared, confused.

"I don't see why we should be wishing them well," Marty said. She sipped, however, thirst overcoming scruples. "Biggest drug company in the world doesn't need our goodwill."

"Oh, but that's exactly what they need," Brian gloated. "That's *precisely* it."

"Okay, I need some more clues," I said. "Fill me in here."

"Drink up first, there's more where that came from," Kam said, as he refilled their glasses. "To put it bluntly, directly, and concisely, we've been bought out." He and Brian clinked glasses again and emptied another round of wine.

Rather than share their elation, I was alarmed, and shook Brian's arm. "Wait a minute! This can't be good! I mean, won't there be layoffs? You could lose your job! And you've always gone on about their bad reputation and . . . and . . . everything! Why aren't you worried? Stop drinking that champagne and tell me."

"It's all upside," Brian answered. "They do have a crappy reputation for their pricing policies and for their waste treatment problems. That last lawsuit was very bad press for them, and it was clear that they needed to do something about it. The old CEO was voted out and a new one with some fairly advanced ideas voted in. And if everyone loves a good villain, then everyone also likes a reformed villain better. United is making a big splash in the media right now, lots of ads about their new outlook. Heavy on the New Agey imagery, medicines from nature, etcetera taking a page out of The Body Shop's book. And that's why they want us, all of a sudden, to bruit about their new approach to things and new policies on testing. We've got the reputation and they've got the money. Better yet, to keep all that goodwill coming in, they are retaining all of our employees—"

"Except for Kelley," Kam interjected. "Our aging hippie president will be retiring to her dream commune a very wealthy woman."

"—they are saying that we can inform the staff of the policy changes and they are buying our stock, they are buying our options! They're gonna buy our options, they're gonna buy our options!" Brian continued in a singsongy voice. He began dancing around the room again, little droplets of champagne flying from his glass, and twirled me around again. "So what do you think of *them* apples?"

I could only stare at my husband. "Holy snappers. I mean,

congratulations!" I gulped down some fizzy, and it didn't do anything to clear my already buzzing head. "Holy—"

Kam nodded smugly. "I know. It's called selling out while still keeping your legs crossed. Brilliant, isn't it?"

Then he did something that I wouldn't have bet on in a thousand years. Kam took Marty's glass away from her and set it on the table. Then he took her in his arms, dipped her backward, and kissed her passionately.

Imagine Queen Victoria flicking a spitball. Imagine Henry Kissinger break dancing. That was the extent of our disbelief.

Brian stopped dancing to stare at them. I kept right on staring dumbly, poleaxed for a whole other set of reasons, now. "Hey, wait a minute," I said finally. "You guys have been *seeing* each other, haven't you?"

"Well," Marty said as soon as she was able to draw breath again. "Among other things."

"And how long has this been going on?" I continued. "When were you going to tell us?"

"A while," Kam answered, setting Marty back on her feet and smoothing out his tie. "And consider yourself told."

"I was going to tell you at dinner. That was my news," Marty said, picking up her glass again and emptying it as if nothing unusual had happened. "So there you are." She nonchalantly accepted a refill from Kam and turned to me. "So what was your news?"

I shook my head slowly and shrugged. Brian shook out of his stupor and opened the other bottle of champagne and topped me up. "Nothing much. Let's see. I found that body last week, you all know about that, and then the next day there was the gun-toting loony threatening us—"

"Emma!" Marty and Kam gasped in tandem; finally I was able to shock them, but the best still remained.

"—and just yesterday I think I've just discovered conclusive evidence that I've got the goods on one of the earliest English settlements in America, but nothing much besides that."

"Are you okay?" Marty asked.

I was touched by my friend's concern. "Oh, yeah, fine."

"Well, good." She paused. "So let's order the pizza, then."

"Marty! Don't you even want to hear about the *site*?"

"Well, yes, but I'm hungry," the supremely ahistorical Marty protested. "At least call it in before you tell us everything."

The next morning, when I awoke, groggy from too little sleep and too much celebrating, I found Brian poring over the paper. I watched him for a minute, enjoying the way the sunlight reflected off his dark brown hair, his skin like warm honey. We were such a good match together.

"What's that?" I said, finally. I yawned hugely and fumbled for the coffee, the need for which had driven me from the bedroom.

"Real estate," Brian answered around a piece of toast.

For once something besides caffeine jolted me awake. "What for?" I asked cautiously.

"Houses."

I paused. "Say that again."

"Houses. A house." He grinned briefly as he turned the page over. "We might want to check one of the New Hampshire papers, though, if we're gonna find something equidistant from here and Caldwell."

For the umpteenth time in less than twenty-four hours, I was speechless. Brian rattled the paper down. "You okay?"

"Yeah." I shook my head. "Not New Hampshire. I hate New Hampshire."

"Okay, then we'll see what else we can manage." He continued to scan the listings.

"So. When did this come up?" I asked, still more than a little bewildered.

"When I heard last week. I wanted to make sure it was going to work out before I told you, and so now it is." Brian looked up and took a deep breath.

"I have to go to San Francisco next week, like, tomorrow," he continued apologetically. "That's where United's head-quarters are. But when I come back, a couple of weeks or so, I want to move. I want to move someplace where we do not smell our neighbors' dinners cooking, where we do not hear people fighting across the alley, where we can live together every night and not just on weekends. We will talk about this, if you want, but basically, I've decided. Sound okay to you?"

Actually it sounded damned good, just nigh on incredible. I took a drink of coffee and it helped a little. The only other time I'd seen Brian this adamant was when he proposed. "Okay."

"Good. You have anything in mind?" For the first time he looked uncertain. "I mean, we're not up to real luxury or anything, the options are just enough for a good down payment, but if you like a style or something, we can look for that."

I thought about it, perhaps for the first time since I was a girl. "Nope. Old is nice. I'd like a room for my own office."

Now Brian looked downright uneasy. "Do you . . . do you want to call your father?"

"No." Dad was a real estate agent; we didn't talk a lot. "We can do this ourselves. Besides, he's going to be on Nantucket until Labor Day with Beebee." My father's second wife was just five years older than I.

Brian breathed a sigh of relief and turned back to the papers. "Good."

The weather had cleared up late last night. I looked around the kitchen. It was sunny but small; I wouldn't miss it. "You know what?"

"What?"

"You're sexy when you're decisive," I said.

That got his attention and he set the papers aside. "Oh? Finish your coffee, then, and I'll show you just how decisive I can be."

* * *

I experienced the social schizophrenia of fieldwork late Sunday evening. So far from being half of an affectionate pair, I was back on the lonely peak of leadership. My domestic life and its staggering, fantastic upheavals once again receded in favor of my work and the totality of its demands. Alan was nowhere to be found when I came in, so I resolved to speak with him after fieldwork the next day. His increasingly erratic moodiness was the only fly in the ointment right now.

On Monday morning the fickle weather redeemed itself, promising to be as glorious as our last day in the field. The wind playfully sped puffy little clouds across the sky, as if only for the pleasure of watching their shadows skid along the river. Neal was driving, and I was semi–conked out in the passenger's seat. The windows were down so that we could enjoy the last cool of the day before evening, so the noise in the car was nearly deafening.

The smell of wood smoke was just becoming noticeable. Rob all of a sudden piped up. "Smells like someone's cooking breakfast."

"Some damned tourist letting things get out of hand. They always think they need a yule log to make their instant coffee," Meg muttered.

Suddenly I was awake. "That's no campfire," I said. I couldn't have told you why I was so quickly worried, but the smell was very acrid. "Neal, let's move it. I don't like this one bit." As we tore out of the tree-lined downslope, we could see smoke billowing into the sky in front of us.

The truck tore around the last rise, and we didn't need to see the cluster of fire engines in the road and Pauline's driveway to realize the horrible truth. Greycliff was burning.

Chapter 8

BEFORE THE TRUCK HAD EVEN STOPPED, I HAD FUMBLED my way out of my safety belt and was running toward the house. The heat hit me like a brick wall and slowed me down, threatening to steal my breath away. When the wind shifted, driving the smoke away momentarily, I could see the paint bubbling and peeling near the windows, flecks of soot and ash sticking to it. The flames were huge, unaffected by the powerful stream of water that the fireman aimed at it. Even before a fireman intercepted me, I had stopped, fascinated by the horrible conflagration.

"You can't go in there!" he shouted. "Get those vehicles out of here! We need room."

"This is my friend's house," I said. "What's—?"

He asked quickly, "Are they at home?"

"No, she's away, in Boston."

"Anyone else in there?"

I shook my head.

"Good, now get those trucks away, down the road, past that telephone pole."

I ran back and told Neal and Alan, in the other truck, to

pull away, not interfere. I know Neal said something, but I couldn't make myself focus on it. I barely recognized him.

The fireman spoke into his walkie-talkie, then gestured at me again.

"Who are you?"

"Emma Fielding. I'm . . . I'm a friend of Pauline's."

"Can you tell me what is going on down on the lawn? Is there anything we need to know about? Pipelines or anything in those holes in the ground?"

I looked where he was pointing, down at the tarps, and realized that the site was just sitting there, waiting for attention while the house burned. A momentary panic seized me, as I tried to imagine whether the fire could affect it in any way. "No, they're . . . just holes in the ground. I've been conducting archaeological research here."

"No kidding?" For a moment he was impressed, then the radio crackled again and he began shouting a response into it. I couldn't make anything out over the monstrous noise of the house burning. It was like nothing I'd ever heard before, so huge and destructive, and yet almost fiendishly reminiscent of a campfire.

It was unreal. All of it was unreal.

I watched as the firefighters worked feverishly, a sort of modern dance, where there seemed to be nothing but chaos at first glance, but after a moment of study, deeper logic was revealed. They dragged a hose across the lawn toward the front of the house to attack the fire from another direction.

"Oh! Be careful—" I cried, then caught myself and cursed.

The fireman grabbed my wrist. "What? What's wrong?"

"No, no I'm sorry." I shook my head. "There's nothing. I just wanted them to be careful of the flowers. Pauline's worked so hard—" I began to cry uncontrollably. "I'm sorry, my God, I'm so sorry, this is so stupid, worrying about the stupid goddamned *flowers* . . ."

"Don't worry about it. I see it all the time. Just sit down over here, stay out of the way, and when things calm down, we'll figure out how to reach your friend."

So I sat there on the bumper of the chief's truck and watched the house burn down. I knew I was still crying because I could feel how puffy my face was growing. I had to blink every so often, but I couldn't for the life of me feel the tears running down my cheeks. The air was just too hot. I tried not to think about all the memories I had here. I tried not to think about telling Pauline. She was rooted in this place; it was a part of her and I couldn't imagine her anywhere else.

I was so busy trying not to think about so many things that time seemed to evaporate around me, swirled away and scattered over the river with the smoke. After what seemed like a long time, I realized that I no longer saw flames shooting out through the broken windows and out a ragged hole that left the rafters exposed in the remaining roof. The next thing I noticed was the relative quiet: The roaring had died away and all that remained was the sound of running water dripping and hissing as it hit hot surfaces, the shouts of the firefighters, and the noise of equipment being deployed or stowed away.

I looked up and saw Dave Stannard standing next to me, his eyes glued to the wreck of the house. He looked down. "You okay?"

"No." I sniffed loudly and wiped my eyes on my shirt-sleeves; my handkerchief had been rendered useless long ago. "But I'm okay." I thought about how stupid that was and almost grinned.

"A hell of a hot fire," he said, shaking his head in wonder. "With all that rain we got? Even with most of the exterior shell still standing, Ms. Westlake's going to have to rebuild."

"She's going to be devastated," I said. "She'll be heartbroken. But she'll rebuild, all right, she's like that." A sudden thought seized me. "Oh damn, the students!" I whipped my head around, trying to see if they were still waiting. "I completely forgot about them!"

I started to head back up the driveway when the sheriff

stopped me. "They're fine, I sent them home a while ago. Told them I'd get you a ride back."

"Thanks." I sniffed again and surveyed the ruin of Greycliff. "Oh hell. What a mess."

Stannard nodded. "I'm going to check with Jimmy in there, see if he can tell what started this all."

Suddenly a shout came from where the firemen were examining the inside of the house. That bred more shouting, which seemed to move from person to person up the drive, until I was finally able to make out the words.

"A stretcher! Get a stretcher in here!"

I looked over to where the action was, confused. Two firemen rushed back and were met by a couple of paramedics who, with unbelievable, practiced ease, moved a heavy-looking gurney down to the house and through the opened back door.

"What's going on?" I asked. "Why do they need a stretcher?"

"Probably one of the firefighters got hurt," Stannard said, frowning. "You stay put and I'll—"

The shouting increased, the buzz of activity increased, and unconsciously, I began to follow the sheriff toward the house. Raincoated firefighters began to stream out of the house, and I saw one of the paramedics leading the foot of the gurney out. I could see black rubber on the stretcher, but it did not resolve itself into the boots that I expected—

As I stared I heard a shout: "Jesus Christ! Somebody get her out of here!"

The black continued to emerge from the house until the other paramedic came out at the head of the stretcher. Or where the head should have been. It was just a formless stretch of black plastic, all the way along the stretcher.

I stepped forward involuntarily. Time once again slowed and I heard a keening moan that seemed to continue endlessly. Some part of me realized that I must have been making the noise, but even with that knowledge, I felt myself collapsing; my knees turned to rubber and I stumbled, the world suddenly seeming to spin around me, my vision awhirl.

The more I tried to deny it, the more I knew it was true. I couldn't have said how I knew, but as soon as I recognized the body bag for what it was, I also knew, as sure as my life, that it was Pauline they were carrying out of the burned ruin.

Chapter 9

"**D**R. FIELDING? EMMA? YOU FAINTED," A VOICE SAID.

"I don't faint. I've never fainted," I insisted, as if from a distance. My words sounded blurred and with that recognition, time suddenly snapped back into its proper pace. I sat up.

"Oh my God, Pauline!"

Dave Stannard nodded grimly. "It's Pauline Westlake. I'm sorry."

"But there's no car in the driveway," I said perversely, automatically refusing to believe him and trying to deny what I already knew was true. I shoved myself up and stumbled a couple of steps to check. Just as I'd remembered: There was no sign of Pauline's Volvo wagon. I turned back to Stannard, frantic to prove him wrong. "How do you know it's Pauline? It could be anyone—anyone!—we don't know for sure."

The sheriff paused. "I recognized her rings. Everything else . . . was in pretty bad shape. We'll have to do an . . . conduct further investigation, but I'm pretty sure. I thought she was in Boston this week?"

"She was supposed to be back next Wednesday," I said miserably. "She was visiting her sister, I think, among other things."

"Do you know her sister's name?"

I wracked my brain. "Claudette. Peirce, I think is her last name. She lives somewhere in Boston."

He looked pale. "How did *you* know it was Ms. Westlake?"

"I don't know," I said. Tears began to leak out again when there couldn't possibly have been any left. "I just knew. Something told me."

"Okay. I've got to get this place sealed up and a crime lab team in here. Once that's done, why don't you come back to the station with me? I'll take another statement from you, we'll try to contact Claudette Peirce. Then I'll drop you back wherever you need to go. Okay?"

I nodded. Something in the back of my mind told me he didn't actually need to be so polite, but I didn't care.

"Okay. Why don't we see if any of these guys has a drink of water, or something, then we'll get started."

Pulling up to the dorm that afternoon, I had to take a moment to recognize the kids sitting on the dorm steps. I saw Meg and Neal, both still wearing their dig clothes, and I began to resent them for looking like they did every day. I knew I must look a mess, my eyes were dry now but burned like hell, and my face felt swollen to about twice its normal size. The smell of smoke that clung to my hair and was soaked into my own clothes was a ghastly, tangible reminder of what I'd seen.

I leaned my head against the glass, trying to gather my wits, summon a little emotional wherewithal: I was going to have to tell them that Pauline was dead, that she was inside her house when she should have been safely tucked away in Boston at Claudette's or the museum or having a good whiskey in the bar at the Ritz overlooking the Public Gardens. I knew as soon as I opened my mouth, I would have to deal with their questions and their shock too. I wasn't ready for it, but then, really, I never would be, I thought numbly.

"You okay? You need a hand?" The storklike Deputy Sheehan, who had driven me home, was good at concern. I hoped for his sake that he had never read Washington Irving.

"Yeah, I'm good. Thanks for the lift."

"I'm real sorry about your loss. Miss Westlake was a nice lady." He was just a kid, I thought dismissively; he looked like a Cub Scout in his uniform. I couldn't imagine anyone taking him seriously as a peace officer. I felt a flicker of annoyance toward him—what could he possibly know of my loss?—then quashed it. I nodded and got out of the car.

I tried to take a couple of deep breaths, but I couldn't seem to get enough air; weird, when I felt so hollow inside. If I could only breathe, I thought, I would be able to handle this. My baseball cap was still stuck on my head, where it had been all day; I felt stupid and childish with it on, but I left it there, needing the snugness of it to feel like something was holding me together.

I guess I took too long to collect myself, because the students exchanged a look and started to get up. I held up a hand; for some reason, it was very important to me that they stay put, where I wanted them. If I could control that, maybe I could control myself as well.

As I walked to the doorway, I thought of how I should put it, how I could tell them. They already knew, as soon as they saw me up close, that something else was wrong, and so it just came out. "It's bad news," I said. "Pauline's dead. They found her inside."

"My God."

"How could they have—?"

I didn't even look at them, I couldn't distinguish their voices. I needed as much distance as I could get from this moment. "Her sister said that she'd left early," I recited, "she'd finished up some business that she was taking care of. She said that Paul was going to have her car looked at—it was making a rattling noise, or something. The sheriff called the guy at the garage in town and he said that he gave her a lift home yesterday."

"God, Em, I'm sorry." I recognized Neal's voice this time. "Is there anything I can do?"

"Anything we can do?" Meg echoed. She sounded so queer that I looked at her. She was positively green.

"I don't know. We've only got a week left, but . . . it's still a week. But there's going to be an investigation, I've got to stick around for that, help with questions until her sister gets up here. Really, I'm the only link with Paul's life outside Maine. There's going to be a funeral, of course, and we'll go to that, but I just don't know about the work . . ."

I was pleased that my voice sounded so normal, but then realized that I was starting to wander. I tried to get to the point, attempting to keep a tight leash on my emotions, but it was just no good. I threw up my hands.

"I *can't* go back there," I said in bitter disbelief. "I can't go back there now, not with Pauline not there, and the house, the house is gone, it's just a blackened wreck, and I know I should be brave and finish up the work, for her or whatever, and I will, we'll go back and we'll make her proud, but I can't do it now, I just can't! I mean, goddamn it, Pauline's *dead*, and she taught me everything, and she's gone and Oscar's gone, and they put her in this god-awful plastic *bag*, and it's just too bloody bad if I can't suck it up enough to go back there for a while! I mean, it's not just me, the sheriff's guys have got to do their stuff and they asked me to hold off for a bit anyway, to keep out of the way—"

I think it was that thought, that I would be in the way at Pauline's house. It just came tearing out of me and suddenly I really didn't care who was there. "I can't believe this, this is just so wrong! I mean, I know she was old, I knew she was, she was an old lady, and that was fine, I could deal with the fact that one day I'd lose her, but not like this. Never like this, not a stupid *accident*, it just goes against everything she is, was, oh shit!"

I leaned against the railing, head in hands, willing time to freeze because when I looked up, I would be forced to come to grips with their sympathy. But not yet. Someone put a hand on my shoulder and I just shoved it away. I knew I'd have to apologize later, to whoever it was, but I didn't care, I couldn't face it now. I opened the door and ran up to my room.

I dropped my bag outside my door and just kept going down the hall to the phone. I tried to remember what the date was, what time it would be in California, and realized it didn't matter. I was devastated when the phone just rang and rang and Brian never answered.

I leaned against the brick, trying to take it all in, make some sort of plan, but the smell of someone's lunch cooking reached me and made me gag, and I fled into my room before anyone could offer me a meal I couldn't eat. I peeled off my work clothes, still clean but for a couple of smuts and some soot, and climbed into the shower to wash the day from me, but it didn't help. Everything I looked at just reminded me that Pauline was dead. I tried to recall our last conversation and whether she'd smiled at all. Finally I got into bed with my bathrobe on and my hair still wet, but a few minutes later climbed back out again. I put my work clothes and my backpack outside my door and locked it, then pulled the covers over my head and tried to fall asleep without the smell of smoke in my nose.

Chapter 10

I FELL IN AND OUT OF SLEEP ALL THAT DAY AND NIGHT and finally resisted the futile urge to try again around four A.M. As unaccustomed as I was to rising early of my own volition, I got dressed, made some coffee, made a few lists, paced a lot, and cried a little more, until I found that I had no tears left. About seven Tuesday morning I heard the others stirring, so I took a deep breath, armed myself with my notes, and went out to inform the crew about my decisions. I felt ancient and raw, inside and out, as if I'd been scoured with pumice.

Everyone was getting his breakfast and before any of them could say anything, I grabbed a cup of coffee and started right in with my speech. Among my many other reasons for being glad of the coffee, the cup also gave me a useful prop, a distraction when it was needed.

"You probably all know by now that Pauline Westlake was found in the house and that she is dead. I should have told the rest of you myself yesterday, but I couldn't . . . if Pauline wasn't actually a relation, she did as much as anyone to make me who I am today, and, well, it's been a shock for everyone. I've decided that we're going to stop where we are—"

A few surprised noises came from the students and I held up a hand.

"For now. We are close enough to the end of most of the active units to finish and map them in a day or two and so we'll wrap them up and not start any new ones. We'd only get another meter or two done this last week anyway, and if we come across anything really big, well, either it will keep until next season, or we can manage by getting it out on weekends, before the semester is in full swing. So we haven't lost much time, really, and you all will get your full stipends. What we'll do in the meantime is work on getting the artifacts washed and labeled, so we can make the most of our time here and still be around so that if the deputies say we can go back to backfill, we'll be here. There has to be some investigation into the source of the fire, and they won't want us kicking up dust around their data, same as we wouldn't want anyone messing up ours."

That sparked a sudden, panicky thought in me, and I hurriedly set it aside. Not now.

Dian spoke up, and I noticed for the first time that her eyes were reddened. "I know I speak for everyone, Em, when I say how sorry we are for you, your loss, I mean." She looked around and the other students nodded silently. "Pauline was great and we all loved her."

"Thanks." It was easier to deal with sympathy now that I'd had a little time to deal with my own grief. "So. The weather looks iffy, but the order of the day is getting things sorted out to go back to the department. I'll probably be in and out"— my breath caught here, but I was able to master myself—"as I may need to help with the sheriff's investigation."

"Don't worry about anything," Neal said. "We'll get everything in order."

I nodded. "Thanks, I'm counting on that. And I'll let you know as soon as I know anything about the . . . funeral arrangements. That's it, I guess. Thanks, again."

I went over for another cup of coffee, the bulk of the morning's unpleasantness almost done. As if I had forgotten something, I said, "And, oh, Alan? Could I have a word for a moment?"

He didn't get up from the table and he didn't meet my eyes. "What is it?"

I gritted my teeth and thought, Alan, you're making yourself a very large target today; don't push me. Concealing my irritation, I said, "I just need your help with something, for a minute."

I led him down the hallway, to another, empty common area, well out of earshot. "Have a seat." I took a deep sip of coffee, wishing I didn't have this on my plate as well. I just didn't need it. "What's up?"

"Nothing. I was just . . . sorry." I could see a lot of his father in him when he pressed his lips together. "What's this all about?"

"I'll be frank with you. You've seemed really angry about something for the past week or so and I think it's getting in the way of your work for me. I wonder if we can sort this out."

He said nothing. I sighed and continued, trying my best to be fair to him and focus on the matter at hand. "I'm thinking of Friday, obviously. You showed a lot of temper, you weren't particularly polite to me, and then you stormed out. You seem to be having some friction with Rob, and a lot with Neal, and this needs to stop. I don't care if you don't get on with everyone, but you do need to behave professionally."

Alan didn't say anything and suddenly my anger ebbed, replaced by genuine worry. He was such a mess that I hoped he was getting some kind of counseling.

Finally he spoke up. "I'm just sick of everyone . . . running down my work. Running me down."

Now we were getting somewhere. "Who's everyone?"

"Well, Neal, for one. Neal especially. He's always on my back, and everyone else follows his lead."

"Neal's job is to keep everyone moving along. And even I've had to go over procedure with you, time and again." I paused, hating to ask the question I knew had to be asked.

"Are you sure this is what you really want, Alan? It's not like there's a lot of money to be had for all the rigors of this field, not like medicine or the law. It's a lot of effort to go through for something you're not completely sure of."

"Yeah, of course I'm sure." He shrugged. "No, I don't know. I just wish the whole thing would go away, sometimes."

"Have you ever thought about taking a semester off, a leave of absence? Just to think things over?"

He looked up at me. "You're not going to kick me out, are you?"

As much as I knew he wouldn't like the answer, I owed it to him to be honest. "It really seems as if your heart isn't in it, that's why I ask. Think about it. But the next time I see a display like last week, I'll probably reconsider hiring you. It's not just aptitude but attitude, as well."

"Christ, I can't please anyone, can I?" he muttered. "Can I go?"

I could tell things were nowhere near to being resolved, but I didn't have the stomach for it anymore. "Sure. I'll see you later."

I looked at my watch: only seven-fifty. It was far too early to call Brian in California and I couldn't call Marty yet. I needed to talk to someone who could put this in perspective for me. I called my sister.

We're not all that much alike, for sisters. For one thing, there's a good eight-year age difference between us, not quite a generation, but far apart enough to matter. We didn't get the usual sibling interaction because she always seemed to be sick after she was born, late in our mother's life. It was because of that that I'd started spending so much time with Oscar as a kid; Grandpa tried to make things easier on the Maternal Parent. But by the time I reached high school, I noticed that the runt had a will and personality very much her own, and I promoted her from background noise and annoyance to probationary ally.

That isn't to say there isn't the expected competition between us. I had to work hard to get good grades and people called me an overachiever. Bucky's like Mycroft Holmes, a razor-sharp intellect and constantly accused of not living up to her potential except when she's interested. We'd both trade for body parts; though Brian says he likes a womanly figure, I'm envious of Bucky's boyish hips. She bristles every time I stretch and yawn, showing off the fact that I got the bust in the family.

As different as we are, Bucky and I became friends as adults. I know two things absolutely about my sister, that I can rely on her and that she will always tell me the truth. I think she knows she can expect the same of me. Even if I still haven't forgotten the incident involving my underwear drawer and a can of chocolate sauce the night before my SATs.

As I rang up the veterinary clinic where she practiced, I counted the rings like other people tell a rosary, a little prayer with each brrr-ing tone. She was in early so many mornings that when the answering machine picked up instead, I swore and hung up, trying not to get nuts with premature disappointment. What I needed was Bucky's calm to help me wade through this, I thought. I tried her at home.

The phone rang just once before a muffled voice said, "Vet."

"Bucky, it's Emma."

"Emma who?"

"Don't be funny—"

"I'm not. What the hell time is it?"

"Almost eight."

"Shit. I didn't get to bed until five. There was an emergency surgery, dog hit by a car. I got it, of course." I heard a tremendous yawn cut short. "Why are you up? Is something wrong?"

"Yeah, yeah, there is." I took a deep breath and told her about the fire, and about Pauline's death. It surprised me that I could relate yesterday's events so matter-of-factly.

"They think that it happened sometime late Sunday night

or early Monday morning," I concluded. "She probably slipped and hit her head on the butcher block island in the middle of her kitchen. The sheriff said that it was probably the smoke and not the fire that did it."

"Any idea how it happened?"

"Near as the Fire Marshal's Office can tell so far, it was the gas stove that probably started the fire," I finished.

"That doesn't sound like Pauline," Bucky said after a minute.

"I know. I'm betting it was bad wiring or something. Not an accident on her part."

"Damn it, Em, I'm sorry. What can I do? Do you want me to come up? I can swap some of my appointments around, if you need me for a day or so—" Bucky was the most junior partner at a thriving practice in rural Connecticut; she was still paying her dues in terms of the scut work and very early or very late emergency calls.

"No, don't, you've got too much going on. I just wanted to talk to you." A thought occurred to me. "Wait, there is something."

"Name it."

"Keep Ma out of my hair. She didn't know Pauline well, but she didn't like her anyway, not when I talked about her so much. I've probably got to tell Ma sometime, but I don't want her crowding me now. If she hears about the fire on the news, she'll kill me; if she comes up here, I'll end up strangling her."

"No sweat," came the immediate answer. "Say, what do you think of this? I'll take Ma out for dinner tonight, and I'll mention it in passing, downplay it a lot. That way she'll know, but she'll be so busy complaining about the service and whatall that it won't sink in."

"I hate being so . . . so . . ." I began.

"The word you're looking for is *sneaky*," Bucky suggested. "Also *circuitous, conniving*, and *conspiratorial*. Forget it. Ma's a pill, and we deal with her whatever way we can. Anything else?"

"No, this just sucks, is all."

"I know. You'll get through it though," Bucky said, confident in her prognosis. "And for God's sake, don't just wade
on with things like nothing happened. Give yourself some
time to get over it."

"I am, don't worry."

"How's the dig anyway?"

"Over now. But we got some really amazing stuff." I filled
her in, briefly.

"Cool."

It surprised me how much that one little syllable meant to
me, almost restoring the glitter to my gold. "It really is."

"You sure you don't want me?"

"Yeah, thanks."

"You let me know if there's anything else I can do for
you—I'm serious, now."

"I know. You wouldn't give up a night to Ma otherwise."

I heard a short, humorless laugh. "Well, you owe me."

"Whatever you want." I paused awkwardly. "I love you,
Bucks."

"Yeah, you too. See you, Em." She hung up.

Even though Bucky jokes that neither of us is good with
people—her working with animals and me focusing on people who had been dead for centuries—I realized how much
better talking to her had made me feel.

I fussed around the dorm lab for a few more hours, then
tried to call Brian. He had already left his hotel room, so I left
a message to call me right away. I could have used talking to
him, especially since I was soon the recipient of another visit
from Sheriff Stannard, who knocked discreetly at the door to
my room at about one o'clock.

I wasn't entirely sure how I was supposed to greet him—I
wasn't being pulled over for speeding, I wasn't going to him
with a complaint, and I didn't know what he wanted. Surely
there were rules, manners for such a thing, but I had no clue
what they were.

"Uh, hi." I looked around my room in its usual disastrous shape. "Sorry about the mess."

The sheriff looked around. "Well," he said uncertainly, "you've probably been preoccupied . . . for a while. Is there anywhere we can sit down and talk?"

"Yeah, come on down the hall."

After we were settled in the empty lounge, he came straight to the point. "I've got some bad news. We've got reason to suspect that the fire was not an accident. That fire was burning too hot, too fast, considering all the rain we got."

I couldn't believe he was saying what he was saying. "What? Not an . . . ? No." I shook my head. "Jesus, no."

"The circumstances appear suspicious," the sheriff said reluctantly. "That's why I need to verify everyone's statements, including yours, Dr. Fielding. If we can develop a time frame—"

"But who would . . . why? Does that mean that Pauline was . . . didn't die by accident?" The horrid idea was impossible to imagine. Oh my dear Pauline.

"We don't know if her death was intentional or not, whether the arson was the real goal," he said gently. "We don't know what the perpetrator had in mind, but it looks real suspicious at this point."

The anthropological part of my brain, over which I have no control, noticed he used the words *circumstances, verify,* and *perpetrator* the way someone who has been trained to a particular vocabulary would. In my estimation Dave Stannard would never have chosen them out of uniform. I realized that I was taking refuge in analysis and tried to face what the sheriff was telling me. It came to me out of the blue.

"Tichnor!" I stood up out the chair, as if I could invoke the man by saying his name. "Have you found him yet? Where was he this weekend?"

"We have no idea where he was this weekend." Stannard seemed to be choosing his words very carefully. "Dr. Fielding, weren't his threats directed at you? Did he even know who Pauline Westlake was?" He flipped back through his notes. "She only saw him leave the site, and that was from a distance. What makes you think that he would try to attack her rather than you? And if he was what you called a pothunter—why this?"

I was aware that Stannard wasn't asking me what he appeared to be, but it didn't matter: I knew what I knew.

"But why would *he* need a real reason?" I argued. "The man's a nut, running around waving that damned gun! This is probably just some way of getting back..." I let that thought die of malnourishment, as it contained a fundamental truth that I was not yet ready to face. The same one that had occurred to me this morning wasn't going to leave me alone.

Stannard just waited.

"Don't you think he's the most obvious choice?" I pleaded. "I mean, look at all the stuff that's been happening, and he's had his finger in all of it! First Augie Brooks washes up on the beach—"

"That was an accident, Dr. Fielding."

"—and everyone telling me how useless he was out on the water and then Nick down at the Goat and Grapes says that he sometimes hung around with Grahame Tichnor—"

"A coincidence, Dr. Fielding. I spent time with several criminals last week and it doesn't mean that I was tangled up in their business."

"And then he threatens me, with a *gun*, no less, and shortly thereafter, Pauline, Pauline is dead and her house burned, and now you're saying it wasn't an accident and so why aren't you looking for him? It can't be so hard to find him, my God, you can't let him get away with—"

"We were looking for him," Stannard interrupted my tirade. "Straight off, just like I promised you. And we found him." The sheriff watched me carefully.

"Well? What's he said?" A distant part of me marveled that anger freed me to speak so.

"Nothing. When we went to his house this morning, we

did find him, but he was dead. Under suspicious circumstances," the sheriff answered patiently. "Professor Fielding, I need to ask you, again, where were you last weekend, and particularly the night before last?"

After that everything was a bit of a haze. I remember having given Stannard Brian's hotel number and Kam and Marty's names and addresses, and then he must have gone because suddenly I found myself alone. Like an automaton, I found myself clutching my keys and heading for the parking lot. Unfortunately the Civic was in the shop. I took the college vehicle instead.

I don't remember the drive out to the beach. I assume that I had been instinctively heading for Greycliff, and then veered off down the public road at the last moment, remembering suddenly, horribly, that not even the house was there to comfort me. Another gut-wrenching realization in a series of shocks. I couldn't decide whether I was more desperate for the tight knot in my stomach to ease up and give me a chance to take just one deep breath or to keep the sharp bitterness fresh, as a memorial to Pauline. Either way I lost.

The beach was deserted; the fog that had driven away the tourists had been followed by rain that was too much for even the most dedicated of beach walkers. I pulled up to the front of the parking lot, where the margin between it and the beach itself was gritty with sand that had blown over the low bumpers. The tide was very high today, and the river seemed rebellious, impatient to reclaim the land that bound it and channeled its progress to the ocean. I couldn't see the other shore for the fog, and the black water lent a depth and sinister quality to the river that was not imaginable on fine days. There was no comfort in the fact that the summer heat was momentarily stalled; the clammy cold leached directly into my bones.

I sat idling for a moment, reluctant to switch off the engine and be totally alone with my thoughts, though I finally realized I had come out here for just that purpose. To grapple with "words that would be howl'd out in the desert air, where hearing should not latch them."

I put the truck into park and turned the key; the windshield wipers froze in place, diagonal across the glass. Irritated, I turned the key again briefly, just long enough for the wipers to slide obediently beneath the edge of the hood; I wanted symmetry and order. The rain battered against the roof of the truck, echoing my own sense of hollowness.

I listened for a long while, trying to make sense of the patterns of rain that snaked down the windshield, trying to make sense of everything that the sheriff had told me. Pauline was dead: murdered. Possibly killed by a man who had threatened me, who was now dead himself. What the hell could be real anymore, in the face of these things?

As if in answer, I felt a pain in my side that persisted long after I'd stopped being able to cry. Taking a deep breath, I pulled my wallet out of my slicker pocket. I stared at it for a moment and then began to rifle through it, slowly at first, then more quickly. Brian is always saying that I cram too much into it, but it wasn't all that cluttered at the moment. I picked out the picture of me with him, the one of us goofing around at the beach down by his parents' house, where I'm sunburned and laughing, and he's laughing too, so completely in his element. It felt a million miles away now; worse, since he had yet to call me back.

I pulled out the rest of the stuff, license, an avalanche of library cards and college ID, a couple of weary credit cards, ATM card, and a bunch of crumpled receipts. I smoothed out the crinkled paper slips and set them aside, then shuffled the cards and set them out carefully on the seat, arranged in a rough array around the creased photograph. I was trying to read my future.

Suddenly the idea of running away was very appealing. Being nowhere; better, being anonymous. Part of what I love about traveling was the idea of vanishing from the radar for a while, even if it was just for an hour in the airport, the idea being that if I couldn't be found, then neither could my troubles find me. No one knew who I was, no one could remind me of my responsibilities. It was just a game I played, being incognito in my own life, and it was all I desired now. How much a relief it would be to leave my wallet and all its contents on the front seat of the truck and just vanish. If I walked down the beach and headed into Fordham, and hitched a lift to Portland, I could get a bus ticket for anywhere: With some of the cash I had, I could be lost somewhere in New York state by dinnertime. If I pushed on to Pennsylvania, and then even farther, I would be completely swallowed up, beyond the pale. No one would know me.

It is very easy to be devoured once you decide to stop resisting. Being devoured sounded very good to me.

Funny how little distance it took, physically or mentally, to move beyond the narrow scope of one's little world. We are the centers of our own remarkably private constellations, and it was surprising to find, as one did occasionally, how fragile these consensual arrangements really are.

I looked at the photograph again and smiled briefly, then frowned: It wasn't the thought of Brian that was keeping me here, and not my overdeveloped conscience either. There was something else, something big that I was missing, like a bear hiding behind the drapes.

Suddenly I was thinking of Oscar. And Shakespeare.

Of all the memories I cherished of my grandfather, the one that I took out least often was the one of me sitting in his lap while he read from his ancient Riverside. I was afraid that if I recalled those peaceful summer evenings too frequently, I would wear out the recollection, and it would be lost to me forever. He always said that the point of reading those plays was to teach me about context and interpretation and structure, but I knew better than to believe that, even as a kid. What I couldn't learn from all our hikes or the visits to his sites; what I couldn't learn about interpretation from *the* Oscar Fielding was not going to be found in some moth-eaten, dog-eared volume of antiquated, elitist plays.

It was simpler than that. He loved the sound of the words. He read to me for the pleasure of hearing his own voice and for the pleasure of sharing it with me. The purple prose passages suited him down to the ground, appropriately huge text for someone who had always been larger than life. That deep-timbred roar, the one that was the fear and scourge of his students and colleagues, could be harnessed and fed into a Petruchio of outstanding rudeness, the most villainous Iago ever heard, or such a witty Mercutio that if Juliet had been really smart, she would have dumped that other numb-nuts and run off with him instead. And Grandpa's Falstaff was the best.

I shook my head. Why was this coming to me now? It tortured me that Oscar wasn't here. He was the only one who would have known the precise region of hell in which I was presently lodged. But why this particular memory?

Shakespeare? I thought about that for a minute. I had, of course, been dredging up lines associated with every outrage, every blasphemy, every—go ahead, I thought, say it—every *murder*, since that terrible moment on the site. The images evoked by "the soul's frail dwelling-house" and "cold and empty veins, where no blood dwells" haunted me—the words popping into my head unbidden at inopportune intervals. But that was only natural, these were the only words big enough to express my feelings. My own feeble attempts couldn't begin to accommodate them.

And what else? What are you leaving out that you shouldn't be? What's behind the words? Think about it logically. A little voice in the back of my head became more insistent, pushed and prodded for attention.

Grief, of course. Huge loss. Guilt, I suppose, but . . . my God, I'm so *angry*, I just don't know what to do.

More, the voice urged, *even more than that. What's stronger than that? What is the common thread running through all those lines that keep coming to you?*

Duty? Oh come on, *revenge*? Tichnor's *dead*, for chrissake . . .

Does that mean he gets away with it? And if the sheriff isn't convinced, perhaps neither should you be. And you're the one in the middle here. You're the one who knows things, who holds the key to all of this.

I thought about that as another fusillade of rain beat a tattoo on the roof of the truck. I slowly picked up the keys, then decisively turned her over. I was freezing. As I waited for the ineffectual heater to warm up the cavernous vehicle, I began collecting up the miscellany that defines me in this culture and jammed it all back into the tired wallet without regard for the tidy little plastic folders that are there for other folks to use.

I suppose, having made a decision, I should have been relieved, but I was nothing but mad: Why me? I flicked on the wipers again and backed out of the parking space. But it certainly had been a surprise, me actually going so far as to entertain the idea of letting myself off the hook. I don't know why, it must have been exhaustion that was making me dither. Deep down, I knew that I had to find out the truth; the alternative was unthinkable. I certainly hadn't needed to waste time and gas money to bully myself into the decision to look into Pauline's death for myself.

And being a scientist, I only believe in ghosts for other people.

"So when is the funeral?" Brian asked later that evening. I'd finally been around when he returned my call.

"I don't know. There's got to be an . . . investigation." I couldn't say the word *autopsy*. "When can you get here?"

There was a long pause on the other end. "I'm going to do my damnedest to get there as soon as I can, but I honestly don't know. We're right in the middle of things, but I'm trying for a day or two."

"Can't Kam cover for you?" I was ashamed to admit to myself that I hoped the desperation in my voice would influence him.

"Not at the moment. His schedule's all over the place. He's still in Chicago for a couple days and won't be out here until next week."

"Shit."

"It's not hopeless, and I swear I'm doing everything I can to get away. Has the sheriff come up with anything else yet?"

"Just a lot of questions. I've got an appointment to go down to the station tomorrow to answer some more questions about times and things; I'm also going to try to get some more details from them. What I know so far is that the fire was arson; whether Pauline's death was intentional is still up in the air. Tichnor's dead, but that could be an accident, they don't know yet; it looks like food poisoning. They don't even know if the two are connected, but I do. I'm sure of it. There are too many coincidences." I bounced my fist gently against the wall in frustration. "But every time something else pops up, it only seems to confuse the matter."

"I know, Emma. I know." Brian paused, and I knew he was trying to find the right words. I tried not to be impatient with him even though I knew whatever he was thinking was probably for my own good. "But look, do me a favor?" he began. "I know your instinct is to try to wrap up all the loose ends at once, but I really want you to try and just deal with what you know for sure right now. You've got plenty to cope with, without adding more to your plate. Just get through packing up the dig and dealing with the fact that Pauline's gone. The other stuff will still be there once you've had a chance to . . . get that sorted out."

I hated that he was right; it went against every inclination I had. "I'm just going to tell them again everything I knew of Pauline's plans and when I last saw her and stuff. I don't know any more."

"All right." He didn't sound convinced.

"What is it?"

Again there was that sense that Brian was choosing his

words carefully. "Emma, I hate to ask this, but has anyone said anything to you about your being a suspect? That you might have—"

I was stunned. "Brian, how could you say such a thing? Why . . . how could you even think . . . ?"

"It's not what I think," he said quickly, "God, no, never. But I'm just worried that your relationship with her might prejudice them against you and I want you to make sure that you get a lawyer if anything like that comes up today. Give Mark Regan a call; if he can't help you, he'll know who can."

I couldn't say anything for a moment and the silence stayed between us like an icy chasm. "That's just so cold-blooded that I can't even think straight."

"That's why I bring it up," he said. "This looks like it might be murder and I just want you to be careful, that's all. I know you can't imagine that anyone might think you did it, but that doesn't mean they can't come up with some stupid reason. Do you see what I mean?"

"Yes, and it sucks."

"I know. I love you, that's why I told you. I want you to look out for yourself, until I can get there."

"So, what, you're going to take care of me then?" Brian didn't deserve bitchiness, but I couldn't help it.

"Yes."

He said it so plainly that I couldn't make any argument. That way was easy and it let me be angry, which was so much easier than grieving. But I knew what he meant anyway, and it was no indictment of my capabilities. I decided to be as adult as Brian.

"Okay. You get yourself up here as quick as you can. Yesterday."

"I promise. I love you so much."

"I love you too. Come home. I need you."

* * *

I got more of the answers I wanted Wednesday morning, but not nearly enough to satisfy me. And worse yet, it seemed, not quite enough to satisfy anyone else.

"Do you recognize any of these things, Professor Fielding?" Sheriff Dave Stannard laid out a small collection of objects on his blotter for me, a moment after I was seated at his desk.

"Well, it depends on what you mean," I said. "I can probably tell you what most of them are."

I was becoming very familiar with the inside of Stannard's office. I was also becoming accustomed to the sheriff and his questions, but I just went along with them, letting the misery of the past couple of days be compartmentalized into an orderly set of details, trying to figure out just what angles he was working from. "I think you want to know something else."

"You are right about that, but humor me for a minute," he said. "I want to make sure that I've got them listed properly for the evidence inventory. Then I'll ask you what I really want to know."

Oh, real subtle, I thought sourly. I looked at the objects and then at the sheriff, puzzled. The little bags held artifacts, nice ones, as far as I could tell. They were collecting quality and not what I was used to finding in the ground. He nodded for me to go ahead.

"Well, that's a porcelain tea bowl. Is it okay to touch?" I was surprised and a little disappointed that the evidence bags looked like nothing so much as the artifact bags we used. I had hoped for something a little more glamorous, I suppose, more high tech or esoteric.

Stannard nodded, and I picked up the plastic evidence bag with a thin porcelain cup and had a close look at it. "It's Chinese and I'm not real good with the exact dates without my books, but based on that interior rim decoration, I guess it's early eighteenth century. It's pretty. It also looks expensive, I mean, it's not chipped or cracked and the gold leaf is in good shape. Good enough to be in a museum."

I put it back, and after he nodded again, I picked up the next bagged object, long and thin with some moving parts. A glint of bright metal caught my eye. "This is valuable," I said right away. "A silver and red coral baby pacifier. The smooth coral bit was to suck on, to relieve teething pain, maybe, and they had little silver bells and a whistle to amuse an older child. It's probably English or European, and again, it might be eighteenth or nineteenth century."

Then it hit me that I actually recognized this piece. "This is Pauline's!" I quickly looked at the rest of the objects. "These all belonged to Pauline! That's what you wanted to know, wasn't it?" I studied his face; it was grim.

"We were pretty sure of that when we found them but we needed an identification." The sheriff avoided my searching glance. "Just keep going through the things, though, make sure they are all hers."

What's going on here? I wondered. Then it struck me. "Wait. These things weren't in the house! They're not burned!"

Stannard nodded again. "What about the other objects?"

"I wouldn't recognize all her stuff, you know," I said. "Pauline collected thousands of things, objects from all different periods and everywhere on earth. I can only give you my best guess on some of them."

"That's all I'm asking."

I went through the remaining objects quickly. A pair of gold-bound tiger claw earrings from India, a small jade statuette of a fish, a small Egyptian scarab pendant, an ornate Venetian dagger. Before the memories of these objects and the sorrow of remembering the stories that Pauline had told me about them could overwhelm me, I picked up the last object. And gasped.

It was a brownish clay figurine. It was roughly the shape of a woman, with pendulous breasts and a huge belly. It had no arms, and only a suggestion of legs made by an incised line extending from beneath the belly down a narrowing cone of clay. The face was a blank surface and the hair was represented by a collection of whorls and what looked like dreadlocks. Depending on your point of view, it was either dull and rude, or beautiful in a very elemental way.

I had never seen this before—where the hell did Pauline get it? My God, what if it's real! "Can I take it out of the bag?" I asked eagerly.

The sheriff nodded. "You look surprised by that," he said noncommittally. "I've got no clue what it is or what it's doing with that other stuff. It's kinda ugly. You care to fill me in?"

"I'm not even sure if it's genuine, but if it is, it's pretty near priceless. At least in terms of research," I said breathlessly. I set it down reverentially, then had to pick it up again, just to touch the precious thing. "I don't even know how you'd go about setting a price on this."

"What is it?"

"What I *think* it is, is a late Paleolithic figurine, sometimes called a "Venus" figurine. Some people consider these to represent the first organized form of religion." I was lost in marveling over the small object.

"Late Paleolithic?"

"Um, Old Stone Age. This is probably at least twenty-five thousand years old, probably European. Possibly North African." Though it could be from Western Asia, too, I thought—I really didn't know much about this sort of artifact. I had no idea that Pauline was interested in such things; it had to be from an old private collection, for I knew she was too scrupulous to have touched anything that was to be found on the illicit antiquities market.

Stannard still looked confused. He ran a hand through his hair, leaving it messy, something I could see was a habit with him when he was in thought or confused. I could see he had no frame of reference for that scale of time.

"If you think of the Egyptians as having built the pyramids five thousand years ago," I explained, "then this shows up twenty thousand years before that. The first anatomically modern humans only appeared about fifty thousand years ago. That gives you some idea of its importance."

The sheriff let out a long whistle. "Pretty darned old. I would have thought a kid made it. It's not real impressive-looking."

"Well, you're right about that," I said, turning it over and thinking that I should really be wearing gloves to handle it. It seemed stable enough, though, and clay wasn't nearly as susceptible to body oils as glass or metal or paper. "It's got all these exaggerated features, and it's small and looks dirty, but on the other hand, it's got a lot of subtle style to it. Look at the detail in the hair. The proportions of the body are well balanced, even with the huge breasts and belly. It's very well executed, and it's been fired too. A lot of thought went into the making of this."

"I can see that, now that you're showing me. You look at your evidence the same way we look at ours," he said. "But how many people would recognize a thing like that?"

"Oh, any number, I suppose," I said distractedly; I wished Stannard would be quiet for a minute. I couldn't imagine the next time I'd be allowed to examine such a wonderful thing. "Anyone who's taken an art history course, or a course in prehistory or maybe anthropology. Possibly some collectors, but it's a pretty rare sort of item. They do come up on auction blocks, but that's not something I really follow."

I failed to attribute any significance to the silence coming from the other side of the desk.

"That's a real small percentage of the population, you know," Stannard said finally.

"Not in the circles I travel in," I said, grinning slightly. The sensation was odd: Eventually I would have to get used to smiling again.

Suddenly I got the point the sheriff was making, and my grin vanished as quickly as it came. I put the figurine down, very carefully. "Where did you find this? Why is it in with all these other things? Why aren't they burned?"

Stannard got up and began to pace. "I was kind of hoping you could tell me something about that. We found all of these other things stashed under the bed in Grahame Tichnor's house."

"I knew it! I told you, of course he did it!" But vindication meant nothing now; I clenched my teeth to resist imagining how Pauline died.

He nodded and continued his measured progress back and forth across the floor. "It certainly suggests to some of us that he was the one who killed Pauline Westlake. But—"

"But what?"

"Most of these things here make sense, if you are a regular crook without too much imagination or smarts." He walked over to the desk to look at the objects again. "Valuable-looking stuff, with gold or silver or precious stones on them. That clay figurine is a different thing altogether. Not too many people around here would recognize its value. Even that teacup is a stretch—who'd know that an old blue and white cup was valuable?"

"Tichnor might have," I pointed out. "He was a pothunter."

Stannard frowned. "Those aren't pots, are they? Least-wise, not the sort of thing that crops up around here. What if he was the one who's been digging up the park at Fort Archer? I mean, there are all those rumors about pirate treasure or buried gold around here, right? I always figured that's what whoever was doing it was after. But none of this stuff is the sort of thing you'd find there, is it?"

"No, of course not. But you said all this was found in his house, right?"

"Yes. That's not to say that he put it there."

"Why wouldn't he have put it there, then, if you found it in his house?" I was thoroughly confused now.

"Someone who wanted it to look like Tichnor had killed Pauline Westlake and set the fire. It's pretty convenient he's dead all of a sudden, wouldn't you say?" The sheriff sat on the corner of his desk and crossed his arms over his chest. "You seem to be pretty eager to blame him yourself."

My jaw dropped, and I struggled to make sense of what he was saying. "Well, yeah, but he was crazy, he threatened me, he had a gun—"

"But Mrs. Westlake wasn't shot, was she?" Stannard said reasonably. "I just think there's a little more going on here than appears on the surface."

Before I could digest that the phone rang, startling us both. The sheriff got up, a little angrily, I thought, and snatched the receiver. "Yes?"

At the same time the door to his office opened and the gnomic medical examiner stumped into the office. "Ooooh, weee! Boyo, when you bring 'em on, you bring 'em good! If I'da known it would do this much good, I woulda set up complaining long ago."

"Thanks for trying, she's already here," Stannard said shortly and hung up the phone. "Ever heard of knocking, Dr. Moretti? How about procedure?" His voice was mild but I couldn't miss the rebuke. Dr. Moretti apparently couldn't have cared less.

"I gotta hand it to you, this is a pip! No interesting work since old lady Ballard fell cold off her chair at work last year, then, bang! First Augie and two now suspicious, little ducks all lined up in a row! What a hoot! Next you'll be handing me the brides in the bath!"

I watched the sheriff take a deep breath. "Best behavior, Terry, we've got company." He nodded in my direction, and she quieted down. Dr. Moretti regarded me suspiciously after she recognized me.

"Oh, yeah, you," she rasped. "You're the one out at the Point, the archaeology lady."

I tried to erase my dislike of her. I'd spent a huge part of my professional life trying to develop a sympathy and respect for the dead, a respect that she clearly didn't share. Considering her profession, her cavalier attitude exasperated me. But she obviously had information I needed. "No one's told me how Grahame Tichnor died," I said.

The woman seemed delighted to have an audience outside her regulars. "Near as I can tell—" She broke off hurriedly and looked at the sheriff, who shrugged.

"I'll start," he said. "This is what we've got: It looks like the victim had just finished clearing up from dinner—all the dishes were washed and in the rack, and there was some fresh garbage in the pail—carrots, potatoes, some small bones, and a beer bottle in with them." He added wryly, "Not only was the deceased given to violent behavior, but he didn't recycle either.

"The deceased was found lying on the floor, and he had convulsed, kicking a chair over." The sheriff hesitated, considering his evidence before he revealed his hypothesis. "I'm beginning to think it was the potatoes."

"What, did he choke?" I asked.

He turned to me. "No, that much I'm sure of. Some of the skins were a little green. Most people don't know that green potatoes, or their eyes, can be every bit as deadly as drinking Drano. They're in the same family as deadly nightshade." He glanced at the medical examiner for confirmation.

"Well, it was poisoning," Dr. Moretti began, "but where the hell are you coming up with deadly potatoes? Belladonna's a whole 'nother kettle of fish! This is convalla-toxin."

"How can you be sure?" asked Stannard. His immediate challenge told me that pathology wasn't any more cut and dried than archaeology.

"I couldn't at first." The medical examiner settled in to her story, now that she had us hooked. "First thing I noticed was his heart looked dicey to me. This stif—deceased had vomited, so I figured, no problem, he was an old coot, maybe it was his ticker. I looked at the crime scene report, and for once they'd checked out the wastebasket and the medicine cabinet—you need to ride those little wieners every minute! But! No heart medicine in the cabinet and based on the trash and the dish rack, it looked like homemade soup for dinner. Next I have a squint at the kidneys: no digitoxin or digoxin, which was what this was looking like to me. Okay, then we

have a wee peeksy in the gut, and we find the remains of din-
dins."

Dr. Moretti eyed us sternly. "Always chew your food, children. It makes my job more difficult, but it saves wear and
tear on your innards. In this case, Mr. Tichnor did not chew
the required forty times per mouthful, nor did he seem to
chew any better for lunch, which was a little further down
the intestinal tract—"

"Dr. Moretti, cut to the chase."

"Calm your liver, Sheriff, I'm getting to it. Well, I'm taking
a tour through dinner and there wasn't a lot. Bingo, I figure
something didn't agree with him, so I have a closer look at
what was going down and I found carrots, potatoes, a little
beef, some celery, whatever. Matches what was in the garbage
can. Also some chopped-up herbs, but the only one I could
clearly recognize was some curly parsley. There's some other
greenage but I'm about to give up when I say to myself, remember, in spite of those washed dishes, there wasn't really
enough for a whole dinner, he didn't make it all the way
through the meal, something's wrong, keep looking. But
how the hell am I going to identify chopped, chewed greens?
Not on cell structure, that's for sure, and the uncooperative
son of a bitch hadn't conveniently ingested any roots or seeds
or whole leaves to make my job easier—"

"Dr. Moretti—" The sheriff was trying hard to keep his
patience and was losing. I just kept my mouth shut and
watched the exchange with all the fascination of one watching a train wreck.

She waved him off dismissively. "But then I poke around
one last time, before I take a sample to send back to Augusta,
and I find this." She produced a small vial filled with clear
liquid. There was something small, round, and orange-
brown suspended in it.

"What is it?" Stannard squinted at the mangled object in
the vial. I peered over his shoulder.

"A berry. From lily of the valley, *Convallaria majalis*. Toxic
as hell, acts a bit like digitoxin, and is occasionally confused

by the unlucky and the stupid for wild garlic." The medical examiner was positively preening now. "I looked it up. Ingesting it will knock your socks off; even the water from the cut flowers ain't too good for you. A few finely shredded leaves wouldn't look suspicious and would do the job nicely. I think that it confirms that our dead chum was murdered."

"I thought you said it could be confused with wild garlic," the sheriff said.

"I did, but not by this guy. For starters, I don't think anyone would mistake the flowering *Convallaria* for a wild garlic, even past bloom; it's just too commonly recognized. For another, from what I've seen of this guy's sheet, he was a survivalist nut and probably wouldn't have made the mistake in any case; they're usually up on living off the land. Also, it's a little too neat that the dishes were all washed up and put away, right? Even if he wasn't hungry, it seems awful convenient that his convulsions did not preclude doing the dishes. I think that someone poisoned him and was trying to clean up any extraneous evidence."

"Any idea of the time of death?" the sheriff wanted to know. I just sat there speechless, torn between my admiration for the way in which these clues were pursued and revulsion at Dr. Moretti's obvious enjoyment of her work.

"Well, as it so happens, this time, yes," the ME said. "Glycosides like the one found in *Convallaria* act pretty quick, depending on the dose, and the physical condition of the victim, etcetera, etcetera. So based on the blood chemicals, rigor, lack of significant infestation, sanguinary drainage"— she caressed the words, made them sound like blank verse— "I guess that this one deceased late Sunday evening, early Monday morning."

I watched Stannard mull this over; my own mind raced to see how this might be tied in with Pauline's death. "Do you have any idea when Pauline died?" I cleared my throat. "Before you said it was the smoke that did it."

After another silent exchange between the sheriff and the medical examiner, Stannard answered.

"This is what we've got so far. Pauline Westlake got home late on Friday afternoon, stopping by the garage because the car was making a knocking noise; I checked it out with Mike at the Texaco, he gave her a lift home, say about four-thirty or so. It was raining still—that didn't let up until late Sunday."

He tapped his pen against his teeth. "I'm no expert, but like I said, it doesn't seem like a faulty wire would be hot enough or fast enough to get that blaze going; I'm still waiting for a final report from the state Fire Marshal's Office. The Point's volunteer firefighters got the call about the fire from a neighbor early Monday morning."

I finally dared to engage Dr. Moretti one on one. "I didn't think it could be an accident on Pauline's part." I took another deep breath. "What was the real cause of her death?"

This time the medical examiner seemed to notice me as a person. It was her turn to cross her arms over her narrow chest, and she looked me up and down. I held my breath the whole time. An idea must have caught her in mid-chew for she scraped her gum off the roof of her mouth slowly, stretching it over her pointy little tongue contemplatively before she sucked it back in and snapped it loudly. She exchanged a look with the sheriff, who shrugged then nodded.

"When I examined the deceased, I found that there was a fractured skull. The break was very recent and, contrary to our supposition based on the location of the deceased in the kitchen, it wasn't made by anything sharp like a corner of a table. I haven't really pinpointed the exact time of death, but I'm going out on a limb and saying that she died close to the time the fire was set. Call it a hunch." The gum was being worked quickly now, in synch with her reasoning process. "It wasn't the butcher block, but it is possible she mighta slipped and hit her head on the tub, got up, and then wandered into the kitchen, and then fallen. Ayuh, head wounds, concussions, are tricky things, you know. Makes it hard to tell."

"Well, was it the tub?" I was starting to get impatient with the old ghoul's games myself.

"No." Dr. Moretti looked me over appraisingly. "The skull was crushed by something with a broader surface than that," she said slowly. "It was a blow to the frontal lobe with an instrument of broad facies. Something wide, maybe with an edge."

"The side of an ax head," the sheriff offered. I got the impression that he was used to this game of twenty questions. I thought of Dr. Moretti leaving a trail of clues like bread crumbs, and that brought to mind Hansel and Gretel and their short-term landlady. More witches to compare with Dr. Theresa Moretti.

"Look, please tell me what you know," I begged. "Pauline was my friend, I have to know."

The medical examiner considered. "I wouldn't be so sure of that, lady."

"Why the hell not?"

"Terry—" Stannard was trying to step in now, but it was too late. The genie was out of the bottle.

"My best guess, and my guesses are pretty damned good, for your information, is that her head was crushed with a shovel. Boys in blue over here claim they found signs of a struggle outside and that wound had to be made up close." She snapped her gum loudly again. "Maybe by someone she knew well enough to approach. And there were an awful lot of people running around the Point with shovels lately, weren't there?"

For a moment I couldn't believe what she was suggesting. "You can't be serious! You don't know what you are talking about, my crew would never—and neither would I! There's not one of them I wouldn't vouch for!"

"Oh, yeah, the momma fox swearing her babies wouldn't go *near* the henhouse," she answered sarcastically. "And just who are you to be vouching for anyone?" She flipped through her report and then stared at me, gum temporarily silenced. "Wasn't the first thing out of your mouth, 'Oh my God, Pauline'? Right off? How could you have known it was her?"

I looked at Stannard, who said nothing. My mouth opened and shut several times of its own accord. "I just . . . I just knew. It was just a feeling. I wish to hell I'd been wrong."

The sheriff cleared his throat. "Dr. Moretti, I think it's time for you to leave. This isn't really your part of the investigation."

"And all I'm saying is that I'm always reading how these archaeologists always got their noses into weird things, old things." She turned from me to the sheriff. "It's unnatural what they do, digging up old garbage, poking around other people's business."

I could only gape, but Stannard just shrugged. "Not so different from what you and I do, Terry," he said carefully, "and let's not forget the small matter of evidence, all right?"

The medical examiner backed reluctantly toward the door. "I'm telling you, they're all loopy, probably repressed as hell, hunched over their bits of things." She didn't even notice me in the room anymore; I had been downgraded from sparring partner to hypothesis.

"Out."

"I'm going, I'm going." She reached for the door handle. "Jeez, try to do someone a favor . . ." She took her gum out and threw it at the sheriff's wastebasket. It bounced off the edge and onto the floor, and she made no move to recover it.

"Good-bye, Doctor."

I watched as she scuttled, crablike, from the room, jamming that cigarette she had stashed behind her ear into her mouth before the door shut behind her. The sheriff went over and closed the door after her, then with a piece of paper, picked up the gum and deposited it in the trash.

"*She's* the one who examined Pauline?" I couldn't help asking.

The sheriff smothered a sigh. "Dr. Moretti is more than competent in the lab. I wouldn't have her if she wasn't. But . . . you could say her people skills aren't all we'd like."

Someone knocked at the door, and the gawky deputy I'd seen before stuck his head through.

"Sheriff Stannard—?"

"Yeah, Den?"

"Time."

Stannard looked at his watch, and his shoulders drooped slightly. "I've got another appointment I'm already late for. Can we get together tomorrow, say, after the memorial service?"

I was stunned. "Memorial service?"

"You didn't know? Tomorrow, ten A.M., at St. Jude's."

"This is the first I've heard anything about it. Who—?"

"The sister, Claudette Peirce. She's made all the arrangements. Everyone else in town seems to know." He frowned. "I'm surprised she didn't tell you." He looked at his watch again. "I've really got to run."

"Fine, I'll see you tomorrow." I nodded vigorously, and for a moment wondered if I could stop nodding. "After the service."

I walked out, bowed over by the onslaught of unwelcome information. Several things were clear to me. Even if the sheriff wasn't coming right out and saying it, he didn't actually believe I'd had anything to do with it. Just as clear was the fact that, for whatever reason, others weren't so convinced. I also couldn't believe that I'd found out about Pauline's memorial service by chance—everyone in town knew about our relationship. I shook my head, trying to clear it. Once Brian got here, he'd help me make sense of all that was happening.

Chapter 11

BRIAN DIDN'T MAKE IT.

He called me from Pittsburgh early Thursday morning, frantic with worry, because against all his good efforts to extricate himself from work, he'd been foiled at the last moment by mechanical failure and the inconveniences of airline schedules. He said that he'd be in late that night and apologized profusely. There was no help for it, but it was just the bad start to an awful day.

Reverend Dyson made a point of introducing himself to me before the service. Even though we'd never met, he couldn't have missed me, not with the graduate students crowded around me in the parking lot, and not with the way that almost everyone else clustered in a large group on the other side of the lot. And although he politely made no reference to my many visits to Sheriff Stannard's office, it was clear that his consideration was specifically because so many others were convinced that I was in some way connected with Pauline's death. News traveled quickly, rumor even quicker than that, in a community the size of Penitence Point, and even though I knew what I knew about human

behavior from years of study, I still wasn't quite prepared
that so many acquaintances were willing to equate smoke
with fire.

The reverend was a stout man with a cherubic face and
kind eyes that even his present sober countenance couldn't
altogether extinguish. I suspected his wife spent most of her
time chasing him around, trying to tame his tufts of wavy
salt and pepper hair into respectable repose.

"I'm glad that you came, I knew what good friends the
two of you were. I know that Miss Westlake didn't like fuss of
any kind, but I couldn't let the occasion of her passing go entirely unnoticed, especially with the circumstances surrounding her death." He coughed delicately. "Better to have a
little closure now, and have a quiet burial once the matter is
settled."

I noticed that he didn't seem worried about closure in
Tichnor's case. No one seemed to miss him at all.

The weather had clouded over again and was almost un-
bearably humid. The skies threatened to open up at any moment. Following the students, I slipped into the end of one
of the pews about halfway down the aisle, for once thankful
for pantyhose: I always hated when the backs of my legs
pulled on the edge of the waxed bench during summer services.

I found myself falling heedlessly into the rituals of the
service, and I was surprised to find that it calmed me. I don't
believe and haven't spent any regular time in any church
since I stopped going precisely twelve years ago, but the
rhythms of checking the hymns and pulling out the kneeler,
the hushed voices and the creak of the pews were comforting
to a startling degree. Although I had been taught that rituals
are a solace, I didn't realize that that rule applied to me too,
and I was grateful for it.

I risked a quick glance at the altar and was pleased to see
there were no carnations, a flower I loathe and will always as-
sociate with orchestrated emotion—instant nostalgia for St.
Patrick's Day or the school colors for enforced loyalty at a

pep rally. But someone in the ladies' guild, with good taste or good luck, had chosen wildflowers, something I liked and of which Pauline would have approved for simplicity. In the vestibule were tributes from others, including one rather splendid bouquet from Tony Markham. Apparently he'd heard from Rick Crabtree, who'd heard from Alan, but aside from a note from my friend Jenny Alvarez, there was nothing else from the department.

A few people that I knew from Fordham and Penitence Point stopped by to exchange condolences with me. Nick the bartender from the Goat and Grapes pressed my hand briefly, looking supremely uncomfortable in an ill-fitting sports jacket and tie. "Stop by later, and we'll wake the old girl in style." I nodded thanks.

A slight commotion erupted at the back of the church, and the heads in every pew swiveled around as one. Claudette Peirce had entered and paused, looking around.

I was momentarily stunned by her similarity to her sister. It was almost enough to crack my heart. She was fleshier than Pauline had ever been, and her hair was more gray than white, but she carried herself with the same relentlessly straight back, and I recognized that determined line to her jaw.

She leaned over to someone in the back row, who whispered in her ear. Claudette's eyes caught mine and she strode over to me, her lips compressed with restrained emotion. I extended my hand in that ambiguous way that suggests I was open to either a handshake, a clasping of arms, or a full hug, but didn't even get a chance to stammer out my name before I got the next rude shock of the morning.

"I'm surprised you have the nerve to show yourself here." Her voice was low but powerful and her words carried easily throughout the church. None of the congregation even tried to conceal their amazement or their relish for the scene. "Pauline lived a foolish life, but I never thought her eccentricities would get her killed in her own home! It makes no difference, though. Once that fraudulent will is exposed, the police will find out how you did it, and you'll get what you deserve."

The force of her words was a blow. Amazed, I could just barely grasp the fact that she was calling me a murderer.

Reverend Dyson quickly ushered Claudette down to the front of the church, throwing me a pitying glance over his shoulder. All around us, heads whipped back and forth, like they were watching a fast hockey game and anticipating blood.

As the service began, I felt Dian squeeze my cold hand, but I just shook my head absently and sat down, still digesting what had just happened. "No, no, it's okay. Really. It was bound to happen. I'm fine."

Well, that's what everybody's been thinking, isn't it? I thought. Now I knew why Pauline didn't much like her sister. And what the hell did she mean about a fraudulent will? She of all people should have known about Pauline's money going to her charities. It had absolutely nothing to do with me.

I sat numbly through the opening of the service, the frail comfort of ritual shredded and no longer effective; I hardly registered the glowing eulogy that Dyson had memorized. Then something in the glow of the stained-glass windows reminded me of that damned mask. I suppose it was just the events of the previous week, followed by Claudette's verbal assault, but the mind is a funny thing in any case. I hadn't thought of the bloody thing for years.

It was my first introduction to Pauline. After Oscar made the introductions, I sat quietly, and for a while it was interesting listening to them talk. But I guess I seemed like I was on the verge of a fidget because he told me to look around the curiosities in the house while he and Pauline visited. He knew better than to tell me not to touch anything.

I was relieved to escape Pauline's sharp eyes, which so casually evaluated me, and I was dying to get a closer look at the things that filled the house, so I didn't need to be told

twice. I wandered from room to room in awe. I won't say
that the place was like a museum, though most of the objects
in Pauline's house were certainly of that quality. There was
just too much soul and emotional effect in the way in which
everything was arranged.

Perhaps there was a little too much effect for an eight-
year-old with an overactive imagination. Snow had fallen all
that morning, deadening sound around the house, and by
afternoon the shadows were long and sharp. I remember
wandering into one room to sneak a touch of the green robe,
embroidered with white cranes, that was hanging on the
wall. On another wall was a case filled with frail pieces of
porcelain that glowed with a pale blue sheen in the dying
winter light.

I immediately loved the coolness of the room, the quiet-
ness of the objects, and the sense of remoteness and the unknown that they inspired in me. Here were things that had
nothing to do with my life, objects that did not look like
those that were in every house on my block. They beguiled
me into wondering about their makers and their purposes.
Alien yet recognizable, I could see what some of them were
made for, yet I knew that there was a step that I was missing,
a layer of meaning that remained hidden from me. This en-
thralled and frustrated me, and I stood relishing the
mystery—a word I would capitalize later in embarrassing,
impassioned teenaged diaries—that surrounded me. Why
was it that that sensation seemed dangerous? I spent quite
some time lost in the vastness of all these worlds beyond my
narrow experience.

Then I saw the face on the wall.

Of course it was only a mask, just as the robe was only a
festival kimono and the eerie porcelain only an eclectic collection of second-tier teawares, representing Pauline's earliest, tentative attempt at connoisseurship. I know now that
the mask was a decent example of Nō art, and I've even read
the play for which it was made. And although memory of the
mask magically shrank and dulled over the past twenty-two

years, I firmly believe that intellectual understanding can't totally erase emotional impact. I remember precisely how that thing terrified me.

Much of its horror stemmed from the fact that, at first, it seemed welcoming, warm and red. When I got up closer, I could see the fading darker details, the scowl lines painted around sightless eyes and open mouth. The light raked across the mask, emphasizing the empty socket on one side, the other half left in darkness. It was like being tricked into running into the devil's embrace.

I stood frozen, fascinated, knowing at one remote level that it was just wood and paint, while the rest of me knew, absolutely, that if I moved another inch, the thing would consume me. You might, if you are lucky, be able to remember that childish sort of silent impasse, where you believe you are facing the means of your own destruction. Movement will only hasten the end, stillness only invites the demon to enjoy itself and linger over the process.

I don't remember how long I stood there, rooted by fear. I can remember the confusion of the moment when I decided I must run or perish. Adrenaline practically lifted me off my feet and the nearly impossible act of stepping backward—who would turn her back on such a thing?—seemed to trigger a wail from somewhere. I didn't care if it came out of me, I only knew I had to get out of there. I turned finally, only to slam into something rough and prickly. I sat down hard and opened my mouth for a true scream, and closed it just as suddenly, surprised to see that it was Pauline's wool skirt with which I had collided.

"Emma, what's wrong?" She leaned over and flicked on the light to get a better look at me. The dull yellow light from the lamp overhead banished the dramatic shadows and reduced the magical objects to mere curiosities. I felt a profound sense of relief and a little cheated. I was just trying to figure out how honest I could be with this grown-up, how she might react to my fears, and simultaneously concoct a convincing story to use if necessary, when my calculations were abruptly interrupted by more caterwauling. At least I knew it probably hadn't been me howling, and I again felt relief, this time that I hadn't embarrassed Grandpa.

"Hector! Get out of there, you wretched creature! Stop that racket before I roast you!" Pauline let go of me, went over to the cold fireplace, and reached behind the firescreen. When she straightened, a lithe form dangled, struggling, from her hand, hind legs inelegantly splayed out straight. Hector was a very irritated Siamese squirming to escape her grip, sapphire eyes ablaze as he continued to cry. This time, however, he sounded more like an animal than the vocalization of my fears, the echoes of his yowls no longer reverberating up the chimney. His owner dumped him unceremoniously on the carpet, where he promptly lifted his hind leg for a quick cleaning and, dignity being at least nominally restored, sauntered casually out of the room. Only his flicking tail betrayed his annoyance.

Pauline turned back to me. "I'm afraid he's put out with us for interrupting his music. Hector was announcing to the world that he is the pinnacle of evolution and a force to be reckoned with." She smiled at that thought. "A typical male. Are you all right?"

I smiled back. She said some other things that I didn't understand, but I was pleased that she wasn't making a fuss over my panic, or laughing that I had been scared by a stupid cat.

"I was looking at the dress on the wall. It's very pretty," I said.

While she listened to me, I could feel her scanning the room, observing my trajectory and deciding for herself what had happened. The dress was on the wall closest to the door, in the path of my flight, directly opposite the mask. She kindly ignored my edited version of the matter.

"It is pretty, but it's called 'kirumono.' It's from Japan, I brought it back with most of these other things on one of my first trips away from home. How about this, what do you think it is?" Pauline held up a neat stack of interlocking black boxes with painted decorations. I shook my head. "It's used to carry food, like a lunch box."

I shook my head again. "It doesn't look like my red plaid lunch box. Where's the handle? How does it stay shut?"

"Good questions. It's tied up with a piece of cloth. That keeps it shut and the knot is big enough so that you carry it. Sometimes you might have rice and pickled vegetables, or—"

Suddenly I was swept up with Pauline's descriptions of the objects that filled the room and the people who made and used them. The sound of her voice was comforting but not lulling, bringing a sense of what the collection meant to her and of the culture from which it had come. When we finally made the circuit of the room and ended back at the mask, I wasn't even disturbed when she put it up to her face, showing me how the actor would have fastened it behind his head, and telling me that the mask represented a benign peasant spirit. It didn't seem any more appealing to me than before, but the immediate terror was stripped away. That had been the start of everything, really. Despite all of Oscar's efforts, that was the first time I had been seduced by culture.

But of course, now the mask had been incinerated with everything else. That started the tears flowing, and I quietly began to mourn my friend in earnest.

The service done, Claudette strode down the aisle and into her waiting car without a glance at another soul. The rest of the congregation followed, front to back, and I found I was subjected to a lot more averted eyes than before as I waited for our turn to file out.

Neal wanted to know if I wanted to go for a drive with them, but it was clear what was on all of their minds.

"No, I'm fine," I said. "You guys were great in there, thanks for coming. I'll see you back at the dorm, in a bit, okay? Got a date with the law."

"Emma, don't," Dian protested. "It's not funny."

"Don't worry about me, I'm okay, really." I tried on a

smile, but it disappeared when Sheriff Stannard caught my eye. I turned back to them all. "Really. Scat."

I watched as they filed out and then steeled myself to face the sheriff, who had been waiting patiently at the back of the now empty church.

He came straight to the point.

"That meeting I had yesterday. It was with Claudette Peirce. She told me that the contents of her sister's will indicate that you had a clear motive for Ms. Westlake's murder," the sheriff said in his unadorned fashion.

"Bullshit!" The word escaped me, ringing out through the church before I thought about editing my response for emotion or location. "Pauline's sister doesn't even know me! How can she possibly imagine that I'd done this? There is no reason in the world that could make me want to hurt Pauline!" I finally moderated my voice out of habit, not lack of indignation.

"According to Mrs. Peirce, you stood to inherit quite a bit," Stannard said. "Money is a tremendous motive."

"No way," I denied absolutely. "I know for a fact that Pauline was leaving her whole estate to her causes and museums and things! And anyway, if I were going to inherit something, if I even *knew* I was in her will, why would I burn her house? Wouldn't that be a stupid thing to do?"

The sheriff looked uncomfortable, as though he might be parroting someone else's words. "Not if you were interested in the cash value of everything—"

"Cash value! The things in that house were priceless, and I don't mean what they cost!"

"—and not the objects themselves," he continued doggedly. "There was a lot of insurance on that place, and remember, the murderer would have needed to cover up his tracks in the first place. Did you know most murders are committed by relatives or close friends?"

I opened my mouth to protest, but Stannard cut me off. "Listen to me. I was informed by Mrs. Peirce that Ms. Westlake was leaving all of her estate to different organizations, but one of them does have something to do with you. She left $500,000 to the Anthropology Department at Caldwell College to endow a chair in archaeology."

He rifled through his little notebook, looking for the precise wording. I slumped against the doorway, stunned.

"More specifically, for a chair in New World archaeology, to bear her name, and to be offered to you as the first recipient. If it wasn't offered to you first, the cash would revert to the rest of the estate with only $10,000 going to the college general fund in her name. So you see, a lot of people might think that that was more than enough motive, for a lot less of a crime. I've been getting phone calls from high up, no doubt courtesy of Mrs. Peirce's concern about her sister's death. I'm finding out she's an influential person."

I stared outside for what seemed to be a long time; the threatened rain had arrived, in torrents, but didn't make things any cooler. No wonder Claudette made such a scene, if she knew that was in the will, I thought. Funny, I never even suspected Pauline would do such a thing. She must really think I—

My thoughts were interrupted by Stannard speaking again. "You okay, Dr. Fielding? I hate to dump this on you all of a sudden, but I thought that, well, it would be better to hear it straight from the horse's mouth. Once this sort of news goes beyond two people, everyone in town knows. And I've got to run; this isn't the only thing keeping me busy these days."

I looked at him warily. "You said a lot of people. What about you?"

The way Stannard sighed told me I'd gotten to the heart of the situation. "Even with this I still don't buy you as a suspect. But I can't believe that Mrs. Peirce is going to leave this alone, and she's bringing a lot of pressure for me . . . to explore every avenue thoroughly. Even with this will, a lot of things aren't adding up for me right now, and I need to find out what I'm missing. You're going to help me sort this out. You are the key to this, one way or another."

I recalled the little voice that chided me with these same words a billion years ago. Tuesday.

"I'll see you straight off, nine tomorrow, then." He put his hat on outside the church, touched the brim, and I watched as he walked over to the rectory.

Chapter 12

I REMAINED IN THE DOORWAY OF ST. JUDE'S, DIGESTING this news, until the noise of the ladies' guild cleaning the flowers off the altar spurred me out to the parking lot. I sat there in the truck for a minute, fighting down my delayed reaction to Stannard's new information. Oh Pauline, what have you done? This was meant as a fantastic gift, but . . . I gripped the steering wheel tightly and rested my head against it, barely noticing the new ache that was creeping through my scalp. I struggled with thoughts that threatened to choke me and blind me.

I waited until the wave of nausea had receded and my vision cleared somewhat, and then I began to back the truck out of the parking space behind the church. The rain that had finally burst out of the sky was gone as suddenly as it had arrived, but made visibility a thing of the past. That's what I get for breathing, I thought wryly. On top of everything else, the antiquated defogging system in the truck hadn't made much of a difference with the fogged windows. A blur caught my eye, and I slammed on the brakes just in time to avoid being sideswiped by a black car that had come tearing around the corner.

Pauline's death and the surrealness of the service, along with a row of sleepless nights, caused me to react more out of anger than the fear that would ordinarily accompany such a close call. I flung open the door and boiled out of the truck, not even caring if the other driver had been hurt in the near-miss: I hoped the idiot got a good scare for his stupidity. I stormed over to the other car, one of those muscle jobs, completely unmindful of the fact that I was ruining my only good pair of summer shoes. I slammed my fist on the trunk of the other car, enjoying the fact that it stung like the devil, and made my way to the driver's side. The windows were steamed up from the humidity and I could barely make out a form inside.

"Hey, what are you, crazy? You could've killed me, you maniac! You couldn't wait ten seconds for the light to change, you had to go bombing through here? Jesus Christ—"

That was when I saw who the driver was, as he opened the door of the car with a loud screeching protest of rusty hinges.

It was the guy I'd seen driving past the site.

As I'd described to Nick, Billy Griggs was about my age, about my height, and skinny, but with a beer gut just managing to creep out over the top of his faded jeans and from beneath his T-shirt. His blond hair was dirty, and it curled around his ears, which seemed stuck to his big, square head almost as an afterthought. I could tell even with the torn Budweiser gimme cap that his hair was sparser than the last time we had met; that chance meeting had been unpleasant too. He had grown a mustache since then, but it was thin and sickly-looking, hovering uncertainly over his thick lips. Billy'd never been an attractive specimen, and age hadn't improved a damned thing.

"Are *you* mouthing off to *me*?" Disbelief, as well as beer, perfumed his language. "You fucking nearly took the side off my Cam, you stupid bitch!" He didn't appear to recognize me, but hey, it had been twelve years or more. I certainly hoped that I had changed somewhat since then.

Under other circumstances, I would have done almost anything to avoid him. But all that meant nothing now. I was so thankful for the confrontation, I could have screamed "hallelujah." It was like the sum of every Christmas and birthday that ever was to have such a deserving target for all my pent-up rage, frustration, humiliation—my fury tasted so sweet that I invited it in to stay. I found myself *aching* for the chance to knock the teeth out of this son of a bitch.

I turned to him, and for once, I said just what was on my mind, rather than fuming about lost anger and missed chances hours later.

"You miserable piece of shit! I'm surprised they haven't put you away yet, you psycho, because the better part of you was left on the mattress your mother used for work!" My blood was singing and I felt *good* for the first time in a long while. This was the sort of berserker rage that the Viking warriors prayed for.

Dim awareness that he had been insulted competed with clouded semirecognition of me. I knew Billy didn't require any provocation, but it was like the band compressing my skull was finally being loosened.

"Oh, fuck this." I could see the idiot bunching up his fist, telegraphing his next move like Western Union. I tensed, ready with a little surprise of my own, when we were both distracted by someone calling out my name.

"Emma! What's going on here? Is there a problem?" A dark, slender man sidled alongside of me, coolly appraising my opponent.

"Jesus! Kam, get out of here! I can handle this!" But my surprise at seeing him was so great that all the bloodlust drained away, and was being rapidly replaced by dread. "Kam, don't, I—"

"Back off, nigger!" Billy spat. "You got about three seconds to get out of here."

Kam looked put out. "How bloody typical. Emma, you *can* pick them." He turned to face Billy and continued, enunciating, in his fluid Oxonian tones. "I am not a nigger. However, if you insist on employing such scurrilous epithets, you might at least do me the courtesy of a little specific accuracy. For example, in my particular case, the appropriate words might be *wog*, or *Paki bastard*, or perhaps even *rag-head*, although you will notice I am not sporting the headgear that some of my countrymen sport, and *really*, even that expression is generally reserved for my dusky brethren farther to the west. In any case, it is sheer ignorance to use such a term, never mind confusing your racial slurs—"

Only momentarily transfixed and confused by this unexpected lecture, Billy suddenly turned from me and launched a well-practiced fist at Kam's head. He missed completely, only to receive Kam's tremendous blow to the solar plexus. The force of it knocked Billy backward onto the driver's seat, smacking his head against the roof of the car. He slumped forward and sprayed beery vomit all over the gravel in front of him.

Kam hopped nimbly backward and avoided being splashed by the filth. I was not so quick, and the spatter effectively ended the useful life of my poor shoes. I stared a shocked moment at the shoes before I ripped them off and stuffed them into a green metal trash can spray-painted "St. Jude."

"Anyone coming?" I demanded curtly.

"Not that I can see." Kam politely ignored the fact that I hadn't said a proper hello.

I reached up under my suit's skirt and pulled off my pantyhose, wadded them up, and tuck them with the shoes on the top of the trash. Kam stood watching me silently; I glared back at him. I was in the process of splashing some of the sick off my foot in one of the tepid puddles when that gangly Deputy Sheehan meandered around the corner.

He paused to survey the parked car, noticed the mess on the gravel, and blanched—Deputy Denny Sheehan looked like he was a sympathetic puker. "Miss Fielding, what happened here? Oh man, that's Billy again! You"—he gestured at Kam—"will you give me a hand with this?" He pulled the moaning Billy all the way out of the driver's seat, set him, not too gently, on the sidewalk: Billy wasn't going anywhere anytime soon. Denny put the car in neutral, then, with Kam's help, he pushed the Camaro off to the side of the lot. By the time he came back I was prepared for the questions I knew he had for me.

"Could you tell me what happened, Miss Fielding? As if I didn't already have a pretty good idea."

I took a deep breath. "Griggs came bombing through the parking lot and almost rammed into the back of me. I got out to give him a piece of my mind, when he threatened me, and then attacked my friend here. Dr. Shah reacted in self-defense."

Just saying it aloud drastically oversimplified the morass of emotions that had consumed me. But even simply repeating this abbreviated version, I managed to scare the hell out of myself pretty thoroughly. What had I gotten myself into? I started to tremble. It didn't occur to me until just then that I stood a much better chance of being badly hurt than of doing any real damage.

Deputy Sheehan scratched his arm and nodded. "This isn't anything new for Billy here, but you acted pretty silly, getting out of the car like that." He turned to Kam. "You want to press charges?"

Kam shook his head.

"We'll get someone to tow the car and let Billy sleep it off. We can charge him with DUI, not that it matters any, because his license is already suspended, but maybe he'll spend a little time in the tank. Not much we can do with him; he seems to spend more time with us than at home, though maybe that's a blessing for his wife." Deputy Sheehan scribbled down a few of the details we gave him, and radioed into the sheriff's department for a tow truck. He turned back to me, and I imagined that I was now looking every bit as worn out as I felt, now that the excitement was over. My bedraggled dress felt like it weighed about a hundred pounds in the humidity.

"Miss Fielding, I came back here to see if I could catch you. The sheriff needs to change your meeting to nine-thirty, okay? Schedule conflict." The young deputy shifted his weight from one foot to the other for a moment, considering his next words. "Miss Westlake was a nice lady. I know that you were close to her, and since you've only been answering questions for us, you shouldn't mind that old cat in there. I'm sorry for your loss." He nodded at Kam, a gesture he had clearly acquired from his boss, and left us alone.

Steam rose off the puddles in the gravel. My feet now hurt me like the dickens from standing in one place on the gravel for so long, and I sat on the fender of the truck. Kam leaned over to me.

"You care to tell me what was going on there? I don't think I've ever heard you talk like that before."

"I always try to use small words and easy clichés when I'm insulting the intellectually challenged," I explained. "If I'd had a minute to think, I might have been able to work his dog and his car into it too."

"Emma—" Kam started.

"I didn't need you to come barging in like that!" I snapped. One might have said I sounded ungrateful. "I was on top of things, okay? I didn't need you to flounce in and save me!"

"No, you weren't on top of things, you were picking a fight with an inebriated redneck who was intent on pounding you into jelly," Kam said. "I've no doubt that you can handle yourself, but there are easier ways to commit suicide than by courting trouble like that."

Those words had been flinty, the next were coaxing, softened with concern. "C'mon, it's me. Tell me what's wrong."

That simple command broke the seal on Pandora's box.

My breath caught once, and all of a sudden the tears that before had come only sporadically came surging out. I caught the lapel of his jacket, and my howls were muffled by his arm around me. I couldn't stop weeping, and for a long time he rocked me, making absurd, reassuring shushing noises.

It was a while before I quieted and sat up. I snuffled again, loudly, but finally. "I hope the dry cleaner can get snot out of your Armani."

"Never mind the jokes, girl. We've got to get you someplace where you can clean up and then we are going to talk." He looked pained. "Besides, it's not an Armani. It's Hardy Amies, and you'd better never confuse the two in front of *him*. Give me the keys." I started to protest but caught the look on his face and thought better of it. "We'll come back for the Jag later. Now, which way out?"

Chapter 13

I TOOK MY TIME CHANGING INTO DRY SHORTS AND A sweatshirt after the silent trip back to the dorm. The air had cooled off after the rain, making everything uncomfortably clammy, and I knew that I would have to come across with some answers for Kam. In a further attempt to gather my wits, I dawdled over making two cups of tea. I knew he wouldn't wait for me to go through the whole ritual to create the coffee I craved so badly . . .

"Why are you here?" I asked finally. "Isn't this a little beyond the reaches of civilization for you? I mean, you can't even get *cornetti e cappuccino* up here."

When I saw that flippancy wasn't going to get a smile out of Kam, I said simply, "I thought you were still in Chicago."

"I finished up and left for home early," Kam said, removing the tea bag from his mug. He took a sip from his tea and wrinkled his nose at the stale flavor. "Brian caught me when he got stuck in Pittsburgh. He was going off his head when he finally caught up with me, and so to keep him from having an aneurysm, I told him I'd come up and see how you were doing. I'm glad I did too."

"And what's that supposed to mean?" I demanded.

"It means that, obviously, you've had a series of dreadful shocks and we thought someone should be here for you," he said. "Now, no more fooling around. Tell me what I walked in on back there."

I gave him a marvelously succinct description of the week's events, including the scene with Claudette Peirce at the church and the news about Pauline's endowment.

Kam said nothing for a moment, sipped his tea meditatively, more out of polite habit than desire, I suppose. It wasn't very good tea. "That was a pretty remarkable thing for Pauline to have done," he said reflectively. "No more struggling. You'll be able to do whatever you want."

It worked precisely as he expected: I exploded. "You're missing the point entirely! You just don't get—"

Then I figured out what he was up to and shut up in a hurry. But it was already too late.

"What don't I get, Em?" The infuriating man looked all innocence as he pulled out his cigarette case. It was silver, an antique, no doubt, but one I had never seen him use before. It suddenly occurred to me that things might be heating up between him and Marty.

The words came very slowly, reluctantly, but only because I knew he wouldn't let me off the hook now. I stared, fascinated, at the etched detail on the cigarette case, seeing it and not seeing it, wishing I was anywhere but here.

"It will only make it harder," I said slowly, "for me. To establish myself on my own terms."

"Go on."

I heard the snap of Kam's lighter, smelled the smoke of the Dunhill he lit; there was no way I could meet his gaze now. It took me a minute to summon up the courage I needed to reveal my thoughts.

"I mean, first it was Oscar, right? He called the chair at Coolidge University to help me get into graduate school. I wanted to go so badly, I didn't even think about what that might mean later on. Then the Caldwell job came up, and of course, it just happens to be near where Oscar did most of his really important work. Then the fact that Pauline had this amazing site on her property and let me excavate it. You see now?"

"I'm afraid I don't, quite." Kam exhaled and was veiled in cigarette smoke.

I frowned at him frustratedly; he was being obtuse on purpose. "All my professional life I've had everything handed to me on a silver platter!" I shouted. "Everything I've ever done has been because someone else has done or given me something! Just when I thought I was going to be able to do something, get tenure, get *my* program established at Caldwell on my own, all that, Pauline steps in again and paves the way. I mean, she even gave me the site, but I found the fort, at least that much was my work. And now this—"

"That rotten cow," he offered with mock sympathy.

"Kam, I'm serious!" I slammed my mug down on the table. "How will I ever know that I was able to make it on my own!"

"Oh for Christ's sake, Emma! Don't be such a horse's arse!" Kam was usually as impeccable with his language as he was with his clothing. "What, were you hoping to live in a vacuum, so you could prove yourself?"

"That's just my point—" I started.

"Shut up a minute," Kam commanded. "Now, listen to me. Was Oscar the sort to tolerate flummery? Carry a dead weight?"

This was idiotic. I didn't answer.

"Was he?"

Truculently. "No."

"No, of course not," Kam said, unmollified by my acquiescence. "He had a reputation for being an exacting son of a bitch, did he not? I seem to remember Brian being rather intimidated the first time he met your grandfather, and we both know what it takes to daunt Happy Boy, right? So Oscar must have thought you had something to offer, or he wouldn't have bothered. Don't you intercede on behalf of talented students?"

"That's different—"

"Oh come now, Emma!" He took another long drag on the cigarette, as if fueling his argument. "If it were really just a favor to your grandfather, the department at Coolidge needn't have given you all that funding all those years, need they? If you were the drooling imbecile you seem to imagine you are, they could have just let you pay your tuition and flunk out, yes?

"And what about Pauline?" he continued. "Did she suffer fools, gladly or otherwise? We both know the answer to that, don't we? And while we're on the subject, what about your husband and friends? We're not ninnies, so why would we waste our time loitering with someone who was?"

Suddenly Kam calmed down, and while his words were no less forceful, at least he was smiling to take some of the sting out. "Look, you. You've got your share of faults: You can be pigheaded, selfish, and didactic. I'm not denying that. You make revolting puns. You are an amazing slob, and I can't imagine what kind of survival skills I'd need to deal with you before eleven in the morning," he added.

"Hey, have a heart!" I protested.

But Kam grew serious again. "But you are also a brilliant, beautiful, kind woman, with a drive that scares the dickens out of most everyone you meet. That and your generosity and your curiosity will make you into the kind of person you are so afraid of not being. It is for those reasons that you have people rushing to do you favors. So forget proving yourself to the world, the world is convinced. Here endeth the sermon." He leaned back and calmly swallowed some more of his tea.

I wasn't pleased with most of his lecture, but the kindly ending made me feel even worse. Tears started oozing out of the corners of my eyes again, and I brushed at them impatiently. The hard wood of the bench was starting to wear my butt flat and I was getting tired, but I wasn't done.

"There's something else," I said.

"Tell me."

I finally said out loud the thought that I had been too loath even to think. "It's Pauline. I can't help feeling responsible . . . I'm convinced it was Tichnor who killed her, and he wouldn't have ever bothered her if I hadn't been there first." I took a deep breath. "It's my fault Pauline's dead. All of this stuff, everything, has happened since I got here. Bodies, site robbers, Billy, arson . . . murder . . ." I lifted my hands helplessly.

"Don't be such a git." Kam sighed and stubbed out the tortured cigarette. "From all that you've told me, Pauline should have called the sheriff, not tackled this guy on her own. Most people would consider it extraordinarily foolish to approach a violent trespasser, with a criminal record yet, unarmed and alone."

I flushed angrily and stood up, ready to leave before I had to listen to any more of *that*.

Kam pulled me back down onto the bench. "Calm down," he said exasperatedly, as he dug out another cigarette. "I'm not blaming her at all. I'm only pointing out that there are a lot of ways of looking at this. She could have stayed in Boston, she could have stayed inside the house. Tichnor could have run when he saw her, he could have stayed in bed that day. And yes, you could have dug someplace else this year.

"But blaming yourself is an exercise in self-glorification. There are too many random occurrences that make up the circumstances in any one day for you to take the blame for this particular chain of events. Chances are, he would have been wandering around looking for artifacts or whatall even if the dig weren't on her property, right?"

I shrugged and looked away impatiently.

"I know what she was to you," Kam said, grabbing my hand to emphasize his point. "Emma, I *know*. And I am damned sorry. But what would she think about *anyone*, anyone at all, trying to take responsibility for how she lived her life?"

That made me smile.

"Right," he said. "And if anything, she is probably haranguing the devil himself to make sure that rotten little sneak thief gets an extra portion of whatever they're doling in hell. So you're straight out of the running. Don't give it another thought."

I mulled it over for a minute. His reasoning was logical, maybe even convincing, but it wasn't entirely comforting. "Okay, you win," I said tiredly. "Where'd you get your degree in psychology, anyway?" I wasn't ready to thank him just yet.

"Oh, you know, Himalayan lamas and all. Same place I learned to sustain a woman in a continuous state of orgasmic pleasure for hours on end. The usual." He leered pleasantly over the cigarette as he lit up again.

"Oh yeah. Marty told me all about that."

Kam choked on the inhale and began coughing violently.

"Just kidding," I added.

"Hmmm. Well, I know for a fact that you've driven Brian to distraction on more than one occasion with this nagging self-doubt of yours." Kam had recovered himself for the moment and continued in a jocular tone. "Frankly, I've always recommended a good sound beating, but he seemed to think that he could reason with you. Maybe hearing it from someone who doesn't have his obvious biases will help. Otherwise I've got the leg irons and the riding crop in the car," he said, and stretched indolently. "Nope, no more of this soft, lovey-dovey Western nonsense for you, m'dear. As Brian's best man, it is my duty to help him through these little ups and downs." Kam sounded smug and secure in his evaluation of the subject.

I smirked. I'm sure you think you're a real terror, you big muffin, I thought, but Marty'd knock you sideways if she ever heard you talk like that.

Aloud I said, "So what else has Brian told you that he shouldn't have? You two are the worst gossips."

"Well, he never told me about that fellow down by the

church," Kam said lightly. "Emma, you were scaring me. Who was he?"

I swore inwardly. I had hoped that because I left out any reference to Billy, Kam would have forgotten about him. Looking back on the situation, I marveled at how far out of hand I had let myself get. The problem was that I understood completely why I had welcomed that confrontation. I chose my words carefully, now convinced that Billy's drives past the site had more to do with his erstwhile friend Augie's death than anything about me.

"Billy and I had a . . . run-in . . . ages ago," I said. "He's mean, he's stupid, and he's vindictive, and since then he's believed—still believes, I guess, if he actually remembers me too—that I wronged him. He's probably certifiable. After the week I've had, when he nearly bashed into me, something just . . . snapped. The fact that it was him, that he is such a maggot, just made the prospect of . . . lashing out . . . so much more tempting." I shrugged, downplaying the affair as much as I dared. "What can I say? I lost it. Sorry I snarled at you. Like I said, it's been a rough week."

"I see," he said, nodding. "And once again, someone stepped in and did what you thought you should have been able to do yourself. But my God, Em, he must have had fifty pounds on you, and who knows what kind of previous experience! Unless you've had a secret life scrapping in biker bars, you could have been killed! What were you going to do, debate him, barehanded, into submission?"

"Well, not entirely barehanded." I went back into my room and brought out the light summer suit jacket I'd worn that morning, drawing forth my "surprise" to show him. It was an antique hat pin I'd been wearing as a stickpin, eight inches of its shaft and razor-sharp point concealed in the lapel of my jacket. I twirled it around so that the deep blue stones, in the shape of a fleur-de-lis, shone in the dull light.

Funny I should have this today, I thought. I wore it for Pauline.

I continued out loud. "Don't forget he was drunk out of his mind too, and I was really wound up. Besides, this is a non-issue. You showed up, my knight in shining armor, and whether I got to bash him, and despite my sarcasm, I am glad to see you." I kissed him quickly on the cheek, and squeezed his arm.

Kam received that tribute, as all else in life, with equanimity.

"Besides," I said, "what made you think *you* could take Billy, aside from your insufferable male ego?"

"Besides the fact that I did? You forget, woman, that I learned—"

"Yes, yes, I know, from Himalayan lamas . . ." I laughed, anticipating another line of charming bullshit.

He leaned back and stretched luxuriously. "No, impudent one. At Oxford, I earned my blue pummeling weak-chinned youths from Cambridge. C'mon, put on some real clothes, and I'll take you to dinner before Brian gets in."

Chapter 14

"OKAY, HERE'S THE DEAL—" SHERIFF STANNARD BE-gan Friday morning.

Once again I was sitting in his office, rubbing my head wearily. Brian had come into Boston late Thursday night and after we discussed it, we agreed that he should come up to help me move back to our place for the three weeks or so before school began and I had to move back to my apartment on campus. The students had already packed up everything and left.

"You with me, Dr. Fielding?" He interrupted my distracted thoughts.

I nodded.

Stannard leaned back in his swivel chair and stared at the ceiling. "I've got a real problem. On one hand, there's a bunch of circumstantial evidence pointing to you in Pauline Westlake's death: the will, your proximity to that death and that of Grahame Tichnor, and the fact that you have access to a couple of unusual sources of information about poisons—"

My jaw dropped. "I beg your pardon?"

The sheriff nodded. "It didn't help your case any when I found out what your husband does for a living—"

"But Brian works for a pharmaceutical company—" I stopped.

He looked at me grimly and nodded. "There's very little difference between what you might call a medicine and what you might call a poison. The other is that one of your students presented you with a thesis last year on Native American plant use."

I opened my mouth and then closed it again, trying to think. "Alan's thesis was really more a caloric study than a focus on medicinal plants, though. Everyone on the faculty read it."

"Well, when we had our little talk, he seemed to know quite a bit about the local plant life and what it was used for. I don't think he's a bad sort," he added, "but something's troubling him, for sure."

I threw my hands up in the air.

"The other thing working against you is that you had a grudge against Grahame Tichnor. Even if you didn't have anything to do with the Westlake death, you had plenty of reasons to murder him, maybe even revenge, if you really believed that he had killed Ms. Westlake. And there's also the possibility that you killed her and then killed him and planted evidence to make it appear as though he had done it. If Dr. Moretti's right and Tichnor died about the same time as the fire was set, you and your students would really be the only ones who would recognize the meaning of that brown clay statuette. I mean, who else would have collected that batch of things? No ordinary house thief did this, that's clear."

"Okay, that's it. I want a lawyer," I announced, jumping up. "I'm way out of my depth here—" I remembered Brian's warning and realized that I was in hotter water than I ever imagined possible.

Stannard shook his head. "Sit down. You don't need a

lawyer. I said that was one hand, and I've got to consider it. There's a lot that works for you, even in the face of all this circumstantial evidence. For one, you couldn't have known about the changed will. I called Boston. The lawyer told me that the codicil was dreamed up right then, that day, spur of the moment, they cooked it up to reflect your common interest with Ms. Westlake."

I shook my head sadly.

"And according to the phone company, there were no phone calls from Boston to the dorm you've all been staying in. So you wouldn't have known that she was leaving early or that she had included you in her will, and frankly I can't see her just calling you up and saying, 'Hey, look what I just did for you.' "

I had to nod in agreement.

"Some people might have done that, but she was one of the old sort, everything all done quietly, discreetly. She might have had you in for tea in a couple of years, and told you then, or wrote you a letter or something. So that motive doesn't work for me."

I had to admit he was good at this. Paying attention to things like that.

The sheriff continued, pacing the length of his office. "I can't believe, even if you had known, that you would have been stupid enough to do it while in the middle of your project, *with* a shovel. That would have been lunacy, and that is out of your character—"

How about me killing Pauline being out of character? I thought bitterly.

"I've confirmed that you were at home until late Sunday night, and then the students vouch for you until morning. And besides, Miss Westlake was old; why not just wait?"

"I'm up for tenure in three years," I said, committing care to the wind. "What if I didn't get it before she died?"

Stannard was adamant. "Nope, I'm not convinced. I've been doing some calling around, asking about this work you've been doing. I checked with a couple of folks who are

experts in this stuff—" He ruffled through a thick file folder
and found the names. "There's a Dr. Fairchild down at the
Smithsonian in Washington, D.C., and a Professor Wilson in
North Carolina—"

"You talked with Laurel and Rob?" I asked, astonished.
The man was prying into every corner of my life and I was
feeling more than a little exposed, despite my innocence.

He nodded. "Both confirmed the significance of this project. Both said that someone like you, with your qualifications
and skills, would have no problem getting tenure with a discovery of this magnitude. Both also were vehement in
protesting your innocence."

He carefully closed his file and made a wry little face.
"Robert Wilson was quite polite about it. Dr. Fairchild . . .
was not. She's got quite a mouth on her."

I smiled in spite of myself, imagining what she might have
said. Good for you, Laurel, I thought.

Stannard continued. "So I'm not accusing you of anything. I can't prove that you did it. Motive is what tells us
where to look. And if I don't believe you did it, then I have to
examine what other motives are there that might explain
why this happened. All I know is that for whatever reason,
you are connected with both of these deaths, both of these
people. What I need to do is find out if *they* are connected.
Right now, you are my only link in that direction. You are going to be the one who leads me to the answers in all of this."

I shivered, remembering my own thoughts on the beach.

The sheriff stared at me for a few heartbeats, and then, as
if resolving something, pushed his seat back resolutely.
"Okay, come on."

"Where are we going?" I asked.

"I want you to see something. It won't take long." Stannard got up and quickly left the office. I had to scramble to
catch up with him.

"Why take me?"

He stopped in the hallway and studied me closely. "I like

the way you look at things. Like that figurine. You see things other people wouldn't think of."

We went out to the parking lot, where he unlocked the new Cherokee I remembered he drove out to the site. The interior smelled of Armor All and coffee, with no sign at all that the pine tree–shaped air freshener was contributing anything to the olfactory melange. A plastic travel mug sat in a holder on the dash, and seeing it immediately made me wish for my midmorning cup; I sensed a caffeine-deprivation headache lurking in the wings, waiting to make its debut.

Stannard took a sip and replaced the cup. We had been in his office for at least an hour. Although I remembered the collection of mugs on my desks at work and home, half filled with coffee-derived biology experiments, I reckoned that if he wasn't even going to offer to share, I didn't need to take any moral high ground. "Isn't that a little old to be drinking?" I asked crabbily, wishing I'd thought to stop at Dunkin Donuts on my way in.

"Naw, just got it this morning." He smiled broadly and made a point of taking another big slug. "Now it's iced coffee. Like some music?"

Before I could reply, he shoved a CD into the player. Soft, electronic music overlaid with an eerie, drifting voice echoed through the Jeep's speakers as the truck's large tires dug into bumpy track.

"What is this?" The music grated on me, another high note lingering and morphing into further undulating passages. I picked up the jewel case, trying to divert myself from the morning's events.

"Enya," he answered. "I think it's very relaxing. My kids like it too, they say it reminds them of fairy stories. What do you think?"

Another cycle of repetitive piano notes droned on. "It's very nice," I said, with as much enthusiasm as I could muster.

Dave Stannard laughed out loud. "You are one rotten liar!"

I relaxed a bit. It was true, and for once it might be a point in my favor.

Sheriff Stannard drove with an efficient carelessness that came from familiarity; quickly and with purpose. "I said before I believe that there's more going on here, and the more I think about it, the more I'm convinced of it. We just don't know who or why."

Finally coming around to my way of thinking, I thought.

"You are the key to this, even if neither of us knows how just yet." He peered closely at me. "You *don't* happen to know, do you?"

"No, but I'm damned if I don't find out." The choice of words made me shudder. I knew what I had to do.

The sheriff stopped rather abruptly at an intersection and turned to me. "Now, hang on. Let's talk about that for a minute. This is not an invitation for you to run around and conduct your own investigation. In fact, the first I hear that you're bothering people, we're going to have a little chat, maybe with consequences."

I shrugged. "So what kind of invitation is it?"

"All I'm saying is that you knew Pauline Westlake better than any of us," he said finally. "Someone seems to have gone to a lot of trouble to make you look like the guilty party. There's a connection, and by occasionally running things past you, to see how they might fit in, I hope to find out what's going on here."

I nodded quickly. "Put together a sort of contextual framework, to hang the facts on."

He nodded, reluctantly. "Remember what I said about taking the bit in your own teeth."

We drove in silence. I realized after another ten minutes that we were heading to the site. My heart pounded—it was the first time I had been back to Greycliff since the fire, and I prayed I would be able to control my emotions.

"We're here," Stannard announced. "I'm assuming that

you'll need to do something, to finish up your dig. Let's have a look and I'll let you know what I want you to leave be." We got out and walked down the driveway to the site.

The light on the site struck me as odd, and it took me a minute to figure out that there was a large empty space in the place where most of the house had been. Certainly there was still a hulking shell of charred rubble that would remain until the probate was worked out, but it was disconcerting to have that extra sunlight where there had been solid wooden walls for longer than my lifetime. I felt a tightening in my throat, but it occurred to me that I would have felt worse if the house had stood intact without Pauline, its genius loci. I couldn't have borne it if Greycliff had faded into anonymity with another family in it and me never to darken its doorway again.

The sheriff's voice dragged me back to the business at hand. "We've already been over the lawn, and looked in the pits that you dug, and it's fine if you want to continue to fill them in, or collect your tarps or what have you."

"We haven't done any backfilling yet," I said absently. "We'll probably do some drawings of the walls of the units and then backfill them before the winter," I said, glancing around at the site. I could barely remember when we had been out here last. "Will it be a problem if we came out over a couple of weekends, to wrap up? The weather hasn't turned yet, and even with classes starting soon, I'll be able to get some willing bodies out here. But . . ." I paused worriedly. "What's going to become of the site? Will I still be able to work on it until it's sold, or whatever?"

Stannard nodded. "I think so. And I think that you won't have any problem with coming back. The land has been given to the state. I don't know what the logistics of it are, but my guess is that it will be protected as a historic site. Another part of the codicil."

I nodded, marveling again at Pauline's forethought. It was positively spooky.

By this time we had reached the southernmost of the still-opened units, those with the earliest material that had been found so far. I stopped short and lifted back the blue sheet, not realizing that I was pulling back a shroud.

"What the hell is this?" I sputtered, gesturing at the excavated area. I whipped back the tarp from Meg's trench.

Where had once been uniformly excavated trenches with razor-sharp walls was an unholy mess. The excavations had been rudely expanded from the original works, and the backfill thrown into the already open pits, destroying the critical stratigraphic information in the surrounding area.

Someone had torn up the site. Somebody had been looking for something.

"Did your people do this? Please, tell me you didn't do this—" I didn't wait for an answer. "Do you have any idea how much work was lost here? The whole reason for working so slowly, so bloody carefully, is that we need to record where everything was found! There was a point to all this, you know!" I was practically stomping my feet, but the sheriff just stood there, appraising the wreckage.

I swore acidly. "I mean, why bother putting the tarp back over it? If you're going to turn my project, the most important site north of Jamestown, into the freaking mosh pit at *Woodstock*, why bother trying to keep the *rain* out? This is the most sensitive, the most critical, the most important area on the whole site! Why not just get a small tactical nuke and clean it off down to the rock ledge! This . . . this . . . this . . . oh hell!"

It was too much. I was too outraged to form another complete thought. I stomped off downslope to get away from the disaster area, began peeling up the plastic in other areas to check for damage.

"We didn't do it." Stannard called, watching me interestedly. "It was like this when we got here."

It took a moment for his words to sink in. "What?" I said impatiently. "Christ, just look at this mess! At least it's not much further than the top couple . . . What did you say?" I halted my inspection of the site.

"I said, we thought you did it," he said matter-of-factly. "Had started backfilling before the fire. We didn't touch it."

"Oh God. Then who—?" Then it struck me. "Oh Pauline," I whispered. I sat down, hard, on the trampled, bleached grass. The sheriff squatted next to me, straining to pick up my words.

"It *was* Tichnor," I said. "He came out to the site with his damned metal detector and started digging, looking for buried treasure. Maybe he was even trying to look for artifacts we might have missed, and I'll bet he made extra sure he destroyed our work in the meantime. He saw no car in the drive. It was raining, and we weren't around, so he didn't have to worry about being seen. But then Pauline came home and surprised him, and—"

My voice caught and Dave Stannard continued for me. "And when she confronted him, he killed her. Then he recovered the pits to cover his tracks and burned the house down to try and make the murder look like an accident." He nodded. "It makes sense to me. He probably just couldn't resist grabbing those things—artifacts—after he got her into the house. I suppose he might even have recognized the value of that statuette . . ." he said slowly. Things seemed to fall into place.

We walked back up to the Jeep, and he pulled another plastic evidence bag out of the glove compartment. "This one of your tools?" Inside was a rusty gardening trowel with a peeling green-painted handle.

I shook my head numbly. "No. We only use mason's trowels, the ones with flat, diamond-shaped blades. You can't keep a good, flat surface with something rounded like that. You find it around here?"

"Yeah, in that vandalized trench," Stannard said. "It was partly covered by dirt. We weren't able to lift any clear prints off of it. Do you think it was Ms. Westlake's?"

Again I shook my head. "She would never let any of her gardening things get out of repair like that. She was meticulous about putting everything away, taking care of them. Besides, she used a lot of fancy, expensive tools she ordered from England."

I stared at the trowel in his hand, torn between abhorrence and curiosity: It was a mute witness to Pauline's encounter with Tichnor. Then the sheriff hit me with something totally unexpected.

"So why don't you tell me about your little to-do with Billy Griggs?"

I did a double-take. Why was he bringing that up now? "There's nothing to tell," I stalled. "Deputy Sheehan took down everything . . ."

"No, you know what I mean," the sheriff said confidently, and I knew immediately he wasn't talking about yesterday's scene in the parking lot. "I saw his priors on his sheet when we booked him. Why don't you tell me what happened back when you were seventeen?"

Chapter 15

"**W**ELL," I SAID, STALLING, "IF YOU SAW HIS SHEET, then you also saw my statement."

"Humor me this once more, why don't you?" Stannard suggested.

Why do you care about this? I wondered. I took a deep breath and began.

"The last day of my summer vacation Oscar, my grandfather, dropped me off up in the woods on Cape Mary. I was going to finish checking out a parcel of land that we had been walking over, and he was going to meet me by the road at lunchtime; he had some business to wrap up before we left the next day.

"Conditions weren't too bad, it had rained the night before, so I was fairly sure that I would be able to see any sites that had been eroded out of the surface. The weather was clearing up, so the mosquitoes weren't dreadful in the open areas, but they were going crazy, whining in the wooded-over patches; between them and the late morning crickets, you could hardly hear the birds. I was concentrating pretty

hard too, so I suppose that's why I didn't pick up on the crying and shouting coming from a clearing until I was almost
in the middle of it."

I paused, almost feeling myself back there again. Stannard gestured for me to go on. Easy for him, I thought. I
continued.

"It was two kids, not much older than me, I, arguing.
There were beer bottles all over the place. I later found out
his name was Billy and his girlfriend was Amy. She was the
one who was crying, and he smacked her a couple of times in
the head, sort of offhanded. Without thinking too much
about what I was doing, I yelled to them, to see if I could
help."

Dave Stannard winced.

"My life up to that point had been pretty sheltered," I explained sheepishly, "I don't know what I thought would happen, but I expected that people could be, well, reasoned
with."

"Most people can—it's hard lesson when you meet those
who can't," the sheriff said.

"Billy told me to butt out," I continued. "Amy shouted to
me to get the cops, and Billy hit her again, really hard. I
couldn't believe this was happening. Amy'd started to bleed,
from a cut over her eye, so I went over to help her. Of course
I didn't think that he would hit *me*; we didn't know each
other, right?"

I shook my head, wondering again at my naiveté. "Billy
shoved me, hard, and I fell back and smashed my head
against a rock; he turned away to slap Amy again for egging
me on.

"I should have just left at that point, but after my head
stopped spinning, I just got so mad. I wasn't even thinking—
I'm surprised to this day I did what I—well, I picked up my
walking stick and whacked him across the shoulders. Amy,
the girlfriend, screamed again, and I thought I must have
about killed him because my hands were stinging like hell;
later Grandpa told me I should have hooked him in the, ah,

nuts, instead—his word, not mine. Anyway, Billy turned around and came after me; I hadn't even fazed him. That really put the fear of God into me."

Sheriff Stannard grimaced pityingly.

"This time I didn't hang around. I dropped my stick and ran faster than I would have believed I was capable. It could only have been fear that that made me move so quick, but it became clear pretty quickly that that was not going to be enough. Billy was *right* behind me. I could just see the road ahead of me and I could practically feel him, a foot behind me, when I barely missed being hit by a pickup. I swerved at the last minute; it must have been the adrenaline."

I paused again, remembering. I could hear the squeal of brakes, see the sudden blur of the truck, and feel how warm the hood was, feel just how close it had come to hitting me.

"Billy wasn't so lucky; he ran smack into the side of it, and flew across the hood. Lucky for me, it was one of the rangers going to work into the state park up that way, and he radioed for an ambulance. Funny thing was, I needed five stitches where my head hit the rock, and Billy got off without a scratch. Not a mark on him except for a little road rash on his hands, when he landed. It was like a bad dream, where nothing slows down the monster that's chasing you."

"That turned out to be the first time that he was actually charged for assault. But I was the one who filed the complaint, not Amy, his girlfriend. She didn't say a peep against him, and worse, later said that *I* had picked the fight with *him*! I couldn't believe that she would've let herself get mixed up with a guy like Billy in the first place, never mind pull a stunt like that after I'd tried to help her! And when I even found out that she married him the next year . . . well, it was my first big lesson in the apparent perversities of human nature."

The sheriff nodded, encouraging me without interrupting. He would have made a good ethnographer, I thought.

"I also got a few lessons in dirty fighting from Grandpa. He was able to convince my mother that I had fallen and cracked my skull on the deck of the sailboat that we some-times rented. I had this big shaved spot on the side of my head, just in time for senior pictures, so Mother decided that there would be no more summers with Oscar. Too much roughhousing for a young lady. But that didn't matter, be-cause college started that next fall and, well—"

I realized I was getting off the subject. "Anyway, that's my side of things—" A thought hit me from out of the blue, jarred loose by my own memories. "Hey, wait a minute! Didn't Dr. Moretti, the medical examiner, say that Augie Brooks had a cracked skull? And that maybe it wasn't an ac-cident he fell off his boat?"

Sheriff Stannard looked thoughtful. "You been eaves-dropping on private conversations, Professor Fielding?"

I blushed but stood my ground. "No one needed to strain to hear that conversation. All I'm saying is first Augie Brooks, then Pauline . . . she had a fractured skull, didn't you say?"

"Yes," he said slowly. "But you have to admit, even if Augie's death wasn't an accident, the two situations don't compare, not for motive, not for execution. I mean, someone set that house on fire and tried to make it look like an acci-dent. And there's a world of difference between the amount of planning between them."

I nodded but said nothing.

We walked up the slope toward where the Cherokee was parked. I hoped we were going to head back into Fordham. "Why are you so interested in this ancient history anyway?" I asked, getting back to our previous conversation.

"Not so ancient," the sheriff pointed out. "It seems as if you've got a lot of history around here, that's all. More, whatchacallit, context. Useful for me to know, given the pres-ent circumstances."

He got into the Jeep looking thoughtful, and didn't say a word as we drove away from the site. Suddenly, instead of taking the road that headed back into town, he took a hard left and went west instead. I grabbed the armrest and just avoided banging my head against the passenger side window.

"Hey, take it easy there!" I said indignantly. "You're going to get us killed!"

"Sorry." He put that Enya CD back in and turned the volume up a couple of notches, acting as though I weren't even there.

"Where are we going, anyhow?" I asked, a little more subdued. We went up a steep dirt road riddled with potholes. "I've got to meet my husband soon." As if that would make a difference to him.

"This won't take long. Relax."

When we reached the top of the hill, I saw a small one-story house, a cottage really, nestled in among the pine trees and hidden from the main roads below. It was a summer residence being fitted up for year-round use but not yet completed. Tyvek paper covered half of the house and new shingles covered the finished part. A small shed, now acting as a one-car garage, was crammed to the gills with rusting tools, paint cans, and other rubbish. It leaned precariously to one side and looked like the next winter's snow would bring it down. The grass around front grew unchecked and unexpectedly dotted with wildflowers, but a small garden plot in back looked reasonably well tended, save for a couple of weeks' worth of weeds. A yellow plastic police line ran across the path leading up to the doorway from a tree to the garage, and a notice was pinned up on the front door warning trespassers away from a crime scene.

I looked around for a moment. "This is Tichnor's place, isn't it?"

Stannard nodded.

"I have never been up here before."

He nodded again. "None of the tire print casts we took matched any of the vehicles that you could have used. Right now I'm just forming some other impressions"—he grinned sheepishly—"and I'd like yours too."

By way of an answer, I wandered around outside, getting a feel for the place. It wasn't tidy, but not completely run-down either. The house had been adequately repaired in stages, perhaps the garage would have been next. I peeked in there first.

In around an old green Nova, stacks of magazines and newspapers were tied in neat bundles, but were mildewing all the same. I took a peek and the titles didn't surprise me, given my personal encounters with Tichnor. A few stacks of *Guns and Ammo*, one of the local paper, a stack of *Survivalist!* were all interspersed with cheaply colored copies of *Big and Bouncy* and *Milk Fight*. An ill-spelled, angry, photocopied pamphlet warning against an imaginary "Zionist Conspiracy with Negroes" was tacked to the wall, with an assortment of aging tool company calendars. The newer tools bore the same label as the trowel that Stannard had showed me by the ruins of Greycliff.

I sauntered around back to the garden, but couldn't make much of that. I recognized the tomatoes and a compost heap, but that was about it. "What was he growing?" I asked.

Stannard looked a little surprised—I guess I came off like a child of the suburbs—but answered politely enough. "Tomatoes, squash, potatoes, carrots, lettuce, some other stuff. Nothing fancy. Let's go in the house."

It was small; we could see virtually all of the ground floor from where we stood. We walked in the back kitchen door and could see that the front room, a pine-paneled living room originally, had long sheets of plywood set up as work surfaces on sawhorses. A bedroom door opened beyond that and at the end of the kitchen, opposite where we entered, was a small bathroom. The place surprised me by being tidy—I'm always vaguely surprised when I find that not everyone likes my system of clutter—but I somehow imagined that Tichnor would have been messier.

The kitchen was decorated in the same knotty pine paneling that had probably been put up when the house was first built. The sink was vintage from the late fifties or so, and the linoleum on the counters and floor was dark red, cracked and worn. Greasy little smudges of gray and white spotted these surfaces, evidence of the investigation that had taken place.

I walked into the former living room *cum* workspace and looked down at the objects on the tables. I looked over at the sheriff, who nodded. "Well, I guess we know who's been digging those loot holes over at Fort Archer."

"We were wondering about that," he said. "But why would anyone want these broken bits of pottery and nails?"

I shrugged and picked up a piece of corroded strap hinge. "I'm not sure; I just thought he was one of those people who believed the old folktales of gold around the Point." I put the hinge back in its place. "Maybe he was looking for buttons, maybe he was hoping to find a whole piece. Maybe he was looking for bottles; a lot of folks do, though it drives us professionals crazy. I don't understand what drives some looters; sometimes it's as though they want things only so other people can't have them."

I picked up a piece of gray stoneware. German, by the looks of it. "I wouldn't have thought there'd be too much left to find. The fieldwork that was done during the 1930s suggested that most of the interesting areas, like the ditch or buildings, had been destroyed by later landscaping. Still, you never know. We'll have to get this back to the site manager there."

Stannard nodded again. "I had something in particular I wanted to ask you about."

He led me back into the kitchen, to the one cluttered area in the whole room. A bulletin board by the phone was covered with scraps of paper, mostly notices of antique shows and gun shows and auctions in the area, with a fading list of phone numbers and a wad of coupons tacked to the bottom, obscured by the notices. The sheriff moved some of the more recent ones aside and untacked a piece of paper that had been partially covered by them. He handed that piece of paper to me.

"This looks like it's old. Is it?"

It was a photocopy of a map, I saw at once, but not just any map. It took me a minute to make sense of the scant and faded lines, obviously hand drawn, no more than a series of linear squiggles that weren't heavy enough to be reproduced clearly. A furry smudge darkened one corner.

After I stared a moment at it, I suddenly felt my stomach lurch, as though I was standing in an elevator that has started down too quickly. "Holy sn—where did this map come from?" I turned to him, excitement mingled with dread. "Where did he get this?"

The sheriff shrugged, hands spread wide. "I don't know. I was hoping you could tell me."

"You don't understand, I don't have this one!" I insisted. "I've combed the state archives, local ones, every university and library that has any collections dealing with early settlements. I've written to repositories in England, contacted the best scholars who've worked on early sites like this, and applied every ounce of my training to finding everything to do with my site. So how is it that Grahame Tichnor, a pothunter and class A nutcase, has a copy of a map showing the location of Fort Providence that *I've never seen*?"

Neither of us had any answers for that. I stared down at the photocopy. It was very primitive, but it clearly showed the familiar coastline of the Saugatuck River and even had a few rectangles to represent the fort. These were marked in French, marked as *"les ruines anciennes."* Another set of rectangles just down the coast was marked *"le Fortin."*

" *'Le fortin?'* " Stannard repeated the term with a surprisingly good accent. "Is that Fort Archer?"

"Yeah," I said, nodding absently. "This is probably eighteenth century, judging from the hand."

"Then I guess maybe he had it because he was pothunting at Fort Archer—" Stannard suggested. "I mean, the map isn't really of Fort Providence, is it? It's just a landmark to show the location of the other fort."

"Yes, yes, but that doesn't say where he got it!" I exclaimed. I began to pace back and forth across the small kitchen. "Where the hell did he get it that I didn't look? What else might be there?"

"Maybe they had it at the Fort Archer archive," he offered.

"No, I spoke with them about maps, because I was sure they'd have some showing the old ruins of Fort Providence that might be standing," I said. "I stopped there first, it would be a landmark that any eighteenth-century cartographer would have included. But they had nothing like this, and even if they had, they wouldn't have given it to Tichnor."

I stopped pacing and walked over to the sheriff and squinted at the paper. "Can you read that?" I asked, pointing to the blur on the corner of the photocopy. "I can only make out a d, and maybe that one is a B or an E."

Stannard looked at it. "I can't even make those out; you've got sharp eyes. What is that?"

"It looks like a library stamp to me. When libraries or archives photocopy holdings from their collections, they stamp the photocopy with their stamp to keep people from reproducing the picture in a book without permission. This is a photocopy of a photocopy and I can't make out where he got it."

"Looks like there was another sheet too," Stannard noted. He pointed. "See? That top corner shows that another sheet was folded back on the original photocopy."

"But where did he get it?" I worried, more to myself than to him. "I mean, I've looked *everywhere*. And he's got it stuck next to his coupons! I couldn't have missed it, could I?"

Something else caught my eye. One of the numbers on the phone list was darker, less faded than the others, and I realized with a start that I recognized it. "Holy snappers, how did *that* get there?"

"I was wondering whether you'd notice that," Stannard said. "It's not marked, but you can imagine how surprised we were to find it there."

I felt a cold sweat break out across my back and shivered. "It's the number for the anthropology department at Caldwell! Jesus, was he calling about *me*?"

"I was thinking just that," Stannard replied. "You should check with your department and confirm that he was asking after you. Maybe it was just—you know, like a crank."

He turned back to the bulletin board. "So why is Tichnor dead?" he asked the advertisements and coupons. "The fort. Ms. Westlake. Why is he dead? There's lots going on but no reason for it all yet. We just get more questions to answer our questions . . ."

"Same with archaeologists," I said, equally distracted. "Who, what, where, when, why."

Stannard looked at me sharply. "I don't want you getting ideas about playing Nancy Drew here! This is a matter of information, not action, you got that?!"

"Well, yeah, but you wouldn't have brought me up here if you didn't think I could help."

"I brought you up here to satisfy myself that you'd never been here before, that's all," he snapped, "and to get your impressions of the place. There's no reason for you to get any more involved than that."

But I wasn't going to be put off now that he'd given me the idea, and I could tell he wasn't so convinced himself. "I'm bound to hear something, people around here talk and they know me. All I'm asking"—and it wasn't until that very moment that I realized I was asking for something—"is that you tell me about whatever *you* discover. Then I'll tell you whatever I find—"

I clammed up suddenly, aware that I had just blown it.

The sheriff turned on me. "I expect you'll tell me whatever you know in any case! Anything less is obstruction," he said shortly. There was a long pause while he debated. "If I come up with anything *I* think *you* can tell *me* about, I'll be in touch. You hear anything, you call me *immediately*. No messing around! Don't make me regret trusting you like this."

He looked worried, like trusting me was going to get him into a lot of trouble. I just nodded, grateful for his admission and grateful for a sense of direction at last.

Chapter 16

CLASSES BEGAN THREE WEEKS LATER, AND THAT FRIDAY, I was trapped in a faculty meeting. This was surely the sort of thing Dante had in mind in filling the rings of his hell with poetically just torments: I had slaved my whole professional life to be in that stuffy little room. As individuals, the faculty members of Caldwell College's Anthropology Department couldn't have been more different, ranging from our soon-to-be-emeritus chair, Daniel Kellerman, to me, the newest member. Kellerman was indeed, as Brian had once described, a "dried-up old mummy man," with great tufts of white hair growing out of his ears and nose that gave him a vaguely rabbity look as well. Rick Crabtree, with his plump, dissatisfied face and dark hair slicked over a wide bald patch, sat with his lips pursed so tightly it made mine ache just to look at him. Next to me was Jenny Alvarez, long gray hair caught up in a leather tie, still wearing the same clothes she'd owned in the 1970s—styles that were just now coming back into fashion. Gretchen Renekker, our doe-eyed pre-Raphaelite princess of political correctness, sat next to Rick Crabtree, setting us an example, I was sure, of how we ought to value his age and wisdom, and look past his bigoted nature, narrow mind, and dated research. Larry Chapman sat across from her, a lanky Cockney in a bolo string tie, a linguist who pined for the Old West of cowboy movies but settled for New England.

Tony Markham, of course, looked as cool as ever, and I noticed that some of the others were already referring their questions to him, as if he had already taken over sleepy old Kellerman's position, as we all expected. It made sense; Tony seemed to be the only one capable of getting things done with the administration, after all, and he just seemed to be a born leader. I thought that it was funny; even in a room full of hardheaded academics with big egos, Tony still came off as the one in charge.

But as a single entity, trapped en masse, the rest of my colleagues were indistinguishable from one another, monochrome in dull shades of boredom and irritability. Most of us were eager to have done with the petty details involved in the day-to-day business of running the department and ready to abandon the campus for the weekend. The first hour of such a meeting can be borne with dutiful energy, the next with grim fortitude. Any half hour after that must be got through by any means available. For some, this meant shifting in chairs and doodling, waiting for their business to come to the table; for others, it meant a display of power, dickering over small and large points; for still others, it was taking refuge in daydreams.

Even Chuck, our department's administrator, usually curious about everything, must have picked up the scent of frustration and boredom, because after he dropped off the coffee, he all but scampered away from the room, Birkenstocks flapping down the hallway. I wished I could follow him.

I was particularly eager to flee; I had already had a hellish day before the faculty meeting began, and a rushed week before that. No sooner had Brian helped me move my things back to our Massachusetts apartment and I had delved into preparation for classes, than it seemed I had to move back to my campus apartment in Maine and begin our second year of weekly autumnal migration for conjugal weekends. We were trying to re-create a normal life after a dreadful summer, but there is nothing normal to begin with about a commuting marriage.

Classes had started, and while I was pretty well on top of my lectures, rumors about the events on the site had begun to fly. There had been talk, hushed, unofficial, and pernicious, about what was being called "the Westlake bequest" and my proximity to her death, and only that morning Dr. Kellerman had suggested a leave of absence on half pay, until "things were cleared up." I startled both of us by giving him a curt response in the negative, and then, having no doubt that it was the work of the dean, went to pay him an unannounced visit as well. Having nothing to lose, I marched into Dean Belcher's office and told him that he could fire me, in which case my lawyer would be on the college like white on rice, or he could leave me alone, and I could continue to be a productive member of the campus community. He agreed quickly, and I left, surprised at my preemptive strike. It felt like the beginning of things, or maybe the end, and so I was feeling particularly penned up, irritated with my colleagues arguing over academic minutiae.

I looked at my watch surreptitiously; there was nearly half a page left to the agenda by two-thirty. The meeting had started at ten, with only a half hour for lunch. I was dying a slow death of boredom and exhaustion; I'd spent the night in my office trying desperately to catch up on all the little crap jobs that had been shoved my way because I was the junior member. It was just a sort of professional hazing, with no conscious thought but to reinforce department hierarchies and take a little of the load off my fellow professors, but it was grueling work. I pounded through the memos I needed to draft on introductory textbook recommendations, computer equipment acquisitions, and language exam schedules. By four A.M. I had finished proofing the departmental newsletter, and had just enough strength to crawl over to the couch and collapse. At eight forty-five I awoke, cursing the birds that sang in the ivy outside my windows, even though they provided me with the opportunity to scuttle back to my apartment and shower hastily.

Finally, just as I was trying to figure out whether dire boredom actually reduced the amount of oxygen in the room, Kellerman wrapped things up with "If that's all, people?"

No one said anything. The others would have killed him.

"Well, have a good weekend."

People stretched and collected their belongings, and shuffled out of the room. I all but ran for the ladies' room for a much-needed break and then hurried back to my office. I flung my notepads down on the desk, where they were immediately camouflaged amid the surrounding clutter. I called Brian at work and got the terse, vexed-sounding message on his answering machine. It never sounded to me like the sweet man I knew at home.

"I'm busy. Leave a message if you have to." There was, as usual, the background noise that was never meant to be recorded, the sounds of Brian fumbling to turn off the machine as he half-sang to himself, "o-ther-wise, leee-eave me-eee a-lone." The righteous dub of a Ziggy Marley song playing somewhere in the vicinity didn't make the message sound any more professional.

I started in with my usual preamble. "Brian, you promised me you'd change this wretched tape. People will think—"

"People will think that I am a rude boy and want to be left alone, which is entirely correct. This ain't the diplomatic corps." Brian had suddenly picked up his phone, interrupting my recital. "Hey, pork chop, you just caught me going out the door. What bus are you going to be on?"

"The early one," I said. "I'm not sticking around here any longer, I'll go crazy."

"Good for you; why risk a trip to the funny farm if you

can be home with me? How was the faculty meeting, or should I ask?"

"Not until you hand me a largish drink, unsullied by additives or ice. I'm still in the throes of the backlash. And I'm just realizing what I said to the dean."

"Ouch," he said sympathetically.

Jenny Alvarez stuck her head in the door. "Have a good weekend, Em," she whispered before making her own escape. I waved to her.

"It's not all that bad," I said. "I'll tell you all about it later, I just wanted to check in. Do you need me to pick up anything on the way, or should we go out?"

"We're staying in. Kam is coming over tonight, so he and I will cook. You can swing by the bakery outside the station, if you think of it, and pick up a couple of loaves of bread. We might get a movie or something too."

"Where's Marty going to be, if himself is with us?"

"New York, working late with the Wilmerdings."

The thought of a normal weekend was almost too much to bear, and I felt myself tearing up. "Look, I've got to get going or I'll never make the bus. I'll see you in a couple of hours, sweetie. Love you."

"Okay, see you in a bit. Love you too. Bye."

I sighed; living apart was very trendy and all, but it was getting harder and harder to carry off cheerfully. Still, it kept a marriage from becoming stale through familiarity. I could use some of that familiarity right now myself, though, I thought vehemently. Well past time for it.

I stuffed a couple of books into my briefcase, thought better of it, and decided to celebrate by dumping them back onto the desk. They could wait until Monday. I wouldn't be any more behind than I was already, and I felt as though life was very nearly on an upswing.

Purely by reflex, however, I decided to have a quick look in the storage room on my way out of the building, to check on the state of field supplies. I'd be heading back to close up the site next weekend, and it was amazing how a little thing like no artifact bags could throw a project into chaos. I unlocked the door to the small room and flicked on the light. The metallic smell of dusty field equipment tanged with musty canvas assaulted my nose. Shovels and screens lined the wall on the left, and the back and right sides were covered with metal shelving and cases for smaller gear. After mentally noting that I'd need to order more marker pens, I turned to leave the room when I noticed something out of place out of the corner of my eye.

Early in our relationship, after observing the postapocalyptic state of my apartment, Brian, in frustration, asked how I could be successful in a profession that depended on the rigorous maintenance of order. "How can you live in such a sty and yet be such a control freak in the field? I would have thought the two concepts would be mutually exclusive," he'd asked.

I'd shrugged. "It's not the same. At home, everything is a known quantity. I know what is clean laundry and what is not; I know which pile has what sort of books. If you don't throw anything out, then you don't have to worry about not being able to find it again later. You know it's all there, and the randomness occasionally helps make connections between things you wouldn't have thought related before.

"On the other hand, everything in the field is an x-factor. You can never take anything for granted, never assume anything. It's the unknown that requires precision." My messy habits were an issue that had never been fully resolved, and still occasionally flared up between us while we were forced to share office space.

It was that sense of something inherently out of place that caused me to glance over toward the back, where a wide gray metal map file stood. The middle drawer was partially open, caught on the corners of a pile of maps sticking out.

Wretched students, I thought, with a momentary flicker of irritation. The drawer that was open was the one that held maps of New England, and so subsequently contained many of my own personal maps. The students were allowed to use them only as long as they treated them carefully. But these had been jammed in any which way, left to tear.

I opened the drawer fully to reorganize the maps and began to sort them out. My ire grew as I realized that they were the maps of the site at Penitence Point; someone's head would roll when I found out who'd been in here last, I thought. I separated the maps, straightened them, and settled them back in, long bottom edges aligned so that the names were easily visible. My fingernail caught on the edge of a map that had been shoved deep between two large USGS sheets, and I pulled it out to set it flush with the others.

It was a photocopied map. Just like the one that Sheriff Standard had shown me in Grahame Tichnor's kitchen.

I pulled it all the way out and stared at it in confusion. It can't be mine, I thought, I would have remembered this, it's not in my map notes.

So what the bloody hell is another copy of it doing here?

I scowled at the inoffensive piece of paper and slid it into my briefcase. I didn't have time to worry about it now; I'd be late for my bus. As I was sliding the drawer shut, however, the doorknob to the storage room rattled, startling me, and I slammed my thumb in the drawer.

A rainbow arc of pain shot across my vision, and I barely managed to get my thumb out before the drawer slid back shut again. "Oh Jesus, that hurts!" I yelled, sticking my thumb into my mouth. I looked up to see who had come in, wishing no good upon whoever it was.

Tony Markham was taken aback; I had scared him too. I held up my thumb, which was hot with throbbing, to show him. "I caught myself good in the drawer," I said. At least the skin wasn't broken. "I'm sorry, I didn't mean to scream like that."

Collecting himself, Tony was solicitous. "Oh no, *I'm* sorry," he drawled. "I didn't mean to startle you so."

"No, not your fault," I said, a bit shakily. "I guess I'm just overtired. It's been a long week."

"Can you wiggle your thumb?"

I did, although it was painful to do so.

"You should get some ice on that," Tony suggested. "Have you got time for a drink now? One for you and one for your hand. There's a couple of things we should discuss."

I made a disappointed face. "I'm sorry, I can't, Tony. I'm running late now. Maybe a rain check?"

Tony frowned. "Well, I don't like to leave it, you really ought to know. Rick Crabtree's been acting strangely when your name's come up lately."

"Ah. How, strangely?" It had to do with Alan, I guessed, but I was wrong.

"He was the one who suggested to Kellerman that you ought to withdraw for a while. I don't know his reasons," Tony said briefly. "This really isn't the time or the place, but you need to be aware of that."

"Thanks." I mulled that over for a minute, my thumb in my mouth. "I had no idea he felt this strongly against me." I'd really have to find out what was making Rick act so irrationally.

"I'm a little worried about it myself," Tony agreed. "Actually, I'm more worried about you. You've been under a tremendous strain lately. Are you really all right?"

"Yeah, I'm doing okay, I think." I didn't want to tell him how frustrated I was in trying to discover what interest Grahame Tichnor had in Penitence Point; if I got on that riff, we might be in the storage room all day.

"What can you pare off your schedule? How about your lectures, have you got them all under control?"

"I'm in pretty good shape there—"

"Can you leave off work at the site until next spring, for example?"

"That's the one thing I can't leave, Tony. I'm doing all right, though, thanks." I was starting to get a little irked with his offers; I really did prefer to take care of things myself. Perhaps he thought I was too green to manage on my own.

"I'm sorry, I'm keeping you from whatever you were going to do in here," I apologized.

"Not at all. I heard noises," he explained. "I wanted to make sure that no one was in here before I locked up. Everyone else has left."

"That's funny," I said, picking up my briefcase. "Chuck usually makes the pretense of staying until five, or at least until we're all gone. It must be the nice weather."

"How about a lift to the bus stop?" Professor Markham asked.

Again with the looking after me, I thought. Maybe it's a Southern thing. Em, maybe the man's being nice to you and you're too fried to appreciate it, I chastised myself. "No thank you, Tony. I've got to go home first, then the bus. I need the fresh air anyway."

"Fair enough. See you Monday?"

"Sure thing."

Time was getting close, so I practically ran out of the building and trotted down the path that led to the apartment complex, steadily gaining speed as the campus blurred into the background, my briefcase thumping awkwardly against my legs as I accelerated. Even with a prepacked bag and a world-class sprint, I was just barely able to make it down to the stop as the bus pulled up.

After sucking some air into my oxygen-starved lungs, and cursing Amtrak for eternally taunting me with the promise of regular service connecting Portland and Boston, I stashed my bags in the overhead rack and began to think furiously as the landscape tore by.

Where had that map come from? And, never mind how Tichnor came to have it, how did a copy of it show up in that file when I clearly hadn't put it there?

Although the puzzle of where that map came from in the first place was eating at me, the fact that there was some connection between Tichnor and my life apart from the dig was really starting to bother me. It didn't matter that he was dead; it was the fact that the connections between him and my life kept piling up, first with Pauline, then with the department's phone number, and now with another copy of that map in the department itself. Why should this link exist? Apart from me and the students, there was no human connection. No one from the department had even been by to visit me at the site, except Tony.

He called the day I'd stumbled over the body, I remembered. Coming out to the site, going to the sheriff's department with me after the incident with Grahame Tichnor, sending the flowers to Pauline's memorial. And then warning me about Rick. He really was going all out, trying to take me under his wing. Except he probably didn't really know, and I'd have to be careful about telling him, that I wasn't the sort of chick to be gathered under someone else's protective wing. Just a big stubborn streak, I guess. I like doing things on my own. Probably just one more thing I'd inherited from Oscar.

I watched the fields and suburbs go by, letting my thoughts wander as they would through my tired brain.

It was funny, although Tony reminded me a little of Oscar, I couldn't imagine Oscar suggesting I leave a site as important, as fragile, as Fort Providence opened to the elements for a whole Maine winter, never in a million years. The idea was ludicrous. Even if the site wasn't so significant, no archaeologist would do it. Usually we conspired to get in as much fieldwork as possible, if necessary, to the detriment of students and home life.

I frowned. So why the *hell* had Tony suggested *that*?

No one from the department had been to the site except Tony . . .

Oscar had always told me to pay attention to the exceptions in a situation, for they'd tell one at least as much as the rule. Tony had been there at every turn, every juncture, with me. Tony had been in the map room when I discovered the photocopied map, the one that I knew I'd never seen before. What about the telephone number at Tichnor's house?

Could that have something to do with Tony, rather than me? When I'd asked if anyone unusual had called for me, Chuck had told me that everyone who'd called had left a message. I thought about the piles of looted artifacts at Tichnor's house, the day I saw the number and the map. My jaw dropped as an even more dire connection came to mind.

The artifacts from Pauline's house. The ones found under Tichnor's bed. Dave Stannard was right; there was a chance that Tichnor would have recognized the value of some of them, but probably not the Venus figurine. The sheriff had pointed out that the number of people familiar with such things around here was bound to be small.

Tony would have recognized the Venus in a heartbeat.

For a moment I couldn't focus, couldn't believe what I was thinking. There was no logical connection, surely? Coincidences, just the same as the others . . . What could Tony Markham have to do with Tichnor, they didn't know each other . . .

Me. They both knew me.

Well, let's not be dramatic, I curbed myself. That doesn't mean anything, and this was starting to sound really crazy. Any couple of people in a circle of acquaintances, no matter how it was formed, were bound to have things in common. I mean, look, I said to myself, they both had interests in archaeology, though admittedly from rather different angles. There were probably lots of similarities. You could even say the same thing about the students, for heaven's sake . . .

I continued to list the possible connections anyway. They both lived in Maine, both were men, had both been to the site on occasion, both—

Had even been on the site on the same day.

A tingling wave of adrenaline raced through me as I recalled the day I had encountered Tichnor. Tony had been there later. In fact, it dawned on me, he had practically insisted on accompanying me to the sheriff's office when I made my first complaint about Tichnor. It couldn't be possible that they had *known* each other back then?

I let myself think about that for a moment, tasting the idea. It was the only thing that suggested that I wasn't the only connection that Tichnor had with the department. It might explain the telephone number, even if it still didn't tell me where that cursed map had come from. I patted my briefcase, reassuring myself that it was still there. When I got home, I was going to look at that map very carefully indeed.

But what about Tony? What interest could he have in Tichnor, if he was in fact the connection?

Tony hadn't become interested in me or my work until I'd begun out at Penitence Point.

Could he be connected to Tichnor's death in some way? That question tore at me and led me to the next logical, horrible step: If my suspicions about Tony knowing Tichnor were correct, did that also mean that Tony knew something about Pauline's murder?

Chapter 17

A S IF REFLECTING THE ABRUPT JOLT IN MY THOUGHTS, the bus jerked to a halt at Boston's South Station; for once it was on time. Wearily I gathered up my pack and briefcase and followed the ant line of passengers into the main station, trying not to get swept away by the throngs of commuters attempting to get home or away for the weekend. As I negotiated the crowds down into the subway, I forced my mind away from my as yet unfounded but profoundly disturbing speculation.

The subway station was almost as sticky as it was outside; the air-conditioning was broken. I sweated my way into the crush on the car, air-conditioned in name only, and let my mind go blank until I got off for my stop in Somerville. As I walked up the sidewalk, I could see that a little mud had dried onto our gnome, making him look as though he'd gone for a long, dusty run. I brushed off a little of the mud, and some of his paint flaked off along with it. Alas, poor gnome, I thought. Gnome just winked back at me, a new, clean, white spot on his red hat.

I had barely made it into through the door when Brian

swarmed all over me, kissing me repeatedly and sloppily. In spite of my stale, bus-sweaty state, I responded eagerly though I was scarcely able to keep balanced in the process; my husband's enthusiasm made him the better lever. He had just started nibbling my neck, and was on the verge of heading further south when a murmur of protest was heard.

"For God's sake, man, at least close the door!" Kam insisted. "There may be small, easily impressionable children in the street who will be startled and confused by this unseemly display, as well as people on their way to eat dinner. They have no desire to see you mauling your wife." He closed the door and gave me a prim buss on the cheek, by way of example. He stepped back and eyed me in commiseration. "You look like you could use a drink. Did you stop for bread?"

My smile faded as I remembered why I had been distracted away from the errand. "No, I'm sorry, I, I completely flaked out. I . . ."

"No need to get broken up about it, I'll just run down to the corner." Kam started, then reached into his trousers pocket for his beeper. He looked a little sheepish, but recovered quickly, and turned to Brian. "I've got an errand. I'll be about an hour and I'll bring the bread on my way back. If you finish up in the kitchen, we can eat when I get back."

Brian did a passable scrape and bow. "Anything else, sir, while I'm at it?" he asked sarcastically.

Kam appeared to consider. "Get Em a drink. Draw her a bath while you're at it."

"Yeah, I like the sound of that," I said. "Two husbands to wait on me!"

"You can get your own bath," Brian said to me. "Kam, you can get stuffed. I bet you arranged to get beeped to get out of cooking dinner."

"Sixty minutes," Kam said, then headed down the street to his Jaguar with uncharacteristic speed.

Brian and I played grab-ass up the stairs and I headed straight for the shower. Turning the water on as hot as I could stand, I stood, willing my reluctant muscles to unknot. As I toweled off, less icky but no less unruffled, I heard a glassy clink and looked up. Brian set a glass of dark liquor on the wide edge of the sink and settled himself on the toilet to watch me dry off.

"You really look wiped," he said, looking at my reddened face with some anxiety. "How'd it go today?"

I thought about telling him what happened in the storage room. I wanted to say, "Well, the meeting went rather well, all things considered, but I think I just decided that Professor Markham killed Grahame Tichnor."

But the fact that I had only the slimmest of evidence and absolutely no clue as to why the two would even know each other kept me from blurting that out. I knew I was exhausted, I knew that I was desperate to think I was doing something useful in the hunt for the reason for Pauline's murder. But I wasn't ready yet to expose my tender theories to the harsh light of day, and to be honest, I needed a moment or two of my particular brand of reality before I could submerge myself further in my suspicions about Tony.

"Earth to Emma, come in, Emma." Brian was waving his hand in front of my vacantly staring eyes.

I batted his hand away irritatedly and immediately regretted the action and my annoyance. My tolerance levels were hideously low, but Brian, of all people, didn't deserve to suffer because of it.

"Sorry, sweetie, I took a little trip there. I am feeling burned out." I took a sip of the Maker's Mark and sighed as it burned its way down my throat; I was starting feel cleansed inside and out. Start with reality, then work your way into fantasyland, I told myself. "In a nutshell: There was a little noise about the bequest and my alleged connection with Pauline's death. I told Kellerman I would not consider taking a leave. Then I told Dean Belcher the same thing. At the faculty department they tried to saddle me with a bunch more crap, but I told them to take a leap."

"You did?" Brian asked with incredulous glee.

I nodded and took another sip. "I am bloody but un-bowed, exhausted but triumphant. Mostly." As I finished dressing, I perfunctorily answered Brian's questions, then we went to the kitchen.

"I really don't want to talk about me anymore," I an-nounced, sucking on an ice cube and spitting it back into my glass. "What are we having, anyway?" I peered under a pot lid and smacked my lips. I was starving. "Oh boy! Dinty Moore!"

"That beef stew has never seen the inside of a can!" Brian said indignantly, flicking me on the tail with a snapped fin-ger.

"Ow!" I protested. "Hey!"

"Those potatoes, carrots, celery, and mushrooms were lovingly handpicked by me at the market not three hours ago! There's a full cup of decent red wine in there and it's been cooking for nearly an hour," he continued. "So Dinty me no Dintys."

I rubbed my backside and frowned; I now had a very good idea of what his students thought of him during his teaching assistant days. "For your information, I like Dinty!"

"Well, you'll like this too," he said huffily, "and this way my intestines won't be ravaged by whatever unnamed bacte-ria kamikazed into the vats in Detroit, or wherever that stuff is extruded." He stirred the pot briefly and tasted the stew, then re-covered the pot, satisfied. "So, look, tell me—"

"Nope, I said no more about me and I meant it," I inter-rupted. "I want to hear about your world. What's your sched-ule for the rest of the month?"

Brian looked a little put off, but pulled up a stool and stole a sip of my drink. "Back out to California Monday, for two more weeks of meetings and presentations. Then that should be it. With any luck, things will quiet down after that. But I mean it, Em, I need to know—"

We both heard a knock on the front door. I jumped down to get it. "It's Kam, time to eat, time to eat—" I chanted, as I went to let him in.

It was Kam all right, but I was a little surprised to see Marty right behind him. "Hey, girl! You two are starting to get pretty cozy, aren't you?" I said, giving her a hug.

"You could say that," Kam said, then all but ran into the kitchen with the bread.

"I'll kill the man," Marty said, staring down the hallway. "I swear, Emma, if he wasn't so damned good-looking—" She reached up to adjust her earring in a rather exaggerated fashion.

Since Marty did everything in a rather exaggerated fashion, it took me a minute to catch on, but when I did, I noticed something truly shocking. "Mariam Asefi, what the hell is that on your hand?"

"You mean Mr. Mole?" she asked blithely, waving her right hand, not the one I was so interested in. "You've seen him a thousand times, dearie. Is there any vino to be had?"

I dragged her down the hall. "Kam, what have you done?" I demanded, excitedly shaking Brian's shoulder and pointing so he could see too; reluctantly he put the bread down.

"Oh, you mean the other hand?" she asked.

I looked her askance, head cocked. Damn the woman, she was every bit as coy as Kam!

"*That* is a four-carat, moss-green, emerald engagement ring. Do you like it?" She held up her hand and waggled her fingers briskly, absently, without turning from her search for a glass. "Aha! There you are," she said, filling a glass from the sideboard. "That's more like it. I can't stand those airline snacks, I feel like I'm coated in grease for a week afterward. *Slàinte*, everyone!" she toasted us and settled in to eating.

I was speechless. The best I could manage was a wordless whoop as I threw myself on Marty, who finally put down her wineglass to hug me back.

Brian was exuberant. "When did this happen, you smug bastard?" he asked his friend.

"Damned if I know." Kam was playing it cool as well. "She just showed up with the thing one day and started talking about registering at Shreve's—"

Perhaps a little too cool: Kam was halted in his tall tale by a purely poisonous look from Marty, who released me, turned back to the table, and folded her manicured hands expectantly.

"As difficult as it was to get this on my hand, I assure you that it comes off much more easily," she pointed out to her fiancé. "Sayonara, you know? Not to be high-maintenance or anything, darling."

Kam gave a small, decorative cough and backpedaled with practiced determination. "I suddenly realized that I couldn't go on any longer without the knowledge that the dawn star in the firmament of my life was truly my own, so I feverishly pressed this insignificant token of my eternal devotion on her before her last trip to New York. Better?" He looked questioningly at Marty, who was now beaming.

She filled in some of the blanks. "He proposed at that long light on Commonwealth Avenue, by the Public Gardens. Two weeks ago now."

"You proposed in the car?" I asked incredulously. "At a red light?"

"Power locks: I was afraid she'd bolt," he explained. "I'll make up the romance to her on the honeymoon. Besides, the inside of the Jag is a lot more romantic than the back of the science building at Coolidge."

He made a disapproving face at Brian, who didn't notice. He was cutting up the loaf of bread, intent on getting dinner under way.

And speaking of romantic, I suddenly recalled the ornate silver cigarette case Kam had been playing with during his visit to the dorm. I made a note to steal it and look for inscriptions at the first possible moment.

"Romance is overrated," Brian said, munching away. "Nothing to it; you ask, she says yes, you get on with your life. But I would have thought that you would have learned something from my example. Wives are a lot of trouble, especially the independent types."

Then Brian suddenly noticed that *he* was on the receiving

end of a couple of very icy stares. "On the other hand, the challenge is half the fun. C'mon," he offered, before he found himself in more trouble, "this calls for a bottle of something with bubbles. Let's run down the street. I'll give you some pointers while GirlNet gets all the details straight."

"I'll be interested to hear what he thinks he knows," I said to Kam. "Scat, you two. Hurry back."

Dinner was fun and full of improbable plan making. Kam was all for a quiet wedding with a larger party for friends, after the New Year; Marty wanted six hundred for a sit-down dinner with wandering minstrels and peacocks in Moorea.

"I don't think peacocks are native to the South Pacific, dearest," Kam interjected.

"You would deny me on my big day?" She pouted.

Things carried on until far later than usual, and it was nearly one A.M. before we chased them out and wearily cleaned up. I noticed that Brian was putting on the teakettle.

"Hey, sweetie, I'm just going to crawl into bed—"

I was surprised when he sat down at the kitchen table and pushed a chair out for me too.

"I know you're tired," he said without looking at me. "And I've tried to be patient. But there's some pretty weird stuff going on with you that you're not telling me about, and I need to know. Right now."

I looked at him in amazement; I still hadn't said a word about Tony. "How the hell could you know—?"

"Kam told me everything."

"Kam? How does he know about Tony?"

Now it was Brian's turn to look puzzled. "Tony? Who's talking about Tony? I'm talking about Billy Griggs, that guy Kam found you with in the church parking lot. Wasn't he the one who tried to kill you in high school?"

Light finally dawned, a little late. "Billy—oh hell, I completely forgot about him! I thought I told you about that when you came back . . ." I tried to recall just what had taken place on Brian's return from California. "No, no, I didn't, because by that time you were home and I was having my talk with Sheriff Stannard. Then that trip to Tichnor's house kind of put Billy on the back burner. I'm sorry, hon, what do you want to know?"

Brian stared in disbelief. "You pick a fight with some nut who's ready to beat the stuffing out of you and you're asking what I want to know? You can't believe how worried I've been since Kam mentioned it the other day. He figured that you'd already told me. I didn't know what to think!"

I was startled by his vehemence. It wasn't that Brian was angry; it was just that he doesn't usually get this excited about much besides work . . . and me, I suppose. So I told him what had happened with Billy, including my discussion about Pauline's death with Kam.

"It was a lot to process," I finished. "I really did forget. I'm sorry you were startled when Kam mentioned it."

Brian gave me a skeptical look. "*Startled* wasn't the word that sprang first to my mind, Em. I thought Kam was making it up, for God's sake! He was getting a little weirded out when I kept telling him to knock it off." He set the mugs down in front of me. "Imagine my surprise. Anything else you forgot to tell me about?"

I took a sip of the nasty, unnatural decaf. "No, that's pretty much it. You know everything else. I mean, he swung by the site the day after I found the body, but then I found that he and Augie knew each other. He didn't even recognize me in the parking lot."

"And Tony. What was it about Tony—Markham?—that so suddenly sprang to mind when I asked about Billy?"

"Oh." I looked up guiltily. "Well, now, I was going to tell you about that, but you just kinda drove that out of my mind. It's not like I know anything for sure, I just found something really disturbing before I left school."

Bless Brian; he sat there and listened to every scrap of my supposition, speculation, and suspicion without interrupting. And he waited until I was done to start shooting down my conclusions as nicely as possible.

"You've got some real neat circumstantial evidence, Em, but I don't think you've got anything that is very solid," he said, almost apologetically. "I mean, look at the obvious things. Why would Tony have left that map in the case, where anyone could find it?"

I chewed my lip. "I don't know. Maybe he panicked and didn't want it found on him."

Brian's eyebrows disappeared under his hair. "But who would be looking for it, pork chop? All you've got is a photocopy of a map showing your site and some people who were never within eyesight of each other once, as far as you know. No motive, no evidence, no connections besides a little anxious coincidence."

I got up and led the way into the bedroom. Brian grabbed me in a bear hug and flung us both backward onto the bed. "Ooof, you're a big girl, aren't you?"

I stopped laughing. "You're going too far now!"

"You're right, I'm getting carried away. You're only a medium-sized girl, with a lot packed on. Hey, wait a minute." He stopped wrestling and looked at me seriously. "Do you see my point? I trust your instincts, but I don't think you've got a lot to go on here.

I sighed. "I know. It sounds different, saying it out loud to you. I don't know, maybe it's just stress, guilt, on top of everything else."

"Maybe. If you feel strongly about it though, why don't you just talk to that sheriff who's been working on this?" Brian asked. "You said he was decent, right?"

"Yeah, maybe. I'll think about it," I said, yawning. It was very late.

"Look, just try to take it easy. Pauline's death was a bad surprise, and it's hit you, *us*, hard. Lots of emotional stuff going on inside. Be careful about looking after yourself, okay? I know you've got to deal with this your own way, but just don't beat yourself up for it, it's not your fault. Remember that."

We snuggled for a while, then fell asleep. But around four in the morning, I sat bolt upright with the astonishing, obvious thought that all I'd have to do was have a really close look around the department to make sure that everything was just as Brian had said.

Chapter 18

I CAUGHT AN EARLIER BUS SUNDAY, OSTENSIBLY TO GET back to Caldwell to get some work done and have an early night before another busy week. I also wanted to have a look around the storeroom that night, before anyone came in Monday morning. When I left, Brian had beamed at me approvingly, and I rationalized that I was only doing as he said, taking care of myself, handling things my own way. On the bus I started to get nervous about what I was planning to do, what it would mean if, against all the odds, I found something, and what it would mean for me personally if there really was nothing to find.

The light was starting to fade in the sky and there was the muted sound of competing stereos coming from the dormitories around the quad. There were a few students moving about, though most everyone was probably at dinner. Those I saw scurried with the sort of subdued panic that comes with the realization that the beginning of a brand-new week, with all of its deadlines, loomed but six hours away. A cool breeze picked up as the sun set, a reminder that the interlude between a Maine summer and a Maine winter was glorious but brief.

As I jogged up the stairs of the Arts and Sciences Building, I was steeped in the feeling that I was doing something dishonest, despite the fact that I had legitimate access to the building and to the department. My heart started to pound, and the tingling sensation that signaled an increased level of adrenaline started at my toes, and got stronger and more insistent as it spread up my back. My movements became jerky, and sweating hands caused me to fumble endlessly with the lock on the outer door.

Oh, get over it, Emma, I chided myself. You're not doing anything wrong. A little weird and obsessive perhaps, but nothing that would bruise even the most delicate of moral or legal sensibilities. In fact, you are the good guy here. Straighten up and fly right.

Yeah, but it's scary, a little voice whimpered back to me. *What if I find something? I don't want to find out that Tony's a murderer. Not Pauline's murderer. See? I'm even ready to let him off the hook for Tichnor. I don't care, I don't want to know. I don't want to be here.*

Well, you don't know any of that yet, I soothed myself. And I know for a fact that Dave Stannard will call up tomorrow and tell you that everything is fine and he figured it all out. So no problem. Let's just take a deep breath, go up the stairs, and have a look around, okay? Hey, we can even get some work to bring home if that will make you feel better—

Liar! You're lying, you know Stannard isn't going to call. And what would Brian say? You know Brian wouldn't like—

This is just the sort of careful, logical thing that Brian would want me to do. You're looking for excuses. You can shiver later, when you've got reason. Now knock it off and get going.

Still unconvinced of the sanity of my mission, I forced my hands steady, opened the door, and began the climb to the third floor. The elevators were shut down for the weekend and the hallway lights were on night mode and barely lit up the dim staircase. The familiarity of the surroundings contrasted oddly with the half-lit shadows. I quieted my footsteps unconsciously, not from fear of discovery, but to keep the echoes from intruding on the extraordinary silence of the corridors.

I unlocked my own office and quickly turned on the lights. As my eyes adjusted to the light, I felt reassured. There were shelves and shelves of my books, familiar friends and enemies; there was the little case full of some prized artifacts from sites I'd worked on; there was the couch that was perfect for reading and sleeping. I put down my bags and took a sip out of the open soda can that was the only thing left in my little fridge; it was flat, but the sweetness was a relief after the bout of nerves I had given myself downstairs. I convinced myself that most of my shaking had to do with low blood sugar.

Having established myself in my sanctuary, I was a little ashamed of my trepidation outside, but I couldn't quiet the nerves that still jangled. A thought occurred to me that I had never taken the chance at home to carefully examine the photocopy of the map that I found in the map file, the twin of the one that we found on Tichnor's bulletin board. Perhaps a little focused study would yield some clues and give me a moment to calm down.

I slid the paper out of my briefcase—such a little thing to get so upset about, I told myself. I flicked on the switch to the small light table I had, a relic of Oscar's with which I invoked Grandpa's keen eye and acute mind. When the light stopped flickering and steadied, so, it seemed, did my nerves. The very act of doing something so ordinary, of looking at a document for clues to its origin and meaning, brought calm: I knew what I was doing here. I picked up a small loupe and began to study.

First the paper. It was a modern photocopy, that much was clear enough, and although it had been pressed very flat, the photocopy was a little dog-eared and there were still minute creases in the paper. Okay, so it was new but had been kicking around for a little while. Not years, but more than a week or two, probably. There was no watermark, it was just cheap copy paper, but as I looked beyond the paper itself, to the image, I realized that there were clues there as well. For one thing, there were dark spots on the paper that looked like the small imperfections that one sees in old, well-made linen paper, bits of flax stem, maybe. So my initial evaluation of the handwriting seemed to be confirmed; this was probably an eighteenth-century document. I considered the possibility that the copier on which this was made had been dirty, but realized that I could see the faintest shadow of one of the drawn lines overlying one of the marks—the dark spot had been written over.

The map itself was not particularly revealing and I found nothing more than I had seen when I first looked at the copy at Tichnor's house with Sheriff Stannard. Although the labels were in French, it was clear that it showed Fort Archer and the ruins of Fort Providence along the Saugatuck River. Although I already had some indication that my fort, the seventeenth-century fort, had been destroyed, it was nice to know that it was in ruins by the latter part of the eighteenth century. But it didn't tell me anything more I didn't already know about either site. There were some small marks made along the center of the river, close to the squares that represented Fort Archer, but I assumed that these were indications of channels in the river.

Wait. I looked at those marks more carefully. They weren't channel marks, or at least two of them weren't. Two of them looked like little half moons. I wouldn't be able to find out what they meant until I discovered where the map came from.

The only thing left was the blurred library stamp that was in the lower right-hand corner. I moved the lens over that and was immediately gratified. I couldn't see too much more than I had before, but the letters that I could see were vastly clearer with the loupe. A series of letters resolved themselves for me, the end of a word,—*rid*. The word after that began with an E, not a B as I had believed before: *Esp*—.

An enormous weight tumbled off me as I realized I had not missed the map through some stupid error. It was now clear that the map had come from somewhere I never would have thought to look: Madrid, Spain. A tingling rushed over me, the same way it does when I find what I'm looking for in the library or a hunch has paid off: The game is afoot. For a moment I felt a twinge of guilt that I was getting such satisfaction from this hunt, but then realized that anything that got me closer to the reason for Pauline's death was worth celebrating.

Even as I congratulated myself on having figured that out, I began to wonder how an English document showing fortifications had ended up in Madrid. Spain and England had seldom, throughout history, enjoyed the best of international relationships. I shrugged. It was an accident of history, documents ended up in odd places for the oddest of reasons. It might possibly have been the result of espionage—but it was more likely that this had probably been intercepted en route back to England and had spent the next two hundred years languishing, unnoticed, in the archives in Madrid.

There was one more thing, however, that caught my attention. Like the copy at Tichnor's, the corner of the photocopy showed that at least one page had been folded over. There had been more than one page associated with this map. If I could find what had been on the pages that came before, I might have a much better idea of what was going on around here.

I flicked off the light box and slowly put the photocopy back in my briefcase.

So, I thought. How about a little trip to the storage room now?

I couldn't put it off any longer and there was really no rational reason to. I walked back into the semidark hall, paused before the storage room door, and took out my keys. The key fit smoothly into the padlock and twisted open readily, seemingly eager to reveal the innocence that lay within. I found the light switch easily and switched it on.

The room was just as it had been when I left on Friday afternoon. There was no reason to assume that it should not have been. But something made me open the drawer to the map file in which I'd found the out-of-place photocopy.

At first everything appeared as I remembered leaving it, but then I realized that something was different. Instead of the lower edges being neatly aligned, as I had done when I'd straightened them out, the maps had been shuffled around and were lying scattered across the bottom of the drawer.

Someone had been here since I'd left on Friday. Someone who was in there after Tony and I had left. My mind raced—who could it have been? No one else would have needed anything in this drawer, it was all New England, mostly Maine, and I was the only one doing fieldwork of any sort around here. No one but the faculty and administrator had keys to the room.

Tony had said we were the last ones still around the department. Tony had seen me with the maps. Tony had come back to see if I had seen the map from the Spanish archive.

Quietly, mechanically, I shut off the light and relocked the door. I leaned heavily against it, trying, with no success, to shut off the flood of thoughts that was cascading through my mind. For the life of me, I couldn't decide if the panic spreading over me was the reasonable result of solid intuition or hysteria, blowing perfectly ordinary things out of proportion. After a minute I was left with only the internal voice that had nagged me downstairs.

See? my doubtful self said. *It's every bit as bad as I warned you. You have to admit now, something's definitely up.*

Yes, it certainly looks that way.

Can I panic now?

Well, yes, perhaps a bit of controlled hysteria could be usefully channeled now. Nothing too extreme, mind; we need to keep our head straight.

What do you mean? We're out of it! Remember what Brian said? Just call Stannard and let him do his job!

Don't twist that conversation around. I will talk to Stannard, but he needs some proof. We're going to get it. We need more information.

Wait, where are we going? Where are we?

Well, it looks like we are standing in front of Tony's office door.

Oh, jeez, I moaned to myself. *Snooping around after hours is one thing, this is illegal!*

So's murder. But hey, don't you remember your Berkeleyian logic? Well, this is only illegal if you someone catches you doing it. So pipe down while I see if any of my keys fit his lock.

The question of trying to break into Tony Markham's office didn't trouble me as much as I thought it would. Certainly the panic welled, and I was nearly put off by the fear of getting caught. But the fact that someone, probably Tony, had come back to check the storage room changed everything. I was committed to this; it was no longer an idle intellectual game or an abstract concept or a fantasy concocted in a tired mind. It was real now, and since I believed he had set the rules, I would now play by them.

I ran quickly through my keys; if the size of the key ring was any indication of the power that one wielded, then it was perfectly clear that I was still departmental small fry. I was just contemplating whether I should try a credit card on the creaky old door with the resistant lock when a firm hand clamped on my shoulder.

Chapter 19

I SCREAMED LONG AND LOUD AND THREW MYSELF AROUND to face my captor. I spun too hard, too far, and smacked my liberated shoulder painfully into the doorjamb. I felt rather than saw my assailant stumble against the opposite wall with a muffled exclamation, and I kept on screaming, even when I recognized the owner of the hand as the department's administrator, Chuck Huxley. Still pumped, I resisted kicking him as he lay sprawled only by the narrowest of margins.

"Aaarrrgghhh!" Bang! I slammed into the door behind me with my fist. "Good sweet Jesus, Chuck! What the hell are you trying to do to me? You nearly gave me a coronary!" Startlement and anger temporarily transformed me into the inquisitor and not the almost-burglar.

"Whoa there, Dr. Fielding!" Chuck picked himself off the floor and made what he apparently thought would be the sort of palms-down, calming gestures one might make to quiet a mad dog. "Deep breath, you're shooting some rilly *spikin'* auras there! Baaad energy, the worst kind. Just slooow down, and get those chakras opened up again."

I successfully restrained myself from grabbing Chuck by his long, leather-bound ponytail and smacking his head repeatedly against the wall, chanting "I know" (Bang!) "you were raised in Orono!" (Bang! Bang!) "Do not dude me" (Bang!) "or speak to me" (Bang!) "in surfing syllables!" (Bang, bang, bang!). Some fantasies are better left unexplored.

Fear of whatever phenomenon was causing the frizzy, flyaway hairs to clump together, sticking to the back of his Grateful Dead T-shirt (why *was* that bear goose-stepping, anyway?), as well as the sudden realization that in about a minute, Chuck was going to ask me what *I* was doing there, were instrumental in this decision. Instead I smiled wanly and feigned compliance, while my mind raced to come up with an acceptable explanation for my presence here. Chuck smiled back benignly, taking deep, bobbing breaths along with me.

After a bit more of the pantomime, I took a final—cleansing! Chuck would have said—breath, and started again. "I'm so sorry!" I said. "I was just trying to figure out how I could get some student application files that Dr. Markham said I needed to look at for tomorrow, and I completely forgot. It being Friday and all."

"Total flakage," Chuck sympathized, clearly relating to the experience.

"And you know that sometimes he can be a bit demanding—" I attempted to include Chuck in my personal conspiracy.

He cut me off gently, with raised hands. "Ease off those negative vibes again. The good doctor can be a harsh for structure, but, y'know, that's his road. No need for you to follow." He waited until he felt I had rid myself of the bad thoughts, and then gestured elaborately for me to continue.

"Well, yes, of course." I tried again. "Anyway, I wanted to see if I could get them before tomorrow. And here we are." I shrugged and attempted to laugh it off.

"That's just sooo incredible," Chuck shook his head in

disbelief. It took me a cold sweaty half second to realize that he wasn't professing doubt of my story, but wondering at the multifarious ways of the universe. "Here you are, with a scene, and here I am, with the means. Now, see? I just happened to be walking by, saw the light in your office, and decided to check to make sure everything was okay up here: It's all to an end, never doubt it."

"Karmic." I probably was a trifle sarcastic as I tried to rub the bruise out of my shoulder, but Chuck wouldn't have noticed in any case.

He beamed at our apparent connection and rummaged around in the pocket of his long, baggy shorts to come up with a gargantuan bunch of keys. "Gnarly. I'm in a position of trust, and in a way to help you," he said, pleased with himself, me, and everything else. His key ring, I noticed, was a clanking chatelaine that was positively medieval in its size and aspect.

Again, trust was the word. It wasn't that Chuck was stupid, it was just that he radiated faith in the universe, in his fellow human beings, in the conviction that everything really *would* turn out all right. From the soles of his Birkenstocks to the planes of his granny glasses just over five feet higher, his honest, hobbit cheeks, his busy little fingers, and every other part of him seemed to emit alpha waves of credence. I wasn't certain I would have chosen that outlook for myself, but it was refreshing to see it embodied in Chuck.

It suddenly occurred to me that Chuck had been more concerned with my upset than with the fact that I had shoved him over. His kindness made me feel like a complete schmuck for my violent outburst, my antisocial whimsies, and, finally, my lies to him. But that didn't stop me from following him into Tony's office.

Chapter 20

IT MIGHT HAVE BEEN BECAUSE I WAS RIDICULOUSLY DIS-
tracted or it might have been because, once again, I had
gotten very little sleep, but for whatever reason, my lecture
Monday morning was augering in. A distinct bomb. The
lights were off and there was no note left for the milkman.

To be fair, I had had a lot to think about since my unpro-
fessional raid on Tony's office the night before. And it was an
awkward time in the semester, close enough to the beginning
so that the pressures of midterm did not yet inspire atten-
tiveness, and far enough along so that the initial novelty of
the class had worn off. I faced rank after rank of glazed-over
undergraduate faces and wondered briefly what I could do
to make them love it like I did, but AN103, Introduction to
Anthropology, lumbered into the tar pit and died unresist-
ing, in spite of my best efforts to drag the beast out and re-
suscitate it.

The weather was still warm, the kind of early fall day that
was immortalized on the cover of the Caldwell application
packets, that hinted at collegiality and football games and
gave no indication of the hellish winter that was coming.

The quad beckoned those trapped within the confines of Arts and Sciences 412, including me. Finally, to everyone's relief, the clock dragged its big hand down to the six and I wrapped it up.

"—and if you haven't signed up for a discussion section yet, I suggest you do so immediately. Ms. Meg Garrity, our TA here, eats live, mewling kittens, so don't give her a reason to remember you unfavorably at exam time. And, don't forget, Dr. Chapman will guest lecture Wednesday, so be sure to finish the chapter in the text on Sapir and Whorf by then." My voice increased proportionally in volume with the scuffling stampede of students leaving.

"God," I said, after the last one had filed out, "I thought I was going to have to resort to electroshock there."

Meg shrugged, her rows of earrings tinkling like wind chimes. "It's the nice weather," she said with unconvincing charity.

"Well, given my druthers, I wouldn't be stuck in here either. You're right though, things will perk up when we move out of all this preliminary stuff."

But in spite of my rotten lecture, I felt unaccountably cheery. It was more than the fact that I knew that I would wow the little darlings next time: I always did. I felt positively galvanized, for the first time since I left Penitence Point. Considering the rocket-sled to disaster my life, professional and emotional, had been on, I couldn't account for the feeling. Perhaps things weren't really so bad, after all; perhaps it was the freedom of having committed to my own particular brand of insanity.

I packed up my belongings, jamming notes and texts into my briefcase in no particular order. "You want to make some money this weekend?" I asked my teaching assistant. "I've got to go out to the site and run a few errands in the next week or so before the big closedown at the end of the month. We can also poke through some of the back dirt that Tichnor left to see if he missed anything."

Meg hesitated, and I interpreted her pause to indicate her concern about running into more trouble out at the site.

"I really don't think that there's anything to worry about," I said.

Meg looked up, apparently astonished that I had read her mind.

"Tichnor's gone, and even if he wasn't the only culprit, I doubt that we'll be bothered. You don't need to be uncomfortable about it, we had a bad time out there. Say the word and I'll talk to Rob or Neal . . ."

"Oh, it's nothing like that," Meg cut in brusquely. "I was just trying to figure out if I'll have the time. Shouldn't be any problem, so long as we're back by seven. When?"

"No problem. I'll pick you up, Saturday morning, not too early, well, yes, damn, I guess it had better be. About nine-thirty?"

Meg nodded.

I smiled. "Good, I'm glad you're coming."

I returned to my office to ponder the results of last night's adventure, and consider my next step. Obviously with Chuck in attendance, I couldn't toss Tony's office the way I wanted, but on the other hand, I probably didn't leave any trace of my search either, as I might have done if I'd rooted around to my heart's content. I'd made quite a show of checking the desk and other obvious surfaces for the nonexistent files, but came up with nothing.

Except for one small scrap of paper that was barely visible, stuck as it was under the leather corner of the blotter. I'd palmed it when Chuck paused to comment on the number of arcane-looking books that filled the room.

When I managed to get back to my office, having secured Chuck's promise to forget our meeting and actions ("*No problema*, babe, I mean, Dr. Fielding. Pinkie promise. Catch you later"), I was shocked to see that the number on the scrap was Pauline's telephone number.

But of course it wasn't. The area code was the same for the

whole state, but the exchange was one digit off, and then the three and the six were reversed. The paper was much worn, and the numbers were faded, suggesting some age. And despite my fear that the number would be meaningless, I was convinced that it was no coincidence that Markham had a number for a telephone in Bakersfield, the town immediately to the north of Penitence Point.

I had tried the number first thing this morning, but it was busy. I kept trying, and finally, just before my lecture started, I was startled to hear it ring on the other end. I didn't have long to wait; the answer came before the first ring had finished.

"Ny'ello, Bakersfield Dive Shop," a brusque male voice answered, booming across the line.

"Uh, hello. I was wondering what your hours were," I stammered, trying to make sense of this. A dive shop? Though what I had been expecting, I could not have said.

"Summer hours are still on, ten to seven, Monday through Saturday, noon to five on Sundays," the voice responded, automatically rattling off the information. Though the voice sounded like it was coming from the bottom of a rain barrel, and it had the alarmed quality of the bell on a buoy. Persistent, urgent, annoyed.

"What are the directions from Route 95?"

"Exit 22, east to Point Road, up through three lights, left on the last. Corner of Tucker and Main. You can't miss us." Rain Barrel was clearly impatient to get back to the salacious talk show that was on the television blaring next to the phone.

"One more question. What do you, er, specialize in?" I asked, trying to get a handle on what Tony could want at such a place.

"Sister, it's all in the name. We're a dive store. Scuba gear, lessons, and rentals. What are you looking for?" Rain Barrel demanded, impressive over the din of the television.

"I haven't the faintest idea. Thanks." The unbusinesslike demeanor of the voice's owner squelched any other ques-

tions I might have had, and I returned the receiver to its cra-
dle. It was just as well; I didn't know what to do with the information anyway. Further speculation was postponed by
the realization that I had a class to teach, and I'd scurried off.

Then after my less-than-inspiring lecture, I called the
Fordham County Sheriff's Department, and after assuring
the operator that my call was not an emergency, was forced
to wait through what seemed like an hour of muzak and the
recorded assurances that my call was important and would
be taken as soon as possible. It was really only ten minutes
later that a familiar voice replaced the tape.

"Fordham County Sheriff's Department. Deputy Sheehan speaking."

"Deputy Sheehan, it's Emma Fielding here," I said, wondering if he'd remember me. "The er, archaeologist, ah, out
at the Point. Any chance I could speak with Sheriff Stannard?"

"Oh, hi, Miss Fielding, how're you? I'm sorry, the sheriff is
awful busy right now. We had a lot of excitement last night,
and he's been tied up all day. Is it real urgent? Anything I can
help you with?"

"Nooo, it's not very urgent, but I do need to speak to him
in person pretty quick. It's to do with Pauline Westlake. What
happened last night? Can you can tell me?"

"Oh sure. We got a hot tip about a dealer who's been very
visible in the county lately, and by the time we got the court
order to search the property, we found a whole lot more than
we bargained for. Weapons, lots of cash, and about $200,000
worth of cocaine."

The awe in the deputy's voice indicated that it was a very
big deal, particularly for a small coastal community largely
surviving on the proceeds of a few months' tourist trade. "I
know that Fordham County has its share of problems, but I
never think of drugs as being one of them," I commented
idly.

"Well, now, most people wouldn't, but seems to get worse
all the time. But look," Deputy Sheehan said reluctantly, "I

can get the boss if you want. If it's really important." He sounded as if it would be a big favor, and not one that the sheriff would appreciate him doing for me.

I debated a moment and decided not to start using up goodwill now; my suspicions about Tony were still wonderfully unfounded as yet. "No, I'll tell you what. I've got to come out to the Point on Saturday. Will the sheriff be around then?"

"He sure will, it's his turn for a weekend shift," Denny said with audible relief. "That would be a big help, Miss Fielding. We really are very busy just now. I'll let him know that you called."

"Thanks a lot." I rang off. Depressed, I stared at the phone, willing inspiration to come to me. The telephone number clue was likely to be meaningless, or at very best, meaningless without further investigation. With all of the real evidence carefully cleaned away, I felt as though I was back where I began, save for my increasing certainty that Tony was involved.

The only thing I could do now was to stop by the shop on Saturday, maybe find out some more, but until then, there was nothing to do but keep my eyes and ears open.

An increasingly insistent gnawing in my stomach reminded me that my meager, hurried lunch had been several hours and a lot of cogitation ago. I was just spinning my wheels sitting here, something I could do just as easily while hunting down a righteous cup of Guatemalan and a corn muffin.

I collected some change from the bottom of my briefcase, picked the lint out of my hoard of coins, and made sure I locked the door behind me.

But even as I turned for the elevator, I was diverted from my errand. Alan Crabtree was waiting for me outside my office. "Got a minute, Professor Fielding?" he asked.

It was "Professor Fielding" now. It had been "Emma" in the field all summer.

"How about we walk and talk?" I asked, hoping the growling in my stomach wasn't too loud.

Alan shifted uncomfortably. "It's, ah, kinda personal."

I sighed. "Let's go in, then."

I shut the door behind us and sat behind my desk. Alan sat nervously in one of the chairs opposite. Watching him fidget, I was suddenly struck by a thought. "Actually, before you start, I've wanted to ask you. Did you use any of the maps in the storeroom this weekend?"

Alan shook his head, puzzled. "Why would I do that?"

"I was just curious."

"I haven't got a key to the room anyway—" he said, his eyes darting away from mine.

No, but your father does, I thought.

"—and if that's all, I've really got to take care of this."

I stretched and set my hands on my desk. So much for brainstorms. "Shoot. What's up?"

"I've got to drop your historic documents course," he blurted after a couple of seconds.

I looked up, surprised. Alan's face was paler and more pinched than usual. I recalled my earlier suspicions that he might be anorexic or have some other sort of eating disorder.

"My schedule is really crazed and I have to drop something. That's it, I guess," he finished hurriedly, not meeting my gaze.

"But Alan, maybe there's a way we can sort this out," I offered. "If you drop this course, you'll be down to part-time, which may affect your funding. If you take another course, you're no better off than sticking with me. What if we reschedule the project due dates—"

"Look, I'm just going to drop it, okay?" he said irritably. "If you could sign this . . . ?"

"Alan, something's obviously wrong," I insisted. "If you tell me what it is, maybe I can help you sort it out." As much as I disliked getting overly involved in my students' private lives, it was clear he needed some kind of friend right now.

For a second I thought he was going to tell me, but then he thrust the drop form in front of me.

"Are you going to sign it or not?" he asked, his voice rising like he was going to cry.

I looked at him and then hastily scribbled my signature at the bottom. "I think you're making a big mistake," I said.

"I gotta go." He shrugged miserably and left my office.

I sighed and reconciled myself to not saving him this time. I reminded myself that I couldn't save anyone on a growling tummy either, and started out for Joey's Sandwich Shop.

As I wandered past the main office, I paused to check my mailbox. A box, too large to fit into the pigeonholes where the rest of the mail was sorted, was sitting on the counter next to the outgoing mail bin. I paused to examine it, and was surprised to see that it was from Spain, an assortment of brightly colored stamps taking up most of the upper right-hand quarter of the package. The label was poorly manufactured, and the ink used to mark it had bled into the surrounding paper.

All of a sudden, there were lots of items with a Spanish connection around here. First the map, now this.

"Who's getting fancy packages from abroad?" I asked, but I was already glancing at the label.

Chuck, who was sitting at his desk, halfheartedly engaged in constructing the world's longest paper clip chain, answered halfheartedly.

"Oh, that one belongs to—"

He didn't get a chance to finish his statement, as the door to the office slammed open and Tony Markham stormed in. What's eating him? I wondered.

"It belongs to me. I'll take that, thanks," he said abruptly, all but snatching the paper-wrapped parcel away. He turned to leave, but a flash of inspiration came to me.

"I guess all sorts of neat things come from Spain," I remarked in a clear, neutral tone.

Chapter 21

H<small>E STOPPED DEAD IN HIS TRACKS AND SLOWLY TURNED</small> to face me. A shade, no more, briefly troubled his features, and if I hadn't been looking for it, I never would have noticed it. Dr. Tony Markham casually searched my face, his dark blue eyes revealing nothing but attentive interest.

"You're so right, Emma. A nice observation."

"Well, when the mood takes me. These little things seem to leap out at you sometimes. Occupational hazard, I guess." What the hell was I doing? What did I think was going to happen?

"Lot of them, in our field," Tony replied. "Occupational hazards."

His words were detached, almost unaccented, but they contained a world of meaning for me. I stood leaning against the counter and said nothing. The moment hung heavy between us.

"Always some trouble to get into in the field, from what I've seen," he finished. "Gotta watch out for yourself." Tony picked up his package and was gone.

I unbent out of my rigidly cavalier posture and stretched

painfully, feeling as though I had just gone too many rounds with the heavy bag, and it had started to hit back. Chuck had gone back to his fiddling, and had, for all intents and purposes, tuned out of the conversation. "Too many books, man, not enough life," I could hear him mumble.

He never did say what the package was.

Either I had spoken aloud or was sharing his thoughts because Chuck replied, "It's probably something to do with his trip last summer. The good doctor can be quite the cipher when he wants."

"Tony was *in* Spain?" I turned to him, wariness temporarily forgotten. "I thought he was in the Yucatán the whole time."

"Sure he was, but then he called up, all in a tizzy, and wanted me to send him a ticket the last week or so. Some library dude found an early church letter or something about his site, so he decided he needed to get there yesterday, if you know what I mean."

"When was this?" I asked, trying to contain myself.

"Near the end of June, beginning of July, in there."

My mind reeled, and I held on to the side of the counter to keep my balance.

Chuck flipped back through the calendar on the desk. "Bingo. Yep, here 'tis, Museo Arquéologico Nacional y Biblioteca, Madrid. Put a real boogie in his board, that did. He was there nearly three weeks, till the second week in July."

At which time he suddenly wanted to visit the site, I calculated excitedly. So far I still didn't know what it might mean, but it sure as hell felt like a solid clue. "Must have found something exciting."

"I don't know, I just pass the papers, make the magic happen," Chuck waggled his fingers, as if casting a spell. He looked depressed, not magical though. "I'm the cosmic enabler. Anything I can do you for, now, Dr. Fielding?"

It actually took me a minute to remember why I had been there in the first place. "No, I just came to check the mail. I'm going to hit Joey's. Can I bring you back anything?"

"Oooh, I could rilly go for a carrot bran muffin!" Chuck brightened considerably. "I've been feeling a little, y'know, tight around the middle. Too much cheese, not enough herbage." He patted his midsection meaningfully. "My great-gran used to tell me, 'Charlie,'—she called me Charlie, y'know—'you've got to mind your innards; you can live without a brain, but no one ever made it through life without a clear set of tubes.' "

I wondered if she meant that remark specifically for her grandson, or just as general advice. As he pulled out a clasp purse that had probably belonged to that venerable relative, I shook my head and indicated that he should put his money away.

"This one is on me, Chuck. I owe you at least that much."

I hurried across the campus, trying to sort things out for myself. Alan was clearly pressed to some sort of breaking point and it was going to be messy when he finally reached it. And I couldn't believe how desperate I was, clutching at slim possibilities like the fact that someone, possibly Tony, had messed with the map drawer while the department was abandoned for the weekend. But this new information, that Tony had been to Spain and that he had a number for a dive shop that was close to the site . . . alone they seemed ridiculous, meaningless, but taken together, they seemed, well, at least circumstantial, at best damned suspicious. The map of the fort only seemed to underscore the tentative links between these facts.

But the incongruity of considering such things, on as fine a day as this one, struck me as I opened the door to the campus sandwich shop. As the smell of warm spices and hot coffee assailed my nose, I wondered about the other customers in the shop. None of them knew that I had mortal thoughts on my mind, and there was nothing about me to suggest that I was occupied with things more dire than lecture notes or article deadlines.

Thinking this, I looked around with a little more interest at the others in the shop, and not surprisingly, no one noticed my scrutiny. Who really knew what was going on behind those blank faces, absentmindedly staring out the window or flipping idly through the selections on the miniature jukeboxes that were on each table? Suddenly I made eye contact with Rick Crabtree, who had joined the line in back of me, and he bolted from the shop.

This is ridiculous, I thought. He had been more than usually brusque with me since the news of the events at the site, but each time I had tried to draw him on it, I had been brushed off or ignored. He had tried to get me to take a leave of absence. And now that Alan had unexpectedly pulled out of my class, I knew that something was definitely up.

I didn't stop to think; I left the line and followed him, even though it was nearly my turn to order. The little bell on the door jangled cheerily as I slammed out to confront my second colleague of the morning.

"Rick, this has got to stop!" I shouted. I believe he only stopped scurrying away because of the heads that were swiveling around to stare at us.

"I don't have anythin' to say to you, Professor Fielding," Rick Crabtree squeezed out through clenched teeth. He still wouldn't look at me, staring determinedly down at the pavement, giving me an unobstructed view of his sweaty, balding head.

"That's pretty obvious, but I have a whole lot to say to you," I said. "You've made it perfectly clear that you believe I had something to do with what happened—"

"Not believe, I know, Professor Fielding, and I think it is an abomination, an abomination, that you are still allowed to continue on here at Caldwell. I brought my knowledge—"

"What knowledge?" I scoffed.

"—my knowledge to the chairm'n, and then to the dean, and in both cases, I was dismissed without the slightes' consideration." Now he looked straight at me, venom tinged with something else I couldn't read. "They may force me to work near you, but I won't have any more to do with a murd'ress than I have to. So all I can do is warn others about you."

"Warn others about *what*?"

"Mrs. Peirce called the department to ask what we were going to do about you—"

"Pauline's sister called here?" I was amazed at the woman's audacity.

"—and she told Dr. Kellerman about the undue influence that you exerted on her sister, based on the will she left. That's when he started to listen to me. He and I discussed it and then brought what we knew to the dean. But he wouldn't make you go on leave."

I held up one hand. "Wait a minute. You think that *I* was manipulating"—the very word was comic—*"Pauline?"* I couldn't help it, I shouldn't have, but I hooted at the notion. "You can't be serious—oh, never mind, it's too stupid to say out loud!"

"I know what I know," he said stubbornly.

"You know nothing." The fact that he believed that drivel made me angry again. "Listen, you wretched little man, the only influence going on in that relationship was Pauline's good one on me. It's too bad you didn't have someone to care about you as much, or you wouldn't be so busy looking for evil where it doesn't exist. And now you're poisoning your own son against me, for no good reason. You're pathetic."

I turned and headed back into Joey's, convinced that reason was lost on Rick, and saddened by the patent silliness of the man. He was a lost cause if ever there were such a thing.

Rick, however, wasn't done. He was trembling with self-righteousness and . . . excitement. That's what I couldn't recognize before. I guess he was rattled enough to practically shout across the quad.

"You can laugh all you want, but I know the truth, and I can prove it too! I will prove it! You just watch yourself, Emma Fielding!"

Chapter 22

CONTINUING IN MY RECENT TRADITION OF BEING forced into too close contact with my colleagues' personal lives, I found that Meg was in a deep blue funk Saturday morning. I sighed. Brian was back in California again and there was no point in my going home this weekend. We finally realized that we were going to have to live with the bicoastal commutes until the two companies were comfortably merged. It did nothing for my growing anxiety about what I thought I was uncovering, and it didn't help Brian, who was increasingly worried that I was chasing fata morgana. He'd said so on the phone when I called him Friday evening and told him about my encounters with Tony and Rick Crabtree.

"Just go to the sheriff," he begged, and I finally agreed. I was left with the feeling that he was more uneasy about me than he let on, because he didn't even tease me as he always did about obsessing my way onto the funny farm. The problem was, I knew something was going on. I just needed some kind of solid proof.

Meg acted as though she was about to speak on several occasions and then just sighed and continued to stare dismally out the window. So much for my attempts to overcaffeinate myself into semihuman behavior. That was okay; I had lots to think about myself.

But just as I had resigned myself to a silent trip, Meg suddenly asked "How did the two of you meet? I mean, you and your husband?"

I was taken aback: I usually make a point of not discussing my personal life with my students or anyone else outside of my little circle, for that matter. Her interest didn't seem idle, however; she seemed genuinely curious, even troubled about something. I decided that I wouldn't be in violation of any state secrets if I told her. And maybe it might get her to chill out too.

"Ages ago, we met. In graduate school at Coolidge, in Michigan." I sighed, staring straight ahead as I drove and remembered. "It was spring, right before exams. I was bringing a bunch of books to the library, you know the deal, bring back thirty, check out another forty for my next paper, right? Back then I had this bad habit of biting off more than I could chew, and I was a little overloaded. Backpack and two tripled grocery bags full of books. I think I had a couple under one arm as well. Anyway, I had way too many, but I was managing; I always do.

"Got from the dorm, across the quad, no problem. My shoulders were killing me and I could feel the handles starting to cut through my hands but that didn't matter as long as those plastic bags held together just long enough for me to get rid of those books. I was taking those quick little steps you have to take when you can't swing your arms, but I thought that I was going to make it before the bags broke. Just in sight of the library, I could feel the plastic starting to tear, and once that starts, you're pretty much doomed, so I kept scuttling along like a little crab down the path. I was just congratulating myself on making it up the stairs to the landing in front of the library's main doors when the bag ripped.

"It wouldn't have been so bad except for the fact that the bag emptied out all over the staircase, and all the books went tumbling and skidding down in a little waterfall. The stairs are pretty marble, but they were badly designed, short and narrow. In the wintertime, it's like trying to climb up an iced-over slide. So there I was, standing at the top of the steps, feeling like an idiot in plain view of the entire university, when two of the library guards started nudging each other, laughing at me.

"I couldn't believe it, I mean, why laugh at someone who's having trouble, right? I'm sure I looked pretty funny, but I sure as hell didn't feel the humor of it—my back was killing me and I wasn't certain how I could manage to carry everything now. I started to say something pretty caustic to them, when three of the books were suddenly stacked up on the landing in front of me. Someone was helping me.

"I looked and there was this incredibly sweet-looking guy smiling at me, like he had just heard the best joke in the world and couldn't wait to share it with everyone he saw. He winked at me, then ran down the steps to get the rest of them. That took about fifteen seconds, but I was absolutely blown away. I was mesmerized watching his back, the top of his head, the way his hair brushed his neck as he bent over, picking books up. I remember thinking that he seemed to be wearing a lot of layers, even for April in Michigan, but that only made me want to get to the bottom of them. Don't ask me why I was so blown away; the best answer I can still come up with is that it was fate.

"I couldn't wait for him to come back up the stairs and say something. I just sat at the top of the steps trying to keep everything else together, but I remember that it felt like about a year before he climbed back up to me. What would he say? I only knew that if it was the right thing, I was his forever.

" 'How about a hand with these?' he asked.

"I nodded, so tongue-tied that as he held the door open for me, I forgot to give the guards a really withering look. I knew that I only had about thirty seconds before we got to the circulation desk, and so if I was ever going to see him again, I had to say something quickly.

" 'Thanks. How about a cup of coffee?' I blurted out. Deathless, huh?

"He thought it over and then shook his head.

"I was absolutely crushed, and I had only ever laid eyes on him three minutes before. Then his next words changed my life.

" 'No, I don't think we could balance anything else on top of all the books. But we could get some after we drop these off.'

"I was totally smitten.

"I began unloading my poor backpack, and I noticed that he was looking at the titles of my books. I don't know why it made me so nervous, but I felt like I was being sized up. I *was* being sized up. I looked at them quickly to remember what I had been working on last night: This guy, whoever he was, had driven every other thought out of my mind. But they were pretty safe, pretty straightforward, mostly faunal analysis and books on sixteenth- and seventeenth-century social life.

"Only he didn't think so. He looked all confused and said, 'Okay, I give up? Historian? Biologist? What?'

"It was an easy question, but I could barely think straight. 'Uh, archaeologist. Paper on Elizabethan foodways.'

"Again he seemed to stop and think about it. 'Are you good at it?'

"No one had ever asked me that before. Mostly they tell me all the stories about dinosaurs they read in the paper. I nodded.

" 'Okay, let's get that coffee. I'm Brian Chang.'

" 'Emma Fielding. Thanks for your help back there.'

"I bought the coffee. Brian ate three biscotti. I found out that he was in the chemistry department and that he'd just finished his exams. I'd never met anyone so . . . happy. It's the only word. I don't mean in the ignorance-is-bliss way. Brian doesn't waste time worrying about things. It was a relief just to be with him—it made me feel as though life made some sense, even though I hadn't ever thought it didn't. I guess he was intrigued by the fact that I was curious about lots of things, not just my work. But at the same time, I liked that he reminded me that there were things going on outside of academia . . ."

"It worked from the very beginning. The thing that scares me is that if it weren't for a stupid, ripped grocery bag, I might never have met Brian. There are accidents in life that send you down paths you've never imagined." Like a stupid photocopied map.

I shook myself a little as I finished, startled to find how vividly the details came back to me. I looked at Meg. She wasn't smirking or anything, she just nodded.

"Guys are funny," she blurted. "One minute you think you are right there with them, the next . . ." She shook her head in frustration. "The next, you realize you're a million miles off the mark. I gotta tell you something," she said abruptly.

"Okay," I said warily. Everyone had to tell me something lately.

"Alan's been saying some pretty horrible things about you to people. Did you know?"

My hands tightened on the steering wheel. "No, I didn't. Are you sure you should tell me?"

Meg nodded. "Pretty sure."

A long silence followed, and then she began in a rush. "Okay, here's the deal. I've been kind of seeing Neal for a while now. A couple of dates so far. Things were going good. At least, I thought they were."

Meg looked out the passenger side window as the scenery gradually shifted from college town to more rural landscapes. She began talking again, quickly, as if to get it out before she thought better of the idea. I just kept quiet.

"He cooked dinner for me last night, chili, real hot, you know, but that's okay. I like spicy food. We were talking and talking, and he was telling me about his huge family and I was telling him all about being an army brat, all the weird things you grow up with, like a change of scenery every six months, learning how to shoot—"

"You shoot *guns*?" I asked incredulously.

"Firearms, yeah," she said, surprised at my surprise. "That's what he, Neal, said too. It's fine as long as you treat them with respect." She shook her head in disbelief. "Man, cross the Mississippi and people get silly on you. Anyway, we were getting along, having a great time. And this is good, okay, because I'm used to guys who are a little more gung ho or have something to prove because their parents are in the army or whatever, so this is just fine with me and I'm deciding that I'm going to give the kid a chance. And we eventually got around to, you know, kissing. Whatever. But that's when the trouble started.

"I guess Alan walked in on us, I don't know, neither of us heard right away. And when we did look up, he had this look on his face like someone kicked him."

I nodded, remembering what I'd seen on the site. Alan had a crush on Meg the size of all outdoors.

"It wasn't like we were doing it or anything, not even close," she said hurriedly. "I just didn't realize that Alan, well, that he kinda was getting ready to ask me out or something, and there I was, trading spit with his roommate. But I figured, cool, now he knows, no harm done, asked him how dinner was—you know he goes home to dinner with his folks every Friday?—and he said dinner was god-awful, but that he quit your class and if I knew what was good for me, I'd stay away from you too."

She looked over to see how I was taking this so far. I just stared out the windshield and nodded that I'd heard, keeping my face blank. I thought that he was having problems, but knew nothing about this. What was he telling people?

Meg continued. "So I tell him he's mental, of course. And then *he* says that his dad's been finding out that you were talking Pauline into changing her will and maybe you knew something about that guy Tichnor with the gun and maybe you and he were planning to kill her and it was just a matter of time before everyone found out about it and he didn't want me getting dragged down if he could help it. So I told him he was out of his mind and he should get his head out of his ass and deal with his parental issues in therapy and not take them out on you, or words to that effect. I guess I was getting pretty pissed off. I've been told I have a temper. Well, Alan announced that he was sick of us all laughing at him— which by the way, has been sort of a running refrain for him and is just number one pure horseshit—and then he stormed out after that." She began to run the zipper on her jacket up and down along its track, creating a little counter-point to her narrative.

"And then Neal, *Neal* gets all quiet and serious and every-thing and says why did I have to go and get Alan riled, when he just managed to get him calmed down for the first time this semester and didn't I ever hear of agreeing to disagree and I didn't have to live with Alan anyway, and I've just un-done about three months' worth of compromise? And I said, haven't you ever heard of standing up for what you think is right or standing up for your friends, even, and where was his spine, or words to that effect, and then I sorta decided to leave before I said worse."

She took a deep breath, and I found that I needed one too, having held mine through her whole long monologue. But Meg spoke again first.

"I mean, I suppose you didn't need to know all of that, but I think it kind of shows just how crazy people are start-ing to get, and you really ought to know that much," she ended suddenly and left us both feeling tremendously un-comfortable.

I tried to figure out where I should begin. "For one thing, to start with, if you have any doubts about me in this, you are under no obligation to defend me, or even be near me, out of some sense of loyalty."

"What other sense is there?" she demanded. "Besides, I know you had nothing to do with any of this."

No, you don't kiddo, I thought. We've known each other

less than three months. Out loud I said, "Well, thanks. And Alan, Alan's got a lot going on right now, so it's not real important to me whether he believes me, that's the least of his problems—"

"But he's wrong—" she protested.

"He's allowed to be wrong," I said, and could practically hear Brian snickering, asking me why I didn't always take my own good advice. Other people were allowed to be wrong, to ask for help, he'd say to me, so why aren't you?

"And I'm not running for a popularity contest or anything, I don't need everyone to like me." Again I heard Brian's imaginary hoots.

"Meg," I said slowly. "Is that why you hesitated about coming out here today? Alan's suspicions?" I was careful not to say Rick's suspicions.

"Hesitated?"

"Back when I asked you, after class, you didn't seem too keen at first."

Her face cleared. "No, nothing like that." Then Meg looked guilty and stammered a bit. "No, I just wasn't certain how you'd be, being on the site and all, after, you know . . ." She turned to me and said, with more than a trace of defiance. "So now you know."

I bit my lip and looked out the window, trying not to smile. Meg was funny; not the least problem in the world with revealing the details of her private life, but start dipping into someone else's emotions, and she turned as shy as a rabbit.

"I'll be fine. Here we are," was all I said, as we pulled down the driveway.

"Do you, you know, want a moment alone first?" she asked a little too offhandedly. "Before we get started?"

I wouldn't have thought that she would have dared to suggest such a thing, but she looked a little edgy herself, and I thought that I'd give her a moment to collect herself. She was pretty ruthless with herself. "Thanks. I'll just be a minute."

It was harder than I thought to go over to the ruined part

of the foundation and look around. "I'm still looking, Pauline. I don't know what's going on, but I'll find out."

A little breeze moved the pines that stood behind where the house had been, but nothing more. I noticed that the roses had been trampled by the emergency vehicles, but one was still hanging on, blooms persisting on broken stems. I pulled a piece of string out of my pocket and tried to prop up the stalk against a stake, and a thorn raked the back of my hand for all my good intentions. I returned, feeling calm, and got Meg.

The site, as it turned out, had been very thoroughly picked over; there was virtually nothing for us to salvage from the vandalized units, and we spent most of the morning mapping and making notes where we could about the ruined contexts, and making lists of tasks for backfilling day, when all of our hard work would be carefully buried until the next season. We finished shortly after lunch, when I remembered the dive shop and asked Meg if she could spare the time for a side trip before we headed back.

"I've got nothing waiting for me now," Meg said. That sounded suggestive, but I didn't pry further. Presumably getting ready for the date she'd had was no longer an issue.

"I won't take long," I promised, "and you're on the clock until we get back." I figured nosing around the dive shop wouldn't give me anything, and the sheriff would probably be too busy to see me again. "I'm thirsty, how about you?"

We pulled up outside a convenience store for a couple of Cokes, when an impulse seized me. Noticing that we were right across the street from one of the longer-lived antiques stores on the road to the Point, I decided to find out if Tichnor had been stupid enough to try selling the materials recovered through his looting activities, maybe even something of Pauline's, if he'd been the one in her house.

The store was set up by a pro; there were a few good pieces placed strategically in the window and in the case by the cash register. The rest of the shop was full of stuff that would have been better suited to the last garage sale of the summer, ratty but not priced to move. All carefully designed to lure the unsuspecting, unschooled vacation antiquer into thinking that there would be treasures hidden behind that pile of tiled ashtrays.

I glanced around as I navigated the jumble of rusting fire irons and umbrella stands, wondering what the owner would be like. He was obviously skillful in business because the place had survived a dozen other similar shops over the past ten years; he possibly had a love for the past or at least a love for the idealized image of the past that could be constructed from the nostalgic geegaws that lined the shelves.

The owner appeared to be the woman who walked with her hand outstretched from behind the beaded curtain that separated the shop front from a back room. Stunned, I watched as she marched up and removed the can of soda from my hand, placing it carefully in the wastebasket next to the till.

"I'm afraid that soda is not allowed in the store. We can't have you spilling on any of our items." The owner's voice snapped out briskly, a voice that plainly traced its lineage across generations of schoolmarms who had no other source of pleasure but the authority they wielded over other people.

"Frannie Maggers. Are you looking for something special, or just browsing today?" Her querulous voice suggested a suspicion that I had already pocketed the best of the shop's wares.

"I suppose I am just looking around. I'm really trying to get a feel for the folks at Penitence Point . . ." I trailed off, not quite sure what form my tale should take.

Mrs. Maggers supplied the rest of my story for me. "Oh, a writer. We get a lot of them," She made it sound as though that corner of Maine had to be sprayed for the infestation of writers every year. "Well, we're good people here, most of us, that is. Not that you could tell from this summer, but there you are. Perhaps you might find a little piece of the past here to inspire you with your writing. Take this for example."

She held up a small brass object. "I don't like to part with any of Grandfather's belongings, but times being what they are, well, you can't eat sentiment. This was his grandfather's pipe tamper, very rare. It dates back to the early nineteenth century. When gentlemen smoked pipes—"

"Oh, I know what a tamper is—" I nodded, confident that this is where I could connect with her. We had artifacts in common.

Frannie continued on, like a steamroller barreling through a Monet landscape. "They needed to tamp down the tobacco before lighting. It was a present from his pretty young bride, who died in childbirth, very sad, and he was never the same person again. I'd be willing to sell it to you for fifty dollars. Cash."

I looked at the object, immediately deciding that great-great grandfather probably wouldn't have tamped anything with a lamp finial from about 1940, and his descendant knew it full well. I said nothing about this, figuring that some folks would be happy to pay for the object just for the story that went along with it. She continued on through the store.

I decided that the other woman's skinniness was not from financial hardship. Where anyone else would have been plump from the pickings of unwary tourists that she was obviously raking in, Fran was all knobby bones and parsimony. And by the end of Fran's tour through the rest of the shop, I had counted ten great-grandmothers, five grandfathers, and far more than the usual complement of great-aunts and uncles. High mortality, bigamy, or divorce must have run rampant in her pedigree for such a collection of relatives to have truly existed.

Fran, sensing that none of her engaging and entirely ficti-tious anecdotes was likely to bring her a sale, made as if to take up her position on a stool behind the counter, but I stopped her, mindful that Meg was waiting outside.

"I've heard that you occasionally buy antiques too . . . ?" I left the question hanging, and let Fran's fancy fill in the gap.

"That's true, but they have to be very special pieces. My customers have learned to expect nothing but the very best from me." She busied herself turning china teacups so that the cracks were less visible.

"Have you ever purchased any eighteenth-century things, maybe military artifacts, from a fellow named Tichnor? I'm wondering—"

"Get out! Get out of here right now!" Gone was the smooth patter and the confident authoritarian; the woman's voice was sleeted over with fear. "I don't want anything to do with him, or any of his friends neither. Get going, before I call the sheriff!" Mrs. Maggers practically dragged me to the doorway, her voice rising with every step.

"I'm no friend of his!" I insisted, gently trying to detach her hand from my elbow. "And he's not in a position to hurt anyone—he was killed a couple of months ago."

"Oh, I know all about that, and good riddance I say! It's not him I'm worried about, though God knows, if there was ever anyone wicked enough to come back from the grave, it was him. I know he's got friends and I don't want any part of them neither. I didn't want his bits of rocks and rubbish—"

Gotcha!

"—but he kept coming back and bothering me about it. And the last time he got riled up, stomping around, and damned near smashed the place, ranting about ancient treasures—" She stopped shy of the door, torn between the urge to get rid of any connection with Tichnor and the burning curiosity to know why I was asking about him.

"What happened the last time? I need to know because—" Here I stopped. I certainly didn't want to mention my suspicions about Tony. On the other hand, I needed to give something to keep this greedy woman interested. "Because I'm trying to get all the details I can for the research I'm doing about all the excitement here this summer." Not entirely untrue, I figured.

"Oh." Again Fran was caught between her desire to be shed of anything to do with Tichnor and her intense desire to get a little free publicity. "I told you before, he kept pestering me about his broken bits of things. No collectors around here for that sort of thing, most people are more interested in more refined stuff, genuine heirlooms. The last time he came in here, he was drunk as a skunk, you could smell it on him a mile away. Kept bothering me to buy some of his stuff. He got madder and madder, because this time he had gone out of his way, he'd said, to get some things that I would like."

"When was this?" I asked, wondering if it was part of the collection of objects stolen from Pauline's house. "Do you remember what he had?" I tried to keep the excitement out of my voice.

"Oh, ages ago, last June?"

June was too early for it to have come from my site or Pauline's house.

Frannie continued. "It wasn't much he had, that's for sure. A couple of brass buttons, a china cup or bowl, not Indian this time, and some flintlock parts. He said it was from his attic, but they were so dirty and nasty that I asked him if they hadn't really come from a garbage heap."

Eighteenth-century stuff, it sounded like. My own thoughts turned immediately to Tichnor's metal detector and his collection of things stolen from Fort Archer.

"That didn't sit too well with him, and he asked one more time, would I buy them or not? And I answered, for the last time, no!" she sputtered. "He started swearing and stomping around, and I thought he was going to leave at last, but he just stuck his head out the door and yelled to his friend to come in, have a word with me."

My ears pricked up. "Did his friend come in?"

"No-ooo," Frannie let go of my arm as she tried to remember. "They were arguing."

"Did you see his friend? Did you recognize him? Or her? Was it a man or a woman?" I asked excitedly.

"I didn't see anyone. I think it was a man. Now wait a minute, let me think." Mrs. Maggers pressed her finger to her mouth in a monumental display of self-important cogitation. "His name, I don't remember what Tichnor called him, exactly, but it was something *common*. Nick? Donnie? No name any polite mother would give her child. Mine are all named properly for their grandparents: Margaret, Richard, Lillian, and Gustav."

I reckoned that if any of the little Maggers were anything like their dam, their names would be rendered "Mad Maggie," "Needle Dick," and "Frigid Lily." God only knows what unkindly moniker would have befallen little Gustav.

"Could the name have been Tony? Maybe Augie?" I knew from all of my ethnographic training that the worst thing in the world I could do was give an informant a leading question, but this wasn't a textbook exercise.

Mrs. Maggers considered. "Might have been. Possible, but I don't say for certain. Anyway, I didn't wait to find out what the word might be. I shoved him out the door, hard, and then locked it." She nodded once: Good riddance to bad rubbish.

I looked at the sharp-dealing shopkeeper with a new respect. It took guts to do something like that. "What happened then?"

"I pulled down the shade and listened to make sure that he wasn't going to stick around. He stood out there, hooting and hollering for a while, banging on the door. I called the sheriff's office, and he sent one of his little Cub Scouts around, but Tichnor had left long before that."

She looked me up and down appraisingly. "Are you going to write a book about all the troubles that've been up here? Something for a magazine? Lots of excitement last summer," she pointed out hopefully.

I dumped every ounce of tedium I could into my lie. "Well, it's really more of a monograph, for a sociological journal, you might have heard of it, *Annual Review of Criminal Psychological Pathology*? It's really quite interesting, see,

I've been focusing on the presumed correlation between murder victims and their own criminal activities, I mean, the specific *types* of illicit behavior, and I've found the most fascinating data on—"

"Oh." Clearly it was nothing any of her friends were going to be reading under the dryers down at Ruby's Hair Fair. Fran lost interest in a hurry.

"Thanks very much for all of your help." I almost felt bad for disappointing her. "If it gets published, I'll be sure to mention you." Which was not entirely a lie.

"You're welcome," the prim reply came. "Perhaps you'll stop by another time, when you're ready to buy something nice."

I got out before I was subjected to any more familial fairy stories. Meg was sitting on the bumper of the truck, throwing pebbles aimlessly down the rain grate. Distant plopping noises could be heard after the ping off the grate itself, and the whole endeavor smacked of morose contemplation of things better left undisturbed.

"Ready to go?"

"Well, I did have this sizable stockpile of pebbles that needed throwing, but I s'pose I can tear myself away." I was surprised to hear the glum cast to Meg's sarcasm.

"Is there anything you want to talk about, Meg?" I asked. "You seem a little depressed today. Bummed out, not to put to fine a point on it."

"Oh no. It's just, you know, the personal stuff I mentioned, nothing you can do anything about." She dismissed my offer out of hand. A little brusquely, I thought.

"I didn't think that I was going to solve anything, just talk." I was feeling pretty churlish myself.

Meg stood up, stretched, and with a lightning movement, kicked the rest of the pebbles down the drain. A wet splash was followed by a fetid smell rising up from the sewer. I picked up her empty Coke can and followed her back into the truck.

After a while Meg spoke. "It's only that sometimes people, guys, can be really irrational and it confuses the hell out of me. They like something about you, then when you're being yourself, they get pissed off with you for it."

I thought about Brian, who adored my tenacity in everything but the present situation. I thought about Sheriff Stannard, who liked the way I looked at things, but didn't want me to look at them on my own. "The only thing you can do is keep bringing it up, get to the bottom of things. Negotiate, compromise, look for the answer." I shrugged; I knew from my own experience that it wasn't as easy as that.

"And if that doesn't work? What if there are no answers?"

That one kept me occupied until we arrived in Bakersfield.

Chapter 23

THE VOICE ON THE TELEPHONE WAS RIGHT, THERE WAS no way that I could have missed the dive shop. It was a sprawling shingled house, the lower floor of which had been converted into a storefront. A giant plaster sperm whale with a sailor's hat winked from the roof of the front porch. It was old and weathered, half of its tail missing. Seagulls had obviously found it a compelling target for years, and the once-bright blue body was faded with white smears all over it, adding a perverse sense of realism to the thing. A yellow electric sandwich board hummed in the late afternoon light, boasting the words "Bakersfield Dive Shop/How Long Can You Go Down?/Winter Classes Start Nov. 1."

I pulled in and was out of the truck saying, "Just wait here, I won't be a minute."

"But—" Meg protested. I ignored her, not wanting to bring up Tony with her.

The inside of the place was as random as the outside, with the same sense of iconoclastic decor. The walls, like the exterior, looked like they had been decorated with the castoffs of a thousand defunct clam shanties, the ornaments running largely toward fishnets, buoys, and lobster traps. A few other oddments added to the sense of clutter, including a bizarre example of taxidermy in the shape of a stuffed and mounted basset hound. This occupied the place of honor behind the counter with the television that had blared talk-show inanities into the phone the day that I had first tried the number.

The stock, on the other hand, was in good order. I didn't know anything about diving other than recognizing some stuff that Brian used for snorkeling. I could tell, however, that the wet and dry suits, hanging like scarecrows, were expensive, and the smaller accouterments were well organized in their individual bins. The whole place smelled of chlorine, rubber, old carpet, and the unpainted wood of the walls.

The television was on again, so I knew for sure that this was the right place: It was tuned to a professional wrestling match. The man behind the counter was seated precariously on a stool, and could have easily passed for one of the contestants in the bout being shown. He was of enormous girth, the top of the stool being lost under him, and had a head of hair that looked as though it had been combed last in 1970, and then with an imprecise gardening tool.

A group of pictures formed a shrine behind the stuffed dog, and with a little squinting, I could just make out a common figure in all of them, a much reduced version of the man in front of me. The pictures were mostly on boats and beaches, a few murky greenish ones underwater, but all clearly from the premier diving spots in the world: Hawaii, Australia, the Keys, the Caribbean, and other places that I didn't recognize. Whoever the guy was, he was certainly a long way away from his previous life.

"Nice pictures, ain't they?" I was caught staring too long for casual interest. The voice that rumbled out of his chest was no less impressive than it had been over the phone, gravelly thunder trapped in a cavern. "I been a lot of places, seen a lotta things. Now I just make sure that other folks get to see them too, and don't get mangled doing it."

"You don't dive anymore." I made it more of an invitation than a question.

"Nope, can't do it. For one thing, there ain't enough neoprene on the planet." This was followed by a tumultuous guffaw. "For 'nother, doctors found a spot on my lungs, and between that and losing half my foot to a shark, I kinda lost interest. Kind of a long shot, that shark attack, and I figure, if you gotta defy the odds some way, I myself would have picked the lottery, but what are you gonna do?"

A little wistfulness tinged his voice, but his overall tone was one of making the best out of life. "Name's Johnny. What can I do for ya, Red?" He reluctantly turned the wrestlers down.

I ignored his use of the repellent nickname. "Well, it's sort of a surprise. A friend of mine dives, and he shops here, and I wanted to get something for his birthday. Of course, I don't know anything about diving, but I figured you might be able to help me out there." I was disconcerted by the cajoling feminine helplessness my voice had taken on. Not my usual style at all, but it seemed to be working.

"That might take a little doing," Johnny said doubtfully. "What's his name, darlin'? Does he dive around here? If he's smart, he'll be heading about two thousand miles south aways, otherwise his balls might not come down again till next Easter!" He bellowed at his own sally, making me wonder if there were a volume button or an amplifier I could turn off.

"His name is Tony—it might be under Anthony— Markham. I know he's come in at least once."

But Johnny's eyes lit up. "I know him all right—you the one called the other day, right?"

I nodded.

"Sure, he's been in here a bunch of times, and always picks out the good stuff too," he said. "Might be kinda difficult finding something he doesn't have, he's a guy who believes in treating himself well. You a close friend of his?" The inquiry suggested that his mind was more than half made up on the subject of my precise relation to Tony.

"Oh, you know," I said coyly offhand. "An old friend of the family's, known him forever."

"Then you got some idea of where he's likely to be doing most of his diving? Same places?"

I was at a loss, having no idea where the same places were, and began to feel, well, like a fish out of water. "Well, I know he's been doing a bit around here lately, but I don't know what his plans for the winter are, and I thought—"

"We thought that we could find him something that he could use anywhere, in case he decides to go back to Kauai this winter too," a voice piped up, saving me from . . . floundering.

I whirled around and nearly crashed into Meg, who apparently had come into the shop almost directly on my heels and had discreetly moved behind one of the displays. She had heard everything, and for some reason was playing along with me. I glared at her, but there was nothing I could do to chase her away without blowing things with Johnny.

"Has he already picked up a watch?" she asked.

"Yeah, sure, first thing," he replied. "And a timer. He already has all the basics: mask, fins, BCD, tank. But he's been by for a couple of bags, an Oakley dry suit, and a *fine* selection of knives." Johnny snickered. "You know, I'm about half convinced that the biggest thing that gets people into diving is that they can walk around with the knife strapped to their leg. A lot of them get off on the big, bad explorer image," he explained.

"Well, that's Uncle Tony to a T," Meg chimed in, giggling. "Computer? How about a pony tank?"

"Natch."

"What about a good map? Has he bought any of those waterproof ones from you?" I asked all of a sudden, noticing a basket on the counter. I was starting to feel left out; I couldn't, er, *fathom* what a pony tank did, I couldn't tell from BCDs, but maps I understood.

"Hmmm. I think he's all set for them too. Let me check." Johnny rifled through a cluttered ledger, looking back several months. "Nope, he's covered there too. Got the ones of the river up to Noggintok, and the coast outside the river mouth."

"So he's got one of Penitence Point, has he?" I asked, thinking quickly.

"Yep—"

Bingo, I thought. It all comes back to the river.

"—he asked for that one the last time he was in, back in July."

"C'mon, Emma, he spoils himself too much, I told you already. He's got all the good stuff that we could have afforded. I still say we should go for the book we saw." Meg smiled wickedly, passing the hot potato to me.

For once I didn't miss a beat.

"You mean the one of Victorian nude photographs?" I asked sweetly. I turned to Johnny. "He's a photography buff too."

Meg snorted with laughter, then started coughing. Got her.

"You're right, Meg. We'll have better luck with that. But Johnny." I turned back to him a moment, putting my hand on his forearm in a conspiratorial gesture.

For a moment I was afraid we were going to see how fast Johnny could move when he sensed danger, but I shouldn't have worried: He was riveted.

"If you could keep our little shopping trip here a secret, just in case we do figure something out? Or better yet," I said, pulling out a scrap of paper, "if you could just give me a call if he comes back. His birthday's in a month, so anytime before then . . . ?" I thought about batting my eyes, but didn't think I could pull it off convincingly.

Fire-engine red crept up through Johnny's face, and he agreed with alacrity. "Yeah, sure, I can always use the business. There's always a gift certificate or coupons for tank fills, if nothing else comes up. Nice, uh, meeting you ladies." He pulled away reluctantly and turned up his wrestling match.

Meg had been picking through the baskets on the

counter, and she placed on the counter a key chain shaped like the whale on the roof. She glanced up at the stuffed dog. "Hang on a sec, Em. Hey, Johnny, I gotta ask—" Meg began as she pulled out her wallet.

"His name's Jake and he was the best damned dog anyone ever had. Stung by a jellyfish. See ya later." He slammed the cash register drawer shut, overcome either with emotion or with the engrossing nature of the bout, and we found ourselves dismissed.

Outside, I found myself faced with another problem. "Thanks for helping out in there."

"You gonna tell me what you were up to?" Meg asked, not able to conceal her curiosity.

I stalled. "Where'd you learn to dive? I wouldn't have thought there was much opportunity in Denver."

"I learned a lot of things moving around with Dad, and once we ended up in Hawaii for a year. I make the most of my opportunities. So," she said, not deterred by the sidetrack, "what's up with 'Uncle Tony'?"

I thought about it; she'd already heard an awful lot. "Get in. Look, I don't know what to tell you. I've got an idea that Tony Markham's somehow tied in with everything that went on this summer. Wait," I implored, cutting off Meg's exclamation as I pulled out. "I don't know how, I don't know why, but he's got an interest in Penitence Point that is beyond absorption in my own sterling work. I'm just trying to find out what that interest is."

"Do you think he killed Pauline?" she asked, stunned.

"I think it's possible that he knows something about it. You cannot, I repeat, cannot, tell any of this to anyone, under any circumstances. Do you understand?" I pinned her down with a glance; there could be no mistaking my intent. "I could get into a whole lot of trouble if this got out. I don't *know* anything. I'm only chasing down what appears to be a bunch of red herrings because I can't think of anything more useful to do in looking for Pauline's killer." And when it came right down to it, I liked the guy. I had a hard time admitting that.

She just sat there, staring out the windshield, deep in thought.

"Meg, promise me you will *not* say *anything*. I'm dead serious about this, my professional life depends on you," I said. "I'm already pretty messed up about this, I don't need to lose my job too."

"I promise," she said finally. "And I keep my promises. But shouldn't the sheriff's department be looking into this?"

"They are, and they're not crazy about my interest in it either, so there's another reason for you to keep close counsel. One more detour to see them, and then we can head out. You still game?"

"Sure!"

"Okay, you might as well come in this time, now that you know what I'm about. Just keep it buttoned."

"I already said I would, didn't I?" Meg said irritably.

"Yeah, I know, I'm sorry. This is still a bit of a strain. I'm sorry, Meg." I felt a couple of centuries old and couldn't seem to straighten up my back.

"I shouldn't have snapped at you."

"Never mind."

A few minutes later I pulled up to the red sandstone monstrosity that was the sheriff's office. The shadows were getting longer, and there was definitely a touch of fall in the air, and I imagined that schoolkids would be moving past this place on Halloween with a quicker step. "Time to start wearing long johns soon," I said, pulling up the collar of my coat.

Meg burst out laughing unexpectedly. I looked at her quizzically.

"I was just trying to imagine our friend in the shop back there in his woolies," she announced.

I shuddered. "Jesus. With that damned stuffed dog, he'd look like a demonic tooth fairy."

We saw Sheriff Stannard almost immediately. He obviously was not in the mood for company, and the way that he was snapping out orders to scurrying deputies and administrators struck me as uncharacteristically brusque. The way some of his brown hair stood up would have been comical, save for the fact that the frustration that had caused him to make it so was still present on his face. The sheriff walked blindly past me, having dispatched the last of his trailing entourage, and stared dismally at the coffeemaker. I could smell burned coffee from where I stood, and watched as he poured himself what was probably his tenth cup of the day. And as much as I longed for a cup now, there was no way I'd drink that garbage.

"Now how did I end up here again, I wonder?" he asked Mr. Coffee, sucking down a slug of the syrup. Then he saw I was there and slumped down where he stood, clearly not any less busy than he had been when I had called earlier in the week. "What can I do for you, Dr. Fielding?"

"I'll just take two minutes. I just want to ask you a couple of questions."

It was not in his nature to deny a request when he could honor it. "Okay, but I got to tell you, it's a zoo here. When the coffee's gone, so am I. What's up?" He sat down on one of the blue plastic-cushioned waiting room chairs, looking like he was glad to have a reason to sit.

I took a deep breath. "I wanted to know if you had found out anything more about Pauline Westlake's killer."

"I'm afraid I don't have any more leads on that." He exhaled deeply. "It's a long way from being closed, though."

"You seem to be busy with the drug bust I've been reading about."

Stannard sighed with resignation. "It's been breakfast, lunch, and dinner for the past two weeks—lots to mop up yet. Why do you ask?"

"I was just wondering how the stuff got here. Do people fly it in, or what?"

"Naw, too risky," he explained. "Usually they get a mule to drive it up from New York, or Providence sometimes, or even all the way from Florida. If they don't get bagged for speed-ing, there's no way we can tell if they're smuggling anything at all."

Alarm bells were going off in my head and I knew I was on the right track. "What about boats? There's an awful lot of inlets, coves on the river—"

Dave Stannard broke in. "Too expensive, too risky. The Coast Guard is all over the place out there and that's their main business these days. What is your interest in this?" He looked at me sharply.

"I was just wondering about a possible connection." Quickly as I could, I recounted my findings. The sheriff ap-peared intrigued by the map I'd found in the storage closet and its subsequent reshuffling, then a little worried when I told him about my odd verbal joust with Tony. And he took out his notebook when I described what I learned from Frannie Maggers. He only looked amused when I told him about Johnny at the dive shop. I carefully edited out the part about the midnight raid on Tony's office and my little white lies to the area merchants. Meg's jaw dropped as I mentioned the map of the site that appeared at Tichnor's house.

"You know, maybe Tony Markham found the map and got the idea for the smuggling," I said. "And what about that guy I found dead on the beach back in July? He might have seen what was going on and they killed him!" I said excitedly. "Or maybe, maybe he was in on it too!"

He closed his notebook. "What guy? You don't mean Augie Brooks?" Stanndard asked, working hard to mask his frustration with me. "He's been drinking and getting into trouble for dogs' years. It was only a matter of time before he got himself into a real fix—"

"But you have to admit that it makes sense, right?" I de-manded. "All the pieces fit together!"

Stannard shook his head. "That is all completely circum-stantial. Why would Professor Markham be connected with anything that happened last summer, anyway? Now, that stuff that Frannie Maggers said, that might be a big help in learning more about Grahame Tichnor's actions. That could be a real clue. And maybe I could see Augie following him there, that could work. But there's nothing in the world I can do with the rest of that information, 'cept to warn you about jumping to conclusions. And, besides, all our leads in this operation suggest that the traditional routes are being taken, straight up I-95. You got too many unrelated things going on here."

"I know, I know." I was impatient for him to get the point of all of my logic and solve things. "But it just seems to make sense, and I thought that with his recent sudden interest in the river area, and diving, and all, that there might be a connection with your recent troubles. There are an awful lot of good, I don't know, *unobservable* hiding places out there, by the Point. And the diving . . . And all his years of archaeological work might have got him drug connections in Mexico or Central America, don't forget," I added as an extra bonus, proof of my rightness.

Stannard looked surprised for a moment, like someone whacked him in the head. Distractedly he put up his hand to halt me and hurriedly wrote something else in his notebook. That same hand rose to rub his hair, then, just as quickly, he read what he'd written and shook his head.

"No. It's gone now," he said to himself. He looked up, staring blankly at Meg, who was fiddling with her new key chain, and scribbled down another note. Stannard turned to me.

"What you've concocted is a nice story, but there isn't a scrap of evidence. Just means this Markham fellow might go diving for his dinner, or for fun, or for any number of things. Not bad, but I'm sorry, I think you're way off base. Thanks for telling me about Frannie Maggers, though, that's a help. I'll check that out, and let you know if I find anything else." He stared at his notebook again, caught himself being absentminded, and shook my hand sheepishly.

He intercepted another harried-looking officer, and they

both went into his office, closing the door with some finality. I sat, chewing my lip thoughtfully. Meg made an unconvincing attempt at a coughing noise, and I looked up.

"I think you're reaching, Em. I think that you need to let this go," the younger woman said quietly.

"I know I'm on to something," I said stubbornly. "Maybe it's not drugs, okay, that was a bit of a stretch, but there is a connection between Tony and all of this. I just know it."

"I think that you miss Pauline, and you want to see the killer pay for it. I think that this might be clouding your judgment. Just a little."

"Of course I bloody well want to make sure the killer pays for it!" I exploded. "Of course I miss Pauline! This has been driving me down a sewer and I want a rope! And the only way I can do that is to figure out this whole mess, so I can get a little peace of mind, and maybe a little bit of my life back. So sure my judgment is for the birds, but I haven't got anything else left."

I looked away from Meg bitterly, but she didn't back down.

"It's not your responsibility—"

"Don't be simple," I snapped. "It's everyone's responsibility, and if I think I have a few of the pieces to this puzzle, then so much the worse for me. Let's get going." I abruptly got up and left Meg to follow if she would.

The ride back to Caldwell was long and uncomfortably quiet.

Chapter 24

SUNDAY AFTERNOON ON THE PHONE, I WAS BEGINNING to sound pathetic and I knew it. "I'm just tired, that's all," I said to Brian.

"You been getting to bed on time?"

At the same time as I was comforted by Brian's instinct to look after me, I was irritated by his lack of perception. "No, not that kind of tired. I've just . . . run out of angles. I don't know what else to do. I mean, I can't even get the sheriff to listen to me anymore."

"Oh."

My husband was doing his best not to say anything, but his forbearance was so heavily painted with self-restraint that I knew he was getting impatient with me too.

"Why not just go down the list," he offered, "and we'll see if I pick up on anything you hadn't thought of."

Brian's offer suddenly made me possessive of my bits of clues. I was afraid that they wouldn't stand up to his scrutiny, and even if they hadn't impressed the sheriff, I couldn't bear not to have Brian's imprimatur. I also knew I couldn't continue on as I had been, chasing odds and ends in search of some resolution that was going to let me off the hook.

"Okay, first there's the map that we found at Tichnor's house . . ." I ran down the list: finding the same map in the storeroom, the fact that Tony and Tichnor had also been on the site on the same day, Tony offering to go to the sheriff's department, finding the department number at Tichnor's house, the presence of the Venus figurine, Tony's sudden interest in the site, his connection with the local dive store, Mrs. Maggers's revelation that Tichnor had some sort of partner in his site-robbing endeavors. Maybe the drug-running idea was a little off, but there were just too many coincidences, including the timing of all of this. Maybe Pauline stumbled onto something that had nothing to do with looting the site.

Brian listened in silence. I knew even as I finished how weak it sounded; it was as though I just needed an audience whose opinion I instinctively trusted in order to see the gaping holes in my theory with open eyes.

"Pretty lame, huh?" I said, finally bracing myself for the truth.

"I don't know," he answered slowly. "You've got good instincts for people. Usually, right? Once you've a chance to watch them for a while, I mean. And if you think Tony's been acting strangely toward you all of a sudden, you're probably right to notice it."

My heart soared. "Right."

"Any idea why? When did it start?"

I thought about it. "After we met up in the storage room."

"But there was nothing else?"

I considered carefully. "He said some odd-sounding things about the package from Spain."

"From what it sounds like to me, you were saying some pretty odd-sounding things yourself," Brian replied. "Are you sure he wasn't just reacting to that? I mean, Em, everyone has a bad day."

"Maybe," I admitted. "You're right, he's not really given me a second thought. He hasn't acted one way or the other toward me. I mean, look at the way that Rick Crabtree acts like my presence is an insult to the department—"

"Right. So maybe you're getting the right impulse for the wrong reasons," Brian concluded. "I think what's going on, Em, is that you've got some coincidences that seem to implicate Tony Markham in Pauline's death. I think that those *are* probably just coincidences. But I think that you might be right to be shy of Tony—it's just that from what you've told me, he's a smoothy, a political animal, and that's never been your style, right? And he's been a little too chivalrous, a little too protective. What if maybe he's still smarting from you rejecting his dinner offer? Guys like that don't metabolize embarrassment easily. So my guess is that you are just mixing this up with your desire to do something about Pauline's murder. It all makes sense, it's just two different things that you need to separate."

As much as I wanted to hang on to my theory, I suddenly felt a weight tumble off my back. Not only was I not nuts, Brian made it all sound so logical. I was wrong but for the right reasons.

Still, it was with reluctance that I set my obsession aside. "I just worry that Sheriff Stannard isn't taking everything into consideration. I keep thinking that there's something I can do, something that I'm missing—"

"You can chase your own tail forever looking for something you're missing," Brian scoffed. "You'll end up at the funny farm doing that." Then his voice dropped about an octave. "But how's about I attempt to distract you from all that?"

"Okay, distract me," I said hopefully. "Make it good, Bri."

"Come out for a visit next weekend. One lousy plane ticket won't make our financial situation any worse than it already is! I miss you and it's warm out here. Don't say no."

"Sugar, keep talking!" It was more than tempting, for in-

stead of my usual levelheaded assessment of the family ex-
chequer and my own schedule, I had already drowned the
little puritan who lives in my head and was planning my escape. "I have class until two-thirty—"

"There's an American flight out of Portland in the afternoon," Brian supplied eagerly. "You can just make it if you
leave straight from class. Better yet, don't risk it, can't you get
someone else to take over for you?"

"I bet I could!"

"Good, do it, whatever it takes! We need this, Em." Brian
sounded eager too; I kept forgetting that all this drama must
be taking a huge toll on him as well. "I'm going to run out
right now and buy a red silk—"

"Oh, not red, sweetie," I interrupted. "I look heinous in
red."

"I was thinking for me," my darling interrupted right
back. "I look *great* in red! But you raise a good point, I'll have
to find you something too, in the grape-peeling oeuvre, I
think—"

"You hate grapes," I pointed out. Fine, so I was on a fishing expedition. Sue me.

"You know I'm not in it for the fruit, sweet thing. You just
make sure you get yourself on that plane, and leave the details to me—"

For the first time in I don't know how long, I could actually feel how tight my shoulders were. And I was just sick of
feeling, well, *pursued* by all my fears and worries and suspicions, which were probably just a result of chronic self-doubt
compounded by panic. Brian convinced me, and even just
making that tiny little decision, I felt a ray of sunlight might
be shining through a crack in that big stone wall that I had
built around myself lately.

Sunday afternoon passed peacefully, not filled with morbid thoughts. The next couple of days went just fine, just
how I imagined my life would be once I landed the Big Job.
Okay, so Brian and I weren't currently in residence together,
but we were working to change that. It would only be a cou-

ple of months before we figured out about a new place together, and I could stand on my head for that long.

But anticipation made Friday afternoon seem forever away.

Early Thursday afternoon at the office I was just putting on my coat to go over to the library when I heard a knock and saw my friend and coworker Jenny Alvarez come in with a small package.

"Found this in your box, and thought I'd drop it off," the anthropologist said cheerfully.

"Thanks. No return address, no postage. Weird," I said, shaking it. The package was about the size of a shoe box and was wrapped in brown paper. "The slides I asked Chuck to have copied?" I tore the wrapping and opened the box.

"He wouldn't bother with paper, would he?" Jenny said doubtfully.

Inside I found something swathed in what was probably a black plastic trash bag. It was Scotch-taped around in three places, and I fumbled with the scissors a minute to cut through one of the bands.

"Emma, don't," Jenny said, suddenly wary.

I should have listened to her. What I found inside the black plastic was obscene, unthinkable. Someone, possessed by some revolting fancy, had placed a Barbie doll in what was now clearly meant to be a parody of a body bag. Only it wasn't just the doll, it was one that had been given a rough bobbed haircut, and worse, had been burned, until the short hair on one side had melted and curled and its poor little blackened face had blistered.

I dropped it, making a noise that couldn't escape my throat, revulsion crippling me.

Jenny reached out a hand to me, but I was already backing away. "Tony" was all I could say.

She looked confused. "Tony? Markham? What about him?"

"He sent it." I bumped into the filing cabinets and then realized I would have to walk past the damned thing if I were going to leave the room. It only slowed me down a scosh.

"Emma, he couldn't have. He left right after a meeting with me this morning. It was only in your mailbox just now—" she tried to tell me, but I was already running down the hall.

Fear propelled me out of the building and across the quad. I was hurtling up the stairs to my apartment before I even realized that I'd left my bag in the office, but luckily I had my keys in my pocket. I slammed the door behind me and threw the bolt, then leaned up against the door to catch my breath, but by then I was hyperventilating and had to sit down on the floor. As my chest heaved uncontrollably, I suddenly realized that whoever sent the doll was sending me a message: I wasn't safe. Tony sent the doll. He knew the gruesome details of Pauline's death and was letting me know that I was next.

That thought practically stopped my heart. I ran into the bedroom and grabbed my suitcase from under the bed. I dumped clean laundry out of the basket and started throwing items of clothing into the bag haphazardly. If I called the airport, maybe I could catch an earlier flight to California. I didn't want to stick around my apartment; that was too obvious, I was too exposed there.

Into the bathroom. I grabbed my toothbrush and bag of toiletries and flung open the medicine cabinet to see what else I needed. Speed was everything: The longer I waited, the more of a target I was, and it was starting to get dark outside because of the bad weather. There was nothing in the cabinet that I couldn't get in San Francisco. Move, move, move.

It was when I shut the cabinet door that I got my next shock of the day. I hardly recognized the face that stared back at me, those panic-widened eyes and two feverish patches on pale cheeks. Jesus, I looked like an animal that knew it was running into a snare.

And that was just what he wanted.

I went out to sit on my bed to consider. That thing in the box was not a subtle message, not something sly that someone like Tony might think of. It was meant to provoke a blind-running terror and it had worked just fine.

Well, to hell with that.

I emptied my suitcase and began to pack in a more orderly fashion. Folding clothing, I studied the situation. Running wasn't the answer; I couldn't just expect my problems to vanish by hiding in California. And appealing as that was, it just wasn't realistic to imagine I could just chuck everything and never come back.

The more I thought about it, the more the doll bothered me. Apart from the vulgarity of the thing, it just didn't make sense. That wasn't the way that Tony would make a threat. He was too erudite, too cagey, and this was just too . . . obvious. The only reason Tony would do something like that was if he were spooked, in a panic.

Then I must be getting close to something.

By the time I finished packing properly, I was much calmer. I knew I had to keep after this thing; the doll only underscored the fact that I was onto something. I wasn't going to dismiss my suspicions about Tony now; my instincts were right, and for the right reasons. No one's sent burned toys to Sheriff Stannard. There must be a clue that *I've* overlooked.

I got a package of frozen macaroni and cheese out of the freezer and heated it up. While I ate the comforting, gooey mess, I decided that I'd fly out to Brian tomorrow, but I'd be back Sunday night as I planned. He and I would find the key to this mess. Monday I'd hand the doll over to Stannard and let him take a crack at this. I wasn't done here by a long shot, and if Tony or anyone else wanted to scare me, well, they'd just have to come up with something a little more impressive than tortured dolls to do it.

In spite of my good intentions, however, the next morning I was a zombie. After tossing and turning all night, I finally fell asleep at five, only to have the alarm go off an hour later. I tried to go for a run before I ate, usually a sure cure for what ailed me, but I came back limping and winded rather than clear-headed. My beloved java burned my tongue. The weather didn't help any, the oppressive low-pressure bank threatening to open up with another corker of a storm, and now it was suffocating and damp. I crossed the quad feeling thick and stodgy and was irritated to find out that the elevator wasn't working. Huffing and puffing, I had just enough awareness to be glad that I made it to my office without seeing any of my colleagues: By now word must be getting around that I was losing my mind. Jenny had agreed to take my intro class, telling me I needed to ease up on my-self.

Nothing I did dislodged whatever it was I supposedly knew from the deep recesses of my brain. I was driving my-self crazy to no good effect, so I did the best I could, staring at an unread book on my desk, waiting for the clock to tell me it was one o'clock and time to begin the trek to Portland. Three hours to go.

As the skies finally opened up outside, my glance fell on the scrap of paper with the Madrid archive's phone number. After all the trouble with Rick the day Tony and I butted heads in the main office, I'd forgotten to ask for it and Chuck Huxley dug it up for me later. The only thing about it that suggested a connection between Tony and Penitence Point was the fact that it was just days after he returned from Spain that he telephoned me at the dorm so suddenly. The package from Spain. The archive stamp on the photocopied map.

I'm such an idiot, I thought. Ten to one the stamp on the map is the same archive that Tony visited. They could tell me what the rest of the document was.

Oddly, though, it took me a minute to pick up the phone and make the call. This act was my very last glimmer of hope. It takes a long time to decide to play your last card when it's a deuce and the loan sharks are waiting outside. It was my last chance to play a rational part in this investigation and to understand how all these disjointed parts fit together.

I listened to the raindrops pattering against the window for a moment, took a deep breath, then dialed the number. After fumbling a couple of times with the correct sequence of international, country, and city codes, I heard a distant brrr'ing that meant that I got through.

Just as I recalled with panic the time difference, a woman's voice answered. "*Buenas dias*, Museo Arquéologico Nacional y Biblioteca."

I mentally stumbled; it's Spain, of course they speak Spanish. Blame it on the lack of sleep and high-strung nerves. I hesitated, trying to dredge up some remnant from those long-ago high school lessons.

"Uh, hello, *buenas dias. Por favor* . . ." I tried to remember the words for "can you help me."

"Can I help you?" the woman inquired politely in English.

"Oh yes, thank you," I said with relief. "I've been trying to track down a friend of mine and he left me this number. He was going to be doing some research and he said that he would keep his eyes open for some data relating to my work that he thought he might come across, and I need it now for an article that's due next week. Can you tell me, is he still there?" Desperation revealed in me an increasingly impressive capacity for prevarication.

"I might be able to. What is your friend's name?" *Friend's* was pronounced with a sthlight Casthtillian lithsp.

"Dr. Anthony Markham." My heart was pounding as I spun the lie out.

"Oh no. I can tell you right now that Dr. Markham hasn't been here since midsummer. I'm sorry, I don't know where he is now. Have you checked his home or university?"

I gulped; how to explain that I was at the same institution? Easy, I wouldn't. "I have, but they say that he hasn't returned for classes yet." Most European universities didn't start until much later in the fall than their American counterparts. "I thought I'd check the number he left for me. The thing is, this article is really important, and it would be a big help if you could tell me what he was looking at when he was there. Perhaps I could tell if he found any references that would help me," I said, inviting her to rescue me.

"Well, I'd have to check. Can you hang on for a few minutes?" The librarian was reluctant, making it sound like it might take a long time.

"Oh yes, I'm happy to wait." I wondered if I could hold my breath until I got the answer.

"I have to get it from our records. You can't be too careful with the manuscripts, we must keep track of everything."

Often the tracking systems were files of handwritten lists of which patron had looked at which documents. I knew I'd suffocate long before she got back, but at least that was an attractive option to life with this increasing burden of anxiety and suspicion.

Much to my amazement, about thirty seconds later she had my answer. "I have it all right here." Pride and efficiency were mingled in her voice.

"That was quick," I said without much hope. She couldn't possibly have found anything useful in so short a time.

"Well, we just got our tracking system updated, and I am starting to learn the right queries." I heard tapping of keys over the line, and little echoing voices in the background as our conversation bounced off satellites and across the ocean.

"Here we are. Now what do you think you might be looking for? He looked at quite a lot of documents during his stay."

That had me stumped. "Well, it would be on the New World," I started. "A map."

"Of course, most of his research has been on Jesuit accounts of Mayan ruins."

Of course. "He promised he would look for anything that had to do with New England. It might even be called Virginia, or Northern Virginia. Perhaps an early account of the

British settlement on the northern Atlantic coast. It was a long shot, but he said he would keep his eyes open."

Long shot indeed, most of the Spanish activity would have taken place in the Caribbean, Florida, Georgia, possibly as far north as the Carolinas.

"No, nothing catalogued under New England. I'm sorry," the librarian apologized a moment later.

"How about Maine? Maybe Massachusetts?" I was wracking my brains to come up with anything that might work: Maine was officially controlled by Massachusetts until 1820.

"Wait a moment. I have an entry under "Province of Maine.""

Bingo! "Yes, that's right! That's it."

"Well, I don't know. You said early British settlement. This document is French, and dates to the second half of the eighteenth century."

Lady, don't try and be helpful now! "I believe it might have some descriptions of the ruins of the site in which I'm now interested," I replied, thinking quickly.

"Now that I'm looking at it, I'm almost certain that this is what you are after."

How the hell——?

"It's a letter and map, a description written by French priests of military movements along the southern frontier. I know this is what you want because your friend was so excited when we found it. It wasn't in our catalogue, but was tucked into a stack of manuscripts. The librarian who brought the volumes found it and was very excited. Dr. Markham also showed a good deal of interest when he saw it. As precise as we try to be, we are always discovering these treasures, sometimes lost for hundreds of years," she said.

"Is it a very long document?" I asked, my heart sinking at the thought of trying to sift the information out of a long, handwritten report. I doubted I could get them to send it to the Caldwell library.

"Oh no," the archivist reassured me. "It's just a two-page

letter, probably a summary sent back with other official documents. Who knows how it ended up here? We have a transcription that an intern made when we found it. Dr.
Markham must have had his copy made for you."

"Is there any way that you could mail me a copy? It would
be a tremendous help!"

"Well, it would be difficult. It is very late here, and the
Spanish postal system is somewhat antiquated, I'm afraid. It
would never get to you in time." The librarian sounded almost as disappointed as I.

"I don't suppose you could send it Federal Express or
something? I'd be happy to pay for it," I offered, my heart
sinking over the possibility of losing even this thinnest of
potential clues. Why was Tony excited by a document that
had absolutely nothing to do with his work? He certainly
didn't run home and tell me about it.

"Well, that's part of the problem. We are preparing to
close for the weekend, and then Monday is what you might
call a bank holiday and nothing is open."

I was at a loss, when she spoke up again, "I thought all
Americans had fax machines. Don't you—?"

"Of course!" Hope leaped up like a rekindled flame as I
cursed my thickheadedness.

"Well, nothing simpler then. I can send it off as soon as I
find the transcription. I will have to send you a bill for the
photocopy and my time, I'm afraid."

I'd sell my soul, señora. "No problem at all!" I gave the
other woman the information and thanked her profusely.

"I'm happy I could help. Send us a copy of the paper
when it's done. I'll put the proper citation on the fax for you
to use."

For a moment I couldn't remember to what paper the
woman could be referring. "Oh, yes. Of course, thanks again,
er, *gracias obrigado*!"

The librarian laughed. "You're welcome! No offense, but I
hope your French is better than your Spanish—*obrigado* is
Portuguese! And please give our regards to Dr. Markham,

when you see him. We are all quite fond of him here—he's so very gallant. Good-bye."

I tried not to watch the clock, waiting for the fax to come; if it was meaningless, then this was all just delaying the inevitable process, accepting facts and getting on with my life in spite of it. I let my eyes unfocus, staring at my bag packed for California and listening to the wind whip the rain against the building. I wondered if I would get the fax before I had to leave to catch my plane. The wind suddenly knocked a spatter of raindrops against the window, reflecting the urgency I felt. The thought of a long, romantic weekend now struck me as torture, if I couldn't see what was on that fax until Monday. Of course, if the fax meant nothing, then I wasn't certain how much fun I was going to be in San Francisco.

Miraculously, I heard the fax machine through the thin walls of the office, and hurried in to see if it was mine. It was, and the first page after the cover letter took forever to come through, the cramped handwriting and the darkness of the photocopy making the fax creep out from the machine at an exasperatingly slow rate. I snatched the first page and began to read it even as the second page was laboriously churning out. The storm outside was picking up and for a heartstopping moment, the lights flickered as the wind picked up. I didn't hear thunder, but couldn't be certain that the wind hadn't taken a transformer out someplace either. Less than a second later the fax resumed after its hiccough and I breathed a sigh of relief, even as I continued trying to translate the document I already held.

I realized as I scanned the second page that I was holding a ticking bomb. My French is excellent, and after struggling to sort through some of the archaic eighteenth-century idiom, I understood the reason for all the excitement about my site. The hunches I'd had about the river being the focus of all the sudden attention were correct. The original letter was written by a French spy, a priest, recording British ship movements along the river in the early 1750s. Apparently he got wind that a ship's boat was going to be dispatched to the

British fort, Fort Archer, carrying gold to pay the troops in the French and Indian Wars. It never made it to its destination, and had sunk downriver of Fort Archer, near *my* fort, Fort Providence, during a storm. If the spy's observations had been accurate, then it was entirely possible that a fortune in gold still rested at the bottom of the Saugatuck River just off Penitence Point. For once, the rumors about gold on an archaeological site had been true and provided more than an ample motive for murder. And now that I knew for certain, I had to act fast.

Chapter 25

I DIALED BRIAN'S HOTEL NUMBER IN SAN FRANCISCO. "C'mon, pick it up, baby, pick it up," I begged as the phone rang away on the West Coast. Outside, I noticed, the light had changed from gray to yellow-white, giving an eerie cast to the sky.

"Brian Chang," came the curt answer.

"Brian, it's me. Listen, something's happened, I can't come—"

"Emma, are you all right? What's wrong? I can barely hear you."

"I haven't much time, the storm, I've got to get to the site right now—"

"The site?" Brian shouted in disbelief. "The site? You absolutely do not need to go out to the goddamned site! I swear to God, Emma, if you—"

"Look, I know, I know, let me—"

"Emma? I can barely hear you! Don't—"

"I think I know—" I shouted, but it was already too late. After a final earsplitting crack, the line went dead, save for a loud whine, some sort of emergency tone. The lights went out as well. I looked out the window and saw that the whole campus was dark.

I tapped the receiver a couple of times, but nothing. Brian would understand, I reasoned, when he calmed down and I could tell him what I'd discovered. He has to understand.

Hurriedly I grabbed my slicker and a couple of other things, then rushed down the hall. In my haste, I ran headlong into Neal and gave him a few brief instructions.

"Get hold of Sheriff Stannard. Tell him to meet me at the Point. And then you stay put—"

"What's going on?"

"I'll tell you later; I've got to get out there now."

Then, not bothering to curse the stranded elevator, I stumbled hurriedly down the stairs and out into the storm.

Two hours later I left the Civic on the road leading to Pauline's driveway in order to draw less attention to myself on the site. The wind had steadily picked up during my drive; when I'd left campus, it had been blowing in sporadic gusts, now it pushed the rain relentlessly. At first I was pleased that I was adequately dressed to face the weather; soon, however, I found myself completely soaked from the thighs down the moment after I slammed the car door shut.

I had wisely decided to leave the fax in the car; there was no way that it would stand up to one minute of the downpour. I didn't need it any longer anyway, I had practically memorized the contents of the text, and one hasty comparison of the sketch—the same as the one in the map file and in Tichnor's kitchen—with a topographic map had only confirmed what the crabbed cursive of the eighteenth-century writer told me.

It was difficult to squelch the same sense of discovery that I'd felt on the site the day I'd found the silver sixpence or started to understand the stratigraphic sequences. I suddenly realized that I'd been getting the same rush hunting for the clues that had led me here as I had with my regular research.

I decided there was no shame in being proud of the skills that would lead to the discovery of Pauline's killer. What mattered now was keeping a head cool enough to get the job done.

I hurried down the driveway and onto the lawn facing the river, the still-open trenches partly filled with water where the tarps had collapsed in and the surrounding area had become a sea of mud and treachery. I moved along the easternmost line of trees, trying to remain concealed while I searched along the river for some indication that I was not on a self-deluded wild-goose chase. I clutched a camera tightly under my slicker and moved as close to the eroding northern bank as I dared. Under the relative shelter of the pines, I scanned the far bank to the east and the west for as far as the low clouds and rain would allow.

I awkwardly twisted the telephoto lens through the plastic bag I had swathed around the camera, trying vainly to see through the mist. A few small sailboats, tied close to shore, rocked violently in the wind, loose halyards and clips clanging against their masts. There was nothing to see, nothing suspicious, nothing out of the ordinary. The wind died down, briefly, mocking my overreaction to an unlikely hunch and diminishing the dramatic impulse that had driven me out onto the stormy coast when I could be heading toward Brian, San Francisco, and the local red wine. I stood there, dripping and freezing, cursing my own foolishness, when I saw what I had been looking for.

The motorboat was much closer to my side of the river than I had calculated from the eighteenth-century map. Surely I had attributed too much accuracy to the description, or else the water had shifted what I had come to find. The boat's dark color and the size of the chop helped obscure the activity that was going on when sane and legitimate business was being conducted indoors. A diver in a black dry suit, barely visible to the casual observer, hoisted himself onto the side of the boat and dumped in a small, bulging bag.

I was ecstatic. I stepped out of the line of trees to get a better view and made the most of the temporarily slack winds by snapping a succession of shots of the diver moving around on the boat. I had an impression of something yellow. The figure then fiddled with his regulator; it was clear the diver was fed up.

"Please, oh please, look over here, let me get a face shot," I murmured as a prayer. "This is why Pauline died, no one wants a sharp-eyed old lady around when there's gold in her backyard. There's too much for this to be a coincidence. Come on, come on, smile pretty for the camera, Tony, give me one clean head shot, and we'll end this right now." I squinted through the lens, every drop of mental energy focused, channeled, willing Tony to give himself away, when, frustrated with the hookup, the diver removed his mask to get a better look.

It wasn't Tony Markham at all.

Chapter 26

THE FIGURE FINALLY SUCCEEDED IN GETTING HIS DRY suit hood pried off of his head, and was, with the impatience of a young man, exchanging his empty tank for a full one. Billy Griggs looked up at the sky and the horizon, as if gauging the storm's progress, then redonned his hood and mask and clumsily reentered the water.

I snapped two or three shots before I realized that it truly wasn't Tony. I stepped back, stunned, my mind racing to try and explain how I could be so wrong. Of course, Billy had been the friend whose name Mrs. Maggers at the antiques shop so imperfectly remembered. Not Tony? Billy was just the sort to keep company with Tichnor and just stupid enough to be deluded by the dead man's promises of riches and buried treasure. He and Tichnor had lived around here forever, and somehow the two of them must have stumbled onto the wreck . . . It was entirely possible that after Pauline observed them, Tichnor killed her. And if Griggs was another one of those survivalist types, it made perfect sense for him to know about natural poisons, like lily of the valley. He was the one.

And what kind of mistake had I almost made? Had the French text and map just been a coincidence? Jesus, I came this close to, what? Libelous accusation of a powerful colleague? I toted up the charges with which I had been prepared to accuse Tony. Trespassing, site robbery, arson, and murder, just for a start. Brian was right, and I was so wrong. Way to go, Em, just because the man was in a bad mood, a little cryptic, you had him limned for a murderer and turned his every word into an allegation and a suspicion. Tony's an *archaeologist*; he would never have gotten into something as unethical as treasure hunting, never mind the rest.

I guess that all the adrenaline I'd been pumping drained away with the realization of my colossal stupidity. Trying so desperately to absolve myself of guilt I felt over Pauline's death, I had completely misread the situation. I could understand now why I had tried to force Tony into the mold of a murderer: I had been so wrapped up in my own little world of thought that I had ignored the facts.

I felt the cold intensely now, whereas I had not even been conscious of it while I was taking the pictures. In spite of my foolishness, it occurred to me that I did have evidence against Billy and Tichnor, and if I were going to get anything out of this exercise in thickheadedness, I'd better do something while I had the chance. Stop overanalyzing, Emma, for once in your life, and do something useful.

I made a rough mental note of the location of the boat. Though it might be too late to catch Griggs in the act, if I were very lucky, there might be some traces of his activities left after the storm to implicate him, along with my photos. I barely had enough energy or, to tell the truth, interest to do so. My legs were chapped from the salty wind and rain that soaked into my jeans; my nose was numb and I could feel it running inelegantly. Even though I had my hood on, the rain driven into my face was rapidly soaking my hair into a sodden mass under my raincoat.

My thoughts were interrupted by the wind picking up again, roaring along the river. The heavy pine boughs swayed, and in the distance dead branches cracked, and the rain regained its former intensity. I decided that it was time to find Sheriff Stannard and see if he could help me make some sense of all this. I turned to leave.

Brian will be so pleased with my good sense, I thought wryly, as another limb splintered nearby. If I hustled, it was even remotely possible I could catch a later flight, but at any rate I had to get out of here before I froze to death. The rain came down harder now, colder because of our proximity to the frigid river. Even during the summer no one wanted to swim in such cold water, and now that fall was well under way . . .

Against the background noise of the storm, a noise caught my attention. Suddenly it occurred to me that the last sound that I had heard wasn't cracking branches and wasn't snapping lines. It was the sound of someone removing the safety and drawing back the trigger on the pistol that was now pointed at my head.

"I'll thank you to hand over the film please. Just pull it out of the camera so that it is quite exposed, thank you."

I knew that voice.

I turned and stared, slack-jawed, too wasted from cold and shock to react immediately. Tony Markham waggled the pistol meaningfully, and slowly I complied, dropping the roll of film to the ground. I drooped; I didn't even bother to close the door to the camera dangling from the strap on my wrist, unprotected against the elements.

"Very good. Now it seems we have a few things to decide," Tony Markham drawled politely. He looked composed in spite of the weather, like he was taking strength from it even as it left me weak. "Well, I'll be doing most of the deciding, won't I? By the way, I would appreciate it if you would drop the camera as well. I wouldn't want to take the chance of getting clobbered with so solid a piece of technology as that."

I complied woodenly. "What's going on, Tony? I can't figure out if you're a murderer and a site robber or just a moody bastard. I'm really very confused." The words came out in a naked monotone, with barely a scrap of sarcasm to cover them. Damn it, I was right! But I couldn't figure out what was going on now, and I couldn't take my eyes off that gun. Oh Jesus, Brian—!

Markham, of all things, seemed concerned with my lethargy. "Now Emma, that's really been your problem all along, hasn't it? No confidence in your theories. I will admit, that worried me about your taking the position at Caldwell in the first place. You were just too young, for all your experience. I warned Kellerman it would come to no good—"

He smiled, and while any other time I would have been fascinated to know about the process that got me my job, I certainly wasn't in the mood for it now.

"—I could tell just by looking that you were busy revamping all of your previous assumptions as soon as you saw Billy out there. I suppose given a bit more time, you might have reached the correct conclusion, though perhaps not with all the details filled in. If it makes you feel any better, I believed that you were a threat to my little enterprise from the beginning. It's just my bad luck that we were only able to finally locate the wreck yesterday. Still, it's all part of the fun. Quite profitable fun."

Fun? He can't be serious. I shivered; the water that soaked me seemed to be forming icicles against my skin. I thought briefly about trying to dodge away, but there was just no way.

He nodded his head in the direction of the barn, and we moved up toward the shelter of the dilapidated building that had been used for tool storage during another life. I was unsurprised to see that the hasp of the padlock had been cut through. The familiarity of the place seemed incongruous with the situation. Rain dripped in through the failing roof, echoing wetly through the dark of the room, but at least we were out of the wind. The last gray light of the afternoon filtered in through the cracks in the walls.

"You look like pure hell, Emma," Tony offered, concerned. Resentment proved a stronger motivation than I might have expected. "I don't need any pity, not from the likes of you!"

"And just what is 'the likes of me'?" His curiosity was genuine.

The door was not ten feet away, but the gun remained unnaturally large in my vision. "Well, to start with you killed Grahame Tichnor. And Pauline!"

"Oh, come now, think about that, would you?" Tony scoffed, his pride wounded. "Were there any similarities at all between those two deaths?"

"No," I admitted. "But you might have wanted it to look that way. No one who would think of something as . . . as *Borgian* as poisoning a stew would be associated with something as brutish as a bashing in someone's head with a shovel! And making it look like an accident might be right up your alley!"

It was only my anger that let me say the words out loud for the first time and keep my emotional distance. His arm had to get tired sometime, didn't it? I licked my lips and tried to think.

Tony considered my reasoning carefully. "Touché. But let me first assure you, I had nothing to do with your friend's murder. That was entirely Tichnor's stupidity. He got out of hand much sooner than I anticipated and I was forced to take drastic steps to cover up his indiscretions. Though you're correct. The 'accident' *was* my idea.

"That's the problem with working with sociopaths." Markham sighed. "He couldn't keep his mind on the task at hand and nearly blew things all to hell when he wouldn't leave your site alone. I should have known how unstable he was as soon as he told me about that first one."

"First one?" I asked, puzzled. "First one what?"

"Friend Tichnor had killed someone even before the advent of our . . . association. A former chum who got too nosy about his interest in the eighteenth-century fort, Fort Archer. Quite an unanticipated turn of events, as I understand it, but his luck was bound to run out sooner or later. I just didn't think he would melt down so quickly."

My thoughts hurtled back to my second week on the site, and my happening upon poor old Augie Brooks. Somehow the logic of the discussion was keeping me going. It wasn't much, but I tried to keep that flicker of hope burning. "Why the hell would you take up with Tichnor?"

How did the bastard manage to look so calm? Why wasn't his heart pounding like mine?

"After I recognized the location of Fort Archer—and really I was quite surprised to find you out at Fort Providence so soon, I thought you weren't due out there for another year—I started thinking about how to handle this. No, you're right my dear, Tichnor was not someone I would have considered for my first pick of companions. But neither was he entirely without virtue. Tichnor was the perfect shield, a well-known troublemaker with dangerous tendencies. Who better to use as a cat's paw?"

No one's anything but a tool to you, I thought, remembering our conversation at the bar. I wondered how much he believed or whether he created his fictions especially for me. His capacity for manipulation was incredible.

I kept my eyes carefully on Tony and tried to think of what I might use as a weapon. There was nothing. I would have given my eyeteeth for one of the steel probes that we'd stored here during the summer, a pickax, a machete, anything.

"Not a bad choice, really." Tony looked like he was considering how to make inferior ingredients into a gourmet meal, intrigued by the challenge. "As soon as I heard of his exploits on your site, I knew that he would serve my purposes admirably. Once I'd seen his picture, it was easy enough to find him. He was cagey, but lacked . . . subtlety. A little flattery, a little careful handling, and of course the lure of the gold— isn't it funny, by the way, how every visitor on every site ever excavated asks if we've found any gold, and on this one, it just happens to be true?"

He was impressed with the irony of it, but I could only mutter, "Yeah. Funny."

Tony paused a moment, almost daintily considering his next words. "The other thing about Tichnor was that I knew, I just knew that, eventually, I would have to kill him. That made dealing with him bearable and . . . how can I put it?"

He looked at me directly. "Rather thrilling."

I shuddered, not able to think of murder as an existential treat and trying not to think of Tony turning his considerable intellect to murder. An almost sexual eagerness radiated from him.

He went on. "I'm certain he and Billy had the same plans for me, but I don't think he was as capable of the philosophical and aesthetic appreciation of the act as I . . . So you see, it worked out for the best."

"What about Billy?" I had to keep him talking while I figured out a way out of this. My God, the door was *right* there!

"An unfortunate situation for me." Tony shook his head regretfully. "Next time I shan't allow for the possibility of partners. I only found out about Billy after Tichnor's sudden decease. Apparently those two—friends for years—were cooking up some ill-conceived scheme to do me out of my share of the goodies. When Tichnor, ah, left this vale of tears, Billy took it upon himself to blackmail his way into my life. Speaking of which, there's the second reason for you to be grateful to me."

"You'll forgive me if I can't even think of a first." Be interesting, Emma, be a puzzle. Don't let him get bored with you, the man likes a challenge.

"I'm hurt—I've always had your best interests at heart," Tony protested.

"Bullshit!"

Tony frowned, either at my disbelief or my expletive, then explained. "We knew that there was a chance that you would thread things together, and Billy wanted to be the one waiting for you. Seems he did not appreciate waking up in the drunk tank again. Our chum there wanted to renew an old acquaintance with you, I understand—rather strong feelings about you, has our Mr. Griggs."

Oh God. I all but wilted inside. I'd forgotten that Billy was still down at the river and he wouldn't be as eager to talk as Tony. No, don't give up yet, keep thinking. "It's not the first time we met."

He nodded. "So I understand. But as far as Tichnor goes, you can't possibly believe that it was only my anger with his idiotic blunder and a needless cover-up that led me to kill him?"

"I have no idea, Tony."

Tony surprised me by sounding genuinely aggrieved. "I was outraged on your behalf. Ever since last summer, when I discovered the French report, I've been discreetly investigating this area, trying on the idea for size. I thought I recognized the layout from your interview lectures at Caldwell. And I was right. So, from a distance, of course, I'd had the chance to learn a little about your Pauline."

"She was no one's Pauline but her own," I said, but I felt ill. I had led them both to Pauline, however indirectly.

Tony nodded. "Pauline Westlake," he said, "as anybody could see, was an admirable woman and did not deserve so ignominious a death. Tichnor was a fool and a wastrel. When the idiot was finished crowing about how he had recovered such wonderful things from your site and then murdered Miss Westlake, I was forced to cover up his impetuousness by attempting to make her death look like an accident.

"He just couldn't leave well enough alone—imagine being distracted from the search for a fortune in gold by petty site robbery. He was drawing attention to us.

"I have to admit that I rather charmed myself with the solution: I'd noticed the lilies of the valley near the house. It was a shockingly sentimental gesture, but one that I couldn't resist. After I got done arranging the 'gas leak' at Greycliff, I returned to join Tichnor for a late, celebratory dinner. Only he started eating before I did and suddenly began to feel rather poorly. Very quickly."

Markham paused. "I watched him die, Emma. He did not die prettily or well. You may consider your friend appropriately avenged. I'm sure that you would have done the same, had you been presented with the opportunity; I mean, we all saw Allan Crabtree's thesis. I thought you would appreciate my action."

Dear God, I thought. He really is waiting for me to thank him. I tried to keep my legs from buckling, thinking about Tony calmly, interestedly watching a man die in convulsions. Just like he's watching me now, I thought. He wouldn't have any trouble pulling that trigger when it came down to it. I only had a chance as long as I amused him, gave him something to think about.

"He deserved it," I managed to sputter.

Tony looked gratified by that. "It was a simple matter to blur my trail a little," he said. "Unfortunately, it was my one slipup where you were concerned: I was so eager to compare one of the details of my copy of the French map with your topographic maps in the storage room that I didn't wait long enough for everyone to leave. It was funny; that day in the storeroom you thought it was odd that Chuck had already left, that he usually waited until the rest of us had gone before he left. Well, he saw the light on in the storeroom on his way out, and I didn't have time to do anything but shove my map in with yours before he came in to check. I told him I was finished and we closed up the room as we left. But then *you* stopped by on your way out—you weren't the only one to be surprised that day! My impatience was regrettable, but really, it is a fascinating thing to watch in oneself under such a situation."

I shuddered.

"I took the artifacts from Miss Westlake's house and hid them under Tichnor's bed, just to reroute suspicion back to the true source of the trouble. Though, again, I might have been a trifle overenthusiastic when I put the Venus figurine in with the other goodies. I knew I had to resist taking any of her fabulous objects, but I couldn't stand to see that precious thing burn; I hoped it would be overlooked. I've mentioned my hopeless streak of sentimentalism—something I must correct in the future. Do you know, I'd never seen a Venus before?"

The memory of the little clay figure brought to mind that day in Sheriff Stannard's office—what I wouldn't give to be there right now! I knew I had to stall for more time. "What about that burned doll?" I asked. "What had I found that drove you to send that?"

Tony looked puzzled, then his face cleared. "Oh my, you can't believe that I would have done something as tacky as that, could you?" He clucked and shook his head at my foolish assumption. "No, that was Rick Crabtree's idea, I think, to spook you into some spontaneous confession. He warned me that I should keep an eye on you for signs of guilt, the idiot."

Abruptly Markham changed the subject. "Take off your jacket, my dear. Unbutton your shirt. Now, please."

I gasped and clutched at the collar of my slicker. "Tony, you can't—"

Tony rolled his eyes in exasperation and I knew that I'd made a dangerous mistake.

"I may be a man with a well-defined sense of the expedient," he admonished, "but I'm hardly a rapist. Charming as I have previously confessed to find you, I have just admitted in plain language to the murder of one man and to the commission of several other crimes. I am merely determining whether you have come prepared with a wire."

I couldn't afford to assume that he would have any predictable reactions, I couldn't afford such a banal response, not when Tony was so clearly looking for a different sort of thrill. Show a little steel, Emma—he asked politely! This is just business, no prurient interest in the world! I swallowed thickly and did what he asked, as calmly as I could with my knees knocking.

"Damn it, Tony, I never even thought of that!"

He shrugged a little and shook his head in commiseration—my shortsightedness would be our little secret. It shocked me to realize that, even now, Tony was as considerate as ever.

I held his eye as I unbuttoned my shirt and showed him that I had no wire, trying not to think about what I was doing. Then I made a point of taking my time straightening my clothing, though that wasn't difficult with my frozen, fear-trembling fingers.

I'd guessed right, though; he waited patiently for me to finish. That deeply ingrained sense of Southern civility would only approve of a woman who took trouble over her appearance. I'd have to remember to appeal to his sensibilities, not let him see how afraid I really was, how I was dying every second Sheriff Stannard didn't show up.

"Thank you, Emma." Tony checked his watch again, looked at me, and seemed to be deciding something. "Now, put on your jacket, don't dawdle, but button it up tightly—it's very wet outside. We—"

That "we" elated me, and my heart soared. I knew I'd just bought myself another couple of minutes, possibly an opportunity to escape.

"—need to go outside to see how friend Griggs is getting along. He can dive well enough when he isn't reeling drunk, but personally I don't trust him to leave prudently before the storm worsens," Markham confided. "All ready? Let's go. And Emma?"

I looked up, carefully masking the increasing jumpiness I felt: I needed to be ready for anything. My muscles were no longer numb, they were stretched taut, ready for some sudden burst of activity. I only hoped I could live up to my instincts. "Yes, Tony?"

"Stay near," he warned, as abruptly he yanked me close and jammed his pistol painfully against my side. "It's treacherous out there."

We slogged out into the storm. The wind had picked up considerably, and so had the whitecaps. Now it was only just possible to keep the little motorboat in view. We skidded through the mud near the pines, like a pair of contestants in a three-legged race. I was in a torment, trying to seem only as though I was trying to keep my balance, trying to gauge when to attempt to make a break for it. I was freezing, and I had to work hard to keep from thinking about just sitting down and crying in fear and frustration. Now of all times, I couldn't afford to think; I had to stay wired.

Billy spied us and waved; Tony signaled to him to return to shore. My dread increased with every step toward the bluff, and once, before I could stop myself, I stopped and tried to resist going down toward the cobble beach.

"You don't want to be like that, Emma," Tony warned sharply. I felt the gun jab again, reminding me that there was only thin cloth, slender bones, and a bit of muscle between a bullet and my heart.

I got control of myself only with effort, and we awkwardly threaded our way down the old stairs to meet him. The crumbling concrete was slick with rain and mud, the railing long gone. At first I refused to think how these hateful people were moving so casually around this place that was so much of my life. And then I realized that I needed that hate, that anger, more than I'd ever needed anything in my life.

It took Billy a long while to fight the waves and reach the cobbled shore. I watched, praying that a wave would knock him into the river and wash him out to sea. It took him forever, but with Tony's arm around my waist like an iron clamp, there was no chance to do anything but watch and wait in icy torment.

Billy hopped out of the boat on the side closest to us, no more than twenty feet away, and tried to haul the boat the rest of the way up onto the beach. As he struggled in the relentless wind and rain, Billy bellowed angrily, "Give me a hand with this, you lazy old fuck!"

Griggs was clearly spoiling for a fight; Tony looked far too dry and rested to suit him—hell, I knew he was too calm for my liking—and he had to be riding as huge an adrenaline crest as I was.

"I can't, I have to watch her!" Markham roared back. "Just pull the boat up as high as you can, and make sure everything is offloaded."

"I'm not going out there again!" Billy screamed as he heaved the anchor out onto the cobbles above the high-water line. He dumped the diving gear on the beach, then, straining a little, set a heavy bag next to it. "Let's get out of here!"

"Right," Markham shouted. Then he murmured into my ear, his breath warm, "Time to go, Billy-boy."

The pistol that had been boring into my side swung away just long enough to pump three slugs into Billy's chest. Blood and neoprene spattered across the bow of the boat and on the beach cobbles below, only to be washed away almost immediately by the driving rain, first leaving dark rivulets, then suddenly, nothing. Instinctively I turned away in horror but was left with an indelible image of what remained behind on the cobbles, what the rain couldn't wash away.

The shock that registered on Billy's face was only at being outthought; as he clutched dumbly at himself, he dropped the pistol he had concealed in the boat with the obvious intention of double-crossing Markham.

Until that point I don't think I really, truly understood what could happen. In spite of the fact that I'd tried to prepare myself for anything, I simply hadn't believed what I was involved in. The violence I'd just witnessed was so quick, so final, that I was stunned by it.

"All that cheap booze was bound to dull the reflexes, Billy," Tony clucked.

It was only then that it truly hit home for me: Tony Markham was out of his mind.

He turned to me, raising his voice to be better heard. "Now, Dr. Fielding, if you wouldn't mind picking up that bag, I believe we'll just leave Mr. Griggs to nature. We need to get to shelter, as the tide is coming in unusually high and we have a few details to discuss. The sack, if you'd be so kind."

Shaking, I picked up the bag, not because I was that eager to get close to Billy, dead or not, but because of the gun that was pointing at me. Markham retrieved Billy's weapon. He paused to nudge Billy Griggs with his toe and Billy slumped over, his face smacking sickeningly against the stones. The tide was just beginning to lap at the feet of the newly made corpse.

Chapter 27

I FELT MYSELF GROW QUITE CALM. MY VIOLENT TREM-
bling stopped. With surreal detachment I had watched
Markham stand next to me and murder Billy Griggs. I coolly
realized that whatever opportunity I had of escaping while
the other two bickered had evaporated too quickly for me to
exploit. I would die in the storm near the ruins of Greycliff,
far away from Brian.

The inevitability of death cleared my mind, which
seemed to speed up in relation to my surroundings. With
universal comprehension, I observed the progress of the
storm, Tony's heightened color as he climbed back up the
slippery stairs next to me, and the gun that never left my
side. I understood precisely how they all interrelated, what
actions would beget which reactions.

Unfortunately with this comprehension came a resignation and a disconnection from my own body that made survival seem very unlikely. The instinct for self-preservation
had fled, and I was operating on pure intellectual energy
rather than by instinct, which might have saved me.

With this detachment, I struggled up the lawn through

the hammering rain, awkwardly lugging the potato sack–sized bag partially filled with gold. Tony led me back to the old barn, and dutifully I remarked that the rain was now driving horizontally through the spaces in the barn's walls, not improving my shivering, drenched state.

Markham switched on a powerful lantern flashlight and set it on an overturned bucket. "No need to fumble in the dark and wet. You showed some genuine sangfroid down there, my dear, most exemplary. Now what *are* we going to do?"

I dumped the bag down. With difficulty, I found my larynx and tried to recall how to make that organ shape meaningful aural symbols. "I presume you are going to shoot me, though it escapes me why you didn't just do it down on the beach with Billy." I was pleased my preternatural calm hadn't robbed me of words: I knew I was going to die and I didn't want to gibber.

Tony shook his head despairingly. "How unimaginative of you." He considered the matter for a moment. "At this point you are the only one who has any inkling that I am connected with anyone's death. Or any dubious treasure hunting, for that matter. If you choose not to say anything, no one will ever know a thing. Why not fall in with me? Take half of the wreck treasure as an earnest."

I wasn't certain whether he was toying with me or not. There was only the hope that I could parlay this into a chance to get away. The thing was to keep his attention.

"I don't think I believe you."

Tony nodded. "Fair enough. But there's no reason to disbelieve me—why would I offer otherwise? It would save me further . . . trouble if you'd agree." He paused, then added meaningfully. "You can have everything you ever wanted. All for the price of saying nothing about my hand in the demise of two people who have caused incalculable grief in your life."

For a split second I actually saw the logic in what he was saying; he seemed to understand so well what I was going through. I still said nothing, waiting for Tony to give me a hint as to his real intentions.

"All you need is the imagination to see beyond your dull little life and take what you really want. It's all about power, Emma." Tony looked me in the eye. "I wanted it once myself until I got it, and realized how meaningless it all was. Even the control you get over people, letting them know that their futures are in your hands, and watching them agonize as they decide whether to sell their souls to you, pales after a while. It gets boring."

I tried to look indecisive, but probably didn't manage it. "I don't know . . ."

"I can see your future and I can tell you how very unsatisfying it really is," he insisted. "When you finally get to the top, you're all alone, and power's no fun unless you're constantly trying to defend it. And the ivory tower is simply too small a battlefield. I saw that and realized even if I waited for Kellerman to finally retire, I'd have nothing. I could entomb myself in boredom or I could take an opportunity that fate offered."

I couldn't think clearly: Would he believe me if I said yes? He knows me too well. Back in the bar, hell, back in the storage room, I might have bought every word.

"Why toil in obscurity when it won't be what you want in the end?" he asked reasonably. "Learn from my mistakes. Let me save you the effort of finding out for yourself."

There was an honesty to his words that I found intriguing, but the idea was ludicrous. And finally I was too tired to play along; the words were out before I could reconsider. "Sorry, I can't." I shrugged helplessly, watching the gun.

"Of course. You wouldn't want anything you didn't earn yourself." Tony seemed to be talking to himself or the damp, musty air in the barn.

Something about his tone pushed me past prudence. "I don't want anything from you Tony!" I snapped. "I don't need your help."

"No, you don't need help from anyone, do you?" Tony conceded reluctantly, then changed the topic. "You know, long ago, when we went out for our little drink, I was surprised to learn that you could believe that no one would know about the family connection between you and Oscar Fielding. I'm sure I couldn't produce anyone who hadn't heard of his work."

I was confused. "What about Oscar? What the hell are you talking about?"

"How humiliating for him, to have to put himself forward on your behalf in graduate school," Tony mused. "And I'm sure that it would have looked bad if Oscar's granddaughter and protégée wasn't capable of getting a position on her own. Even after he foisted you off on Coolidge, his reputation was at work—"

"*Foisted?*" I interrupted angrily. "You don't know what you're talking about! And you forget, Oscar was gone long before I got the job at Caldwell!"

"I know, Emma. But doesn't that make it all the more macabre?" Tony reproved. "I mean, really, the poor man was *dead*, and he was still dragging you along on his coattails—"

"Shut up! You don't know what you're talking about!" It was a lie.

"I'm sorry, that's right, you don't need help from anyone, do you? You can do it all on your own. The fact that Pauline—"

"Don't you dare say her name!" It only came out in a whisper, though. My throat was too tight. "Just stop it!"

"—was so worried about you, felt she had to buy you a permanent place in the college, is just touching. Very nice for you, I'm sure. And you know, when Chairman Kellerman asked my advice about the Westlake chair, I reluctantly said yes. I was curious to see how anyone who had caused a friend's death—however inadvertently, I'm sure—would decide if she should also *profit* by it—"

My mind reeled. "Stop it! Stop it! That's disgusting!"

"Isn't it though?" Tony agreed severely. "And on top of that, you don't even have the guts to go after her killer—"

"He was dead before I—" I stammered. I couldn't

breathe, my chest felt like it had a chain and padlock around it. "I mean, I couldn't—"

"I really shouldn't have had to kill Grahame Tichnor, should I? Once again, you let someone else do your work for you. How does that feel, I wonder, to be so in debt with no way of paying it all back? Must feel a little like drowning, I should think."

Tony let me think about that for a minute. How could he know all this? He had to be wrong—but he spoke with too much authority, he knew too much. It did feel just like drowning, I couldn't catch a breath, I couldn't think; I could only wait for him to speak again.

"But, of course, you don't need help from anybody, do you?" he asked scornfully. "I don't know how you can cope with the knowledge of yourself. I withdraw my offer—I was a fool to imagine that I should do anything for you too—"

There it was—the lifeline! Something inside me clicked— just the way it did that day on the site when all the data just snapped into place. Tony Markham might be smart enough to imagine the fears that drove me, even enough to play on them, but he didn't know anything of real truth at all. Much as I'd admired him, he didn't know *squat*. I laughed out loud and it was like breathing fresh air after being locked up in a tomb—Antigone with a reprieve. I suddenly heard the rain again and not just Tony's words.

And for the first time that afternoon, he looked disconcerted.

"Jesus, Tony, that was good! It was just like you'd been inside my head for the past ten years, playing me like a fiddle! And you were so close . . ." I stopped to catch my breath. "So close. Damn, you nearly had me." I took another, steadying breath—if I hadn't been so exhausted, I would have laughed again, but the fact that I could feel the cold air again made that inconsequential. "I almost asked you how you could know. But you know, the last thing you should have done was compare yourself to Oscar and Pauline."

A look of relief flickered over his face. "Stupid of me. I

must curb this urge of mine to overdo the dramatic simply for the sake of it. Of course, it doesn't actually change things much, does it, Emma?" Tony smiled and nodded his head meaningfully at the pistol, which had never lowered during our exchange.

That sobered me. I'd won the battle but lost the war. "How do you think you'll get away with shooting me? You can't—" I tried weakly.

"But everyone knows how irrational you've been lately, jumping at shadows at the department, your insane accusations of me," Tony chided. "Yelling at poor Rick in the quad. Running away from dolls. Nothing easier. You called me in hysterics, I agreed to meet you—I was worried about you. But when you drew your gun, I attempted to wrestle it away from you, and shot you quite by accident. I, of course, was horrified to find out that it was the same one with which you killed your old nemesis, Billy Griggs. Who kindly provided me with it, by the way—stolen, of course."

He seemed to consider the scenario for a moment. "I don't think I even need to wing myself. If I wrap your . . . regrettably . . . lifeless hand around the stock and fire into the barn, my story would ring true enough."

His calculations chilled me, and I had no doubt that he could carry it off. I had one more question, however. "Why, Tony? When you've got everything anyone could want? Why get tangled up in robbing a site? You don't need the money, prestige, anything—"

"I told you before, it's not enough," he interrupted impatiently, then sighed. "This little lark, the wreck, just came along in time to rescue me from superlative boredom. A bit of amusing naughtiness, well away from my professional spheres, and I thought, away from everyone else's too. I don't even know whether it was even *illegal* according to Maine's historic preservation laws—"

"It is, actually," I muttered.

"—and then things took a rather exciting turn when

Tichnor's stupidity elevated this little adventure to something else altogether."

Now his eyes blazed with excitement. "I'm tremendously indebted to Grahame, actually, I'll always remember him fondly. This gives me a whole new outlook on life. I don't suppose that you might . . ." He looked at me hopefully, but now I could tell that he was ridiculing me.

I tried again, desperately, to provoke him. "Just how insane are you, Tony? The best thing for you to do is put the gun down—"

"Put the gun down?" Markham laughed. "I'm not that insane. Well, Emma, finally your desperation bores me. A shame, up till now, it's been . . . *fun*."

The bonhomie faded from his face, and he surveyed the situation for a moment. "Get up, my dear," he said finally. "I think the entry wound should be under the chin, close, but not too close to the skin. It needs to look like we were struggling, you see. Head wounds are notoriously dicey, but even if you don't die immediately, this angle will certainly still your tongue."

I felt the metal radiating coldness so close to my face, and felt the chill slink into every part of me that was not already frozen.

"Don't," I whispered hoarsely. "Please."

But Tony couldn't hear me, he was so focused. He paused for a long moment, considering. "I wonder what it will feel like this time. Tichnor was so indirect and Griggs was self-defense. This is something else entirely . . ." Tony's words trailed off as he lost himself in the experience.

He *caressed* my cheek with the end of the pistol, as another blast of wind shook the old shed to its beams. I prepared myself for the shot, wondering if I would live long enough to feel the pain of it. The calm that enveloped me was now quite complete, the kindly numbness that shocks a creature into immobility before inevitable death.

Chapter 28

THE INTIMACY OF THE MOMENT INSIDE THE BARN WAS broken by a dissonant, persistent blare of a car's horn breaking through the storm. Tony started from his concentration, and swore. "That stupid tart Amy will have the whole county down on us. Something's wrong, even she wouldn't make that racket." He grabbed me by the arm and shoved me out before him into the rain. "And whatever will I tell her about her poor Billy?"

A set of headlights accompanied the honking as a truck moved down the driveway. Unfortunately Tony recognized the driver a split second before I did, and the pistol swung up again.

"Jesus Christ, Neal! No!"

Awareness came to me too late, my warning too feeble against the fury of the storm. Two quick shots shattered the windshield and I could see Neal thrown back against the seat, then slump forward over the steering wheel. The truck slammed into the side of the burned-out house, and rested there motionless, the headlights illuminating the torrents of rain and low, dark clouds.

Even as Tony squeezed off the second round, I slammed into him, knocking us both into the mud. I managed to scramble away, kicking blindly at Tony as he grabbed for me. My foot connected with something solid and I heard a grunt behind me as I struggled to my feet.

I skidded down the slope, barely able to believe that I had freed myself, slipping in the mud and tripping over wind-tossed debris as I tried to avoid the tarps that marked the dangerous, still-open pits. With my hair plastered against my face and heavy raindrops slamming down unremittingly, it was more through memory than by sight that I located the stairs down to the cobble beach. I had nowhere to go but down.

With a sudden, gut-wrenching jerk, I found my progress violently arrested at the top of the stairs. My heart stopped beating and a scream tore from my throat, only to be sucked away by the wind. I whirled around and found nothing more sinister than my slicker caught on the rickety iron post that was all that was left of the staircase's railing. I impatiently ripped the coat loose, but in all that haste the momentum of the motion pitched me off the stairs and down onto the beach.

I fell precisely as I should not have, with one arm flung out ahead of me to break my fall. My full weight crushed the delicate bones in my left wrist against the anvil of the beach cobbles, the sound like walnuts being cracked in a vise. I completed the somersault by tumbling over onto my back, my full weight momentarily resting only on that broken hand. Landing forced the breath from my lungs at the same moment the excruciating pain in my wrist revealed itself and my head smashed against the wet stones.

The pain was so overwhelming that for a moment, the only comfort I had was that I was spared the trouble of trying to isolate the worst of it. Freezing water soaked every stitch of clothing that wasn't already wet and raced over the collar of my slicker, snaking its way down an icy path along my spine like a surprise attack. I lay there for a moment, the rain pelting me in the face, unable to believe the encyclopedia of physical anguish currently revealing itself to me. At the same time I was dimly aware that I needed to move before worse things came to pass.

I almost regretted that I wasn't going to pass out when I tried to sit up. My throbbing head was not improved by uncontrollably chattering teeth, and my broken wrist was an arc-lamp of brilliant agony. I didn't dare imagine what the bruises on my back would look like. No doctor could prescribe a compress colder or heavier than my own clothing at this particular moment, I thought giddily as I struggled against the waves to stand up.

I noticed a faint light bobbing around up on the cliff, illuminating the raindrops, and realized that Tony was now looking for me. I sloshed through the water and hoped the storm's wrath would cover the sounds of my splashes. Cobbles clattered and rolled in the surf, the tide attempting to suck my feet out from under me. I tripped a half-dozen times trying to cover the minuscule distance between the site of my crash-landing and the relative cover of the staircase, but one of my stumbles brought with it a possible means of escape.

I staggered over the outstretched leg of Billy Griggs, who was now being rolled about by the waves as the water tried to pull him into the main current of the river. Another blast of pain almost knocked the eyes out of my head as I tried to break my fall with both hands, but after wrestling myself out of the snare of legs and lines, my good hand brushed across something hard against the resiliency of Billy's dry suit.

He had strapped a knife sheath to his leg, whether for show or some practical purpose, I would never know. But now if Markham wanted to get close enough to make my death look like an accident, I would have the means to make it difficult for him.

I spat salt water and gingerly examined the knife by touch. The blade was nine inches long with a serrated tip and an edge so sharp it could split atoms. I wasn't altogether certain I could actually use it, but I did know that I wanted every opportunity to get out of this alive.

I had only just concealed it up my left sleeve when I saw Tony's light shine onto the water over my shoulders. I turned around slowly, clutching my hurt arm to my chest with my good one, holding the blade up that sleeve with its handle close to hand.

The light passed over me and for a moment I believed that Tony hadn't seen me—it was getting darker by the minute—but those thin hopes were rent when the beam returned to rest squarely on my face. Markham obviously was no longer interested in creating the illusion of an accident, for a bullet whizzed past my head. I rushed to get out of the light and into the shadows on the beach side of the staircase when I heard a second and then third shot that seemed to come from another direction completely. The light played wildly across the water and up the slope, and either the wind was playing acoustical tricks or Tony was moving with supernatural speed. Neither thought cheered me much, and I decided to risk wading along the bluff's base, away from the stairs and the beach. The water was deeper there, and churned more violently with the steep drop-off of the river's bed very close to the shore. I was counting on Tony believing that I would be moving closer to the beach and toward relative safety from the storm.

Pausing to try and catch my breath, I hazarded a glance back toward the stairs, where the waves that accompanied the high tide smacked against the crumbling concrete. To my surprise Tony had started down the stairs, but did not appear to be looking for me. Instead he turned his attention back up the slope toward where the wreck of the house stood, drawn to someone or something that I could not see.

A beam from a flashlight lit him, and with a sigh of relief, I realized that Neal had succeeded in contacting the sheriff's department. If only he had listened to me and stayed away after that!

I began to move cautiously back toward the stairs, fearing

that unless Stannard moved quickly, Tony might be able to dodge him and flee toward the beach himself, probably to Amy Griggs and a waiting car. I had to slow him down long enough for the sheriff to make it down the slope.

Another shot came from upslope, and this time Markham clutched at his left side. I struggled, hopping and sloshing through the surf, feeling as though I was moving in slow motion with my body weighted down with cold, exhaustion, and leaden clothing. The dark below the cliff was nearly impenetrable, and the light from the flashlight served to illumine only Tony's face, distorted with pain from the bullet wound. I noted with vehement satisfaction a gash on his forehead where I had kicked him, still oozing blood that mingled with rainwater running down his face.

Then I heard something that paralyzed my heart in spite of my exertions. I renewed my efforts to reach the staircase. It was not Dave Stannard on the slope.

"Bastard! Bastard! You stay there, or I swear to God, I'll blow your fucking head off! You stay right there! You drop your gun where I can see it!"

It was Meg.

I have to hand it to him, Tony didn't miss a beat. "Meg! Miss Garrity!" he called out as if in piteous relief. "Thank goodness! Emma, Professor Fielding's in terrible trouble! I only just—"

"Fuck off!" she screamed. "I *know*! You shot Neal! Now throw your gun over the cliff! Do it now!"

I watched Tony toss his pistol, but so feebly that it landed a few inches from the edge of the bluff.

"Shit!" Meg screamed. "Stay there, stay right there, or I will fucking blow you away!"

It was only when she carefully edged over to retrieve his pistol that I realized what he was doing. Tony's right hand snaked almost invisibly into his pocket to the pistol he had removed from Billy's corpse. I found my voice as I reached the staircase.

"Meg! Stay away from—!"

Too late! Her scream rent the storm as the bluff, eroding and unstable for as long as I had known it, surrendered several tons of soil and rock to the violent river, taking Meg with it.

With the last niggardly shred of strength I could ever hope to have, I hooked my good hand around Tony's ankle before he realized what was happening and pulled as hard as I could, toppling him from the stairs.

Markham landed on top of me, flailing wildly. My head went under and something hit my shattered wrist, forcing a soundless howl from me and a gout of seawater down my throat. I had released my hold on Tony when we collided, and now I fought to get my head above water for a lungful of air. Another wave slapped at me, but I finally found a firm foothold and managed to heave myself up, gagging up salty water and stomach bile.

I sucked in one deep breath, only to have it knocked from my lungs as a tremendous blow landed across my back. This time I fell forward and heard someone else splashing heavily in the water nearby. A third, huge swell swept me toward the base of the cliff, and it took all of my concentration to keep from being slammed into the wall of coarse sand.

As I struggled up I was surprised to see my left hand still attached to the end of my arm. Vaguely I remembered Billy's knife, but that was long gone, lost during my ill-considered attack on Tony. Worse yet, I realized dully that he was now nowhere to be seen.

I felt increasingly warm and tired and distantly recognized the signs of shock and hypothermia. The thought floated through my tired brain that I should try to move: Meg might still be alive. But I had nothing left in me to move toward where the bluff had been.

I stood dumbly, buffeted by the surf, as I vainly tried to sort out what I should be doing, and what I was now capable of doing, when I heard another roar over the waves. My head ached so that I couldn't be certain that the noise wasn't just a result of concussion. The noise, a low throb, continued, and

I turned, remotely interested, toward the source and was surprised to see Tony gliding easily over the water not ten feet from me. Nothing made any sense anymore, and I stood unsteadily in the surf, the rain still pounding my head, trying to figure out what was going on.

It took a moment, but after brushing a tangle of hair from my eyes, I saw that the motorboat that Billy and Tony had used to haul their treasure from the bottom of the river had been lifted by the tide and was now moving away from the beach. As the small craft headed into the steam rising from the center of the river, Tony turned and looked over his shoulder and I could have sworn I saw him grinning at me before the mist obscured him totally. But of course it was too dark for me to have seen any such thing, and I was so tired and hurt *so* much . . .

Chapter 29

HARD AS I TRIED, MY BRAIN WOULDN'T WORK. AT FIRST I struggled a few steps farther over toward the cliff side of the stairs, but it seeped through the mush of reason that I was incapable of digging Meg out of anything like two tons of earth, even if I managed to find her.

I sloshed on.

Then I heard the cries. "Help! Shit! Goddamn it, where are you? Emma!"

"Meg?" I croaked in disbelief. "Where are *you*?"

But she wouldn't have heard my amazed whisper on a calm day, so I started back toward the steps. I knew that there were fourteen of the cement steps, and oddly, I remembered that Sherlock Holmes knew how many stairs led down to the rooms at 221B Baker Street. Might as well have been a hundred, from where I stood in the water. A wave shoved me in the right direction and I fell against the wet, gritty stairs.

Meg had called. Meg had called. I used that as a mantra, a focal point as I tried to make the most of the wave's push, since I was already a mess. Only I couldn't feel the hurts I knew I had, and that bothered me. I started to count the stairs, try and mark my progress to the top, but the only real thing that kept me moving was the fact that Meg was still out there.

"Coming," I muttered. I pushed myself up carefully, if not on all fours, then unsteadily on three, and hauled myself up four more stairs. I sat on the fifth as a reward, but realized that if I didn't want to risk the rest of the bluff crumbling away from the stairs, I would have to keep moving.

I hauled myself up another three stairs, only to be surprised by the feel of grass under my hand. One more effort and I was at the top, where I fell over into the sharp, wet weeds. All I wanted to do was sleep. I forced my eyes open again, and that simple act brought with it a ray of hope.

Or at least a ray of light, which was just as welcome. Meg's flashlight spilled a beam along the ground away from me, illuminating her as she clung, almost on her belly, to the edge of the bluff. She seemed to be trying to edge forward without moving too much. Suddenly I saw something appear on the bluff a few feet from where her head and hands were. Had Tony returned? No, it was Meg's foot, followed by her backside, as she, in one move, pulled herself up and over, and rolled away from the edge to lie on her back about fifteen feet from where I had collapsed.

I must have checked out for a moment, for I heard Meg yell hoarsely, "Emma! Where are you?" and couldn't remember how she came to be standing up.

"Over here!" I tried to holler, but a hacking cough was all that came out. My stomach rolled as I raised my head.

She started, not expecting to find me so close by. Meg's chin was badly cut, and the front of her was unevenly covered in coarse, wet sand. Water soaked her leather jacket, and even as my vision closed I was transfixed by the way the rain beaded on her glasses and earrings, spattering them with dark jewels. She picked up her flashlight and came over to me.

I waved tentatively, trying not to lose my balance and fall again, but my head was buzzing and I couldn't see very clearly. Through the warm fuzzy feeling that seemed to envelop me, I lazily tried to remember something that seemed rather important at one point. "Tony . . . I think Neal's . . . I wasn't . . ."

Meg didn't bother to stifle her exclamation of dismay when she reached out for me. I looked down and saw that my left index finger was jutting out and back in a sickening fashion. My stomach heaved and I looked away.

"Shhh. Neal's not okay, but he's not dead, not by a long shot," she said. "We've got to get the two of you to a hospital though, or we'll have a couple more specimens for the faunal collections." She half-pulled, half-carried me up the slope, away from the edge of the bluff. "Damn, you weigh a ton," she gasped.

That irritated me, but I couldn't think of any suitable retort.

"I was just getting him, Tony, lined up when the ground collapsed under me. I could feel the vibration and chucked the light and Sally, but I got the wind knocked right out of me, I didn't think I was gonna be able to hang in there—"

Meg was rabbiting on and on about climbing, and blankets, and whatever, and I was glad to have her there, but I really wished she would just shut up and let me drift off. I'd had enough. I tried to explain this politely to her, but apparently the words weren't coming out properly, because every time I tried to stretch out on the slick grass for a little rest, she would just start swearing and yelling at me. Then she would yank me up again, which was annoying, but at least now it didn't hurt.

Then, just as I had decided I would really have to be quite short with her, Meg shouted again, but this time not at me. Dozens of people, it seemed, came swarming toward us, asking me silly questions, and poking and peering rudely. I lost track trying to watch them, and got more muddled when I tried to talk to them. I caught words that I recognized, but most of it made no sense, like I had missed the beginning of a word game. In the midst of all the to-do, I felt something

sting my arm and cursed the virulent Maine mosquitoes that
seemed not to fear either the dark or the stormy weather. I
abruptly decided that if no one was going to take the trouble
to deal with me politely, I would ignore them too, so I
slipped away into the dark.

Chapter 30

SATURDAY EVENING I WOKE UP TO SEE SHERIFF STAN-nard standing in the doorway of my hospital room for a moment, sort of taking in the view, I suppose. He shook his head slowly in disbelief.

"Well, the doctors tell me that you'll be all right."

When I'd come to that morning, it had taken me a while to sort out just which parts of me were actually damaged and which were just along for the ride in the blur of pain. The official inventory was three fractured metacarpals, a smashed third carpus, and a simple fracture of the left humerus—that's a busted wrist, crunched index finger, and a broken arm for those of you without an abiding professional interest in skellies—a mild concussion, a sprained right ankle, a couple of bruised vertebrae, and a fine collection of assorted contusions and scratches. The most impressive-looking, though by no means the most painful, injury was a monster bruise all over the back and right side of my noggin from my crash landing. It peeped out along my hairline like a black and purple aurora borealis and scared the dickens out of me the first time I made it to the bathroom by myself and got a load of it in the mirror.

I nodded at the sheriff, immediately regretting the action. My head still felt sore and dizzy—they wouldn't let me have any painkillers worth a damn because of the concussion—and it seemed as though the slightest movement triggered coughing bouts. It would be a long time until I had the urge to go swimming again.

"My wife made these." He moved into the room carrying a brown paper bag. "Blueberry muffins. People walk in front of trucks to get Barbara to make muffins for them. She made some extra at breakfast, and thought you might like a break from the hospital chow."

I was about to tell him that I hadn't been eating anything, that I didn't have much of an appetite at all, when I got a whiff of them. Magnificent, rich, with coarse sugar on the tops of them. Those blueberries had been picked by real humans. Carefully—they were still hot—I pulled the top off one and stuffed it into my mouth. I couldn't remember the last time I'd eaten, and had certainly never tasted anything so good in my life.

"Maybe you can tell me how you finally got yourself into this state?" Dave asked, as patiently as he could. "What possessed you to drive out there in that god-awful weather?" He settled down in the hideous blue plastic chair at the foot of the bed, making himself comfortable.

"Mmmmm—" I chewed up my mouthful of muffin.

But the sheriff let his anger or frustration or worry get the better of him, and without waiting for me to swallow and translate, he quickly added, "You know, you could've gotten killed, rather than just getting the crap kicked out of you? You don't know how lucky you are—"

"There was nothing else I could have done," I said tiredly. I waited a second to see if the muffin would stay put. "I wanted to call, but the lines were down and I didn't want to waste any time. I did send Neal, but now I kind of wish I hadn't. But I did try."

The emotion on Dave's face shifted to something softer. "I know. I think you're one of those people who can't help themselves when they get an idea in their heads. Staying alive out there was a real trick, though. I'm just glad you had the sense to tell *someone* else you were going . . ." he trailed off thoughtfully.

"You've seen Neal?" I asked eagerly. "Is he okay?"

"He's fine, though he won't be doing any bench presses anytime soon. I got a statement from him before he was released," Stannard answered. "The, ah, young lady who pulled your fat out of the fire the other evening was with him. Ms. Garrity. I'm not real sure, but I think that I may have interrupted a make-out session."

I laughed in spite of my sore throat, for the first time in days it seemed. "What century are you from?" I asked after I got done coughing. "Make-out session!"

The sheriff got serious again. "That accounts for nearly everyone who was out there when we showed up. We pulled Billy Griggs's body out, but we're still trying to locate Markham's body. It hasn't washed up yet. And Amy—"

"What about Tony?" I demanded. A lead weight settled in my stomach, and I set the muffin down. "You haven't found Tony yet?"

"No, not yet, but I'm sure it's just a matter of time," he said confidently. "That was a bad storm, the worst this early in years. No one could have survived it in an open boat, especially if he'd been shot. We found the wreckage of the motorboat he was using down the river a ways."

"Yeah, but you didn't find Tony!" I said, becoming increasingly more nervous.

"We didn't find a body. But I'm sure we'll find him, there's no way he could have survived that mess."

My head began to throb again. Jesus, he was still out there! "What about a car? He didn't walk to the Point—"

"Not yet." A sympathetic look crossed Stannard's face. "Look, this is just another loose end that I can't tie up yet. I will, though."

"You don't know him!" I insisted. "I saw him escaping, and he didn't look like he was getting ready to just up and drown! He looked like he was just starting to enjoy himself! You don't know, he's out of his mind!" My voice was getting high with hysteria.

"Hey, hey, it's all right," the sheriff soothed. "Calm down, I've got all the bases covered. I've notified the FBI, the Coast Guard, and even they told me I was crazy, that there wasn't a hope of him having made it through that nor'easter. So not only do you have the assurance of the Fordham County Sheriff's Department," he said, smiling, "but two federal agencies as well. The boat was a complete wreck."

I wasn't mollified. "That's not the only boat in the world," I pointed out. I practically expected Tony to crawl out from under my bed at any moment.

"No, no, course not. In fact, I was just down to the marina, getting an assessment of the damage down there. Lots of boats were wrecked, pulled right off the moorings." Suddenly he frowned.

"What?" I demanded. "What did you just think of?"

He shook his head. "It was nothing to do with this case."

"Tell me!"

Stannard shook his head. "It's really nothing, you just knocked a thought loose in my head, something to check on. One of the missing boats had been tied up, but I don't remember seeing any rope left on the cleat. I'll have to go back and have another look." He carefully pulled out his notebook and jotted down the note. "Probably just a loose knot," Dave said. "The owner is a weekend sailor, with more boat than he knows how to handle."

"What kind of boat was it?" I asked nervously. I no longer believed in coincidences, not anymore.

"A Wayfarer," he said. "But look, you're making a whole lot out of nothing. And I've still got some holes to fill in on my report." Dave reached over and helped me peel the paper off the bottom of the muffin. "I found the fax in the car when we found you. I translated it, but I'm still missing some of the pieces. How come no one went after it before now, I wonder?"

"For whatever reason, the report and the proposed plans to recover the bullion never made it back to France," I explained. "They were probably picked up en route by a Spanish ship, and that's how they ended up with a bundle of church documents in the archive in Madrid—it's amazing how often things end up in weird places like that. There they rested, with their veritable treasure map, for better than two hundred years, until Tony happened upon them."

The sheriff looked confused. "What was his connection with Grahame Tichnor? How did they ever end up together? I'd've thought they were the original odd couple—oh. The mug shots."

I nodded. "But the thing that slowed me down before I found the map in the storage room was that I couldn't understand why Tony was so interested in Penitence Point— there was nothing there that should have caught his attention, professionally or . . . otherwise. Tichnor, he was just there to hunt pots, I figured. Even when I thought they were working together, I couldn't understand why Tony, an archaeologist of the first water, would bother looting my site—nothing valuable there for them to sell, really."

"The Saugatuck River has got a bunch of forts all along it," Stannard said. "And there's lots of other rivers in Maine. How could they tell which one was the right one?"

I took another sip of ginger ale, another bite of muffin. "You're right. Unless you're familiar with the area around Penitence Point, the letter might have referred to anyplace in Maine—it only mentioned the *'le fortin Anglais au cote du fleuve de Sauckatuc.'* And based on the map, it would taken a lot of computer hours to recognize that particular point on the river. Unless, of course, you immediately recognized the shape of Penitence Point and the relationship of the two forts. Once you knew the location, it was a simple matter of a little patience and discreet diving to get you a couple hundred pounds of gold and silver. Tony knew the location,

Tichnor knew the rumors of gold around here. I thought they were just the same sorts of rumors that spring up around any historic site, but this time they had a grain of truth to them. But even knowing all this, it took them a while to find the exact resting place of the ship's boat."

"I don't understand why they didn't just wait until after the storm to go after it."

"I think Tony was nervous that I was getting too close. He wanted to get something, before I actually found him. Remember, he said he'd been out there on Thursday too. If he'd had all the time he wanted . . ." I paused, marveling at what he'd almost won. "With the crew of the boat drowned, the only ones to know about the loss would have been the British Admiralty, and they wouldn't have known where the wreck was. The letter was lost, so the French couldn't have found it. I guess the Spanish wouldn't bother with it; too little a prize to risk a ship in wartime."

"And Markham recognized it from the descriptions of your work," Stannard supplied.

"Right. The first time I started to think about Tony's connection with the map we found at Tichnor's, I didn't understand the attraction. But he did. Dr. Markham knew about my research from the lecture I gave when I was being interviewed for the Caldwell job a year and a half ago. I had slides, handouts, maps, everything one could want to make the location on the fax abundantly clear to someone trained to put those data together. Tony was an unscrupulous bastard, but he had a brilliant mind. It's not surprising that he put things together so quickly—I don't think I would have, without my familiarity with the site."

I chewed my lip, remembering his sudden phone call to the dorm back in mid-July, even allowing myself to remember how much I was looking forward to his visit. "I guess that explains why he was so surprised to find that I was working out at the Point: As far as he knew, I wasn't supposed to be out there for another season. He thought he'd have the whole place to himself. Instead, he found half the department camped out there."

The sheriff chuckled at the irony of that, and I continued. "Not only would Markham have had to worry about nosy Yankee neighbors, but there was a whole *slew* of folks who spent their time looking for tiny little details. *And* every one of them knew his face. I'd have panicked in his shoes too. But it's surprising how close he came to getting away with it. If it hadn't been for Tichnor killing Pauline when he went back to check out what we were finding, they both would have gotten clean away."

"You know," Stannard said, "I think I can fill in a few details for you. Your instincts if not your facts were right on target, but I think I might have reached the same conclusions from a totally different angle."

He settled back into his chair and began to recount his side of the adventure. "About a week ago, I ran into Amy Griggs. I try to 'run into her' about once a week, keep an eye on her. I worry about her, but there's not much I can do unless she makes a complaint or I have good cause to believe that Billy's been hitting her again." He grimaced. "But this was after you stopped by the office and knocked a couple of thoughts loose in my head. It was pure chance I should have run into her just then. You see, I was leaving the Bakersfield Dive Shop, just as she was going in."

My jaw dropped. "What . . . how did you end up there?"

"I got the idea when Ms. Garrity and you stopped by last week. You kept insisting it had something to do with the river, and she just kept fiddling with that key chain whatzit Big Johnny Serino sells. That bothered me at the time, but I couldn't figure it out. I didn't know anything about Markham, but I sure as hell—pardon my French—could find out what Billy'd been up to.

"See, I hadn't heard a peep out him all summer, not since Denny Sheehan ran him in after Ms. Westlake's memorial service. And being so well behaved wasn't like him. So I checked in with Johnny and asked if *Billy'd* been buying any gear, or renting it. And wouldn't you know it, he'd been in a couple of times since July—"

"Just after Tichnor and Pauline died," I pointed out, then briefly told him about Billy's thwarted plot with Tichnor to steal the entire hoard.

"Right. So I began to wonder where he'd got the money for all of that, and what he was up to. And when I really did just run into Amy going into the dive shop, I gave on to her like I knew what they were doing—I doubt she knew everything herself—and she was excited. All she'd say was that they thought they were close, and soon Billy wouldn't have to be worried anymore and they could be happy."

He paused again, angry, barely able to contain it. "That's the way she looked at things, Billy only hit her because he was anxious about money, and she made it worse by worrying him. Poor thing was broke up yesterday, finding out he was dead, when she should have been dancing in the street. Anyhow, I just kept my mouth shut and let her talk—she was too excited to even be shy around me, like she generally is. But all she kept saying was, Billy's got a new friend, teaching him about old stuff."

"Old stuff." Dave laughed humorlessly. "When she said it, at first I thought she was talking about that New Age mumbo-jumbo she tends to go in for. But when she said it again, I remembered you talking about Professor Markham, another archaeologist, and then the two sort of . . . overlapped . . . for me." The sheriff sat back drumming a pen on the sole of his shoe while he remembered. "And that reminded me of the phone number at Tichnor's place. That's when I started wondering about a possible connection to the department besides you.

"And I think that, considering what you said Markham told you, we need to reexamine Augie Brooks's body. That looked like an accident, but now that we have—"

He was interrupted by voices, a scurrying outside my room, and an "Emma!" as Brian came hurtling through the door. He brushed past Sheriff Stannard, stopping short of my bed for a heartbeat, shocked by the picture I presented. I stuck out my good right hand and pulled him over to me slowly, feeling for the first time that I might eventually stop aching, itching, and just plain hurting so completely. I could feel bone knitting up, just at the sight of him.

"Oh God, look at you!" he said. "Your poor head! Your hand! Are you okay?" With his free hand he moved to touch the bandaged and bruised parts, but wavered and pulled back each time, not wanting to aggravate anything.

I scooched up the back of the bed to sit up straighter. "I feel pretty crappy, which is apparently a good sign, but a hell of a lot better than I did yesterday. It's good to see you, love."

"She'll be tangoing again in no time," Marty said reassuringly as she surveyed my situation.

"Which is a miracle"—Groucho Marx's voice came out of Kam's mouth—"considering she couldn't tango before!"

I burst out laughing. Unfortunately that started me coughing again, and I shoved Brian's hand away to cover my mouth with my good hand.

Brian wheeled angrily on his friend, bringing his face to within an inch of Kam's. "You shut up! Can't you see she's in pain?"

We all stared in shock. "Brian, it's okay, I'm fine! Kam's just trying to cheer me up!" I said.

There was an awkward pause, then everyone spoke at once.

"Kam, I don't know what—"

"Don't give it another—"

"Good heavens! Timmy just *kicked* Lassie!"

A giggle broke the tension just long enough for Marty to suggest to her fiancé that she was desperate to explore the delights of the hospital coffee shop. "We'll be back in half an hour, okay, darling?" she told me. "Don't tell any good stuff till we get here."

Dave Stannard cleared his throat uncomfortably. "I'd better be going, I'll come back tomorrow if you're up for it." He paused a minute, sizing up Brian, nodded, and left.

I couldn't help feeling a little bereft to see him go; in spite of the fact that we didn't always agree, Sheriff Stannard had been through all of this with me.

"Hey, it's okay," I said, grabbing Brian's hand again. "No harm done."

Brian shook off his anger, exhaled deeply, then dragged the ugly blue plastic chair to the side of the bed, never letting go of me. He sat down and rested his head against my hand in his for a minute and looked up at me. "Jesus, I was so afraid you were going to die. Even though Kam told me the hospital said you'd be fine, I was afraid I was going to lose you. If I could've gotten out and pushed that damned plane, I would have . . ."

I couldn't see the lower half of Brian's face, but I could feel him chewing gently on my knuckles, making sure I was still there. His eyes were red-rimmed.

"It was all an accident," I said softly. "I didn't think that anyone would be on the cliff, that's all. I was trying my best to stay out of trouble, just so you know."

"I know you're careful, that's the only thing that kept me from going totally nuts, was knowing you're not stupid," my husband said. "But if you could please not do it again, I'd appreciate it." He sniffed. " 'Kay?"

" 'Kay."

"I love you."

"I know that. I love you too."

Brian sat there for a long while, and I knew instinctively what he was going to ask. "They got Tony Markham, right?"

When I didn't answer right away, he started getting agitated. "Tell me Tony's dead, tell me he's in jail—"

"No, not yet," I said lightly. "But the sheriff is sure a body will wash up soon. It's just a matter of time."

Brian scowled and I knew just how unbelievable I sounded. Despite the odds, I couldn't believe that Tony was dead or that anyone would ever capture him. He had used everything I'd ever admired in him, found—God help me—attractive in him, against me and might do so again. He had a head start, a small fortune in gold probably stashed somewhere, and had just consciously shed the last of whatever moral restraint he might have possessed.

The Wayfarer is a sweet, salty little craft, capable of coastal and deeper water travel. It's the sort of thing folks who know what they're doing buy when they get ready to retire and sail off to the Caribbean in their retirement years.

Or when they're just setting off to discover the wide world.

Chapter 31

THE NEXT AFTERNOON MEG KNOCKED TENTATIVELY AT the door. My back was to her but I could see her reflection in the bathroom mirror. I sighed and decided, finally, that I wouldn't pretend to be asleep and rolled over.

"How are you feeling?" she asked quietly. She had a small Band-Aid on her chin.

"Not bad, considering," I said, too quickly. "Bit like a Kleenex that's been used to clean the hull of a battleship. Give me a minute, would you? I have to use the, er . . ." I nodded my head toward the bathroom and swung my legs stiffly over the side of the bed.

"Need a hand?"

"No, I can manage." I hobbled over without the crutch and shut the door behind me, turning on the faucet for camouflage as I stared into the mirror. I needed a minute to think.

I'd spoken with Brian about my reluctance to see Meg. At first I assumed that I had just been scared that she could have gotten herself killed—rushing around during a storm by herself like that! He let me keep talking about how angry I was that she had risked herself so foolishly, until even I realized that I was repeating myself and started thinking about what I wasn't saying.

I was mad because Meg had, to use Sheriff Stannard's words, pulled my fat out of the fire.

Brian, sensing that I had hit on the real reason for my anger, kissed my hand and went off. To get a soda, he said. To let me think privately, I knew.

It didn't take me long from there to figure out that I resented her rescuing me. It took another half hour before I acknowledged that she was the one who had come closest to actually stopping Tony. The rest of the day until I accepted the fact that she had come out to the site better prepared than I, in every way. She was not only aware of the potential for danger, but also willing to meet it with the force necessary to survive: She'd found a gun and had even used it on Markham.

In the end it was just my ego, that tenderest and most fragile of organs, that was suffering. But in confronting the fact that she and Neal were the reason I was still breathing, I was also forced to realize just how skilled Tony Markham had been in manipulating me. He made it very plain, knowing precisely my mania for shouldering my own burdens, that *he* had been the one to gruesomely punish Pauline's killer, that *he* had slain the monster of my teenaged nightmares. It made me wonder what would have happened if I hadn't come out to the site, if I had put my suspicions of him behind me. We might have continued on in the department together, a true sadist's feast, for who knows how long.

But as for Meg . . .

I gritted my teeth and slapped a big, stinging dose of honesty to the shreds of my pride. The trick is knowing when to be brutal about it, and when to lay off and let it heal gradually, and this was no time for niceties. I washed my hands and went back out.

Meg sat in the repellent blue plastic chair now, and looked up expectantly.

"How are you doing?" I asked. "How's Neal feeling?"

"He's good, though you'd never know it from the amount of bitching that I hear in a day." Apparently fearing that she sounded too disloyal, Meg added, "It can't be easy for him, though, he's used to being in charge of things." She took a deep breath and blurted out, "I'm moving into his place, just to look after him for a while. Might even stay on." She shrugged with elaborate carelessness, daring me to gainsay her decision.

"I didn't know," I said, not surprised by anything but the speed at which this event had come to pass. "And, ah, where's Alan?"

"Alan and I swapped, he took my dorm room," Meg answered. "It was a good solution, I mean, he's pretty seriously messed up . . . I mean, I think his father wanted him to be an anthropologist, now he just has to decide if that's what he wants too."

"I hope he figures it out." I didn't tell Meg that Alan had already been in to visit me, and before I could stop him, apologized for his behavior all summer, bringing in far too many details about his family life and his father's suspicions about me for my pleasure. But I figured if he was brave enough to do something like that, I could ignore his discomfort until it went away through daily wear and tear.

"It might be easier," Meg added, "because I heard his father is taking an early retirement next semester."

Again I didn't say anything. Once news of what had happened at the Point reached the department, events transpired quickly. I got a call from Jenny Alvarez, who said that the incident with the doll had prompted Dr. Kellerman to suggest an early retirement as a means of graceful withdrawal for his friend. Harassment of that sort made for ugly headlines and lawsuits. It wasn't the censure I'd wanted, but it was as much justice as I could hope for in the face of Rick Crabtree's seniority and influence. At least I wouldn't have to look at the old sourpuss for much longer.

"Have they moved forward on the topic of the bequest?"

I'd asked Jenny idly. I didn't really expect that any decision about me being offered Pauline's chair would be made for some time, until all the legalities had been sorted out.

"Well, that's going to be up to the college of course, but the new department chair will also have something to say about it," Jenny had replied. "You've caused quite a stir in the chain of command, Emma, clearing the next two candidates out of the running. First Tony Markham—I *still* can't believe *that*—and now Rick. Kellerman's not thrilled, I can tell you. At first he was grumbling over divvying up your classes for the next week until you get back, but that's paled with replacing two senior positions. He's worried about his retirement plans now . . ."

"Oh God," I said bleakly, sinking back into my pillow. "*That*'s going to endear me to the new chair, whoever he is. That's the end of my career. Give me the worst, who's it going to be?"

I could hear a long pause, and a terrible thought occurred to me. Anyone but Gretchen the Wretched, the syrupy suck-up, the Queen of PC . . .

"Well, there's nothing official yet . . ."

"Jenny, you've got to tell me," I said weakly. "Who is it?"

"Me." Before I could take that in, Jenny rang off, laughing and saying, "God bless, Em. Get well soon."

"—okay?" Meg asked worriedly, bringing me back to the here and now. "Emma? Do you want me to call someone?"

I shook my head. "Sorry, I'm just a little drifty right now, the doctor said it'll go away in a couple of days." Then, before I could lose my nerve, I quickly blurted out, "Meg, thank you for being at the site. No—Meg, thank you for saving my life." I felt better and immensely foolish all at once.

Meg fidgeted, supremely uncomfortable. "Well, I didn't go out there intending to be the cavalry, you know. I just went along because Neal was tearing off and I've gotten in the habit of tagging along with him. I almost lost it when he got shot."

"Where were you? I couldn't figure out where you came from."

"I'd been looking under the seat for a flashlight. I heard the windshield shatter, then the truck smashed into that wall, and when I saw Neal bleeding—well, I saw Professor Markham and just got pissed off before I got a chance to be scared," she said, shrugging. "That's another bad habit with me."

"Wherever did you find that gun?" I asked. "I lost track of the ones that Tony had."

"Emma," Meg said incredulously. "That was mine. Sally's a Heckler & Koch P7 M8. I've been shooting for years. I told you this."

I gaped.

"My father taught me," she continued, "I'm very good, even better in daylight, with no wind and rain, unfortunately."

Meg saw my look of—what? surprise? horror? marveling?—and sighed, then began reeling off what sounded like a well-practiced monologue.

"Emma, I've got all the permits, I follow the NRA regs. I keep it locked up in a gun vault at home, and besides, it's my constitutional right—"

"You're not serious!" I broke in, recovering from my shock. Holy snappers! I'd been rescued by a member of the NRA? I had long sensed something of the conservative about her, but could this be the final indication that Meg was a *Republican*? "I didn't think that College Housing allowed guns," I finished lamely.

"Well, I'm not living *there* anymore," she said without a trace of guilt. "I don't see why you should be so surprised. If I'd had it with me that day Tichnor had you cornered out on the site, none of this might have happened. It's a scary old world out there, and the lieutenant, Dad, I mean, wanted to make sure that I could take care of myself. Better to bend a few stupid college rules then end up on a slab."

Meg appeared to be struggling with something too, a little

more serious perhaps than my own present astonishment. I recognized the telltale signs: It was a bit of basic truth fighting its way to the surface. "But I'm learning that self-reliance isn't everything, is it?" she concluded.

What could I possibly say to that?

Epilogue

"**W**HAT'S GOING ON?" I ASKED SLEEPILY A COUPLE OF days later. Brian was bringing me to Somerville for the rest of the week, to keep an eye on me, he said. The Civic had left the smooth pavement of Route 95 and was bumping down a much quieter road. "You're not going to detour to see that place with the plastic cows again, are you? Route One is too slow this time of day . . ."

"No, we're not going down to see the cows, but getting a steak later would be a good idea. Help those bones and muscles of yours," Brian answered. "I just want to show you something."

We followed the road away from the interstate a ways farther, came to a medium-sized town with the traditional New England layout—center green, boxy white wooden church, and town hall—and passed straight through to the other side. The tree line got denser, and fields in various stages of use appeared, delineated by low stone walls.

I couldn't resist trying to be the expedition leader, even when I had no idea what we were looking for. "There's nothing out here, sweetie. I think we've moved beyond the fringe of civilization."

"That's the general idea. Hang on a minute, okay? Trust me."

I sighed and snuggled down into the passenger seat to continue drowsing, for once relinquishing command and content to be led into the unknown. Earlier that day we had swung by the little graveyard at St. Jude's to look at the place where Pauline had finally been buried. The plot was pretty enough, but in the end I decided not to leave the flowers I brought because as far as I was concerned, Pauline wasn't there. We drove through town and back out to the Point, where I set the bouquet down on the surviving front doorstep of Greycliff. It didn't matter that I knew the roses would fade in a day or two on the wreck of the house; my final and best tribute to my friend would be the book I eventually wrote about her site.

Two minutes later Brian pulled onto a tertiary road. It had been paved, but not in the recent past. He stopped the car in front of a white wood-framed house, at least one hundred years old, classical revival with a series of attached buildings on the back of the house. "Big house, little house, back house, barn" was the way the rhyme went.

"What do you think?" he asked.

I looked at Brian, eyebrows raised. He shrugged his shoulders, answering my question with one of his own, looking excited and nervous.

Not daring to hope that he really was asking me what I thought he was, I looked at the place again with a critical eye.

"It's gorgeous!" I blurted.

Then reality forced me to be objective and I looked hard at the old place. "But the exterior needs work. The barn is in bad shape, but the rest is better. The roof looks sound and the foundation is all right, though we'll want to check to see if that's a creek or pond behind that line of trees back there, in case of floods. But," excitement took over again, "we could have flowers! You and me, together, could have *flowers*! Of our own! And things! For *our* house. Like a rake! Or . . . or a trash can, a new one, not something nasty that came with the apartment!"

But Brian, having had an opportunity to digest all of this potential, had already passed the apartment dweller's obsession with land and had moved on to practicalities.

"*We* could have *offices,*" he announced proudly. "And I could keep mine nice and clean, and we could just close the door on yours until the EPA comes to mitigate it."

That inconceivable bit of luxe knocked us both into silence for a moment.

"What about the commute?" I finally asked. We really did have to consider the practicalities now.

"Forty-five minutes to Boston before the rush hour. And I just timed us coming from your apartment at Caldwell at fifty minutes, taking it real easy. The commuter line to Boston runs through the next town over, but I've been talking to Roddy down at the lab, and he's looking to get rid of his pickup truck." He paused. "We could use that for the renovations too. We'd both have a longer drive rather than a walk—"

"But we'd be coming *home*, to each other," I finished. I unlocked my side of the car and hobbled carefully across the front yard to peer, hands cupped around my eyes, into the window. It looked okay to me, but I wasn't the one with the contractors in the family. "Have you been inside yet?"

"Just once, a quick look on the way up last week. The neighbors down the way have a key, they saw me and let me in. I haven't called the realtor yet."

"We have neighbors? Like across the yard, instead of on top and all around us?"

"Half a mile back the way we came, a quarter mile farther on too." Brian was smug with pride; he'd taken a chance and come up big. "We could dance naked in the backyard and no one would see us!"

"Bit cold this time of year, but I do like the idea of privacy, sweetie. Could we manage the repairs?"

He looked thoughtful. "Yeah, I think so. Most of it's not major, just some updating and cosmetic remodeling, but that can come later. The barn should probably come down, though, right away. We could do most of the stuff weekends, and my dad offered to come out for a couple of weeks when I called him about it."

"Lotta work." I thought about how busy we both were already.

"Different work, though. It will make a good break," he said. A greedy look came into his eyes. "And we'll need power tools! Lots of them! I'll get you a reciprocating saw for your birthday! You'll love it, once your hand is better."

I left him to consider an imaginary array of circular saws and power nailers and looked inside again, into what had been the parlor. There was some yellow striped wallpaper, not my style, but not hideous cabbage roses either; I could live with it for a while. A respectable fireplace, the sort of thing you could imagine having quiet tea next to of a Sunday, or whiskey of a winter night. Lovely complex molding that looked like it was the original was trapped under layers of paint. In the central hallway beyond I could see a staircase that obviously once had been someone's pride and joy. I thought about how a cat of our very own would look on a couch and liked the picture. Bucky had called almost every day since she'd heard I was in the hospital, wild for something to do for me; maybe I'd tell her to keep her eyes out for a suitable feline companion.

Stepping back, I glanced around the front porch, a later addition that spread across the entire width of the house. There were a couple of trees along the driveway and a huge oak in the front yard. It appeared as though it had been there for better than a century, and good for at least that long again. Permanence, at last.

I sat down on the steps, rested my crutch against my knee,

and felt the sun warm my face. A mockingbird hissed and chattered, then swooped down from a maple and across the street. I looked up and saw two large, rusted S links hanging from the inside of the porch roof, five feet apart. It took me a minute to figure out that it was for a bench swing. I couldn't imagine anything more perfect. Across the street was nothing but a field and woods.

Then I tried thinking about all the raking, the repairs, the potential plumbing problems, and the tax bills and decided that I would happily trade them all for the possibility of a porch swing. Any day.

"How much?" It took me a couple of moments to ask the all-important question: I was already starting to feel possessive and couldn't bear the thought of someone else in our house.

Brian hesitated, then gave me a figure. "It's on the far side of what we can afford, with the repairs, but I think we can do it. I want to."

When I heard his answer, my fears vanished. I smiled lazily and leaned against the porch railing: Brian might have found our dream house, but I would secure it for us. "No problem at all, sweetheart. That's only the asking price. I can knock that down, wail about all the work it needs, how remote the place is, and *then* start gouging into the commission. I'll play this limp and the cast for every cent they're worth. Just watch me, it'll be epic." I made a show of cracking the knuckles on my right hand, a display of ready, capable aggression. I knew real estate agents well enough to play their games like a pro.

"I'm glad you're on my side," Brian said. He didn't even like mentioning bill discrepancies to waiters when we ate out. "I never thought that listening to your father yammering about real estate would be anything but an exercise in ripping hangnails."

"Well, this is my one chance to make use of all that, and I want to be sure I squeeze it for all it's worth!" I nodded to my darling. "Let's do it."

He helped ease me off the stairs and we walked slowly around the place, taking note of the garden in the back, the earthy smell of the field beyond the back courtyard, a splintery pile of firewood already stacked and seasoning. I noticed there were a lot of exterior doors, and that made me frown briefly.

Brian noticed and read my mind. "You know, if you really think you can reduce the price by a bit, I think we'll have enough to cover a good alarm system." He shrugged. "We don't know anything, but it never hurts to be careful. There's crime in the country too."

I nodded, relieved that he was the one to bring it up first. Since I had left the hospital, I thought long and hard about getting a gun of my own, but decided that I just couldn't do it. I settled for asking Meg to show me how to fire hers, just so I'd know the mechanics of the things, and decided to arrange for some private lessons in self-defense. As Brian said, it never hurt to be careful.

Because I knew, sure as I breathed, that Tony was still out there, alive and waiting.

We let the subject drop, wanting to enjoy this moment, so we spoke idly and inconsequentially, flitting like butterflies from the subject of curtains to the question of drainage, from supermarkets to linoleum, without lingering so long on any one topic that the talk could pall. Details are anathema to castles in the air, and so we wandered back to the car, content to leave the real planning and calculating for later.

I looked back at the house: Our place wasn't typical, architecturally speaking, and I loved its eccentricities.

Brian echoed my thoughts out loud. "It's a little different, isn't it? It's got that extra side addition I've never seen around here."

"And it looks like someone finished the attic. Maybe raised the roof, even."

"It's a bit quirky." Brian added quickly, "Quirky, but nice. I love it."

"Quirky, but nice." I thought about it a minute longer,

made a connection with a long-ago memory, and smiled contentedly. "And you know, it's only what you warned me about all along."

He looked at me quizzically as he fastened his safety belt and turned the key in the ignition.

"You always said that one day, if we weren't careful, we'd end up at the Funny Farm."